PRAISE FOR THE MOONFALL MAYHEM SERIES

"*Falling of the Moon* is a fantasy fairytale like nothing I have read before. Mystery and secrets take you to a fantastic mystical world sure to have a book two. It is *Pirates of the Caribbean* meets Cinderella. Looking forward to Ascot's next adventure. Strong and determined with her loyal friends she will certainly make the Moonfall Mayhem a great series of books. I am ecstatic that this is just the start to what will be a truly great trilogy."

— Girl + Book

"I'd say it's like Shrek meets The Wizard of Oz if Dorothy were Wednesday Addams and Toto a talking cat with bat wings. Fun and funny with many laugh-out-loud moments. Can't wait for the next book in the series!"

— Susan Abel Sullivan, author of the
Cleo Tidwell Paranormal Mystery series

"A unique and clever fantasy, *The Falling of the Moon* is a thoroughly entertaining read from first page to last. Very highly recommended and certain to be an enduring favorite."

—Midwest Book Review

"If you're looking for a great Autumn and Halloween read then look no further, this series has everything you need for a cozy fall evening spent reading. This one is 5/5 stars for me, it's absolutely perfect and a must read!"

—*Hollie Ohs Book Reviews*

Into the Moonless Night

Moonfall Mayhem, Book Three

A.E. DECKER

World Weaver Press

Published by World Weaver Press, LLC.
Albuquerque, New Mexico
www.WorldWeaverPress.com

Edited by Laura Harvey
Cover designed by World Weaver Press.
Cover illustration by Nicole Vandever.
Additional cover images used under license from Shutterstock.com.

First Edition, March 2018
ISBN-13: 978-0998702254
ISBN-10: 0-9987022-5-0

Also available as an ebook.

This book, in its odd way, is about parents. So this dedication is for Debra and Richard. Thanks for the love and support!

And to Charlie Daugherty, mentor, martial artist, and friend.

INTO THE MOONLESS NIGHT

A. E. Decker

CHAPTER ONE:
THE DEVIL YOU KNOW

A cramp threatened to double her over.

No. Clutching her ribs, Ascot galloped up the rise, leaden feet dragging. She burst over the crest and stubbed her toe on a rock. Stubbornly, she staggered another three steps before folding and gripping her knees. Her breath came in gasps.

Sere yellow earth stretched before her. Wind stroked its sparse coating of grass, like a hand sliding over satin sheets. *Go ahead*, it seemed to whisper. *Take a listen.*

Musn't succumb. Ascot gritted her teeth. But Moony was off chasing insects in the brush. Rags-n-Bones and Dmitri hadn't yet reached the summit.

She was alone. No one would see.

Must. Not. Succumb.

The grass rippled again. Sunlight struck a piece of mica embedded in the dirt. It winked like an eye.

Ascot succumbed. Kneeling, she pressed her ear to the ground. A glossy, black beetle scurried past her nose. *Hmmm, some sort of vibration*, she thought, listening intently. But was it the pounding of far-off feet, or merely the mountain suffering some stone-based indigestion? And if it was footsteps, was it the footsteps of three shifters, or a herd of deer?

"What are you doing?" asked Dmitri, directly behind her.

"Miss! Are you ill? Did you fall?" cried Rags-n-Bones, loping to her side.

"Don't give up now. You nearly caught that beetle." Moony scampered over excitedly, bushy gray tail swishing. "Just stick out your tongue and you'll have him."

Ascot closed her eyes. *They showed up the instant I crouched. Of course they did.* She lifted her head, sweat-damp hair peeling reluctantly from the ground. "I was looking for tracks," she said, combing out mud clumps with her fingers.

Dmitri sat on his haunches. When the big wolf's tail curled around his forepaws, Ascot braced herself. *You were playing ranger, weren't you?* he would say. *You've read about people who can deduce what their quarry had for breakfast by the depth of their footprints, and thought to do the same.*

"Ascot," he said, gently. "It might be that we can't catch up to them."

Catch. She didn't break, but the word—the *name*—struck the barrier she'd erected inside herself, hard. Six days of running, now. Six days of chasing Catch, Cavall, and Savotte over increasingly rugged terrain, ignoring blisters and side-stitches, never pausing in their relentless pursuit.

Except to eat. And sleep. And to reorient themselves when they realized their southward track had drifted east or west or—once, and most embarrassingly—north.

Don't forget the ladybug's funeral, she reminded herself. They'd lost an afternoon to mourning when Rags-n-Bones accidentally stepped on it. She bet rangers never gave a thought to the bugs they squashed while charging gazelle-like across the wasteland.

"We don't have to catch up to them," she said, forcing confidence. "We know they're heading to a city called Holdfast, somewhere to the south. Even we can't miss a city."

Except, the way things were going, they probably could. Ascot was beginning to think the moon could wander whistling across their path, and they'd be so busy singing a dirge to a fallen dragonfly they wouldn't notice.

"Can we take a break, miss?" asked Rags-n-Bones, glancing toward the bushes. "I need to..." He fidgeted significantly.

Another function rangers never seem to need to perform. "Certainly," she replied. Since they'd stopped anyway, she might as well attend to her blisters.

"Thank you, miss." He headed for the bushes at a grateful galumph.

"Ranger." Choosing a flat rock, Ascot sat. "Means 'one who can run endlessly without emptying his bladder.'"

Catch would like that, she reflected, yanking a clinging sock free. She'd have to remember it to tell him. Abandoning the beetle, Moony headed for a stand of conifers. Some kind of leaping cicada haunted the tough, saw-edged grass between the trees, periodically venturing forth to menace the trail, making hostile *bloc, bloc* noises. They terrified Rags-n-Bones, but Moony loved them. He'd already eaten four.

Dmitri's gaze remained fixed on her. "Ascot. You're not thinking clearly."

The underbrush beneath the trees rustled. Ascot turned her head sharply. Grass and peeling gray bark waved innocently back. Dismissing the noise, she peeled off her second sock, spread it beside the first, and edged away when the wind carried a whiff of them to her nose.

"Ascot," said Dmitri.

She hurled her boot. Not at Dmitri; just away, and hard. It bounced across the thin grass and yellow clay before clattering to a halt against a chunk of rotting bark. "We must get him out of there!" she cried. "He never wanted to go back. He called it an abattoir."

Dmitri waited until the puffs of dust settled around her flung boot before speaking. "And yet he went back, of his own volition. Perhaps he's concocted a scheme of his own."

Ascot stared at her bare feet. Wiggled a toe. Perhaps. Catch had told her he'd escape. But Catch lied. She was *never* going to believe his story about being taken captive by sentient teddy bears in Fluffendale.

Rags-n-Bones came loping back like a lopsided crane, scuffing his foot along the ground every third step. "Are we leaving soon, miss?" He tugged the ends of the purple muffler wrapped around his shoulders, exposing Nipper's furry back. Squeaking irritably, the rat burrowed deeper. "Only my shoe's gone floppy," Rags-n-Bones finished. Hesitantly, peeping up through his rusty forelock, he lifted his foot to display his peeling sole.

Rangers' boots never wore out in the stories. And all right, she'd given up believing stories were true, but why did reality have to be so bloody-minded and unforgiving? Ascot bit off a curse. The grass rustled again. But when she glanced at it, it instantly stilled.

"Something wrong?" asked Dmitri, noticing her shift in attention.

"I think we're being spied on," she replied in an undertone, watching the brush.

Moony burst out of a spiny hawthorn bush, in hot pursuit of a *bloc*-ing cicada. It looped toward Ascot. Without pause, Moony raced straight up Dmitri's backbone, leaped off his snout, and snatched the cicada in mid-flight.

"Oof," grunted Dmitri, shaking his head. But an idea struck Ascot. Almost before Moony's paws hit the ground, she grabbed him up.

"Oh, Moony, must you?" she demanded, turning him and his mouthful of wriggling, jointed legs into full view of the others.

On cue, Rags-n-Bones began wailing. Moony, unrepentant, crunched down cicada number five. "What's the sudden concern with insect rights?" he asked, licking his lips.

"Nonexistent," Ascot told him under the cover of Rags-n-Bones' sobs. "We're being watched. Investigate under that cedar—carefully!" she added, when he began wriggling with excitement.

"Count on me!" he whispered, fur crackling with sparks. She set him down. He spun around, licked the base of his spine, gave a ridiculous hop straight up into the air, and bounced off toward the cedars. "I'm going to eat more bugs!" he sang. "Bugs, bugs, bugs!"

Keeping an eye on him, Ascot patted Rags-n-Bones' arm. "There, there." She hated taking advantage of his sentimental nature. His sobs were already fading. Even Rags-n-Bones could only muster so much sympathy for the horrible, *bloc*-ing cicadas. "Maybe we can glue your sole with pine tar."

He smiled timorously. A baby screamed.

No, not a baby; it was a chicken getting murdered. Or, possibly, a pig that had decided to take up yodeling. Or—and this was beginning to seem the most likely—a dreadful combination of the three, mixed with the scrape of chalk against a blackboard.

Rags-n-Bones dashed to hide in Ascot's shadow as she leaped up, staring wildly about. Dmitri jabbed his nose toward the cedars. "It's coming from there," he cried just as a dark and terrible creature rose from the underbrush—hardly larger than a pillow, but stocky and powerfully built.

Moony recoiled, ears flat against his skull, as the creature's mouth opened in a wide pink triangle lined with white spikes. Still screeching, it dashed forward, jaws snapping.

And Moony—Moony, who'd throw himself at a bear!—scuttled back before its onslaught. "Help!" he cried, cupping a protective paw over his nose.

Shaking off her shock, Ascot grabbed up a branch and ran over, the saw-edged grass tearing her bare, blistered feet. Screaming, the creature spun to face her. It resembled a badger, but with a larger head. Black fur covered it, save for crescent-shaped white patches on its chest and rump. Ascot swung her branch at its notched and tattered left ear.

Whipping its head around, the creature caught the branch between its teeth and bit down. *Crunch.*

Ascot stared at the stub remaining in her grip. *That was thicker than my wrist.*

"No good," shouted Dmitri as he and Rags-n-Bones raced up. Rags-n-Bones kept going, straight past her and up a cedar tree, where he clung to a branch. "It's a Tasmanian devil," Dmitri continued. "Their jaws can bite through steel."

Moony set down the threatening paw he'd just lifted and retreated. For lack of other ideas, Ascot picked up a rock. Cocking her arm, she circled to the devil's left, while Dmitri paced right.

"Oh, please!" begged Rags-n-Bones, dangling off his branch. Tears poured down his face and dripped off his chin. "Please, Mr. Devil, don't be angry. We're nice people. Listen, I'll sing you a lullaby. *La, la, hush, little devil, don't be…evil. I'll give you a biscuit without any weevils.*"

The devil's screams petered out. It stared up at Rags-n-Bones who, as was his wont, became so enamored of his own off-key wailing that he forgot all else. Swaying lightly, knees hooked over the branch, he continued. *"If you're good, little devil, we'll be bestest friends evel—ever. I'll never pull your tail or feed you bevels—*Are bevels some kind of nasty berries?" he asked, cocking his head.

The wind brushed the summit softly, almost furtively, seemingly unsure of its welcome. Even the cicadas ceased *bloc*-ing. Into the new silence came a moist, disjointed, pop-and-crackle, like someone mauling a ham inside a paper bag. Too late, Ascot realized what it heralded.

"A bevel is an angled slope," said the dark-haired young man who materialized in the devil's place. Grimacing, he tugged his left earlobe, which was just as tattered in this shape. "Hang it. I intended to reveal myself eventually. Lost m'temper."

Reveal himself. Ascot fought down a hysterical giggle. Of course; the young man was a shifter. Why else would a Tasmanian devil be following them? And, also of course, he was completely naked. Shifters' clothes didn't transform along with flesh. Rags-n-Bones hid his flaming cheeks in his hands.

Dmitri took charge. "Why are you following us?"

Completely ignoring the nudity factor, thought Ascot, going to fetch a blanket. But then, Dmitri only cared about attire when he could offer fashion tips. Moony's tail thumped the fallen pine needles twice. Lifting a paw, he commenced savagely washing.

The devil-shifter kept tugging his ear. His human form was slimmer than what was suggested by his stocky devil-shape. Scars tracked the left side of his neck, starkly white against his tan skin. Even more horrifying was the slanting capital "F" branded across his left cheek, half-concealed by the fall of his dark hair. Mutilations aside, his face was symmetrical, with a straight, wide-bridged nose balancing out a square jaw.

"Right." His chin jerked in a nod. "M'name's Jolt Blackavar. I'm part of a group of rebel slipskins called the Hide Aways. You savvy 'slipskins'?"

"Shifters who refuse their allotted place in society," said Ascot, returning with the blanket. She held it out to Jolt. "Mind wrapping this about…about your middle?" Rags-n-Bones was going to combust shortly, otherwise.

"Humans and their weird fetishes." Jolt rolled his eyes. "Everyone has a body."

Ascot forebore from pointing out that she was half-noble Shadowvalian as he wrapped the blanket loosely about his waist and crouched on his heels, propping his elbows on his knees.

"Right," he said. "We keep an eye on Sniffers—slipskin hunters— like Cavall and Savotte. We noticed those two making trips to that human town—"

"Widget," said Rags-n-Bones, slipping off the branch. A sigh escaped him as he glanced north. Guilt pinched Ascot. This winter, in Widget, he'd just reconnected with a group of old friends known as the Meddlers of Moonshine. Yet when she'd asked, he'd left them to chase after Catch, smilingly, without a murmur.

"Right, Widget," said Jolt. "This last time they left, someone else came with them. Is it...?" He nodded to the amber ring on Ascot's left hand.

She spread her fingers and the tourmaline sparkling in the center of five petal-shaped bone slivers caught the sunlight and threw it back. The ring weighed so little she often forgot she was wearing it.

"That's the Starthorne crest," said Jolt. Looking back up, Ascot managed to meet his eyes. They were large, if narrow, pale as clover honey, and he always seemed to peer out their corners instead of facing people directly. "This is the year of the Moonless Night. Is the bloke with Cavall and Savotte Catch Starthorne?"

"What's the Moonless Night?" asked Dmitri. Beside him, Moony had worked up to a rude place in his washing, tail slapping the ground hard enough to raise dust.

"Supposedly, it's when Magden Le Fou's prophecy will be fulfilled," Jolt replied. "It's a lunar eclipse occurring three nights after the vernal equinox."

The prophecy, thought Ascot. The frabjacketing prophecy. Something about a golden star and—well, Catch hadn't elected to tell her much else, save that the shifters of the Clawcrags thought he was the golden star. Which was ridiculous. Had any of them ever *looked* at scruffy, roguish Catch? Heard him lie with a straight face, or seen him guzzle more coffee than anyone's kidneys could stand?

Frabjacket, how she missed him.

Dipping his head, Dmitri scratched the ground. Abruptly, his nostrils flared. "That's only nine days from now."

Ascot's throat turned into a stretch of dust. "Nine days?" It came out as a dry squeak. She worked some saliva into her mouth and swallowed. "What will become of Catch if nothing happens on the Moonless Night?"

She didn't want to hear it: the confirmation of her worst fears.

Had to hear it, just so she'd know. Jolt lifted a brow, seeming surprised that she'd even ask. "If he's not the golden star, then he's just another slipskin. There's only one penalty for slipping your skin in the Clawcrags." Jolt gave his earlobe a final tug. "Execution."

Ascot fell away inside herself. The world, shadowed and dark, floated at a distance, as if she stared at it through the cavern of her own skull. Every sound droned and echoed. Only the *bloc, bloc* of yet another cicada came to her, crisp as the ticking of some mocking clock.

She almost didn't hear Jolt speak again. "Want us to help rescue him?"

But she did hear him. Seizing hold of his words as she might a lifeline, she resurfaced in a world that contained light and hope, and took a breath.

"Yes," she replied.

CHAPTER TWO:
PITTED FOES

Catch droned:

> *"A raindrop dripped into a bucket with none.*
> Splash! *Went the droplet, and that made one.*
> *A second droplet dripped as a cold wind blew.*
> Splash! *Went the droplet, and that made two.*
> *A third droplet dripped off a branch of the tree.*
> Splash! *went the droplet, and that made three."*

Ahead on the trail, teeth ground. Cavall's black-gloved hand clenched a little tighter around the hilt of his sword.

Catch had learned the song from his old friend, King Alastor of Albright. Alastor had known a lot of inane songs—he hadn't appreciated exactly how many until this trip. It took a thousand droplets to fill the bucket. At five hundred, the *splashes* changed to *splooshes*, but Catch suspected he wasn't going to get that far.

> *"Another droplet dripped off the old sycamore.*
> Splash! *Went the droplet, and that made four.*
> *A fifth droplet dripped in a steady, wet dive.*

Splash! *Went the droplet, and that made—*"

Cavall whirled. "Shut up, shut up, shut up *now!*" he snarled, teeth bared.

Catch blinked innocently. "Does precious not appreciate music?"

Cavall punched him in the eye. Catch kicked Cavall's knee. Swearing, both went down in a flurry of flailing fists, churning up dust and dead pine needles in the trail's center. Cavall never noticed the moment Catch's hand snaked into his jacket pocket and removed the little leather drawstring pouch secreted there.

"That's enough." Sighing, Rainy Savotte stepped forward to break up their fifth brawl in a week.

"Why?" Cavall demanded sometime later, nursing a bitten hand. Lying on his back in the middle of the track, he could've been addressing Savotte, the sky, or any helpful philosophers who might be passing by. "He agreed to return to Holdfast. Fur and fangs, he made the bargain to return to Holdfast. So why is he trying to drag out the journey as long as possible?"

Because Ascot's out there, somewhere, thought Catch, sprawled panting against a tree stump. She was, wasn't she? Gingerly, he massaged his throbbing eyelid with the tips of two fingers. Of course she was. The last time someone she'd cared about was threatened, she'd ridden a hell-horse into a mob armed with pitchforks. His mind shut down trying to picture what she might be up to now.

Catch just hoped she hurried. The woman possessed many talents, but a sense of direction wasn't among them. And Cavall was right— he *had* made the bargain to return to Holdfast, meaning that if he attempted to escape, Alph Gildar would be within his rights to resume terrorizing Widget. But if Ascot's merry band stole him back, well, that was Cavall and Savotte's fault for not watching him closely enough.

Making soothing, if exasperated, noises, Savotte hauled Cavall to his feet. Cavall swatted dust off his shiny trousers. His face was a collection of narrow angles, with thin lips and pale blue eyes that gleamed like reflections thrown off ice. "I have a new curse," he grated. The man always did sound like he'd swallowed a bucket of sand. "Want to hear it? It's *Starthorne*."

"Precious is testy," said Catch. "Means 'cross,' 'irritable,' or 'cranky.'"

Cavall stepped forward, raising a fist, but Savotte grabbed his arm. "Don't," she said. Her gunmetal hair flowed as sleekly as ever over her shoulders, but the tightness of her bow lips said that even her temper was beginning to wear. "You're only playing his game. Besides, another fight will delay us reaching Highmoor and fresh coffee supplies."

Both she and Cavall directed glares at Catch. He grimaced. "Accidentally" dropping their coffee over Laststand Rise yesterday had required almost more fortitude than he possessed.

But it bought more time, he reminded himself. Before he'd done it, they might have avoided the little town of Highmoor. Now they were certain to stop, and once they were there, Catch was sure he could contrive further means of delay. *Perhaps I'll get myself arrested.* Getting arrested was a skill of his; he'd once managed it for drinking black coffee out of a white mug. *Fur and fangs, but I hated Twitmire.*

"Get up, Starthorne," said Savotte, aiming a kick at his side. He rolled out of the way before it connected—no one could kick like a horse-shifter. As he did, the letter in his inner left coat pocket rustled.

Careful, he thought. If Ascot didn't reach him in time, that scrap of paper could be the last bargaining chip between him and execution. He couldn't afford to give its presence away.

They started walking again, Cavall leading the way through the pine woods, Savotte falling in beside him. The wind, still bearing winter's bite, wove through the spindly trunks, tugging the tail of Catch's long, brown coat about his legs, and lashing his hair against his cheeks. He shivered. He wasn't cold—the wind couldn't penetrate the Smilodon fur he always wore, even when it didn't show—but it had a lonely sound.

"What I want to know is why he's playing this game," Cavall grumbled, kicking aside a large pinecone. "I assume he's not stupid. I assume he knows his life depends on his being the golden star."

The golden star. Catch stared fixedly ahead, his fist clenched around the lump wrapped in soft leather that he'd stolen from Cavall. *Prophecy, fate. No choice. Your life a fixed track leading to an inevitable destination—*

Pulsing, red threads surged up, choking his thoughts. *I came so close to dodging Magden Le Fou's ridiculous prophecy. If I could've kept away from the Clawcrags for another month, or if Ascot had agreed to journey on to Buenovilla rather than stopping in Widget last winter—*

But of course Ascot had chosen otherwise. She was a life-wrecking lunatic wrapped in pale skin and a black coat.

Or, at least, life-changing. Catch smiled, imagining her tangled black hair and expression of indignant determination. The red tide in his head receded, becoming a faint wash rather than saturation. Closing his ears to Cavall and Savotte's conversation, he examined the purloined pouch. He'd first glimpsed it their second night of travel, coming back to the campfire with an armload of wood, to find Cavall bending over the flames. A branch had snapped under Catch's boot, and Cavall spun around, but not before Catch noticed him hastily tucking something into his pocket.

The fool should've realized that pretending it didn't exist was the quickest way to gain my interest, thought Catch, touching his eye again. Spider-lines of pain flared through the socket. *Damn the black-clad nightmare. If he didn't insist on wearing skin-tight leather, I could've simply picked his pocket while we walked instead of having to goad him into a fight.*

An embossed blot of golden wax sealed the pouch's strings. Recognizing Alph Gildar's insignia of a pawprint inside a rising sun, Catch took great pleasure in prying it off with his nail, flicking it away, and, for good measure, trampling it deep into the fallen pine needles.

The pouch's silken strings unknotted easily. Catch glanced up at Cavall and Savotte through the lock of hair that always fell in his face, then shook the pouch's contents into his palm.

A silent explosion erupted in his head. His breath rushed out of his chest and into his throat, choking him. "Where'd you get this?"

Distantly, Catch realized that he'd stopped in his tracks. The roaring in his ears drowned the patter of needles raining from the branches. It didn't drown the strangled, gargling noise Cavall made. "How'd you get *that*?" he gasped, blood draining from his face.

Savotte looked from him to Catch. The elegant arches of her brows, like two swipes of ink, drew together. "What's going on?"

In three swift strides, Cavall closed the distance between him and Catch. "That was my father's," he rasped, grabbing the cord of the moonstone pendant resting in Catch's palm.

Catch hooked a finger in the opposite loop, stretching the cord tight between them. "And that was *my* father's," he said, pointing to the ring threaded through the cord. A black pearl, centered between five amber slivers shaped like sharply-pointed petals, seemed to suck in sunlight. Tiny, carved thorns jutted from the bone band. It was the twin to a ring he'd last seen on Ascot's hand, reversed in color. A peach pit with a coppery sheen dangled between the ring and pendant.

He and Cavall stared at one another. Savotte's fists went to her hips. A foot began tapping. "I repeat; what's going on?"

"Alph Gildar told me to give this to Starthorne after we reached the Underway," said Cavall. An entire beach's-worth of sand seemed stuck in his throat. "I watched him drop the ring in the pouch and seal it up. So, how—"

Catch lifted a brow. "How did Gildar get his paws on my father's ring?"

Cavall's gaze dropped. Savotte's toe ceased tapping. Blades of saw-edged grass, ruffled by the wind, made little rasping sounds.

"Your father's dead," said Cavall.

Catch frowned. "No, he isn't."

A muscle in Cavall's jaw jumped. "He died a year after you…left Holdfast."

Lethe Starthorne, dead. The idea fell into blackness without an echo. Catch stared at the ring swinging off the cord. He remembered the bubble trapped near one petal's tip. "Let's pretend I believe you," he said, untying the cord's knot. "If you watched Gildar put the ring in the pouch, how did it come to be tied to your father's pendant and a custard peach pit? Did Gildar take up prestidigitation while I was away?"

He removed the ring and the peach pit and retied the knot. Only as he gave the cord a little jerk to secure it did he realize that it was taking a long while to answer a simple question. Glancing up, he met Cavall's eyes, blue and staring in a slack face. "What?" asked Catch.

Cavall shook his head. "That's not a custard peach pit."

Catch ran his thumb over the hole that had been drilled in the pit for the cord to pass through. It was heavier than a normal pit. A richly bittersweet aroma came off it, clinging to his fingers. "Yes, it is." He remembered pilfering custard peaches from the Alph's grove as a cub, with Gildar's son, Glim.

He was *not* going to think about Glim.

"Can't be." Cavall turned away, making a show of running his fingers through his hair. "I know the tree this came from."

"Impossible," said Catch. Custard peaches were the royal fruit of the Clawcrags. Every tree in existence grew in the Alph's grove. Only a few elite shifters ever saw them, and such a group did not include hound-shifters like Cavall.

Mutely, Cavall transferred his gaze to the ring and pit lying on the deflated pouch in Catch's palm.

Good reply, thought Catch. He scratched his jaw. "Where is this tree?"

"Highmoor."

"Your hometown."

"Yes," said Cavall. A muscle still twitched in his jaw, but aside from that, he'd hardened his face into an expressionless mask. "My father was stationed there, to apprehend slipskins. He was killed there." He looked down at the moonstone pendant, attached to the cord by some braided knotwork of thread or hair. His voice thickened, growing raspier. "This was on his body when…"

His father was killed. Mine—again Catch's thoughts wandered into a hollow black void, lost and confused. Lethe Starthorne didn't die—he killed. Shaking off the sense of disorientation, Catch tucked his father's ring into a pocket. An amber petal caught the light, glowing palely yellow. It was a colder hue than Ascot's ring.

Ascot. You are *looking for me, right?* Hating himself for asking, his eyes went northward, tracking the jagged slopes of yellow earth and sparse conifers clinging to the mountainside. Of course she was looking.

Deliberately, he put her from his mind and turned to Cavall. "We're headed to Highmoor anyway. Let's have a look at this tree." It couldn't be a custard peach tree. Cavall had to be mistaken.

"Yes." Cavall's hand tightened around the pendant. He drew a breath. "Yes. I never learned exactly what happened. Maybe whoever sent this knows." His lips bent into something that wasn't exactly a smile. "Perhaps I'll finally learn the truth."

"If precious is ready for the truth," said Catch.

Cavall's not-smile transformed instantly to a scowl. Pivoting, he stalked up the trail, kicking weeds and snatching up the latest cicada to come *bloc*-ing out of the woods.

"Is it scrumptious, precious?" Catch called. "Is it crunchably delicious?" Cavall ignored him. Catch released a silent breath. Thank goodness. He and the leather-clad nightmare had almost been bonding there for a minute.

A pinch on his upper arm made him hiss. Savotte, forgotten until now, had crept up and administered it. Rubbing his bicep, he looked down into her eyes, clear and brown as a cup of strong tea. "Galen's too distracted now to wonder how you got the pouch," she said. "But I'm not. You picked his pocket, didn't you? What else have you stolen?"

"Nothing," he replied, mentally tallying the brooch, comb, ebony pen, pocketknife, and bag of molasses sweets he'd lifted from her. *I was bored,* he replied defiantly to the reprimanding voice in his head. She wore the Sniffers' usual two-toned gray uniform, making her an easier target than her leather-clad partner.

The curve of her mouth flattened, pulling down the beauty mark on her upper lip. "Very well," she said, and quickened her pace.

She believed him? Before Catch could comfort himself with such an obvious lie, she spoke again. "I've been watching you. You're due to shift, probably before we reach the Underway. When you do, I'll go through your pockets. All of them."

Catch stiffened. *The letter.* It didn't rustle, but he was abruptly, painfully aware of its slight weight in his inner left pocket. He heard the voice of Tipper Petroyvan, the ghostly owl-shifter, whispering to him in Equinor Cemetery. *"It's the real reason I fled the Clawcrags. Bad enough to live a life you loathe. Worse to discover it's all a façade."*

If Savotte found it, there went the only thing he could possibly use to buy his life if Ascot didn't save him and he wasn't the golden star.

Which he wasn't. So, there went the only thing he had to buy his life. *Bored now?* asked the voice in his head, and laughed.

CHAPTER THREE:
FISHING FOR TROUBLE

"Almost there." Jolt pointed to a wooden post hammered into the roadside as the wagon juddered along.

Half-standing on the driver's bench between him and Bellmonte, another Hide Away, Ascot cupped her hand over her eyes. Afleeta, the third Hide Away present, pulled the wagon, shaking her black mane and snatching weeds as she clomped along. Ascot had never seen her in human form. Apparently, she wasn't fond of it.

"Highmoor, one mile," said Ascot, reading out the name painted in weathered, white letters down the post's side. She rubbed her rump before sitting again. A patina of bruises had built up there after two day's jouncing over bumpy mountain roads.

Seven days until the Moonless Night. She only hoped they'd beaten Cavall's group to Highmoor. "Are you sure they'll stop here?" she asked Jolt—again.

Sighing, he shifted the licorice root he was chewing on to the other corner of his mouth. At least he was dressed now, in a sleeveless shirt, drawstring trousers, and soft boots. Plain, dark attire, save for the vermillion mantle patterned with white dragonflies draped around his shoulders. "Our group's been watching them. Starthorne tossed their coffee supply over a cliff three days ago. They must be about ready to eat each other. Highmoor's the last place they can restock before they enter the Underway."

Ascot, who'd watched Catch gnaw on raw acorns when deprived of his coffee fix, nodded. But Dmitri, curled amongst the crates in the wagon's bed, lifted his head. "What's the Underway?" he asked. Rags-n-Bones sat beside him, singing his devil song and twanging his flapping sole. Moony, braced on his hind legs, peered over the bed's rear, watching the road unfurl behind them. He'd been very quiet ever since meeting Jolt.

"It's a series of tunnels through Mt. Skylash," said Bellmonte. He was a tall man with dark hair and features so chiseled he should've carried a bottle of polish to go with them. His broad shoulders and cleft chin could've graced the covers of the sort of volumes Ascot often saw girls giggling over when she accompanied Dmitri into a bookstore.

"The Underway leads into Holdfast," Jolt added. "But its entrances are sealed alchemically, so once they enter it, we haven't a chance of overtaking them."

Rags-n-Bones' fingers stilled. "Alchemy?" he asked, leaning forward. One of his Meddler friends, Master Porpetti, was an alchemist. "You might be able to open it with water. Water talks to rock."

Jolt gave Rags-n-Bones a side-eyed look. Ascot gathered he was impressed. She was blinking herself; she had no idea he'd actually been learning alchemy while staying with Master Porpetti and the Ashuren siblings this winter.

"Maybe so," said Jolt, "but you're also more likely to run into Sniffers around Mt. Skylash. We'll stick to the plan of ambushing Cavall and Savotte in Highmoor."

"Simple, but effective." Dmitri settled his chin on his crossed paws. "Cavall and Savotte are only two, and if we abduct the captain, he can't be blamed for absconding. The Alph's deal to leave off harassing Widget should hold."

Ascot hadn't even considered possible retribution to Widget. *When did I grow so selfish?* she wondered. Fretting over Catch, she'd barely talked to her new companions. "What kind of shifter are you, Bellmonte?" she asked, hoping to belatedly make up for her rudeness.

"I am a cow-shifter, miss," he replied gravely.

Ascot shook her head. Had a cicada just buzzed past, blurring her hearing? "Cow? Surely you mean—"

Jolt nudged her. "He doesn't," he whispered. "Shifting's complicated. Sometimes things get a bit mixed up."

A cow. Ascot glanced sidelong at tall, rugged Bellmonte and pinched herself.

"I like cows," said Rags-n-Bones. "They chew grass and gaze off into the horizon as if they know something deep and secret."

Bellmonte beamed. "We do."

There really wasn't anything to say to that. Ascot occupied herself in studying the rough, rugged countryside, seared yellow by the sun, with the sky spreading like a wrinkled blue kerchief overhead.

Isn't Highmoor Cavall's hometown? she thought, remembering words overheard in a graveyard. Surely there was some mistake. Cavall had to have grown up in a cold, wet country of somber, green forests and gray stone—

Frabjacket, was she believing life should be a story again? She sighed. Would she ever outgrow that habit? But the notion only grew more ludicrous as the the wagon passed under a swinging sign and Highmoor unfolded around them. Single-storied, slat-sided buildings bordered rutted, yellow dirt streets. Pine trees provided shade for tiny yards enclosed by ramshackle fences.

Cavall, with his strut and black leather, grew up here? It seemed such a…plain place.

Afleeta drew up before a bait and tackle shop. "They're rather keen on fishing here, you may discover," said Bellmonte.

"Good coffee, though," said Jolt, jumping to the street and stretching.

"So long as they don't have rules about public wolfy-ness," grumbled Dmitri, leaping off the wagon bed. The wagon springs *sproinged* gratefully as he shook off a cloud of loose fur.

"This isn't Twitmire," said Ascot. They wouldn't allow fishing in Twitmire, or for that matter, much of anything else. Before Twitmire, Ascot would never have imagined it was possible for anyone to get arrested sixteen times in a single day. *Catch must've been trying to prove some asinine point.* She looked up and down the street. Plaid-clad passers-by nodded, offering friendly "Mornin's" before continuing on.

No sign of Cavall. Perhaps they *had* beaten his group to Highmoor. Buttery black leather would show up here like...well, like buttery black leather in a sea of plaid. "What now?" she asked Jolt.

"They'll get fresh coffee at The Nook," he replied. His brand was garnering curious looks. Dipping his head, he combed his hair to screen his left cheek. "Best breakfast spot in town. Pancakes so large they flop over the edges of the plates."

"Breakfast?" Rags-n-Bones looked around hopefully, licking his lips, as if he expected someone to bustle up and offer a plate of jam-filled doughnuts.

"Yes, why don't you go there with Bellmonte?" said Jolt. For an instant, Ascot thought something flashed through his expression, like the shadow of a shark passing beneath the ocean's surface. "If they're not there yet, get something to eat."

"And if they are?" asked Dmitri, acting all brisk and focused. But Ascot, knowing his love of sweets, could tell his imagination had been piqued by the mention of plate-sized pancakes. She had no appetite herself. Someone was turning a fork in her innards, twisting it tighter and tighter. *Catch might be here, now.*

"Then come back and wait by Alfeeta," said Jolt, patting the bay horse's side. Grunting, she swished her tail and continued munching down weeds from the side of the tackle shop's porch, without a care for their thorns. "We don't want a confrontation in front of the locals. Meanwhile, I'll scout the town."

"And what if you find Cavall's group?" Ascot called as he started up the street.

Jolt grinned over his shoulder. "If I find them, I'll scream," he replied, and ducked around a corner.

Not much of a plan, she thought, staring after him. She wanted certainty, definition…she wanted too much. *Really, we're lucky the Hide Aways came along to help us, considering we were well on on way to wandering back to Twitmire and getting arrested again.* Forcing down her misgivings, she turned to the only one remaining in the wagon. "Want to get some breakfast, Moony?" Perhaps smoked salmon would coax him into a better humor.

Moony's big, orange eyes stared past her. His bat-wings beat the air once. "I smell fish offal," he said. Jumping out of the wagon bed, he slithered under the bait shop's porch.

"Moony, get back here," said Ascot.

His tail twitched once and slid out of sight.

"What's the matter?" asked Bellmonte.

"He's still angry about the fight with Jolt," she replied, crouching to peer under the porch. As a kitten, Moony had once come out rather the worse in a scrap with an overgrown warg-rat. He'd spent the next three weeks dashing out to the stables at odd hours, challenging her father's carriage horses to single combat. She still remembered their bored expressions as Moony clung to their backs like a furry, four-legged starfish, trying to pierce their leathery hides with his tiny teeth.

If Moony was under the porch, his gray fur camouflaged him perfectly. "Frabjacket!"

"Perhaps you should leave him to explore?" said Dmitri, cocking his head.

"He's not looking to explore. He's looking for trouble." Ascot dusted off her knees. "I'd better find him before he finds it. You go ahead to The Nook as planned."

"Mm," said Dmitri, but it was one of his considering "mm"s, not an annoying one, as his love of pastries vied with his more intellectual self. Ascot almost saw the moment the scale tipped toward gluttony. "Perhaps that's better. Come along, Prince Myshkin."

Rags-n-Bones scratched his head. "You always call me Prince Mushkin. I like mush, especially with jam, but it's not my favorite. Shouldn't you call me Prince Avocado-kin?"

Sighing, Dmitri took the hem of Rags-n-Bones' garrick coat between his teeth. "You keep Moony from terrorizing the town," he said to Ascot. "Meanwhile, I'll try to explain Dostoyevsky to the prince here, while we watch for Cavall."

❧

Catch's skin felt tightly stretched over his body. His eyeeteeth ached, and when he'd awakened this morning, he'd had trouble tearing his gaze from a deer he spotted through the trees.

Plus, he had a caffeine headache. Growling, he massaged his temples. The chill morning air smelled sweet and faintly smoky, like a dissipating whiff of cherry incense. It came from the spiny-leaved pink flowers clustering the ground under the trees. Cavall, as usual, led the way, his pace brisk as a hound straining at the leash. Ahead stretched the small town of Highmoor, composed of simple, slat-sided houses with bark tile roofs and split wood fences.

"The Smilodon wants out, doesn't it?" asked Savotte, walking beside Catch, hair swinging in a sleek sheet about her shoulders. She smiled, too sympathetically.

"Maybe I'll let it eat you," Catch retorted, dropping his hands. There *was* a primitive part of his Smilodon brain that insisted horses were delicious.

Savotte snorted like the horse she currently wasn't. "You're not a killer, Starthorne. Blame yourself for starting this pocket-picking game." Snatching up a flower—sleepyheads, he remembered, so-named for the inwardly-curling petals that gave their yellow centers a drowsy, lidded appearance—she set it between her teeth and moved up to walk beside Cavall.

"I wouldn't suggest going through my pockets," he called at her back. "They're booby-trapped with alchemical bombs. Plus, I've hired a saber-fanged mini-otter named Opie to guard them. I pay him in raisins."

Both ignored him. Maybe he *should* eat her. Or sing "The Prickliest Hedgehog." *If I sing that, she might beg me to eat her.* That particular inane ditty not only stayed in your head; it virtually set up camp there.

His mad little snicker told him exactly how strong his need to shift had grown. Shoving his hands in his pockets, Catch scuffed his toe against a sleepyhead. Pink petals clung to his boot. The muddy pong of the Wandering River, a flat, silver snake rippling to the east, clogged his nostrils, blocking the scents of pine tar and dust, and the oily over-tang of fish. He kicked another flower and the paper in his inner left pocket rustled.

Bones and shards, what was he going to do? Still no sign of Ascot, and he couldn't put off shifting more than a couple days. And even if Cavall and Savotte missed the hint contained in the letter, they'd notice the signature at its bottom. They'd confiscate it and turn it over to Gildar, who would not miss the hint.

Not only will he not miss the hint, but he'll probably make sure Cavall and Savotte experience some "unfortunate accident," just in case they noticed the hint, thought Catch, kicking a pinecone. Some satisfaction, he supposed, except he'd likely be too dead by then to care.

His toe scraped Cavall's heel, startling him from his thoughts. "What?" he said, stepping back.

Cavall had stopped at the foot of a long drive covered in flint chips. Here, on the last flat piece of earth between the river and the town, someone had built a sprawling, single-story ranch house and left it to decay. Its front door hung crookedly off its top hinge. A spider had woven a splendid web in the bottom corner's gaping black space. For Ascot's sake, Catch tried to make out letters in it, but the morning dewdrops just sparkled on the usual whorls.

"Lousiest coffeeshop I've ever laid eyes on," he said.

"We'll get coffee after," said Cavall in a queer, tight voice, his gaze nailed to the gaping doorway. The moonstone pendant hung from his fingers, gleaming milky blue.

A patch of missing tiles on the ranch house's roof made a lopsided plus sign. The longer Catch stared at it, the harder something nipped the undercurrent of his thoughts. It made the space between his shoulders itch. Made him want to run.

"Your father's house." Savotte sucked in a breath through her nose. "Well. Let's get this done with."

"I say let precious explore the old ruin if he likes," said Catch. The nibbling in his head turned to outright gnawing; old memories gobbling up new thoughts, resurfacing like some hideous sea monter. His eyes dropped from the gap in the roof to the rickety railing of an old corral around the house's corner. His muscles jerked briefly, as if part of him had already bolted.

Cavall walked toward the house's rear. Savotte prodded Catch's back. "Move, Starthorne," she said, her tone promising a kick if he balked. Shoving his hands deep in his pockets, he complied, feigning indifference even as sweat prickled under his armpits.

This is ridiculous. I've never seen this ranch house before, have I? No, of course not. He shook his head. He was only going along with this to waste more time. Cavall had to be wrong about a custard peach tree growing in Highmoor. It would turn out to be some kind of aberrant apricot.

When Cavall stepped over the corral's wobbly, split-log railing, the rotting wood fell right out of the post's socket. As Catch followed with Savotte, he glanced up at the hayloft. A beam with a hook swinging from it jutted out over its open, square door. Particles of old hay swirled in a sunbeam, as if recently stirred. Catch stared at the hook. The itching between his shoulders grew nails.

Cavall strode across the corral, eyes locked on a tree growing up against a corner of the barn. Its thin branches, covered in shiny, elongated-teardrop leaves, crooked tentatively toward the sky, like a blind man feeling for an object just out of reach. Cavall laid his palm against its bark. His shoulders swelled and subsided with a heavy sigh. "Here is it. Is it a custard peach, Starthorne?"

Catch stared into the barn's open doorway, at the soft piles of straw and old rope coiled any which way, and the big, elliptical knothole in one board. The breeze wafting from the east rustled the tree's leaves, carrying a striking scent to his nose. Both sweet and golden, it seemed composed of apricot jam and caramel, with a touch of rum, a pinch of lemon peel, and a double pinch of cinnamon.

Whenever he tried to gather his thoughts, they combusted in a brilliant, red explosion, so he hugged himself and shook, listening to the wind whistle through the cracks in the barn's side, bringing with it a curious, rich-sweet aroma.

"Oh, yes, precious," said Catch, still staring into the barn. "It's a custard peach."

He began to laugh. It was indeed a custard peach.

And he'd seen it before.

CHAPTER FOUR:
PEACHY KEEN

Ascot meandered southward down Highmoor's main street, pausing to peer under porches or into yards. "Moony?" she called, spotting motion under a scruffy alder bush. A big-eared streak of gray-brown fur darted out and dashed down the street. Just a hare.

Sighing, Ascot straightened, swatted a cicada, and continued on her way. *Where could Moony be?* she wondered, passing a house topped with a weathervane shaped like a leaping trout.

She hardly cared. Let Moony have his fun. How much trouble could he get into in this sleepy fishing town? All that really mattered was that this interminable, frustrating period of waiting passed, passed soon, that they reclaimed Catch, and returned to happily wandering the continent of Alumbria.

Does Rags-n-Bones really want to keep traveling? Maybe he'd be happier in Widget, with Master Porpetti and the Ashurens.

She had no reply to that. Reaching the end of the street, she stood staring south. The wind, blowing damp, tangled her already disheveled black hair with its new white streak by her temple. The scent of freshly blossomed flowers almost cloaked the prevalent, ammonia tang of fish.

I should go back, she thought. But she couldn't pull her gaze from the mountain's curiously split peak, which seemed to be making a rude gesture at her. *That's Mt. Skylash, the one with the tunnel leading through it.* Through conversations with Jolt, she now knew the city of Holdfast stood on a plateau between it and the next mountain, Mt. Snagtooth.

The wind keened again. Another sound rose above it. Ascot stiffened as she recognized the distant, but hideously familiar cry of a furious baby mixed with a chicken getting murdered.

❧

Savotte shook Catch's arm. "What's the matter with you, Starthorne? You've gone white."

He shrugged her off. "Oh, I'm grand." Almost drunkenly, he crossed the corral. A small lump crunched underfoot. He lifted his boot. A pit glinted through the corral's yellow dust, oval and corrugated with a coppery sheen. Except for the lack of a drilled hole, it was identical to the one strung on Cavall's pendant. Catch picked it up and laughed again. "A custard peach in Highmoor."

"Are you sure?" Cavall yanked his palm from the tree as if it had stung him and stared up into its branches. "The fruits always wither before they ripen."

"They would, with only one tree." Catch tossed the pit at Cavall who flinched out of its path. "I suppose Daddy never made you custard peach custard for dessert."

Cavall glared, gloved hand tightening on his sword. "My father couldn't have known it was a custard peach. That—"

"Would've been an act of defiance worthy of the greatest slipskin," Catch finished for him.

Some expression beyond anger flared in Cavall's face. "My father was not a slipskin."

A tiny motion overhead made Catch lift his gaze. Twelve feet above him, a man peered around the hayloft's opening. If Cavall hadn't been glaring at him, and Savotte watching Cavall worriedly, they might've spotted the intruder, for not only was he exceedingly pale, white-skinned and white-haired, he also wore a long and flashy, if faded, red coat. Grinning, he put a finger to his lips.

A rescuer? Beneath the red coat, the pale man wore a sleeveless shirt and drawstring trousers: shifter-garb. *Maybe Ascot sent him,* Catch told his stupidly sinking spirits. What mattered who rescued him? The important thing was—

A breeze rustled the custard peach tree. Another waft of brandy-sweet scent blew past, mingling with dusty hay smells from the barn. Catch's brain threw up another memory.

He lay in the darkness, shaking. The barn door creaked open. A young man, probably only a few years older than himself, entered, bearing a steaming bowl between his hands.

"Father thought you might be hungry," he said, crouching, eyes two slits of blue in the dimness. His nose was thin and beaky. Black hair fell to his shoulders.

Staggering forward, Catch grabbed Cavall's shoulder for support as the taller man stalked up. "Hey," growled Cavall, pulling back.

Catch's grip tightened, black leather squeaking between his fingers. "We met," he choked. "Here, in this barn, twenty-five years ago. You brought me a bowl of smoked trout chowder."

Breath hissed between Cavall's teeth. "That was *you*?" He leaned forward, scanning Catch's face. "You were so bruised, your eyes virtually swollen shut."

"I could barely see," Catch replied. "No wonder I didn't recognize you in Widget, either." But they'd felt something, instantly. They'd been like ticks under each other's skin since their first meeting.

No, not our first meeting, thought Catch. They stared at one another. Down by the river, a baby screamed.

❧

Ascot was running. She hadn't realized she'd started running, but the gray walls of slat-sided houses flashed past. Her nerves rang, like tight wires struck with a hammer.

If I find them, I'll scream. Jolt had said that, hadn't he? That was definitely a Tasmanian devil's screech. The sound was something like childbirth, apparently; you forgot the pain shortly after experiencing it.

I should go fetch Dmitri and Rags, she thought. Her feet kept pounding against the hard, yellow ground. Hoofbeats sounded behind her. "Afleeta," cried Ascot as the bay horse trotted up behind her. "Wonderful! Go tell—"

She paused, thoughts whirling. Would Dmitri and Rags-n-Bones recognize Afleeta if she shifted to human form? She'd have to find clothes; that would take time. *I should run to The Nook myself. But Jolt screamed! That means Catch is here.* Ascot glanced behind her. Back toward the river.

Afleeta twisted her nose toward her back; a clear "Get on" gesture.

Maybe the Hide Aways have already informed Dmitri and Rags. Yes; that must be it. Relieved, Ascot climbed onto Afleeta's back. The instant she did, Afleeta began cantering toward the river.

Ascot tugged her mane. "Dmitri and Rags are coming too, right?"

Afleeta's ear flicked twice. Was that a "yes?" Jolt screamed again, and Afleeta accelerated into a gallop. Ascot nearly slipped off, reclaimed her grip, and clung on.

Two flicks. Surely she meant yes, thought Ascot, gritting her teeth as the smooth ground gave way to rockier terrain.

Surely.

❧

The baby was very angry. Perhaps it was even a ghost baby. The eerie, echoing shrillness of its shrieks lifted the hairs on Catch's neck.

"What the buzzard's guts is that?" demanded Savotte, running past him and Cavall to stare toward the river. After a moment, Cavall cursed, jerked free of Catch, and joined her by the corral railing.

Catch pressed splayed fingers to his temples. He remembered almost nothing of the time immediately after he…left…Holdfast. He recalled the spinning end over end. The rush of air. Blood, stinking hot and coppery in his nostrils. The alternating flashes of dull pink and deep gray behind his closed eyelids.

Nothing before. Nothing after. Until now.

A pebble struck the ground by his boot. He looked up. The pale man stood in the hayloft's doorway again. *Did you slip the pouch in Cavall's pocket to lure him here?* Catch wondered. If the pit came from this tree, it couldn't have been Gildar. Considering that Gildar had been willing to raze Widget over the theft of the Moonlight Muscatel vines, if he'd known of the existence of a custard peach tree in Highmoor, there wouldn't be anything left of the town, save for a smoking pit with a sign pointing to it reading: "Don't muck with shifters' fruit" for everyone to gleefully misconstrue.

Cavall turned from the railing. "Some rabbit getting murdered."

"If that was a rabbit, it was a possessed rabbit," muttered Savotte. She kept watch a moment longer, shielding her eyes. "We've spent enough time here. Let's go buy some coffee and be on our way."

"Not yet." Dismissing her with a curt gesture, Cavall stepped closer to Catch, expression probing, intense. "My father, Arctic Cavall, was murdered shortly after you vanished from the barn. Did you see anyone suspicious? Speak to anyone?"

"After I vanished from the barn...I vanished from the barn?" Catch scratched his cheek. He'd only just remembered the barn, and it still seemed disjointed, like a sequence from a dream. He tried to concentrate, but a sharp, staccato rhythm kept chopping into his train of thought. Only when Savotte looked toward the barn's corner, irritation creasing her face, did he realize that the sound was real, not the phantom of a long-lost memory.

Hoofbeats, clattering on the gravel drive. "Catch!" called a voice. Ascot's voice.

❧

He's really here, thought Ascot as Afleeta cleared the barn's corner. Really horribly rumpled and bruised and likely stinking of sweat and dirty leather, but right before her. The lines of his face and body were softening with little twitches and jerks, like he'd been knotted up so long he'd forgotten how to relax.

Afleeta pulled up and Ascot slid off her back. "Ascot," said Catch as she ran to him.

And then her arms were around him, and his breath in her ear, and yes, he did smell—she probably did, too—but he was warm and solid, and beneath the pungent odors were the familiar, comforting ones she associated with him: coffee and fresh-cut grass and nutmeg and…him.

Him.

"My diddle-darling," he said.

Smiling, she rested her chin on his shoulder. She'd kill him later.

"Where are Dmitri and Rags?" he whispered.

"Coming," she replied quickly. Too quickly. She hoped it didn't sound guilty. She hoped she wasn't lying. Where were they?

"Miss Nuisance."

Ascot would recognize that sand-and-silk voice amongst the babble of a thousand. She released Catch as Cavall came strolling over. "Galen," she replied. Oh, he was as beautiful as ever, tall and lean and practically painted into his black leather, wind ruffling his silky dark hair. But somewhere along the way, he'd lost that edge of glamour that had captivated her in Widget. He just seemed a man to her, now.

Well, a hound-shifter. And under his lazy, insinuating smile, she noticed marks of strain in his face. Rainy Savotte stood across the corral, her elegant, long-nosed features fixed in a severe expression.

"What are you doing here, Miss Abberdorf?" she demanded. "Starthorne agreed to this. There will be dire consequence for that human town if he reneges."

"But not if he's abducted," said Jolt, rising from a patch of scrub ten feet beyond the far railing.

Cavall whirled, drawing the black-hilted sword that hung at his hips in a blur of motion. Jolt had a rough voice, too; honey-and-gravel as opposed to Cavall's silk and sand. He also had a small, but lethal-looking, crossbow which he leveled with a smirk.

Glancing at Savotte, who'd unsheathed a knife with a curving, wicked blade, Cavall snorted. "You've only one bolt," he said, and, shoulder to shoulder with Savotte, began advancing on Jolt, who stood his ground, still smirking.

I should've waited for Dmitri and Rags, thought Ascot, mouth dry, pulse racing. She reached back, seeking Catch's hand, and found it. Her ring's band cut into her finger as she squeezed his hand, hard.

With a small explosion of hay, a pale man vaulted from the barn loft, twisted mid-air, and caught the pulley one-handed. When he landed, it was on his feet, and with a second crossbow pointed directly at Savotte's head. "Count the bolts again, leather-britches," he called.

Cavall spun around. His shocked expression transformed into one of pure, distilled outrage. "Starley Reftkin!"

Grinning from ear-to-ear, the pale man bowed, sweeping back a tail of his faded red coat. Even his eyelashes were white, as were his arched brows. A somewhat long, pointed nose and a droll mouth gave a look of deviltry to his otherwise heart-shaped face. A red bandana kept his shoulder-length white hair out of his eyes.

Visibly grinding his teeth, Cavall cast a swift glare over his shoulder at Jolt. "I should've—"

Starley held up a finger in the most insolent gesture Ascot had ever seen. It stopped Cavall mid-sentence. Dipping into his pocket, crossbow never wavering, Starley came up with a small jar, undid the cork with his teeth, scooped up a finger-full of the salve inside, and rubbed it over his face.

"That's better," he said, recorking the jar. He squinted at the sun, murky gray eyes narrowing. "Brighter day than expected. I burn so easily. Right." He tucked away the jar and waggled the crossbow. "Yes, Galen, yada, yada, you should've expected, whatsit. Doesn't matter, now, does it? Because I twitch my finger, and Rainy has a fresh hole in her head. My comrade there can do likewise to you. So frankly, since we're starting to look like some great whatsit—centipede—all lined up like this, why don't you two step back and let us walk away with Starthorne?"

"I'll walk away with your *hide*, you damned weasel," snarled Cavall, slowly ratcheting up to an almost demented fury. Ascot wouldn't have been surprised to see a trail of smoke drift out of his nostrils.

"That's *stoat!*" Starley retorted, wrapping his two inner fingers over the outer ones and thrusting his hand downwards. Whatever it signified, Cavall practically exploded. He stepped forward, but Savotte threw out her arm, barring his way.

"Not now, Galen," she said.

Despite her less than convivial history with Savotte, Ascot nodded agreement. "There's no need for anyone to get hurt."

Savotte threw her a look of utter scorn. "There's no need for us to fight now. Not when we can retreat, marshal a party of Sniffers, and hunt you down well before the Moonless Night."

"No," rasped Cavall, straining against her outstretched arm. A moonstone pendant swung from his shaking fingers. "Not yet. Not until Starthorne remembers. Did someone help you leave the barn? Did that person kill my father?"

Catch—the oddly quiet Catch, Ascot realized—seemed to be studying his own brain, so inward-turning was his gaze. Lifting his head, he shook his badly-in-need-of-a-trim hair out of his eyes. The right one was puffed and bruised. "I don't remember your father at all. But if he planted that tree, if he helped me, he was a slipskin."

"No!" Cavall twitched under his black leather. "He—"

Starley sighed theatrically. "Not interested in standing around 'til I burn, leather-britches," he said, empahsisizng his words with jabs of his crossbow. "Work on your daddy issues while the two of you stand under the peach tree and watch us leave with Starthorne."

Savotte managed to drag the glaring Cavall off to stand beneath the indicated tree. Amazingly, it didn't wither from the heat pouring off him. Ascot cast him a regretful glance. This might be the last time she saw him. She hoped he—and Savotte, she supposed—didn't face severe punishment for Catch's escape. *Let's get on with the escape first,* she reminded herself. *So far, it's been smooth.*

She winced. That was a bad kind of thought for such a delicate interval. Hoping no capricious luck-fairy had overheard it, she turned to Catch. "Dmitri and Rags are at The Nook. Let's—"

"Eh, sorry, love." Starley's crossbow swung to point at Catch. "Should've listened more carefully. I said *we're* taking Starthorne."

Even as Ascot fell back, feeling like she'd just been smacked with an invisible brick, she found herself nodding. Yes, this was the way the world worked, all right. *Damn you, luck fairy. I* knew *this was too easy.* "You meant this all along," she said, glaring across the corral at Jolt.

"Yes," he replied without a trace of repentance, crossbow still covering Cavall and Savotte.

"Got a rebellion to win, love," said Starley. "Holding Starthorne hostage gives us a bit of whatsit."

"Leverage," said Jolt.

Savotte laughed softly, mockingly. "Should've chosen your allies more carefully, Miss Abberdorf."

Like I was offered a long list of options, thought Ascot. Her nails bit her palms.

"Get on Afleeta's back, Starthorne," said Starley.

Catch lifted his head. He'd been staring fixedly at an unremarkable patch of yellow corral dirt for the past few minutes, still apparently wrapped in some inner debate. He studied the bolt pointed at his head with apparent disinterest, glanced at Afleeta, and scuffed his toe through the dust. "No."

Savotte laughed louder.

"Get on Afleeta, Starthorne," called Jolt.

One of Catch's brows rose. "If you shoot me, there goes your leverage."

Starley shrugged. "True. Fortunately, we have leverage for our leverage." With a swing of his arm, he moved his crossbow.

Ascot sucked in a breath. The bolt now pointed at a spot right above her nose. It instantly began to itch.

"On Afleeta, now," said Starley.

Catch's shoulders tightened. His slightly heavy eyelids lowered, giving him a brooding, angry look. It softened when he glanced at Ascot.

"I'm sorry," she mouthed.

Sighing, he dropped his arms, went to Afleeta, and took hold of her mane.

Thump. "At last I found you, Galen Cavall!" announced a small, raspy voice. A series of whippy, swishing noises followed.

Ascot spun around so quickly her ankle screamed a protest. She didn't take time to nurse the small pain, for there, standing tall and proud—well, proud—on his hind legs in the middle of the corral was Moony, flourishing his tiny sword. That was the whippy sound. It was followed by a noise she never forgot: the wet click of four people's eyes blinking in tandem disbelief.

CHAPTER FIVE:
SHOWDOWN AT THE ADEQUATE CORRAL

Once, in Albright, Catch had pointed a pistol at Ascot. When Starley raised his crossbow, that image played through his head: that afternoon in Alastor's maze garden with the frogs singing their throaty song. He'd taken her to that spot by the pond, moving like a clockwork man powered by the sickness in his gut. Lord Roebanks had promised to burn the contract incriminating him if he shot her. But in the end, he'd chosen her life over his.

I chose her, then. Back in Widget, I made her promise never to come to the Clawcrags, even though I knew she wouldn't keep it. When had he become willing to risk her life for his sake?

When I decided to run again.

His hand still clutched a handful of Afleeta's mane. He released it and folded his arms.

Puffing out his chest until the crescent of white fur in its center rose a full inch, Moony strutted over to Cavall. "Draw, villain."

"Moony, not now," said Ascot, making frantic "come here" gestures.

Moony responded with a bratty, defiant flick of his wingtips. Catch laughed, low in his throat. Like himself, Moony had it in for Cavall ever since Widget. "I can never rest until I avenge the many insults this man has done me," said Moony, settling into what he probably imagined was a fencing stance. As far as Catch knew, Moony had never had a sword lesson in life. Or, for that matter, opposable thumbs.

The black-clad nightmare, damn him, recovered his composure. One could almost smell the oil coating his brain roasting as he stared at Moony. Slowly, his lips stretched in a crooked smile. "Before we commence with our duel, kitty, perhaps you'd better spare a glance behind you."

Moony's whickers twitched. Then, with the air of humoring Cavall, he glanced back.

He did a double-take, eyes flying wide, then narrowing swiftly. An angry growl boiled out of his throat. Dropping his sword, he crouched. "How dare you!" he yowled, and launched himself at Starley, who, in the fascination of watching a tiny, bat-winged cat threaten Cavall, had apparently forgotten he was pointing a crossbow at Ascot.

"Whoa!" cried Starley as Moony flew at his face. Most people would be content to lift an arm, or jump out of the way. Starley did a back spring. Apparently, he'd never practiced the move while holding a crossbow. The trigger went off the instant his hands touched the ground. The bolt skittered harmlessly across the corral, raising dust before striking a stone and spinning into stillness. Landing well out of Moony's range, Starley smirked before noticing he held a now-useless weapon. "Whoops."

Moony bounced on his landing, flung himself at Starley's leg, coiled his paws around it, and commenced biting. Metal rasped against leather as Cavall drew his sword and faced Jolt.

Ascot dove for Moony. "No, get out of here!" Catch cried, trying to intercept her, seeing Savotte dart forward, all flying, gunmetal hair and deadly purpose.

A grip on his collar jerked him back. Hay-scented breath washed over his neck. He looked over his shoulder and straight up Afleeta's nostrils. She gripped his coat in her strong teeth. Snarling, he wrestled out of his sleeves—

Too late. Savotte dragged Ascot backwards, bending her arm at a painful angle. Her curved knife tucked under Ascot's chin.

Catch froze.

"Galen," cried Savotte. She had a voice like a bell. Whenever Catch had heard that description before, he'd assumed it meant "dulcet." *Melodic, honeyed, sweet.* But bells are meant to awaken. It pierced the tumult engulfing the corral.

Cavall turned. Jolt's shot quivered in the custard peach tree's trunk. Dropping the crossbow, Jolt drew a knife. Starley had just kicked Moony loose. Savotte's cry caught him, rather absurdly, in a split.

"Oh, hell," cried Starley. Moony jumped at him again, and he ducked and pointed at Ascot. "Look, kitty, look!"

Moony did. Snarling anew, he advanced on Savotte, puffed to the size of a large and rather ferocious breadloaf.

"Take another step and I'll cut her throat," said Savotte, pressing down with the knife. A dark red bead ran down Ascot's white throat.

Moony stopped, tail lashing, but whiskers quivering in a way that reminded Catch of Rags-n-Bones. "Captain?" he said, his growl trailing off into a plaintive whine.

It was the first time Catch had seen Moony truly, deeply scared. With reason. Savotte had been ready to break Mr. Cavendish's neck in Widget; no reason to assume she'd show mercy now. Catch stared at the ground.

Oh, Catch, are you running again? How often had Ascot said that to him? When he'd made the deal in Widget, it was with the idea that, this time, he'd hold the course.

That was the trouble with being a dedicated liar: occasionally you fooled even yourself.

His coat lay on the ground where Afleeta had dropped it. Picking it up, he brushed off the dust. The inner left pocket crinkled.

"Starthorne." Starley spoke very softly. Catch looked at him, raising a brow. Starley grimaced, scratching under his bandana. "Look, I'm sorry about this mess. Please. Come with us. We'll save her later."

Turning his back on Starley, Catch worked his arms through his coat sleeves.

"Grab the kitty, Galen," said Savotte, her eyes cold as stones for all their warm, brown shade. "The others are at The Nook. We should take at least the boney one hostage, too."

Ascot rolled her head enough to give Cavall a look that was part beseeching, but mostly reproof. Avoiding it, Cavall strode toward Moony, kicking away Starley's crossbow as he did.

"We have agents at The Nook," said Jolt. "You won't get the others."

"Planning to 'get them' yourself?" sneered Cavall, pinning Moony. Moony snarled and lashed out, to little effect. Coating yourself head-to-toe in black leather had its advantages, after all.

Ascot, Moony, Rags-n-Bones, Dmitri, thought Catch. All threatened because of his selfishness, his damned cowardice.

"Those who get near us die." The remembered smells of coffee flavored with black cherry syrup, soft leather, and salt, filled Catch's nostrils. His father's careless laughter rang in his ears. A phantom hand stroked his head. *"Don't let it worry you."*

Catch pulled up his collar, eliciting another crinkle from the inner left pocket. He'd been so obsessed with the letter that he'd stopped noticing the other sounds his coat made: small clinks and rattles, even a soft ticking. His pockets contained many interesting items.

Including his father's ring. Sliding it onto his finger, he held up his hand so the light shone through its amber petals. "Fits perfectly," he declared, knowing no one was watching his left hand slip into his outer left pocket.

Savotte watched him warily as he walked over, but made no objection when he touched Ascot's cheek. Her cherry-brown eyes regarded him steadily, but the depressions in in her plump lower lip indicated she'd been biting it in silent fury.

"Some reunion," he said, offering a small smile.

She took a breath. Then another. "Shouldn't have been a disunion in the first place."

"Means 'separation.'"

"Parting."

"Division." Leaning in close, he kissed her brow. "I'll miss you," he said, stroking her streak of white hair back from her ear. She winced a little when one of the thorns on his father's ring scratched her cheek.

"Don't be silly," she said, and that was the Ascot he knew—stubbornly defying reality in favor of the way she thought things should be. "This isn't goodbye."

"Yes," he said, softly. "I'm afraid it is."

Her high brows came down, forming a little crease between them. Then they rose again. Stiffening, she reached up and touched the tiny cut on her cheek, making a little hissing sound, as if stung. Her lips parted, but no words came out.

Catch laid his hand over Ascot's heart. "Find the lie," he whispered, watching her eyes go dull and roll back in her head. Savotte fumbled her knife and caught her under the arms as Ascot went limp.

"What—?" gasped Savotte. Her frantic finger jabbed Ascot's neck, searching for a pulse. When she found none—she wouldn't—her incredulous gaze settled on Catch.

"Ascot?" said Moony in a wee voice. "Ascot, what's wrong?"

"You're joking," said Cavall. Darting to Ascot, he took her from Savotte, laid her on the ground, and searched for a pulse himself.

Catch shook off the last drop of clear liquid clinging to his father's ring. It sparkled once, like a dewdrop, as it arced to the ground and made a small, dark spot on the hard yellow earth. "I only knew her a few months," he said, settling his coat about his shoulders with a shrug. The inner left pocket didn't crinkle.

Starley and Jolt, huddled with Afleeta under the custard peach tree, gave him incredulous stares as he kicked Cavall's heel. "We should get going."

"She watched us leave Widget." Cavall spoke as if he had to remember how to form each word. "She was watching from the window. You didn't even turn around."

I knew she was watching without turning around. "It appears I am my father's son after all," said Catch. His smile felt like a dead thing laid across his lips. "Shall we discover if I'm the golden star of prophecy as well?"

Starley came to life. "Better we all die than be saved by the likes of you!" he shouted, kicking a spray of dust at Catch. Jolt grabbed his arm.

"Ascot? Ascot!" Moony began writhing, clawing the ground, turning his head in snakelike twists to bite at Cavall's wrist. "No...it's a mistake...no...Captain. Captain! I'll kill you. *I'll kill you!*" The words mangled into a yowl.

"Bring him," said Savotte, using a very cold voice. "If he flies off, he'll alert the other two, and get the whole nonsense started again."

Jerking his head in a nod, Cavall took a cord from his pocket and lashed Moony's legs together. "Come along, Starthorne." He paused to glare at Starley. "This isn't over, Reftkin."

"Chew tail, leather-britches," Starley spat back. "I know why your father died, and he'd be ashamed of you."

Cavall's face went white, absolutely white, in shocking contrast to his sleek, black clothes. He started to advance on Starley, but Savotte seized his arm and shook her head. Breathing heavily, Cavall glowered at Starley. "You'll pay for that," he said, grating out the words.

Catch stared southward, to the forked peak of Mt. Skylash, every bit of him aware that Ascot sprawled on the ground behind him. Without waiting for Cavall and Savotte, he started walking and didn't look back. This time, there was really no point. Ascot wouldn't be watching him go.

CHAPTER SIX:
WEASEL WORDS

Raindrops pattered on Ascot's face. That was the worst thing about camping; waking in the rain. You could pull your blanket over your head, but you'd soon start feeling the sharp points of every rock you could've sworn you'd cleared away the morning before. Then, dampness would begin soaking through the cloth, making you shiver.

This is an awfully warm rain, however, she thought. *Odd. It's not even spring, yet.* The flowers smelled nice, though; rich and custardy. She flailed an arm, searching for a blanket that didn't seem to be present.

"Miss!"

The cry popped her eardrums. Cold, boney fingers grabbed her flailing hand and practically crushed it. "Oh, miss! Miss!"

Rags-n-Bones. Why was he crying this time?

"Oh, she's alive," said a sharp, not quite familiar voice. "Oh, mange and maggots, thank goodness."

"I told you." Dmitri's unmistakable deep tones, husky with relief despite his words. "I told you he wouldn't actually do such a thing."

"What did you tell me this time?" said Ascot. Dmitri was always telling her things—and more annoyingly, being right about them. *Mr. Smarty-wolf.* Stretching, she sat up and opened her eyes to

44

Dmitri, Rags-n-Bones, and a rough circle of sun-baked ground, surrounded by a wobbly fence.

Rags-n-Bones hurled himself on her. So did the events of the past morning. It wasn't morning anymore. The sun rode high in the sky, looking like it was just considering ambling downwards.

Catch. Moony. Cavall and Savotte. The Hide Aways.

"There, there." She patted Rags-n-Bones' shoulder before pushing him off, having to use force when he seemed determined to cling. Pressing her palms to the ground, she craned her neck, searching the corral, even trying to probe the depths of the dilapidated barn through its open door.

Dmitri put a paw on her knee. "He's not here. Nor is Moony."

Pretending to misunderstand, Ascot looked behind her. There was the tree with the shiny leaves. A fresh hole gaped in the litter of pits beneath it; quite a large one. Two young men crouched beside it, but her heart didn't even have time to leap in hope before she identified them as Starley and Jolt, both covered in yellow dust.

Dmitri bumped his nose under her arm. "How are you feeling?" he asked. "Any dizziness or nausea?"

Her stomach grumbled—emptiness, not nausea. Her head ached, but that was hunger, too. Aside from an irritating itching sting on her cheek, she felt rested, alert—

Her cheek. Her brain had a few more memories to spring on her, after all. "Catch."

"Drugged you," said Dmitri. "Yes."

"You looked dead," wailed Rags-n-Bones, stroking her sleeve. "I really thought you were dead."

Ascot looked at the developing hole beneath the tree. Gauged the size and depth of it. "You were digging me a *grave*?"

"Seemed the least we could do," said Starley, pulling himself out of the pit. He came over with a dragging gait. Dust turned his white hair blond. Stopping beside her, he met her gaze squarely. "I'm sorry."

Leaping up, she aimed a punch at his nose. Something—it felt like a matted clump of dead leaves—fell out of her coat and onto her toe, but Ascot had a target on Starley and paid it no mind.

He stepped aside and caught her wrist. "Sorry for setting you up," he said. "Sorry for using you. Sorry for aiming a crossbow at your head. But mostly sorry my world's such a wreck that I decided such things were necessary." Releasing her wrist, he waited.

Ascot drew back her fist again.

"Listen to him, Ascot." Dmitri's voice stopped her.

"Please, miss," added Rags-n-Bones.

Her fist, poised by her ear, tightened. Starley merely watched her, his murky gray eyes calm. She sensed if she threw this punch, he wouldn't dodge. She lowered her arm. "You tricked me," she said. That was easier to focus on than the fact that Catch had scratched her with some sleeping death potion, like something out of a storybook. Her mind hurried right past that without stopping for a look.

"Yes, we tricked you." Jolt threw down the rotted piece of corral railing he'd been using as a shovel and folded his arms. For the first time, he looked straight at her—no, *glared*, his eyes slivers of frozen amber. The afternoon sunlight gave the raised, white skin of his brand a silvery gleam. "You know *nothing* of the Clawcrags. Of our lives. The laws keep getting stricter. The Sniffers killed seven Hide Aways last year and imprisoned another dozen. Starthorne's valuable enough that Alph Gildar gave up his vendetta against a human town. You'd have run away with him and never given us a thought."

After their betrayal, Ascot wouldn't have believed it possible, but she found herself shrinking inwardly. Each of Jolt's words hit with the cold, impersonal, honesty of hailstones. "You could have told us. You could have asked," she muttered.

Jolt tossed his head, flicking his hair away from his branded cheek. "The words of a lucky person who's always had cause to hope."

Staring alternately at the tree, the sky, and the ragged line of mountains to the south, Ascot wriggled her toes, just to feel them bumping against the unyielding leather of her boots. At last she thought of something to say. "You must have some hope. Otherwise, you wouldn't bother trying to rebel."

Starley broke into a laugh. "She has you there," he said, clapping Jolt on the shoulder. Jolt scowled. Starley rubbed the back of his neck. "Look, we're not whatsit, treacherous by nature. Just desperate. If we'd had more time, we would've approached you more friendly-like. Can we start again?"

Start again? Ascot almost laughed in his face. But Dmitri made one of his irritating, know-it-all little coughs, accompanied by a cautionary glance. Ascot shut her mouth and thought it over. It was either that or receive a lecture.

"Where's Moony?" she asked. Last she'd seen, he'd been pinned down by Cavall.

"Leather-britches tied him up and took him along," Starley replied. "Feared he'd fly off and warn your friends, otherwise." Standing on one leg, he scratched the back of his ankle with the opposite toe. "Eh, that was our fault. Your friends not coming to help you, I mean."

"Bellmonte assured us that Cavall's group hadn't arrived in town yet," said Dmitri. "We assumed you were still chasing Moony."

More treachery from the Hide Aways. *They must've planned to separate me from Dmitri and Rags all along. How convenient we did it for them.* All the scattered shards of her rage began collecting again—but still Dmitri regarded her with that cautionary eye, silently begging her patience.

Something round, soft, and slightly gritty was pushed into her hand. "The doughnuts at The Nook were really good, miss. I saved you one," whispered Rags-n-Bones.

Ascot squeezed it. A drop of raspberry filling oozed out. The gritty stuff was a coating of sugar. Her stomach rumbled. She lifted it to her mouth.

"I don't think Nipper nibbled it at all," Rags-n-Bones added.

Ascot hesitated, then bit down anyway. It was very good. While she was chewing, Dmitri glanced at Starley and Jolt. "Could you give us a moment?"

"Sure thing, mate," said Starley. He and Jolt returned to the tree. Peach pits clicked softly as they began filling in the hole.

"You want to work with them," Ascot said to Dmitri, licking sugar off her fingers. Rags-n-Bones squatted and began chirping with Nipper, who was gnawing something he'd found on the ground.

Dmitri sat, winding his tail about his forelegs. "Jolt's right. We know nothing of shifters or their ways. We know nothing of this prophecy, or what's at stake. We cannot rescue Catch without help."

He was right. Their brief foray into ranger-hood had proved that much. Rolling grains of sugar between her fingers, Ascot watched Starley and Jolt fill in her unnecessary grave.

Nipper squeaked.

"I don't know," Rags-n-Bones replied.

"I don't think they ever meant to hurt you," said Dmitri, following Ascot's gaze. "They were horrified when they believed you dead."

When Catch killed me. Appallingly, she giggled.

"Catch told us little of his past," Dmitri continued. "But if what he did let drop was true, I'm not surprised some shifters have grown desperate."

Ascot sighed. *Yes. When pushed, some people grow desperate enough to slip their loved ones a fake death potion.* She touched the little stinging spot on her cheek and went over to the tree. A rich fragrance, like butterscotch pudding, only fresher, hung about it. "Not a bad place to be buried, I suppose," she offered to Starley and Jolt.

"I plan to spontaneously combust when I reach a hundred and fifty," replied Starley. "But, yeah." He shoveled a final scoop of dirt, threw down his plank, and stretched. "If you must be buried, it's right enough. Glad it wasn't necessary, however."

"Me too." She glanced at Jolt. He said nothing; only watched her silently as he smoothed the ground and scattered pits across it. "We need help."

"So do we." Starley clapped dirt off his hands. "If we help you rescue Starthorne, will you try'n convince him to support our cause?"

It seemed a fair deal. Ascot rubbed her itching cheek and looked back at Dmitri. He nodded. "So long as you don't give us a reason to distrust you again," she said, turning back to Starley.

"Miss?" Rags-n-Bones rose, waving a sheet of brown paper. Nipper danced about his feet. "Nipper wants to eats this, but I think it's part of a book, and I've told him you don't eat books."

"Quite right," said Dmitri. "The few that actually deserve eating would give you indigestion." His black nose twitched. "Odd. Smells of leaves, not paper."

Ascot took the page from Rags-n-Bones. Dmitri was right; the thick sheet, about twice the size of her hand, was made of brown, pressed leaves. She squinted at its surface, covered with faded, spidery writing, made from some odd, purple ink.

"Where did it come from?" asked Dmitri.

"It fell out of Miss Ascot's coat," said Rags-n-Bones.

"Catch," said Ascot. She remembered him pressing his hand to her heart. There'd been the softest of crackles. *Find the lie.* She shook her head. *What a nice change. Usually, he's sneaking something* out *of my pocket.* "What is it?" She scanned it again, and a name at the bottom caught her attention. "Magden Le Fou!"

"What?" Crowding over her shoulder, Starley leaned down until his nose almost touched the paper. "You're right."

"That's the woman who made the prophecy, isn't it?" said Dmitri, straining his neck for a look.

"Yes," said Starley, breathlessly. "She lived five hundred years ago. Jolt," he croaked, running his finger along a line of purple writing. "I'm not sure, but I think this is a letter addressed to Rune." He and Jolt stared at each other, widened eyes seeming to take up half their faces.

"Who's Rune?" asked Ascot.

Jolt tucked the letter back in her coat. "The Great Alph. The lion-shifter who won Holdfast and founded our entire system."

"Not here." Starley shook himself, assuming a brisk, authoritative manner. "If Cavall meets with any Sniffers on his way to the Underway, he'll set them on our track."

"So where do we go?" asked Dmitri.

"Well…" Starley stood on one leg to scratch again. "We do happen to know an expert on Magden Le Fou." He made a sound vague enough to be translated as either a murmur of contrition or a stifled snicker.

Jolt's eyes narrowed. "You're joking. Not *her*."

"She could be a big help, and you know it," replied Starley.

"Oh, I don't like this." Pulling a licorice root from his belt, Jolt bit savagely down.

"Who's 'her'?" asked Ascot.

For answer, Starley rummaged in a pocket and came up with a crumpled rectangle of pasteboard, which he handed to her. Taking it, she squinted at the many lines of cramped writing on the back.

"Are these directions?" she asked, flipping it over. The card's other side displayed a drawing of a rather befuddled-looking vulture with a single eye in its forehead. Beneath it scrolled a line of larger, more legible letters. "Condorella the Very Dark Blue Shading Into Violet?" she read. "Who has a name like that?"

A moment later, she realized *exactly* who'd have a name like that. "Oh, no! Not someone from GEL."

They'd been walking for several hours in perfect silence. Before that, they'd been walking a couple of hours in perfect clangor as Moony attempted to raise not merely the dead, but the undead, the sleeping, and the not-yet-born with the force of his yowls. Now he simply dangled from Cavall's hand, all four legs bound, staring fixedly, unforgivingly at Catch.

Well, and here's a piece of luck I don't deserve, thought Catch, running his thumb over the carved amber petals of his father's ring. *Looks can't kill. I'd certainly be dead if they could.*

And he intended to survive the Moonless Night. He didn't know how, yet, but he wanted the prophecy and the Clawcrags to lose their hold on him forever. He wanted to brush them off his clothes as he walked away from them. He wanted to brush their *rubble* off his clothes as he walked away, with the pleasure of knowing he'd exposed their foundations as cheap façades.

But that was melodramatic, and really, he'd be satisfied with simply walking away. Catch almost smiled, but the impulse slipped away. He rolled the ball of his thumb over one of the carved thorns and pressed down until its point threatened to pop through his skin.

The muffled crunch of Cavall's footsteps over a thick layer of pine needles abruptly stopped. Catch, absorbed in his thoughts, almost banged into that broad, leather-clad back. "Lose the way, precious?" he asked, side-stepping at the last instant.

"What is it, Galen?" asked Savotte.

"Reftkin," said Cavall, staring straight ahead at the looming side of Mt. Skylash, a crooked yellow-gray pyramid against the darkening sky. "That pasty weasel knows something about my father, or imagines he does. I'm going to go back and squeeze it out of him, then skin him, then find any spot he so much as pissed on and set it on fire."

"Oh, tell us how you *really* feel, precious," said Catch.

Tossing Moony aside, Cavall punched him in the eye.

Why is it always the eye? grumbled Catch, reeling back. "And here I thought we were getting to be friends," he said, rubbing it.

"I thought *we* were friends," growled Moony, lashing his tail. Catch looked away.

"You should drop this, Galen," said Savotte after a short silence. He just stared back the way they came, his gaze cutting through the trees as if they weren't there.

Catch took his hand from his eye. So, the leather-clad nightmare wished to hunt the Hide Aways? Good. They'd threatened Ascot. Let them and Cavall devour each other. He shaped a laugh, hard and sardonic. "Oh, yes, precious, you've only been looking for answers for twenty-five years. Just forget that the weasel told you he knows how your father died."

Actually, Starley had said "why." Catch shrugged. *Details.* Anyway, his words had an effect. Cavall's hand tightened on his sword's hilt.

"You mean for me to take Starthorne to Holdfast, alone?" demanded Savotte, incredulous. "What will the Alph say? What about Mist—"

"That's an order, Lieutenant Savotte," Cavall barked.

She fell back. If she'd been in horse form, her ears would've flattened against her head. "Of course, Captain Cavall, *sir.*"

Oh, you deserved that, thought Catch, seeing Cavall wince. But he quickly stifled it. His face hardened as he strode off.

"Goodbye, precious," Catch called after him. "I'll miss that dimple of yours. I'm referring to the one in your cheek, by the way. The black leather shows it off so nicely."

Cavall halted. "Rainy," he said without turning around. "One thing more. Remember who you're traveling with. Remember what he is."

Arms folded, ears still metaphorically pinned back, Savotte did a splendid impression of deafness. After a moment, Cavall's footsteps crunched off over the carpet of needles.

"Did he have a torrid break-up with a cow-shifter in his youth?" Catch asked conversationally, watching him go. "Is that the reason for his attire?"

The silence at his side was of the speaking variety. Glancing sidewards, Catch found Savotte studying him minutely. They were almost of a height, her tea-brown eyes level with his. "What?" he asked.

For reply, she picked up Moony by the rope's end and held him out. Moony swung, puffed and snarling, glaring at Catch.

"Snap his neck," said Savotte.

Bile erupted in Catch's stomach. The world tilted to the left and he slid down the slope, clutching at air.

"Go ahead." Savotte advanced, dangling Moony like an inviting treat. "It's the work of a second."

Glim. Alastor. Ascot. The people who get near us die. No, not Ascot. I chose her life. Catch swallowed the hot muck threatening to rise out of his throat. "Murdering a helpless cat is beneath me."

"You just murdered the lovely Miss Abberdorf." Savotte's lip curled, pushing her beauty mark closer to her nose. Moony's snarls trailed off. His tail lashed less violently. "Surely her cat matters even less."

"I'm my own cat!" spat Moony, writhing.

Savotte studied Catch a moment longer, then shrugged. "Very well, I'll do it." She wrapped her fingers around Moony's neck.

Catch seized her wrist. "No."

Her mouth bent into a hard smile. "You didn't kill Miss Abberdorf."

Catch dropped his gaze. Licked his fangs. His Smilodon-self longed to bite off her face.

"Of course you didn't." Savotte set Moony down, giving him an ironic pat. "You're no killer. I knew that in Equinor Cemetery."

"I hope you're right," said Catch, but far too quietly for her to hear. Louder, he said, "Let Moony go. You don't need a hostage."

"Hmm, what did Galen just say?" She tapped her chin. "Oh, yes, to remember what you are. A *liar*." Taking a shiny brown object from her knapsack, resembling a split hazelnut, she clipped it to Moony's left wing.

"Ow!" he squalled.

She didn't have to stick it right on the joint, thought Catch. His fingers, curling into his palms, felt very like claws. *Another person hurt for my sake.*

"That's an alchemic clip," said Savotte, undoing Moony's bonds. "I know the word that activates it. Try to escape, and it'll bite off your wing." Coiling up the rope, she smiled sweetly at Catch. "There. I let him go."

Pulling his fingers from the small craters he'd gouged in his palm, Catch swept her a bow. "I'm overwhelmed with gratitude," he said, seizing her hand. "Means 'thank you,' 'thank you,' 'thank you.'" He kissed her knuckles.

It wiped off her grin, at least. "Let's get going, Starthorne," she said, snatching back her hand and scrubbing it against her trousers. "It's still half a day to the Underway." Snapping a weed off its stalk, she put it between her teeth and paced ahead.

Catch exhaled. It took effort; his breath seemed to want to congeal in his chest. "I'm sorry," he said, crouching before Moony. "Both for the clip and that charade in the corral. I feared one those idiots would cut Ascot's throat by pure accident if I didn't—" Why was he making excuses? He shook his head. "Let me see your wing." He extended his hand, ready to accept a bite.

Moony rubbed his cheek against Catch's fingers, purring. "No, I'm sorry. Of course you didn't kill Ascot! It was all a clever plan."

A plan? Catch wished he could laugh. His "plan" was a mad dance on a knife's edge, trying not to cut his feet. But Moony pranced about excitedly. "We'll infiltrate Holdfast while she attacks from without!" Forgetting the clip, he jumped with wings extended, winced, landed heavily, and licked a paw to cover his mistake.

Attack from without? No! Catch's whole purpose in secreting the letter in Ascot's pocket was to keep her out of the Clawcrags. He'd felt certain that, upon seeing it, Dmitri would instantly suggest they do research and haul her off to the nearest library—which probably meant returning to Widget.

But even as he opened his mouth to protest, he realized that Moony was right. The letter likely wasn't enough to distract Ascot from her quest to reclaim him. Catch had come to the opinion that if a switch existed that could detonate the world, Ascot would inadvertently stumble across it, set it off with all the best intentions, and then manage to defuse it two and a half seconds before it erupted—with Dmitri dispensing advice the entire time, and Moony challenging people and generally getting in the way.

Meanwhile, I'd probably die of anxiety and be revived by an overly helpful Rags-n-Bones.

So be it. Sighing, Catch turned up his palm, as if releasing a skitterish butterfly into the wild.

"I could've gotten free of the ropes any time I wanted, by the way," said Moony, giving himself a final lick. "When Vicardi cats get really angry, they burst into flames. I could've burned right through them in an instant."

"I know." Catch enjoyed Moony's stories immensely, particularly the one about the opera-singing pirates and the giant tuna he'd lived inside for three days. He ran his thumb over his ring. His father's ring. The murky pearl in the center of the amber petals didn't glow, the way pearls usually did. It hid its secrets, like the moon under a cloud.

"Get moving, Starthorne." Savotte's shout floated back.

Lifting Moony, Catch set him on his shoulder. Moony's tail wrapped around his neck as he trudged after Savotte. "So, what's our next move?" Moony whispered in his ear. "Does it involve dueling?"

"We have two days' journey through the Underway ahead of us," said Catch, watching Savotte slash tall, fluffy-headed weeds out of her path with the blade of her hand. The name "Galen" featured strongly in her disgruntled mutters. "Assuming I don't eat her from lack of coffee before it's done…"

"Yes?" prompted Moony, quivering and crackling. "Can I challenge her?"

"Actually," Catch scratched his cheek, "I was thinking we might turn her to our side."

Moony choked. "You think we can do that?" he said, coughing.

Catch smiled grimly. "Be fun to try." Turn the leather-clad nightmare's partner against him. That could be useful, as well as exceedingly amusing.

"Well, all right." Moony settled, draping across his neck like a furry scarf. His ears flicked thoughtfully as Catch walked. "If you don't succeed, can I challenge her?" he asked after a while.

Catch sighed.

CHAPTER SEVEN:
ANY WITCH WAY

"Why blue flowers?" asked Rags-n-Bones as Ascot tucked the sprig behind his ear.

"Because that's what's specified on the back of Condorella the Blue's—"

"The Very Dark Blue Shading Into Violet," Rags-n-Bones reminded her. "Is that why the flowers have to be blue? Won't the magic work if they're pink?"

He wasn't trying to be difficult. They'd searched the riverbank they were currently sequestered nearby, but the only blue flowers to be had were a handful of hyacinths Jolt ransacked from a window box. Their intensely sweet fragrance made poor Rags-n-Bones sneeze dreadfully.

"It's a wizard thing," she explained, adjusting her own sprig, tucked, per the card's instructions, behind her left ear. Miss Eppicutt, her old governess turned headmistress of the Widget Academy, had many words on wizards' proclivities for drama. If you asked her, ninety percent of wizardry was theatrics, two percent magic, and the final eight percent the mopping up afterwards.

"Oh," he said sadly, and sneezed.

Starley ducked into the overhang they huddled under. "All right.

Afleeta's going to hide out at a local horse farm for a couple days, and Bellmonte's headed to Merryvick. They should be safe. Ish. Are we ready to go?"

"No," said Jolt, yanking on his ear. Sighing, Starley tugged him outside.

A witch, Ascot grumbled as they set out. They were about to consult a witch. Just once, couldn't she come to a new place and discover that all the thaumaturgically-inclined people in the area had accidentally turned themselves into pumpkins in the past week?

The card's directions led them vaguely southwest, following a thin trail that wriggled down a slope covered with spindly pines and rocks that jutted out of the ground at the perfect height for tripping over. Further instructions required them to stop every ten minutes, stand on one foot, and pronounce "Yeowah!"

"Can't," said Dmitri when she read this aloud. "Please don't ask me to attempt it."

"I'll do it for you," said Rags-n-Bones. Putting his fingers to the top of his head to mimic ears, he dropped his voice to a gruffer tone. "Yeowah!"

Dmitri sighed.

"That'll fool anyone who isn't looking. Or listening. Or thinking," said Jolt.

At a squat crabapple tree, they had to stop and spin three times clockwise. Ascot decided that the rituals printed on the card's back had little connection with magic, and more to do with discouraging all but the most persistent of door-to-door salesmen. Rags-n-Bones knocked himself over with a sneeze while spinning. Jolt helped him back onto his feet.

"Master Porpetti's alchemy is much more sensible," said Rags-n-Bones, sniffling.

"Likely true," Jolt replied. "Unfortunately, all the alchemists in the Clawcrags are under Alph Gildar's command."

"Bloody witches," grumbled Starley, tapping his nose twice against a hand-shaped dark splotch on a boulder to the left of the path.

Ascot tapped her nose in turn. "Do you work with this Condorella—"

"The Very Dark Blue Shading Into Violet," added Rags-n-Bones, nuzzling the boulder enthusiastically.

"Often?" finished Ascot.

"Too often," said Jolt.

"We saw her last year, with Fairflax Ashily," said Starley.

"Another member of your group?" asked Dmitri.

Starley shook his head. "She died last summer."

"Was killed last summer," Jolt corrected.

"Eh, killed." Starley waved a hand. "Just a more active way of dying." He spoke lightly, but this time, Ascot saw the truth of it. Beneath all his nonsense, he was holding pain somewhere inside, like a hiker determined to keep going with a thorn in their shoe.

Jolt slid down the last three feet of the narrow path they'd been following, kicking up stones. "We should be nearly there," he said, looking around. "What next?"

Clattering down beside him, Ascot consulted the card. "There should be a stump shaped like a fat man's bottom."

"Right here, love." Starley rapped his knuckles against its bulbous top. "What do we do?"

She consulted. "We find a bent stick and—" She did a double-take. "Oh, no, we're not doing *that*."

"Do what, miss?" asked Rags-n-Bones.

Ascot shook her head. It would just upset him. Unfortunately, no less than four maybe-paths radiated out from the small clearing where the bottom-stump sat. Scratching her ear—the hyacinth's sap was raising an itch—she glanced toward the top of the hill they'd just descended. What little light remained in the sky was swiftly vanishing. "If we can't find Condorella, we're going to have to climb back in the dark."

"Did we do the magic wrong?" asked Rags-n-Bones with a worried sneeze.

A breeze sent pine needles raining down on their heads. Abruptly, Starley's nostrils flared. Something very like panic flashed across his face. "Fur and fangs, she's at it again."

Doing a smart about-face, Jolt started re-climbing the slippery path they'd just descended. Starley grabbed his shirt collar. "Don't you dare. We've come this far."

"Let me go!" snarled Jolt, kicking as Starley dragged him toward the northwards path.

"What's the problem?" asked Ascot.

Glancing back, Starley tapped his nose. "Can't you smell that?"

Ascot sniffed. Pine tar, wood both living and rotted, dust, and the sweetness of flowers. Nothing unexpected. But behind her, Dmitri abruptly gagged and sat on his haunches. "You will in a minute." He padded after Starley and Jolt, shaking his head, as if trying to dislodge a bothersome insect from his ears.

Five steps later, both Starley and Jolt gagged, flinging up their hands to cover their noses. Dmitri groaned. Ascot and Rags-n-Bones looked at each quizzically.

Five more steps, and he, too, stopped abruptly. "Oh, *dear!*" he cried, hands flying to his nose. Nipper poked his head out from under Rags-n-Bones' muffler. Little black eyes widening, he strained forward, all of his whiskers quivering avidly.

"What's wrong?" asked Ascot, beginning to feel left out.

No reply. Just a "keep going" gesture from Starley, followed by another grab for Jolt's collar as he tried fleeing again. The trees thinned, revealing a rough path that curled around the base of the slope. As Ascot stepped onto it, the breeze shifted. Suddenly, without any of the evergreens' piquancy to cover it, a new smell hit her full in the face. Her stomach rumbled tentatively, initially classifying it as edible, then roiled, violently rejecting the idea.

"Oh! Oh! Ghouls and goblins!" Without prompting, her hands flew to her nose.

Cheese. Definitely cheese. Cheese that had not merely gone bad, but had taken up loitering in dark alleys with piercings and a menacing hairstyle. Something vegetable, too, of the long-deceased variety. A glum and pasty sort of odor fought to hold the two together, while a musty-moldy scent attempted to sneak in via the backdoor and join the party.

Did something die? was the usual comment to make under such circumstances, but Ascot knew it wasn't the case. The corpse of an ogre who'd died of explosive flatulence would be embarrassed to raise such a stink as this.

"Oh, miss!" Tears poured down Rags-n-Bones' cheeks. "We must've gotten the spell wrong."

"No, we didn't." Starley pointed to a path of moon-white pebbles between a pair of stately larches. A cottage's peaked roof showed over their tops.

"Let's get this over with," said Dmitri, ears and tail drooping. She'd never seen him in such distress, and that included the time he'd been shot. Nipper, in contrast, stood on his hind legs on Rags-n-Bones' shoulder, head lifted high to catch every last, succulent whiff of the scent.

Snatching the hyacinth from behind her ear, Ascot inhaled deeply as she walked. Its fragrance, cloying a moment before, cut the reek, a little. The stench clung to her skin, seeped into her clothes, and ran fingers through her hair. Her vision took on foggy yellow tints.

But not all the yellowness was the effect of the smell. Soft, golden light shone from the cottage's windows. Despite the stink, it was a cute little building, almost doll-perfect with its thatched roof, cozily smoking stone chimney, diamond-paned windows with red shutters, and—

Lumpy white walls? Ascot frowned as they reached it. Either that was the oddest stucco she'd ever seen, or...

"Cauliflower au gratin," said Dmitri. "It's covered in cauliflower au gratin." Slowly, in a manner that would've looked comedic under other circumstances—and if he wasn't Dmitri—he folded to the ground.

"No," Ascot told the chirpy little memory that was nagging for her attention.

Yes. She remembered the story from the white book she'd brought with her from Shadowvale, the one about the lost children finding a gingerbread house in the woods. Even then, when she believed the stories were a record of actual Dayland history, she hadn't quite been able to swallow that one and assumed the author was simply making some metaphor about bakeries.

The doorbell was a withered radish, suspended on a rope of braided jerky. Ascot was *not* going to touch it. "Starley!" she called. "You know Condorella. Stop mucking about and get up here."

"Ow! Yes—ow! Coming!" Starley came up, his arm locked around the struggling Jolt's neck. He rapped on the door, a large and slightly charred slice of toast, creating hollow, crunching noises. "Oy, Condie!" he shouted.

"Azzcawt." Dmitri spoke in a tiny voice, very unlike him. "I can't tage id much longer." Rags-n-Bones honked into a kerchief like an overgrown goose.

Nipper, also unable to bear it any longer, jumped off Rags-n-Bones' shoulder and started ripping gobs off the cottage's lumpy walls, his eyelids drooping in bliss.

Ascot peered in a window. Gingham curtains shielded the cottage's interior from scrutiny, but at least the windows *were* glass, and not some rancid foodstuff. "Hello?" she called, tapping on it.

A shadow fell over the curtains; huge and vague at first, shrinking into definition it approached. Human-shaped, except humans didn't usually wear giant sea urchins on their heads. "Who's there?" cried a voice, muffled by the layers of cheese. The blue-and-white checked curtains parted, and a tall, boney woman with wild ginger hair—not a sea urchin after all—peered out. "It isn't goblins again, is it?"

Goblins? Ascot had met goblins in Shadowvale. They had an

unfortunate habit of pinching things when your back was turned, and liked to lick walls, for some reason. They'd be piled up three deep, dead, if they tried that with Condorella's house. "No," she replied. "We're the Hide Aways. Please, let us in."

Condorella drew back. The flaring sleeves of her spangled, dark blue gown, swayed. "What's the password?"

Password? Ascot's jaw dropped—a mistake, as the smell promptly took this as an invitation to crawl inside her mouth. She quickly shut it and glanced back. "Starley?"

Starley and Jolt slouched together, shoulder-to-shoulder, propping each other up and groaning lightly. Running a pale red sleeve under his nose, Starley blinked watering eyes. "Uh...poppycock?"

"Poppycock?" Ascot repeated to Condorella.

"No!" she roared. Drawing herself up, she raised her hands dramatically. "Toad time!" An incomprehensible series of gobbledygook followed.

"Sorry," said Starley. He and Jolt slid another couple inches closer to the ground. "Was sure it was 'poppycock'."

Ascot caught her jaw before it dropped again. *Toads, really?* Why did everyone immediately grab for the stereotypes? Especially when combined with Condorella's manner of dress, not to mention her cottage made of at least theoretically edible building materials—

Her brain pounced. Who'd build such a ridiculous thing?

Answer: someone who'd taken the story of the gingerbread house story far too seriously.

Right. Returning to her companions, she propped her sprig of hyacinth under the whimpering Dmitri's nose. "Rags. We need your help."

Rags-n-Bones sniffled. "Should I sing another song?"

"No. Here's what you need to do." She whispered the plan in his ear, waited for his nod, then announced in a voice of theatrical horror: "Oh, dear! There's a small child out here, eating the house."

"Mmm!" said Rags-n-Bones in a high, weedy voice that, thanks to his stuffed-up nose, did resemble a snuffly child's. "I'm so hungry after my parents abandoned me in the woods, and this uh, cheesy stuff, tastes so good."

Ascot couldn't help but note that Rags-n-Bones, who munched down pinecones like cookies and gnawed rocks, stood well away from the cottage wall, giving it the same wide-eyed, terrified stare he'd bestow on an aggressive cicada.

The chanting inside the cottage stopped abruptly. A chuckle rang out, a complicated chuckle, as of a relatively young woman pretending to be an old crone pretending to be a sweet, grandmotherly lady.

Oh, yes. Ascot nodded to herself. "Get ready to run inside the instant the door opens," she said.

The porch floor, which was just a continuation of the floor inside, vibrated under approaching footsteps. *"Chewing, chewing, like a duck-o. Who is gnawing on my stucco?"* quavered the crackly voice.

Dmitri groaned, and Ascot knew it wasn't all because of the smell. But his muscles tensed. Starley and Jolt pulled themselves upright.

With a creak, the front door opened, expelling a rush of warm air, smelling of woodfire and cooking; highly preferable to the outside stink. "Now!" cried Ascot.

Her companions needed no urging. She hoped Dmitri didn't wrench his dodgy leg with his burst of speed. Rags-n-Bones, always quicker than she credited him, practically somersaulted past Condorella. Starley and Jolt got stuck in the doorway trying to enter at the same time, but, after a bit of cursing, burst through together.

That left Ascot. She banged an elbow on the frame as she hurried in, pushed Condorella aside, and slammed the door on the stench.

"Hey!" Condorella scrabbled at her hand. Ascot flinched at the sight of her long, yellow nails before realizing their color was due to a coating of varnish, and not any exciting fungal infection, as Condorella probably hoped. "I was about to snag one!"

I bet she tries to ride that broomstick I see propped in the corner, too, thought Ascot, leaning firmly against the door so Condorella couldn't open it again. Fortunately, its inner surface was made of honest wood. "There's no child. It was just Rags-n-Bones."

Rags-n-Bones waved sheepishly from the hearth, or more specifically, its oven, and all the savory smells issuing from therein, which he'd gravitated helplessly toward. Inside, the cottage looked very, well, countrified, with simple white walls and a wooden floor strewn with rushes. Herbs and hexes hung off the exposed rafter beams of the low ceiling. Dmitri collapsed under a bundle of dried lavender. Starley and Jolt squabbled over a clove-studded pomander, snatching it from each other and inhaling deeply.

Condorella widened her eyes and waggled her brows. After a second, Ascot realized she was attempting to make them blaze with anger. "You dare toy with a witch?" she cried.

The Guild of Enchanting Ladies' latest representative was living down to Ascot's expectations. "Starley?" she prompted.

Tossing the pomander to Jolt, he waved. "Hiya, Condie. Been a bit."

Condorella frowned, scratching her beaky nose. "I remember you. Starkly, right?"

"Almost, love." Starley claimed a chair at the rectangular block table.

Well done. You almost remembered the madcap albino shifter in the red coat. Biting her tongue, Ascot went over to Rags-n-Bones and took the oven hook from his hand before he opened the door and helped himself.

"Miss, Nipper's still outside," Rags-n-Bones whispered worriedly. "Do you think he's all right?"

"I'm sure he's fine," said Ascot, more afraid they'd exit the cottage and stumble over a rat gorged to watermelon-size.

Starley put his heels up on the seat of the chair opposite him. "We were here with Fairflax last summer. She came for that enlarging spell, remember?"

"Oh, yes." Condorella brightened. "Why didn't you say so? How is she? My spell worked, didn't it?"

"Eh," Starley rubbed his jaw. "Well, it worked, but—"

"Not well enough," replied Jolt, flatly, taking the chair beside Starley. "She's dead."

The dangling charms, made from bent twigs and bits of glass, spun slowly in the draft from the chimney, sending colored glints dancing up the walls. "Oh." Condorella scowled at them, tugging a tangle. "I don't suppose she managed to steal one of Magden Le Fou's Seersees beforehand?"

"No." Starley's easy cheer slipped, offering Ascot another glimpse of the thorn in his shoe. But a moment later, his grin returned. "But we have something even more betterer to offer you."

Ascot took her cue. "We think this letter was written by Magden Le Fou," she said, taking it from her pocket and laying it on the table. It had survived the journey surprisingly well, but she decided against smoothing it out for fear of pulling it in half.

"Magden Le Fou's own writing," whispered Condorella, trembling. The many charms hanging around her neck rattled and clinked. She tottered forward, hands clasped to her chest. Ascot recognized a truly magical moment unfolding before her eyes. Amazing how rarely such moments had anything to do with actual magic.

Condorella all but fell forward onto the table, her palms smacking the wood to either side of the paper. Her wild hair obscured her face.

"Well, Condie?" asked Starley after several silent minutes.

Straightening, Condorella drew in a long breath. "I think you'd better stay for dinner." Going to the oven, she pulled out a pan of lumpy white stuff that bubbled and steamed. It looked very like the stuff that coated the house, only not disgusting.

Dmitri lifted his snout for an exploratory sniff. "Cauliflower au gratin?"

CHAPTER EIGHT:
PAST TENSE

The cauliflower au gratin proved surprisingly tasty, but eating without Catch slurping coffee or Moony hunting insects under the table subtracted from its savor. Ascot expected Starley and Jolt to explain the visit's purpose during the meal, but they concentrated instead on stuffing in as much of the casserole, seed-topped bread, and salad of crunchy herbs, as their stomachs could hold. By his beaming, Ascot could tell Rags-n-Bones greatly approved.

But finally, Starley pushed his plate away. "Most excellent, love."

Condorella preened. "My cauliflower au gratin is legendary. You'd think at least one lost child would come by to taste it. I know gingerbread's traditional, but after a night wandering in the woods, children need a healthy meal more than sweets."

Didn't the witch in the story want to fatten them up and eat them, rendering concern over their long-term health moot? Deliberately, Ascot stuck her fork into her leg. It was either that or make a very rude observation. "Was that letter really written by Magden Le Fou?" she asked once she was sure her worser impulses were under control.

Condorella jerked defensively toward the letter, now lying in reverence atop a tall, iron-scrollwork table in the corner, as if Ascot had jumped up and attempted to smear cheese sauce over it rather than asked a question. "The writing matches the two fragments I have of her work."

"And this whole quandry more or less originated with her," said Dmitri around a mouthful of bread. He swallowed. "I don't suppose you remember the approximate wording of the prophecy?"

In unison, Starley, Jolt, and Condorella recited:

"Look northwards to the twin-spiked spire,
Behold the lash of crackling fire.
Three nights after spring's first day,
No moon shall light the coming fray.
Fear to face the thunder's roar,
Unless the star appears before.
This golden star, born of death,
Shall fall, and rise, and yet have breath.
This golden star must put wrongs right
If you wish to last that moonless night."

The fire's pop broke the following silence. "Ah," said Dmitri. "You do." He crunched more bread.

"Everyone in the Clawcrags knows it," said Starley.

"Beautiful." Wiping a tear from her eyes, Condorella raised her glass of cider toward the letter. "Magden Le Fou was an *artist*."

Ascot picked up her fork, tapped its tines against the table, turned it over and tapped the stem. Her ring's tourmaline flashed. "Is that it?" she asked. "Catch got pegged as the 'star' of the prophecy because of a stupid ring?" Suddenly, she wanted to tear it off her hand.

"No," said Starley. "Aside from his fath—family name—"

Ascot raised her brows. What had the brief stutter been about, like he'd changed thoughts mid-speech?

Even now he was hurrying on, as if hoping she hadn't noticed. "—there's the fact that he transforms into an extinct animal, the only shifter in Clawcrag history to do so. 'Born of death,' see?"

"He wasn't the only candidate." Snapping a licorice root in half, Jolt placed one end between his teeth. "Alph Gildar Ambersun's son, Glim, was another. The sun's a star, too, and Glim's mother died giving birth to him. Plus, Glim had a star-shaped whorl on his shoulder when he shifted into his lion-form."

Glim sounded like a better candidate to Ascot, save for all the "wases" and "hads" they were using in referrence to him. "I take it he's dead?"

"Got any coffee, love?" asked Starley, turning to Condorella.

Ascot knew a dodge when she heard one. "Well?"

Starley gazed mournfully at the kettle steaming over the fire.

"Well?" said Ascot a little louder, thinking she'd add a foot-tap if he still didn't reply. Dmitri slapped a big paw on the table, directing an intense stare toward Starley.

"Glim's dead," said Jolt. "He and Starthorne fell off the edge of Holdfast Plateau twenty-five years ago, during a Rising Tournament. Only Starthorne survived."

Ascot's breath hitched.

"You can see how that strengthens Starthorne's 'fall and rise and yet draw breath' qualification." Jolt sipped cider.

There was something more to it, something they weren't telling her. Ascot spun her fork. Having pressed this far, she wasn't sure she wanted to hear the rest.

"They fell off a mountain? And Catch survived?" Dmitri shook his head, scattering loose fur. "How did he manage that?"

Starley shrugged. "Eh, should probably ask Starthorne that."

Ascot almost laughed. *Ask Catch? We'll be waiting a long time.* The fork had looked better the other way around. She flipped it again.

"Excuse me." Rags-n-Bones, hitherto quietly sucking on his own fork, raised his hand. "What is the Captain going to save everyone from? In the poem, it sounds like a thunderstorm. They're not really dangerous, if you don't climb trees."

One of Rags-n-Bones' peculiarities—and there were many—was

that while a bantam could rout him with a halfhearted cluck, he loved thunderstorms, clapping his hands when lightning split the sky.

"I suppose the Captain could make everyone a big umbrella to shelter under." The fork crunched as Rags-n-Bones bit off a tine.

And then Count Zanzibander could add it to his collection, thought Ascot, remembering her would-be fiancé from Shadowvale. She'd never forgotten the pink, sparkly one he'd gifted her with.

Dmitri licked up breadcrumbs. "I expect Le Fou was speaking in poetic terms rather than referring to an actual storm."

"Bit o' both, actually," said Starley. Condorella fetched an applesauce cake out of the oven and placed it in the table's center. Ascot waited as everyone dove for it, then sneaked the biggest slice when they banged heads.

"She's referring to the tengu," Starley continued later, settled back in his chair. "They're a kind of storm goblin, supposedly. You know the type; dark and evil, eat children, cackle viciously, probably play with their own whatsit, yadda, yadda. Anyway, five hundred years ago, we shifters were a disorganized lot. We fought amongst ourselves, but mostly we fought the tengu. The Great Alph, Rune, banded us together."

"Mostly," said Jolt.

Flashing him an irritated glance, Starley continued. "He defeated the tengus' leader, the Storm Queen, drove them out of the Clawcrags, and founded Holdfast. But—and this is all according to legend, remember—his actions angered the sorceress, Magden Le Fou."

Condorella raised her cider again. Her other hand toyed with one of her charms.

"Le Fou was the Storm Queen's friend, and when she was vanquished, Le Fou made her prophecy as a kind of revenge. I guess we get to find out if it's all true a week from now. Where's that coffee?" Starley looked around. Condorella was staring dreamily at the letter, hands tucked under her chin. She'd managed to drag one of her flaring sleeves through the cheese sauce.

"Not much of a revenge," said Dmitri, flicking first one ear, then the other. "Seeing as how she told you to defeat the tengu again."

"Well, yeah, exactly." Pushing back his chair, Starley went to the hearth. "I did say the whole thing's a legend."

"Meaning 'story,'" said Ascot. *Meaning 'lie,' or 'half-truth' at best.*

Lie. She seized on that. "Catch told me to 'find the lie,' when he slipped the letter into my coat."

"Could be the letter reveals a truth behind the myths." Starley picked up the kettle, a pot, and, for some reason, a toasting fork, and commenced making a dreadful clatter with the lot. "Maybe it even reveals the prophecy as a sham."

"Magden Le Fou didn't lie," snapped Condorella. "She may have hidden the truth behind metaphor or—for Merlin's sake, I'll do it," she snarled at a particularly loud crash from the hearth. Jumping up, she grabbed the kettle from Starley.

"Took you long enough to get the hint," said Starley, reclaiming his seat and folding his arms behind his head. "Anyhows, I didn't say Le Fou lied. I said someone may have misinterpreted what Le Fou said." He shrugged. "Where'd Starthorne get the letter?"

Ascot spread her hands. "I suppose he must've had it with him when he fell off the plateau."

"No," said Dmitri. His spring coat was darker than his winter one, the silvery markings around his eyes more visible. Perhaps that was what made his gaze seem so intense. "You never noticed, back in Widget."

"What do you mean?" she asked.

"Catch really meant to run away."

If it had been anyone other than Dmitri who'd said it, she'd have fired back at once. Her nails dug into the tabletop. He regarded her levelly.

"I'm sorry," he said. "But you never worked out the timing. When he told you to read chapter thirteen of the beekeeping book—"

"He'd written a message telling us he'd worked out that Cavall and Savotte were behind everything," she said.

Dmitri's eyes rolled toward the ceiling but, perhaps in deference to her feelings, didn't make the trip all the way around. Catch's message hadn't been nearly so straightforward. "No. Chapter thirteen contained information about the symbiotic relationship between the Moonlight Muscatel and bees. Catch pointed it out so you could find the culprit without him. Think, Ascot," Dmitri went on, gently. "He hadn't time to write the message. He'd only just returned from the graveyard, where he was speaking with Tipper Petroyvan's ghost."

Ascot thought back to that night. It had been a memorable one, containing her first glimpse of the helhest, an attack by an armed mob, and an alchemic draining at the hands of Prof. Smothers, all topped by Catch informing her that he intended to abandon her to deal with the situation herself.

He'd really meant it.

But he changed his mind!

"He changed his mind, obviously," said Dmitri. "He sneaked back into the library, wrote the note, and, I fancy, took something from a hidden compartment. Something Tipper Petroyvan told him about. Petroyvan was an owl-shifter. If I recall correctly, owl-shifters—"

"Work with old documents," finished Ascot, eyes sliding to the letter.

Condorella banged down a pot of coffee and several mugs. "Here."

"Petroyvan didn't leave Holdfast just because he wanted to make wine," said Ascot. "He found something in the letter. Something dangerous. He told Catch where it was, and Catch—"

Tried to run from the responsibility, as he always did. *But he came back!* Starley passed her a mug of coffee. She pushed it aside, so he drank it himself.

"The question's what did he find?" said Starley. "Can you decipher it, Condie? I'm uh, having a little trouble reading her loopy handwriting."

"Nothing to do with your dreadful eyesight, then?" murmured Jolt, *sotto voce*, as Condorella wiped her hands throroughly, fetched the letter, and brought it to the table. Starley gave him a shove.

A wrinkle formed between Condorella's brows as she read slowly, pausing over the missing words.

"To Rune, My former...ved,

My crystal witnessed...I know your reasons, but find them inadequate. A friend is...treason is treason, and to lose the former by the latter...even from you. Perhaps especially...I believed better of you, and can...that belief shattering.

Should I find myself...forgive you, I've kept...your treachery. I've taken what you stole...am going to a green and hidden land, beyond your...Fly as far as you wish...Search until...ache, as my heart does.

...poor Ginkiku!

Magden Le Fou."

"Whatsit?" said Starley.

"That's it." Cradling the letter, Condorella returned it to its special place. "The rest is indecipherable. But perhaps..." Folding her hands under her sharp chin, she rolled up her eyes like she was trying to examine her own brows. "...perhaps I could find this green and hidden land."

Jolt took the licorice root from his mouth. "Wait. Fly. Did she say 'fly'? Rune was a lion-shifter."

"Eh, metaphor." Starley brushed it aside.

"Maybe." But Jolt's eyes remained narrowed. Slowly, he put the licorice root back between his teeth.

Ascot stared at the paper. *Find the lie.* What part was the lie? "It sounds like Le Fou took something from Rune," she said, musing aloud. One of her sudden, bright ideas lit up inside her skull. "You Hide Aways want leverage? What do you think Gildar would trade for something that belonged to the Great Alph?"

The front legs of Starley's chair banged down on the floor. "Hard to say until we know what it is. But likely Gildar would at least listen to us."

"It's a chance," said Dmitri. "A distinct chance. You believe you can find this hidden place, Condorella?"

Condorella nodded, a new gleam in her eyes. "I think so. Give me some time to consult my books."

Starley sipped his second mug of coffee. "Make you a deal, Condie. You keep the letter in exchange for finding this green place, plus performing a few spells for us. For this lot, I mean," he amended, canting his head toward Ascot.

"Deal," said Condorella, spitting on her palm. The gob sizzled. Grimacing, Starley waved her hand aside.

"Spells for us?" asked Ascot. "What do you mean?"

Leaning back in his chair, Starley blew a stream of air toward the ceiling, spinning a string of herbs dangling off the beam overhead. "It appears you're going to be hanging around the Clawcrags a while. With all the Sniffers, and shifters who just plain don't like non-shifters…" He rubbed the back of his neck. "To put it simply, to have a chance of safety around these parts, you're going to have to transform."

"*Transform?*"

At the cry, Ascot shot up in her seat, for a moment convinced that Benny Bikkit of Widget had appeared simply to deliver that single, ear-splitting shriek. A glass on a shelf behind Condorella hummed with the force of it.

But of course the cry didn't come from Benny, although when she located the source of it, it seemed almost as astonishing.

Dmitri. Ruff bristling, ears laid so flat against his head they vanished in his creamy fur. Eyes widened until the whites showed, and so full of blatant fear that, for the first time since she'd known him, there seemed to be no thought going on behind them at all.

CHAPTER NINE:
ENTRANCES AND EXITS

By mutual consent, they walked through the night. Catch and Moony were accustomed to nocturnal travel, and Savotte seemed glad of the exercise, to work off her pique. By early dawn, they reached a shallow canyon in Mt. Skylash's northwestern side. Overhead, the lopsided moon reeled drunkenly home for a good day's sleep.

"I have another idea," said Moony.

Catch glanced over his shoulder before returning to swiping at the debris covering the cliff's side. A few lashes of his forepaw revealed lines etched into the yellow rock. In his Smilodon vision, they glowed foggy blue, like some design scribbled by an absent-minded architect. Savotte looked up from where she was squatting over the bundle of his belongings.

"Nice work," she said grudgingly, and returned to sorting through his possessions with evident and mounting annoyance at their sheer volume. Catch gave his paw a satisfied lick.

"I have another idea," said Moony, louder.

Padding over to the flat rock Moony perched on, Catch draped himself across it. "Do tell."

Moony wiggled his ears. "Tail?" he said, looking at his.

"Tell."

"Oh, sorry. Your accent's peculiar."

Catch shrugged. "Smilodon. My dialect's probably old-fashioned." They were speaking Felinus, of course, the language common to all cats, even the big—or extinct—ones. Ascot always wondered why he and Moony always seemed to be snarling at each other when he transformed. One day, the sly glances and sniggers they exchanged after such a session was going to give their secret away.

Being a shifter, Savotte knew what they were up to, of course. "If you're talking behind my back, I don't care," she said. Abruptly dumping all of Catch's belongings in a heap, she stalked to the cliff wall, tilting her head to study the blue marks. "Entrancing. Entitled."

"Is she trying to open the Underway?" asked Moony.

"Yes," Catch replied. "When she says the right word, it'll remember it's an opening. If she remembers the right word."

"Entangled," said Savotte.

Both Catch and Moony watched her avidly. "Think she'll kick it soon?" asked Moony.

"Oh, yes." Catch's stub-tail twitched. He swatted it, growling under his breath. It was the great disappointment of his Smilodon self. Back when he was a cub, and expected to become a cougar-shifter like his mother, or a jaguar-shifter like his father, he'd so looked forward to having a long, expressive tail. "What's your idea?" he asked to distract himself from it.

"Oh, right." Moony settled into a loaf-shape, his clipped wing folded against his side at a crooked angle. "I've been thinking there's no point in my challenging Savotte. She's just a messenger, after all. I'll wait until we reach Holdfast, and then I'll challenge this Alph Glider of yours."

Catch didn't snort. He'd expected something of the sort. "Gildar," he corrected. "A lion-shifter."

Moony's fur rippled with an unimpressed shrug. "So, he's a lion. Vicardi cats are much faster than lions, especially during full moons. We can outrace cheetahs, then."

"Entrails," said Savotte. The wall just looked back at her, stone-faced. "Enticed. Damn you, Galen."

Rolling onto his side, Moony attempted to lick his clipped wing. "Well, what do you think, Captain?" he asked, his head bobbing like a cork in a stream.

I think your plan's well up to expectations. "Gildar doesn't deserve the honor of fighting you in a duel. I think we should find a horde of bandit clowns to abduct him, dye his mane purple, and sell him to a traveling circus."

Moony giggled. "Are there lots of bandit clowns in the Clawcrags?"

"It's a huge problem," said Catch. "They've been known to glue bowties to their victims. Polka-dotted bowties."

Moony giggled harder.

"Entrelac," said Savotte. Her leg twitched. Both Catch and Moony tensed, but she set her foot down, un-kicked, and took a breath. "Entropy."

"Seriously, Captain." Moony returned to his licking, trying to pin the errant wing with a forepaw. A snowflake-white moth briefly distracted him; he wraggled his rump, clearly considering pouncing, before going back to his grooming. "Once I defeat Glider, he'd have to let you go, right?"

Catch crossed his paws. "There are a few problems with your plan." *Starting with the idea you'd defeat Gildar in single combat.* "First, by law, the Alph can only be challenged on a solstice or an equinox."

"We should reach Holdfast in time for the vernal equinox," said Moony immediately, ears perking higher.

Of course he'd notice the timing. "We call it 'Yawning Day.'" Catch sighed. "It's a festival. Second, you must be a shifter to challenge the Alph."

"Foo." Moony deflated, flopping onto his side. His tail thwacked the rock.

Don't say it, don't say it, thought Catch. He snapped up the moth himself.

"Entertain," said Savotte, pacing before the cliff.

Moony sat up. "Why don't you challenge Glider, Captain?"

He said it. Closing his eyes, Catch swallowed the moth. "Because if I won, I'd be Alph. And I'd rather coat myself in honey and jig through a field of bees than be Alph."

Moony fell silent. He knew it was serious when Catch brought up bees.

"Enterprise." Throwing up her hands, Savotte kicked the cliff.

There it was. Catch snickered along with Moony as she skipped about, clutching her calf and swearing. Standing, he gathered himself back into his human form. "Try 'indigo,'" he suggested, cracking his neck.

With a rumbling crunch, the cliff wall opened up along the blue lines, obliging as one could please.

"You knew all along!" cried Savotte, setting her foot down gingerly.

Catch shrugged. "Sounds like 'in we go.' I suppose someone thought it was clever. I didn't know if it would still work after twenty-five years." He stared into the Underway's dark mouth, faintly lit by luminescent lichen.

With poor grace, she limped over to her knapsack. "Get dressed. If possible, I'd like to make this a record trip through the Underway."

Considering they hadn't managed to refuel their coffee supply in Highmoor, Catch agreed—save that Gildar and the Moonless Night awaited him at this trip's end.

And my past, he thought, starting to dress. That lurked most of all, rising unexpectedly from shadows to snap at him.

Leaping off the rock, Moony bounded over to the Underway's entrance. "Hello!" he called. Echoes carried his voice back to him. Giggling, he scampered back to Catch. "I had another thought," he said, jumping back onto the rock. "Why don't you use that sleeping potion on Glider? We could sneak away while they were burying him."

Shifters don't bury their dead. His father's ring gleamed atop his folded coat. Catch hesitated, then slid it on.

"Or would that still make you Alph?" Moony put his head to one side. "Why'd you have that potion, anyway?"

Catch studied the ring. The whorl in the black pearl's center seemed to wriggle, snake-like, as he moved his hand. "I made it." Rags-n-Bones wasn't the only one to spend a profitable winter in Widget. Hopefully, Master Porpetti hadn't noticed that some of his rarer herbs were missing.

Moony's eyes rounded. "You made it? Who taught you to do that?"

"My father." Catch let his arm drop to his side. "He was Holdfast's most notorious assassin."

Moony's eyes bugged. Catch stared at the ground. His father had taught him many interesting things.

His father had taught him to be a killer.

"Ready?" asked Savotte, waiting impatiently by the Underway's mouth, knapsack slung over her back.

Grabbing up his belongings, Catch shoved them in diverse pockets to sort later, picked up Moony, and joined her at the entryway. "Ready," he said, and waited for her to take the first step. When she did, he seized her wrist. "Not so hasty. We usually don't get to see the lines we're about to cross so clearly. Take a moment to look at this one."

With lowered brows and a roll of her eyes, she pulled free of his grip. "Enough of your nonsense, Starthorne. Let's get going." She stepped into the Underway without a glance down at the groove delineating the inside from the outside.

He ran his toe along it before stepping inside. "Indigo," he said. The door crunched shut and damp darkness, lit by patches of glowing blue lichen, closed in.

"Asassin?" murmured Moony on his shoulder.

"Assassin," Catch affirmed. *Means 'killer,' 'slayer,' 'dispatcher'...*

He looked at his ring. The whorl wriggled, sucking in a gleam of blue.

...father.

CHAPTER TEN:
A NICE CHANGE

Breakfast was gingerbread pancakes. Ascot suspected Condorella chose gingerbread as an unconscious nod to her ongoing obsession to capture lost children in the woods. They were also good enough, studded with plump, golden currants and threaded with veins of melted brown sugar, to make her consider asking Condorella if she shouldn't give up the sorcery nonsense and become a chef.

That'll never happen. She glanced at Condorella, hunched over a spellbook, shoveling in pancakes off-handedly while flipping through its pages. She'd managed to drag her sleeve through the batter.

"Ready to begin the transformations, Condie?" asked Starley, across the table, draining the last of his fourth cup of coffee and attempting to help himself to Jolt's. Jolt smacked his hand.

"Mrghfur," grunted Condorella, holding up a finger.

Don't say the "t" word so loud. Ascot winced. Once, back in Albright, Dmitri had told Queen Bettina Anna that he'd been transformed into a human. He'd never mentioned the incident again, and considering how Dmitri enjoyed pontificating, his very silence spoke a library. Looking around, she located him in the cottage's back corner, staring at Condorella's single shelf of books. Despite his love of sweets, he hadn't joined them for breakfast.

"Is Sir Dmitri all right?" Rags-n-Bones whispered worriedly. "Is his leg hurting him again?"

Ascot pushed back her chair. "I'll go see." She gave her remaining pancakes a wistful glance, wondering if they'd still be there when she returned.

Dmitri's amber eyes remained fixed on the books' spines as she approached, pretending to read them. Ascot knew he was pretending because even he couldn't be interested in *Healing Through Yodeling*, *The Auras of Acorns*, and *Basic Broomstick Maneuvers*.

I knew Condorella tried to fly on that thing. She touched Dmitri's shoulder. He didn't jump. Doubtlessly, he'd heard her come up behind him. "It's not actual transformation, you know," she said. "Just an illusion."

He kept staring. Abruptly, he lifted a paw and rubbed his snout, his dew claw coming dangerously near his eye. "Today could be my birthday."

"Really?"

His ruff rippled with a shrug. "Somewhere around the vernal equinox. Wolves aren't too definite about such things."

Ascot nodded. Shadowvaleans didn't fuss too much over birthdays either, preferring to celebrate deathdays instead, those being so much more definitive. "I'll buy you a book, next time we're near a store."

A scraping noise drew her attention to the table. Condorella had stood. "Come help me prepare." She motioned Starley and Jolt toward the hearth.

Ascot looked back to Dmitri. He'd fixed his stare on the books again, as if drawing strength from them. All along his spine, the myriad white hairs stood stiff as fine wires. "Maybe you don't have to go through with it. Afleeta spends most of her time in animal form."

Dmitri laughed. "As luck would have it, I'm the one who absolutely cannot retain my natural form. It's illegal to be a wolf in the Clawcrags."

"What?" Ascot stared at him.

"I talked to Jolt last night. Five centuries ago, the wolf-shifters nearly drove shifter-kind to civil war. They wanted their own land. Eventually, they left the Clawcrags to its troubles and emigrated to Shadowvale. They're considered traitors among those they left behind."

"You mean—Shadowvale's werewolves are actually shifters?" asked Ascot, dumbfounded.

"Apparently."

She picked at a loose thread on her trousers. One of the local werewolves, Dashiel, had courted her until her father put a stop to it. Catch was going to make snide comments about her evident taste for shifters when he found out.

And he will *find out.* Pulling the thread free, Ascot glanced over at the hearth, where Condorella was running her finger over a line of text in her spellbook. "You could go back to Widget," she told Dmitri. "I'm sure Miss Eppicutt would welcome you at the school."

"No," said Dmitri. Shaking himself, he gave his side a quick lick. "No. Actually…the timing…"

Dmitri, at a loss for words? More confounded than ever, she waited.

"Intellectually, I know the timing is coincidental," he said, spitting out a clot of fur. "But the fact of this particular birthday coinciding with the prophecy…" Again he paused, picking his words with the same deliberation he used before raising the bet in poker. "I see a chance to make amends for my past."

What could sensible, cautious Dmitri have to make amends for— amends that required him to face his worst fear? Ascot didn't believe it. Whatever he imagined it was, he had to be exaggerating it.

"I believe Condorella is ready for us," he said. It still took a moment for him to stand. She saw him brace himself.

"How old are you, Dmitri?" she asked.

"Neither ladies nor talking wolves answer that question," he replied lightly. Padding over to the hearth, he settled on the braided rag rug before it.

Ascot twined the loose thread from her trousers around her finger. She'd become accustomed to Catch keeping secrets from her. Learning Dmitri had them as well was unsettling, even if he didn't, as Catch did, wave them in her face, then pretend they didn't exist.

"Come along, Ascot," said Condorella, beckoning.

Now she's gotten crushed herbs on her sleeve, thought Ascot, walking over. *At least her dark blue gown—pardon me, very dark blue shading into violet gown—hides stains well.*

Noticing that the last of her pancakes had indeed vanished, she sat beside Rags-n-Bones, who trembled, sucking on the remaining stub of last night's fork. "Don't worry," she whispered. "I'm sure the spell won't..." she hesitated. If she even mentioned "hurt," Rags-n-Bones might bolt for the door, and she was sure the smell of rancid cauliflower au gratin was still loitering about, waiting its opportunity to sneak inside.

"Won't what, miss?" he asked, turning his big, gray eyes on her.

"Won't take long," she amended. "I daresay it'll be done before you know it's begun."

He stopped shaking at once. Ever since she'd ridden the helhest to his rescue, Rags-n-Bones' already towering confidence in her had soared. "Oh, good. I'm ready." He bounced up. Ascot swiftly pulled back the hand she flung after him. She'd only meant reassurance.

But Condorella let out a satisfied grunt. "Good, the easy one first." She snapped her fingers. "The herbs, weasel."

"That's *stoat,*" said Starley, holding out a mortar filled with crushed vegetation. His fingers were stained green to the second joint.

"And the potion," said Condorella, ignoring him. Jolt handed her a round flask filled with a pale blue liquid that smelled of buttered violets. Condorella poured some of it into a saucer. "Drink this," she said, giving it to Rags-n-Bones.

He did, quite happily. *He's not going to start shrinking. He isn't,* thought Ascot insistently.

He didn't. "Ooh, yummy," he said. While he licked his lips, Condorella seized a handful of herbs, threw half of them over him, and the other half in the fire. The flames billowed up, taking on strange greenish tints.

"*Protean volo vu!*" cried Condorella, waving her arms.

Rags-n-Bones' outline wavered. Condorella's hand clenched, as if she held the reins of a large animal that was thrashing to get away. "Chose a word," she said between her teeth.

"Biscuit?" said Rags-n-Bones helpfully.

Pop. With a soft wink of light, Rags-n-Bones vanished. In his place stood a small, scruffy dog, its rust-and-white fur all over cowlicks. Its tail wagged uncertainly, and its funny, crooked ears perked. "Ooh!" cried the dog in Rags-n-Bones' voice. A merry, circular chase commenced.

Condorella lowered her arms. "I should've specified a word you won't say or hear often. Oh well." She shrugged. "Next."

"Wait," said Dmitri. The tense lines of his body showed through even his thick coat. "How does he change back?"

"He says the 'b' word. Or someone says it," replied Condorella. "Easy as toadstools."

"Biscuit," said Dmitri.

Pop. Rags-n-Bones blurred, stretching as he was pulled onto his hind legs. In less than a second, he'd returned to his gangly, more-or-less human shape. "Aw," he said, twisting his neck to look at his rump.

Dmitri sighed in evident relief. But Jolt frowned. "Doesn't look or sound like a proper shifting. Can't you make it cracklier?"

"Yeah, and he's still got his kit on," added Starley, scratching his back on the hearth stones. "What's up with that?"

"You next, Ascot," said Condorella, shooting them an "everyone's a critic" look.

It couldn't have hurt, thought Ascot, taking the indicated place before the fire. Rags-n-Bones hadn't so much as yipped. But if pressed, she'd have admitted that her stomach felt like a nest of spiders had taken up residence. It was a good thing the saucer of blue liquid Condorella passed her was indeed tasty—rather like a creamy pound cake with sugared violets crumbled on top—or she might not have been able to get it down.

Condorella tossed dried herbs over her. Ascot fought not to sneeze. "*Protean volo vu,*" cried Condorella.

The syllables ran over Ascot's skin like a thousand excited insects. The tickling swiftly grew more invasive, as if all the invisible bugs Condorella had summoned were trying to burrow under her skin. Painless, but definitely disconcerting.

"Your word," said Condorella.

"Kerfuffle," she replied. *No one's going to say that by accident.*

The insects dove under her skin and turned her inside-out. It didn't hurt. It more seemed like she'd been flipped in some strange way that had nothing to do with her position in space. She looked down at herself. Her usual body was still there, everything in the right place, but strangely transparent. Much more solid-looking, grown up around her and, disconcertingly, through her, was the figure of—"A skunk?"

"Well, you do have a white streak in your hair," said Condorella, defensively.

"A skunk?" Putting her hands on her hips caused a strange resistance, as if something was dragging off her wrists. Looking down again, she saw the skunk had mimicked her action. She knew she was standing straight, yet felt like some invisible hand was pushing her down onto all fours. Over her shoulder, she got an eyeful of fluffy, black-and-white tail. *I'm not going to play with it.*

Oh, all right. She allowed herself to fluff it once. It was like stroking a cloud; not exactly there. Unfortunately, something else skunk-related was very much present. "Frabjacket, did you have to add in the smell?" she asked, gagging.

"Wouldn't be proper skunk without it." Condorella thrust out her chin. "You'll get used to it."

"Could you get used to it later?" asked Jolt, grabbing up last night's pomander.

"Kerfuffle," said Ascot, and the insects shot out of her pores. The vague downward pressure eased off. She rolled her shoulders. "What an aromatic visit it's been."

"All right, wolf." Condorella crooked her finger at Dmitri. "Two forms for you. I'm thinking human and dingo."

Dmitri had started to approach, claws scraping over the floorboards, but he stopped, ears flattening. "I am not a *dingo*."

"Listen," Condorella began heatedly. "I'm the one doing the magic—"

"Eh, not dingo," interrupted Starley, rubbing his neck. "They've recently been reclassified as—" His voice kept going smoothly, without pause. But his gaze briefly flicked toward Jolt, and Ascot's brain inserted one. "—ferals."

"Oh," said Condorella, scowling. Jolt stared toward the front door, void of all expression. "Maybe a fox, then. An arctic fox?"

"That will be satisfactory," said Dmitri. If he'd intended to quibble, whatever strange current had just passed in the room subdued him. He took his place by the hearth. Condorella added a chalky pink liquid to the blue one in the saucer. It didn't smell as good. "Drink it," she told Dmitri, taking up a double handful of herbs.

By Dmitri's grimace, it didn't taste very nice. Condorella sprinkled her herbs. Her back arched. So did Dmitri's. His fur rose, making a sizzling sound. Sweat rolled down Condorella's face. "Your words," she grated out. "Three. One to change to human, one to fox, one to your true shape."

"Fyodor, Alyosha, Ivan," Dmitri managed.

What are the odds we'll instantly run into someone named "Ivan"? Ascot couldn't help thinking, even as Dmitri writhed. He seemed to be sprouting random limbs. His tail vanished, thickened, and reappeared.

"Fyodor!" cried Condorella.

Pop. Dmitri rose on two legs. His hair was still creamy white, his eyes amber, and there was something decidedly lupine about his nose, but the rest of him was all human: tall, long-legged, and broad in the chest. A small, round scar pocked his left shoulder. He was also naked. Ascot whipped her head away, cheeks flaming.

"That's more like it," said Starley.

Ascot's imagination whispered something she really didn't want to hear. Her cheeks burned hotter.

"So glad you approve," said Dmitri. His voice was less deep and gruff in this form, but perfectly recognizable. "Alyosha."

Pop. Ascot risked a peek. "Awwww!" she cooed, ruthlessly stifling the urge to get on her knees and cuddle the small, enormous-eared, bushy-tailed creature standing before the fire. It was definitely foxlike, but much, much cuter.

Dmitri squinted around at himself. "This is not an arctic fox," he rumbled.

"A fennec's close enough," said Starley. "Stop being such a whatsit, drama-wolf."

"Ivan," said Dmitri. With a pop, he returned to wolf form. Ascot squelched a sigh of regret. "Well, it seems to be working," he said, checking to make sure all his bits were in place.

"Of course it worked." Condorella fondled one of the trinkets hanging around her neck. "I'm a disciple of Magden Le Fou. This is one of her teeth, you know." She gave it a kiss. Ascot instantly wanted a bath.

"So, now we're safe in the Clawcrags?" she asked, edging away.

"Safe? In the Clawcrags?" With a short laugh, Starley plopped back into his chair. "Came to the wrong place, love."

"You'll be safer," said Jolt. "After you've practiced a bit, that is." Wrapping his dragonfly-patterned mantle tighter about his shoulders, he surveyed the cottage's single room. "I suppose we can stay here while you do that."

Rags-n-Bones, busy licking out the abandoned mortar, suddenly cocked his head.

"Oh, that'll be lovely. Skunk-stink on the inside, cheese-stink on the outside." Slouching, Starley hooked a finger through a mug's handle and twirled it. "Cut off my nose now."

Condorella put her hands on her hips, knocking over the flask of blue liquid in the process. "How am I supposed to concentrate with you lot stomping around in here?"

Frowning, Rags-n-Bones went to the door, crouched, and put his ear to it. Ascot strained her own ears. Was something scratching at the outside?

"The more we move, the more likely we'll be spotted by a Sniffer," said Dmitri.

Any further comments were interrupted by a soft creak, followed by an appalling aroma. Starley and Jolt gasped and dove for the pomander. Dmitri stuffed his snout under the rag rug. "Who farted?" screeched Condorella, clapping her hands to her nose.

"Um, me." Hurriedly shutting the door, Rags-n-Bones waved. "Um, I mean I didn't, but..." He held up a bloated and greasy-whiskered Nipper.

"Something wrong, Rags?" asked Ascot. Nipper's squeaks had an urgent quality about them.

Another squeak. Rags-n-Bones' eyes flew wide. "It's the Black Knight! Nipper glimpsed him through the trees not fifteen minutes ago."

CHAPTER ELEVEN:
DIVERTING PASTIMES

"Are we there yet?" asked Moony, riding on Catch's shoulder. His small, raspy voice echoed off the Underway's close sides.

"No," said Savotte.

Catch was impressed. Moony had taken the oldest, simplest, and most irritating travel-trick in the book, and made it ten times more annoying than it naturally was. He managed this by purring cutely, staring about with wide orange eyes, and never listening to the answer. If he did hear it, he apparently forgot exactly five point three seconds later.

Most brilliant of all, he'd started it up only an hour after they entered the Underway. Admittedly, an hour in the Underway seemed to stretch an entire day. Nothing to see but endless curved walls, illuminated by pale blue lichen, and pocked at intervals with mossy holes bored to the outside. You'd suffocate without them, but the distant glimpses of sky made the reality of being trapped underground, like a mole-shifter, all the more depressing.

Actually, mole-shifters were spies. The fact that this was general knowledge rendered them useless for their designated task. *Fur and fangs, but we're a daft race,* thought Catch.

"Are we there yet?" asked Moony.

"Will you tell him to stop it?" asked Savotte, pulling at her hair.

"Stop it, Moony," said Catch in the automatic, uninflected sort of way that really meant *"keep doing it."*

"Starthorne." Savotte took a breath.

Catch gave her a look of wide-eyed attention. "Yes?"

"We have two days' journey ahead of us, in cramped surroundings. Let's try to be civil." He laughed. She swore, not quite under her breath. "We have to talk, sometime," she said.

"Not necessarily," he replied. "We could attempt charades."

"This is petty," she snapped.

"Means 'spiteful,' 'malicious,' or 'vindictive,'" he replied. The last seemed particularly appropriate.

"Are we there yet?" asked Moony.

"Gah!" cried Savotte. Catch patted Moony.

The passage branched off in two different directions. Marks etched at the corner of the diversion told you which path led where, if you knew how to read them. When Savotte paused to squint at them, Catch pushed past her, taking the right passage.

"Wait!" cried Savotte.

"It's the correct way," said Catch, not looking back. He slowed his pace, so he could hear her irritated huff when she finally deciphered the marks.

When it arrived, it was more of a sigh than a huff, but it would suffice. "You have the Underway's passages memorized?" she asked, hurrying to catch up to him.

He shrugged. Years ago, his father had taken him blindfolded into the Underway's center, left "just for a minute," and failed to return. After Catch worked up the nerve to remove the blindfold, expecting his father's reprimand every instant, it had taken him four days to find his way out.

"Actually, it was a guess," he said. "I'm a very good guesser. Astounding, really. Once, at this one pub, I guessed a man had a leprechaun in his pocket, and, do you know, I was right. Won a—"

"Starthorne!" Savotte shouted, flinging up her hands. The Underway's close walls carried her voice along them in a series of reverberations, echoing and repeating.

"Are we there yet?" asked Moony.

Savotte sagged against the wall. This was a more difficult proposition than it first appeared, for the Underway's passages were perfectly round, save for a slight flattening of the floor. Walls bowed away from you. But Savotte managed by bending her knees and sticking out her rump. She dropped her face into her hands. "You are such an *ass*. You cannot be the golden star of Magden Le Fou's prophecy," she said through her fingers.

"Oh, well spotted," said Catch.

Her head jerked up. "What do you mean?" she asked, eyes narrowing.

"What do you mean, 'what do you mean'?" he retorted as they resumed their journey. He turned to walk backwards, so he could face her as they talked. There was nothing to trip over in the Underway, anyway. "You're a smart woman. Tell me, do you know exactly where you'll be tomorrow at this time?"

She frowned, jaws working as if chewing an invisible stalk of grass. "Well, most likely I'll—"

"Sorry, that was rhetorical. Means 'oratorical,' 'stylistic,' or 'you don't have to answer.' Yes, we'll probably still be slogging through the Underway. But how will you be feeling?"

"Annoyed with you," she snapped. They passed one of the mossy holes drilled to the outside. Clear, yellow sunlight fell over her face, revealing she had that flattened-ear look about her again.

He nodded; he'd grant her that one. "Aside from that, though. You could twist an ankle between now and then. I could eat all your molasses twists and leave you with nothing but the smell of sugar."

She slapped her pocket with a sudden, panicked movement. Her eyes widened when she realized the small bag was missing. Taking it from his own pocket, Catch held it up.

"Will you stop stealing things?" Savotte shouted, grabbing it back.

"Consider it an illustration of my point," said Catch. "If you can't predict my doing that, how can some woman who lived five hundred years ago—"

His heel struck an unexpected lump. Moony yowled, digging in his claws as Catch stumbled, put his other foot down hurriedly, struck another lump, and fell rump-first on yet more lumps. Hard lumps, with points and angles. Moony's tail swatted him across the face.

Savotte laughed.

All right; he'd give her that one, too. Catch got up gingerly, spitting out cat hair. Rubbing a new, throbbing spot on his bottom, he turned to look at what had tripped him.

"That's imposs—" he began, then shook his head. Clearly, it *was* possible, because he was looking at it: a fall of rock from the Underway's ceiling, completely blocking the path for some un-seeable distance ahead. The rubble obscured the glowing lichen, or perhaps it had scraped off the walls when the rocks dropped, rendering the passage dark as the inside of a mouth.

Savotte's laughter trailed off. It had been sharp and grim anyway, containing little humor. Coming to his side, she stared at the fall-in. "No telling how far it extends."

"No. We'll have to backtrack and take the left fork." He stooped to study a rock, but one lesson his father had neglected was geology, so it told him nothing. *Still, there's never been a cave-in before.* He scratched his cheek, frowning.

"I don't know another route," said Savotte, hugging her elbows.

Gildar likely discouraged people from learning the various bends in the Underway, in case the information got passed to potential slipskins. "I do," said Catch, tossing the rock aside and standing.

"I certainly didn't predict this," said Savotte after a moment. Catch slid a sideways glance at her. Meeting his eyes, she almost, maybe smiled. It was the closest thing to a truce they'd reached.

Sighing, Moony draped himself around Catch's shoulders. "We're not going to be there yet for a while, are we?"

&

Condorella harrumphed, watching with crossed arms as everyone grabbed up belongings. "Such a fuss over nothing. Cavall will never find the cottage. My magic hides it."

There's my knapsack, thought Ascot, spotting it crammed beside a sack of potatoes. *How did it get there?*

Dmitri coughed. "We didn't follow the directions on the card exactly."

"Ah, but," Condorella smiled proudly, "the one that mattered was the blue flower. The cottage is invisible if you're not carrying a blue flower, and Cavall can't pick a blue flower because he's colorblind."

Slinging her knapsack over her shoulder—and stifling an impulse to strangle Condorella for all the whirling and rock-licking her instructions had forced them to perform—Ascot spoke very calmly. "But, if Cavall tracked us to the hyacinths, he's smart enough to deduce we picked them for a reason."

Nipper squeaked. "Um, Cavall was carrying a flower?" Rags-n-Bones translated. Nipper squeaked again. "And an, um, torch?"

Into the silence came a soft, sinister *pop*, followed by a *crackle*. Then a kind of bubbling noise.

Wow. Cavall actually managed to light the cheese, thought Ascot, running to the window. Fleetingly, she wondered if baking would improve the smell.

After a second of frozen shock, Condorella exploded into action, waving her arms so frantically she seemed to have grown an extra pair. "We have to get out *now*," she cried, grabbing up a spellbook and tucking the letter between its pages.

"It's not burning very quickly," Ascot reported, dropping the gingham curtain. The ancient cauliflower au gratin was too mucky, she supposed.

"Maybe we can extinguish it," said Dmitri. "Do you have a bucket of water?"

"Water?" cried Condorella, mummifying the book in several layers of cloth. "I'm a witch! Do you think I want to risk melting into a puddle of goo? I'd sooner keep a bucket of acid in my house." She shuddered.

Ascot closed her eyes. *Of course she'd embrace that story point, too.* "Then, we'd better get out before the flame hits some pocket of gas and the cottage explodes."

With a grunt, Condorella grabbed up her mortar and pestle and shoved them into a satchel. Jolt, too, was busily gathering up various items. He hadn't brought anything to the cottage, but it seemed such a natural reaction that Condorella apparently didn't notice he was nicking dried fruit, bread, utensils, and a glass paperweight he'd evidently taken a fancy to. Rags-n-Bones cradled every jar of jam from the pantry.

Ascot joined Starley and Dmitri at the door. Amazing; even with the cottage on fire, none of them were eager to open the door and face the stench. "Just a moment," said Dmitri, putting a paw on Ascot's hand as she reached for the latch. "Cavall could be out there, waiting to ambush us."

"Six to one, drama-wolf," said Starley, slightly crouched, eyes intent on the door, clearly intending to sprint out the instant it was opened. "He tries it, we take him down, sit on his head, and fart." He made the same gesture he had in the corral, inner fingers wrapped around the outer ones.

I'm almost glad Moony isn't here, thought Ascot. *Him and Starley together in one room might cause some kind of explosion.*

Condorella came to the door, a satchel over her arm, the spellbook with the letter cocooned on her back. Picking up her broomstick, she turned it over and shook off the bristles, revealing a glowing, dark blue crystal.

"Can you do any magic with that?" asked Dmitri. "Turn us invisible, perhaps?"

Condorella shook her head. "Invisibility works fine for stationary objects, but movement tends to give things away."

"If Kay were here, we could just hold his hand and walk away," said Rags-n-Bones.

"Yes, shame he's back in Widget," said Ascot. She didn't mean to be brusque, but a definite sizzling was coming from the outside. They had to abandon the cottage, but if Cavall was out there waiting to pick them off—

Not "us" off, she realized. Starley. She'd bet the last chocolate bar hidden in her pocket that if Starley jumped over a cliff, Cavall would follow with his teeth in Starley's heel. Maybe they could work with that. "If invisibility won't work, how about another illusion?" she asked, turning to Condorella.

❧

"Are my eyebrows really that crooked?" Ascot whispered to Dmitri five minutes later, as they hurried up the mountain path. Behind them, a trail of black, greasy smoke leaked into the sky, staining it gray. The air stank of burning cheese.

"The likeness is exact," Dmitri whispered back. Ascot stumbled over a rock, unable to watch her footing and stare at her doppelganger, pacing ahead, at the same time. As they reached the clearing with the bulbous stump, it paused to glance back at the cottage. Ascot stopped, too, watching with fascination. It wasn't anything like looking in a mirror. Reflections always obediently copied you.

Then it lifted one foot to scratch the back of the other, and the illusion shattered. *Starley,* said her brain. "I don't scratch my heel like that," she objected. Plus, the way he held her head made it look as if she had an earache.

"An' I don't walk like I've inserted a broomstick up my...well, swallowed a broomstick, love," he retorted, and that was even stranger, hearing his voice issue from her lips—which surely weren't that pouty, were they? "Try to loosen up."

"Shut up, both of you," advised Jolt. "If Cavall overhears you, he'll sniff out the ruse." Drawing close to Ascot, he murmured, "If Cavall goes for this, lead him off as far as you can before revealing yourself, to give us time to reach our hiding spot. We'll send Nipper back to lead you to us." He tugged his ear. "You're sure Cavall won't take you hostage?"

About eighty-five percent certain. Maybe seventy. "I'm not the one he wants," she replied, just to keep it simple.

"What were we supposed to do with the stick, miss?" asked Rags-n-Bones, gazing at the stump. At the last moment, he remembered to direct his question toward Starley.

Cupping his hand over his mouth, Starley whispered in his ear, smirking in a way that Ascot knew never happened when *she* wore her face. Rags-n-Bones nearly went up in a puff of smoke.

"Oh, dear," he managed to squeak.

Ascot gave Starley a kick. It just made her—his—smirk widen. "Let's keep going," said Dmitri, pushing her with his head.

Grouchily, she obeyed. She was quite sure the phantom Starley body she wore was trying to trip her with his long, rangy limbs. Off to the right, the brush crackled.

"Watch out!" cried Dmitri.

That was Ascot's sole warning before Cavall, in his great, inky-black hound form, dove straight at her. She jumped back, barely avoiding the snap of his jaws. If she'd actually been Starley, she probably would've added several cheeky spins and backflips to the repertoire.

I'm not even going to attempt it. Cavall snapped at her again. Well, at least he was falling for their ploy. Now she just had to play her part without getting bitten in half.

"Run!" cried Dmitri, butting between Cavall and Starley, who'd automatically leaped toward the hound.

I should be doing that, thought Ascot. She lashed out with a foot and connected with Cavall's ear, harder than she'd expected. She'd misjudged the length of her leg.

Enraged, Cavall flung back his head and howled. For a moment, Ascot simply gaped into that pink, wet chasm lined with white stalactites and stalagmites—right now she wasn't interested in sorting out the difference. Reeling back, she fled, making for a stand of thin trees.

A mistake. Starley never would have run so soon. When Cavall didn't come after her instantly, she glanced back, and saw him standing in the path, ears pricked, head cocked, dividing looks between her and the others, running in the opposite direction.

Oh, frabjacket. Turning around, she mimicked Starley's favorite gesture, with the two inner fingers looped over the outer ones, and a downward jab of the hand. Cavall's hackles rose. A snarl rippled his lips as he crouched.

Ascot wasted no time gawking. She bolted. *I'm going to have to ask Starley what that gesture means, if I survive this.*

Wiry yellow grass tore at her legs. A dry, whippy branch sliced across her cheek. Once, she stubbed her toe on some tough, hidden root, nearly fell, and ran on, ankle twinging. Likely only the fact that Cavall had to dodge around trees kept him from bringing her down.

Must give the others time to escape. She ran out of trees. A clearing of hard-baked earth stretched ahead of her. A warning throb tingled up and down her left leg. Balling her fists, she lowered her head, and charged for the edge.

Cavall brought her down in the clearing's center. Her chest and chin struck the ground while her arms flew out wide, too late to break her fall. All the air grunted out of her chest, and for an endless, terrifying moment, she couldn't get it back. Cavall's teeth worried her hair. His paws pinned her down. Couldn't breathe.

Then suddenly, she did, sucking in a great, painful gasp that croaked in her throat. At almost the same moment, the weight disappeared from her back and the hot breath stopped steam-cooking her neck.

She took another breath. This one didn't hurt so much. Her eyes watered with mingled pain and gratitude. Another, wonderful, breath. This one hardly hurt at all, meaning her chin seized its chance to register its complaints.

Duly noted, she thought. The rest of her pains could wait their turn. She rolled over. The great black hound watched her, pale eyes narrowed, silky ears pricked.

"Peppercorn," she croaked. Starley had chosen the word. His illusory body melted away with a series of tiny, tickling pops.

An answering series of crackles erupted around the hound. Ascot closed her eyes as Galen Cavall, now in human form, rose above her, propping his fists on his very bare hips.

"Miss Nuisance," he said.

"Galen," she replied. She opened her eyes. *I simply must get used to bareness around shifters,* she told herself firmly.

Sighing, Cavall ran a hand through his hair and over his jaw. "I should've figured it was a trick. That damned weasel would've tried to bite my throat out."

"Stoat," Ascot corrected. Taking the fact that he wasn't trying to drag her off and arrest her, or whatever he had in mind, as a good sign, she sat up cautiously, testing everything to make sure it wasn't broken before moving. "You're not surprised to see me alive."

He crouched down on his long haunches with a shrug. "A few miles out of Highmoor, I remembered Starthorne's a liar." The corner of his lips twitched in a rueful grin. "For once, I'm glad he is. We always did have a certain affection for each other. In fact—" A gleam came into his eyes. He moved forward. Like a predator; all sleek purpose and sleeker muscles.

"What?" blurted Ascot, shuffling awkwardly backwards on her rump and hands. He kept coming, rose above her. One long-fingered hand reached out to cup her chin.

"No one would know," he breathed, staring down at her with those blue, blue eyes. No trace of icy gray in them at the moment.

Ascot's heart brushed light, butterfly wings against her breastbone. Hot all over, then quivery-cold, as if sprinkled with a light spring rain. Back to hot. Through this parade of sensations, a part of her sat back and checked items off a list: her travel-stained clothes, sweat-stringy hair, blistered feet sloshing in her boots, dust-covered skin—

She stopped before the list depressed her too badly. It was enough to prove her point: he could hardly find her unbearably desirable right now. "You're only trying to get back at Catch," she said, pushing him off.

He returned to his crouch, still predatory, but perhaps with a touch of regret about it. "Am I? It would be fun."

She stifled a hot retort. "I think you'd enjoy crowing about it to Catch more than the fun itself." Sitting up, she combed her fingers through her hair. *I'm tucking it back, not flirting.*

"He poisoned you." Folding his hands beneath his chin, Cavall regarded her speculatively. "Aren't you angry with him?"

"I'm fine." She backed off a few more inches, just to be safe. "It was *your* partner who held the knife to my throat."

"Ah, so he was just saving you, back there, and now you're returning the favor." Cavall rose, dusting off his skin.

Ascot flung up her hands. "What do you really want, Galen?"

"You won. Catch is returning to Holdfast." *He left me. Again.*

But not willingly, she insisted. *Not truly, really willingly.*

"I want—" He paused. Abruptly his tone shifted. His brows lowered into angry lines. "I'm giving you this one chance. Forget Starthorne. Leave the Clawcrags."

Should I forget Moony, too? The temperature of Ascot's blood began ratcheting up. She bit her tongue.

"Go find your wolf and Mr. Bones," Cavall continued. "Take them back to Widget, and I swear no shifter will harm you. But if you stay with the Hide Aways, I'll hunt you like the Hide Aways. I mean to tear out their throats." He bared his teeth. "Starting with Starley Reftkin."

"I'm sure he'll be delighted to hear it," said Ascot. She'd imagined he was better than this. Maybe, distracted by his looks, she'd been fooling herself all along. "Want to know the truth? Catch may be a liar, but he isn't a killer. That's why he'll win over you every time."

She wished she could walk away from him, after that line, but Nipper had to find her, first. Folding her arms, she stared fiercely off southward, at Mt. Skylash's double peak, pretending Cavall wasn't still standing behind her.

Her shoulders tensed when he walked up behind her, but she kept pretending, even when he whispered in her ear. "You're right, Starthorne's a liar. A good one. Who convinced you he isn't a killer in the first place?"

Ascot concentrated all her energy into staring at a thorny flower, vivid as a purple explosion, waving amongst the grass.

But she couldn't block out Cavall's voice as it dropped to an even lower, more intimate murmur. "Has anyone told you about Glim?"

"What about Glim?" she snapped, trying to sound disinterested and hating herself when she didn't.

"He was Starthorne's best friend," Cavall replied. "Maybe you've heard about Starthorne falling off the edge of Holdfast Plateau? That's one version. Another is that he murdered Glim and used his body as padding when he made his escape by jumping over the side."

The air whooshed out of Ascot's chest, as if he'd knocked her to the ground again. Her stomach felt as if she'd just eaten a helping of Condorella's cauliflower au gratin—the stuff on the walls, not the stuff in the oven.

Cavall went on. "Should you see Starthorne again, ask him to tell you the truth." He paused. "Then, remember that he lies."

He hovered over her a few seconds longer before a brush of cold air replaced the warmth of his presence. There may have been a few soft, whisking sounds as he padded away, but she couldn't be sure, over the buzz in her ears. Alone in the clearing, she staring unseeingly at the forked peak until Nipper scurried up to guide her back to her friends.

CHAPTER TWELVE:
RHYME AND REASON

They'd been walking long enough—it seemed days—for the Underway's endless, rounded walls with their glowing blue patches to start spinning in Catch's vision. Sometimes, he could swear he heard odd thrummings emanating from somewhere deep in the mountain's heart. Fabrications of a bored brain, he supposed.

Their current path was a lesser-used one, narrow and steep, winding through Mt. Skylash's heart. In lieu of openings to the outside, alchemic bubbles pulsed at intervals along the walls; gelatinous, semi-translucent things, resembling some kind of parasitic sea life. They circulated the air, sluggishly. Thick sheets of cobweb clung to the walls, gleaming with odd, electric blue tints in the lichen light.

Catch didn't remember the Underway being infested with spiders before. "What are they eating, do you imagine?" asked Moony, pawing a web hopefully. "I haven't seen any bugs."

"Probably because the spiders have eaten them all," said Savotte. She walked much closer to Catch than she had previously, the whites of her eyes gleaming. Her jaws worked on a lump of molasses from the bag he'd generously returned to her. If she'd been in horse-form, she'd probably be snorting.

Catch frowned. *Have we actually seen any spiders?*

Moony batted at a trailing web, sat on his haunches, and sighed. "Are we there, yet?" he asked without enthusiasm.

"I have little notion where we are." Savotte glanced up at the ceiling, shrouded with webs. "Underneath the chambers where the tengu lie sleeping, perhaps."

Moony abandoned the cobweb instantly. "Tengu?" he asked, trotting alongside Savotte.

"Monsters from a bygone age," she replied. Catch clicked his tongue derisively, but she ignored him. "If Magden Le Fou's prophecy is right, they'll awaken on the Moonless Night and come sweeping down on Holdfast."

"Meaning it's just as likely Rags-n-Bones will ride into Holdfast on a magnificent gold dragon and challenge Gildar to single combat," said Catch. Fur and fangs, he wished his ears would stop ringing, or humming, or whatever they were doing. He swiped webbing out of his face and it clung to his fingers.

"I'd like to see a dragon," said Moony. But the idea of the tengu had clearly captured his imagination. Scampering to the wall, he sniffed at a crack in the rock.

"You don't believe in the prophecy *or* the tengu?" Savotte asked Catch.

He shrugged. He'd been all through the Underway and seen no sign of the fabled chambers where the tengu supposedly slept. Perhaps they'd lived here, centuries ago, but they were gone now. "They only interest me insomuch as that if I'm the golden star, I am supposed to defeat them on my lonesome." He scraped his web-sticky fingers along the wall and froze mid-step.

"You are?" Moony looked up, eyes glowing like a pair of glass cherries. "Lucky!"

"Hush," said Catch, still touching the wall. Faint vibrations ran up his wrist. Apparently, his brain hadn't been lying to him after all.

Mountains rumble, he told himself. Maybe there was an

earthquake upsetting Skylash's bowels, an avalanche pattering across its surface. Aware of Moony and Savotte's curious stares, he pressed his ear against the wall.

Boom. Boom. Boom.

Catch pulled back, his left cheek tingling. Mountains rumbled. They didn't beat drums. "How very strange," he managed.

The walls laughed. It echoed all around: laughter like an array of cymbals being struck with an ax—harsh, metallic, and lacking any of mirth's gentler notes, rattling out of the myriad ruts and crevices. Catch's lingering hopes that his brain was playing a trick died a swift death when Moony's and Savotte's eyes shot wide.

Boom. Boom. Boom.

"The tengu," whispered Savotte.

"The tengu? Where? Hiding in another passage?" Rearing up, Moony clawed the wall, scraping off filmy cobwebs.

"Don't say that," said Catch. "It isn't the tengu. It isn't." *Not my brain's trick, but someone's trick, surely.*

As his mind raced and groped for an answer, fresh blue light, more vivid than the dull lichen, began glowing through the cracks in the walls. Savotte spun on him, white showing all around her brown irises. "We're below Mt. Skylash's peak, perhaps right under one of the secret lairs they've been sleeping in."

Boom. Boom. Boom. The beat came faster now, like a heart hit by a jolt of adrenalin. Then the chanting began.

Run! Run! Here we come!

Give us all, and we'll leave you none!

Another rattle of laughter followed the rasping, metallic, yet perfectly intelligible words. Moony clawed the wall more frenetically.

Boom. Boom. Boom. Each *boom* struck like a tiny hammer, hitting the soles of Catch's boots.

"They're getting closer," said Savotte, trembling.

"There's no 'they'!" snapped Catch, glaring at the walls, the floor, down the length of the tunnel. Cobwebs wafted, glowing like electrified lace in the new brightness.

The horrible, rasping chorus spoke again.

Run! Run! Before you're done!

Fall behind, and we'll have some fun!

"Are you offering a game of chess?" Catch shouted at a particularly bright ceiling crack, fists clenched at his sides. "Whist, perhaps? I fancy liar's dice, myself."

Savotte grabbed his wrist, almost wrenching his arm from its socket, and muscled him along the path. "My orders are to deliver you to Holdfast, not watch you get eaten by tengu."

"There are no tengu—do you see any tengu?" he shouted, clawing at her fingers.

Boom. Boom. Boom.

Moony ran from crack to crack, rearing up to scratch the wall. He ducked behind a great, wafting sheet of cobwebs, leaving only the twitching tip of his tail visible. "Hey, there's a—*merooooo!*"

His tail tip disappeared.

"Mange!" Twisting free of Savotte's grip, Catch dashed over and swiped the sticky web aside. It plastered itself over his bruised right eye. The left was still clear enough to see the irregular gap in the wall, large enough for a small melon, or one average-sized Vicardi cat. "Moony?" Catch stuck his hand into the crack, expecting to receive a spider bite for his trouble. Instead, he touched the sides of a smooth, slick slope, leading downwards.

Run! Run! Or never see the sun!

Heads, you've lost, and tails, we've won!

The words echoed out of the hole. Catch put his clear eye to it, but all was blackness. "Show yourselves!" squalled Moony distantly. Scuffling sounds followed.

At least he's alive. Call it a consequence of the life he'd been leading recently, but Catch had briefly feared that the wall had actually swallowed Moony. "Moony, what's happening? Where are you?"

"Sorry, Captain. Busy showing these cowards what-for," Moony called back. A series of thumps and snarls reverberated up the hole. Either Moony had found an actual adversary, or was putting on one impressive pantomime.

Boom. Boom. Boom.

"Move," said Savotte, shoving him aside. She pushed an alchemic glow-globe, filled with firefly powder, into the hole. It rolled smoothly down the slope. A few seconds later came the tinkling crash of it shattering on some unseen floor.

"Oh, well done," said Catch.

"The firefly powder will provide some light," Savotte snapped. True enough; a faint green light seeped out the hole, Catch again peered through it, but the angle of the slope prevented him from seeing anything beyond a vague yellow-greenness. Moony squalled piercingly. "Can't he just flutter back out the hole he fell through?" asked Savotte.

"Not with your alchemic clip on his wing," Catch retorted.

Run! Run! Our all to your one!
Your life is ending and your death begun!

"Merow! That's what you think!" A definite thump.

Turning from the hole, Catch jogged along the tunnel, feeling the walls. "Where are you going?" shouted Savotte, caught off-guard. She ran up behind him a moment later.

"He's right beside us and slightly below us," Catch replied, stopping by a depression in the wall and studying it. "There must be a way to reach him."

She tried to grab his wrist again. "If those are tengu—"

"There are no tengu," he snapped, shrugging her off. A myriad of cracks traced the depression. *Cracks—indicating fragility.* He rifled through a pocket.

Boom. Boom. Boom.

Savotte shook his shoulder. "No tengu? Can't you see? They've returned, exactly as Magden Le Fou foretold."

Whirling, he pushed her so hard she staggered several steps back, arms flailing for balance. "Nothing will convince me, because believing the prophecy is real means accepting that I am not a man, but a *puppet!*"

Instantly, he wished the words unsaid. The Underway echoed them forward and back, all along its length, as if to carry them to both Holdfast and Highmoor, as well as up into the sky for the birds to gossip over. He closed his eyes, but couldn't shut his ears to the reverberations. They came to him again and again: the bare truth, without the polishing gloss of a single lie. They took a long time to fade.

Boom. Boom. Boom.

"Mur! Stay still!" Moony cried faintly.

Catch opened his eyes. In the bar of blue light painted over her face, Savotte watched him warily, but also, perhaps, with a new hint of understanding. He sighed. "I'm not leaving the Underway without Moony, so you might as well help me reach him."

After a couple seconds, she nodded. "What do you intend to do?"

He patted the depression. "The rock's fractured here. I have some gunpowder—"

"You're carrying gunpowder?"

"I used to have a pistol." He'd flung it in the pond, back in Albright.

"Never mind. You intend to blow a hole in the wall." She rubbed her nose—such an Ascot gesture it made Catch briefly smile. "You might bring the ceiling down on us."

"Possible, but unlikely, if we direct the blast." He smirked at her. "Besides, if I'm the golden star, I'll be fine. Can't die until I fulfil the prophecy."

"Your concern for my well-being warms my heart, Starthorne," Savotte retorted. But she helped him set the gunpowder and construct a rough fuse.

Of course the prophecy says nothing about me possessing all my fingers when I face the tengu, thought Catch just before he sparked the match. But Moony's faint snarls continued, interspersed with that horrible, metallic laughter, so he lit the fuse and quickly retreated a distance down the tunnel to crouch beside Savotte.

Boom!

This one had nothing to do with the not-tengu. Rock shards sprayed out of the depression and struck the opposite wall. Tensing, Savotte watched the ceiling, but only a few small pebbles dribbled down. Several bounced off Catch's head as he went to the depression. The explosion had created a hole just large enough for him to fit through.

More or less, he thought a minute later, halfway through it, constricted around the chest, palms on the rough floor of a new passge, and feet kicking air.

"Want a push?" came Savotte's muffled voice behind him.

"I'm fine," he gasped, since he couldn't glare at her. He walked himself forward, thighs scraping the hole's rough edge. His head banged against the opposite wall before his toes pulled free, thumping down on the floor.

A glow-globe dropped through the hole. Savotte's heels appeared, swinging gracefully to the floor, followed, with an eel-like shimmy, by her torso. She didn't even knock her head on the lip. "Hate you," Catch panted, rubbing his bruised ribs.

"Mutual." Savotte picked up the glow-globe. A matching green-yellow glow emanated around the corner, where the narrow passage they stood in opened into some wider chamber. The grating laughter sounded even more metallic close up. Hooking the glow-globe over her wrist, Savotte drew her knife. "If those are the tengu, maybe you can defeat them now and save time."

"It isn't the tengu," said Catch. "Moony?"

A half-choked grunt answered. *Is he being strangled?* Forgetting the pain in his ribs, Catch raced into the larger chamber, Savotte on his heels, and came to a sliding halt.

Bulky black bodies lined the chamber's wall, lit by yellow sunlight shining through several holes in the high ceiling. Moony, teeth buried in one figure's dangling arm, was doing his level best to tear it off at the root.

"What's this?" gasped Savotte, holding the glow-globe high so its light could play off the low-browed, distorted faces arrayed along the walls. Not a single one reacted.

Oversized teeth jutted from wide, lipless mouths. Huge, clawed hands hung past bowed knees. Stocky torsos clad in leathery, gray rags sagged lifelessly. The creatures fit the stories' description of the tengu: big, lumpy monsters that would tear off your arm simply because they'd find it easier than figuring out how to shake your hand.

Boom. Boom. The vibrations thrummed faintly through the soles of Catch's boots. Spying a glint of copper, he padded over and discovered a series of knobs and levers connected to thick wires running into the walls. He pulled a switch, and the metallic laughter cut off. "It's a trick."

"There's more in here," said Savotte, poking her head into a second chamber. "What are they? Puppets?"

Catch squeezed the elbow of the figure Moony was mauling. There was some sort of armature inside, wood or wires; he couldn't tell. It reminded him of Rags-n-Bones, despite this not-tengu thing being twice Rags-n-Bones' bulk. "Moony, stop that," he said, trying to wrench the little Vicardi cat loose. Moony's jaws ground tighter. "Moony, it's just a doll."

Moony opened his eyes. "A doll?" he asked, dropping to the floor.

"Or..." Propping his elbows on his knees, Catch interlaced his fingers beneath his chin and frowned, studying the not-tengu. *Rags-n-Bones...* "A homunculous. Artificial creatures given a semblance of life through alchemy," he explained when Moony blinked quizzically.

"How long have they been here?" asked Savotte incredulously, returning from her survey of the smaller cavern.

"Not five hundred years," said Catch. "The damp would have rotted them away." He glanced up toward the ceiling holes.

A pair of baleful eyes glared back, set in a dark face. Two-toned eyes, fierce and strange. Even from fifteen feet, Catch felt their burn, like hot copper. Uttering a startled cry, he leaped to his feet.

Savotte and Moony spun around. "What?" asked Savotte, following his gaze. But the face had already whisked away. A feather dropped through the hole, straight down, without fluttering or wafting, as if it possessed less air resistance than the average rock. A trail of fine, white sparks sizzled after it. Hitting the ground with a soft clang, it rocked on the curl of its spine. Moony sniffed it, jumping when a spark snapped.

Cautiously, Savotte picked the feather up. "It doesn't feel like metal," she said, bending it between her fingers.

"It's probably been altered alchemically," said Catch, his liar's brain expertly concocting an explanation. This one sounded plausible even to him. But he kept searching the holes for further signs of movements. The eyes he'd glimpsed still burned in his memory, with their two distinct rings of color in each iris. Eyes no shifter possessed.

"Alchemically?" asked Savotte. He could almost hear her brow lift.

"They're always blowing themselves up with their experiments," Catch replied, still speaking automatically. "One of them was probably trying to turn chickens into silver, or something like that."

Not so much as a leaf blowing past the openings. Catch finally dropped his gaze and saw that, indeed, one of Savotte's ink-swipe brows was raised. "Chickens into silver?" she asked.

"Seems a waste of chicken," said Moony, sneezing and rubbing his nose.

"You can't deny there is alchemy involved." Catch swept a hand around the circle of lifeless, craggy faces. "Someone with power and authority set this up."

It took her a second to catch his subtext. When she did, her brows shot higher. "You think this is Gildar's doing?"

"All Clawcrag alchemists are in his employ."

"Like Ebon Porpetti?" she shot back.

Catch sucked in his cheeks, disgruntled. Point to Savotte. Why did the slipskin they'd encountered in Widget have to be an alchemist?

"No," she continued, pocketing the feather. "It's just as likely this is the work of some rebel hoping to scare the populace."

Catch pursed his lips. Savotte sounded more like she was trying to convince herself of Gildar's innocence than actually certain of it.

"Feh!" Moony swatted one of the not-tengu. "They're not scary at all."

"They write perfectly dreadful poetry, too," said Catch. "I hope they never consider publishing a volume."

Savotte rolled her eyes. "With that comment, I officially declare you recovered from any shock. Let's be going. I fear this unexpected detour will add half a day to our journey."

"Hope you have enough molasses candy to see you through," said Catch.

She clapped a hand to the pocket containing the bag—which meant she wasn't paying attention to the pocket she'd put the feather in. As they returned to the narrow passage they'd broken through, Catch deftly liberated it from her. He stroked his thumb over its vanes before he tucked it away. Savotte was right. It didn't feel quite like metal. And none of the dolls possessed wings.

CHAPTER THIRTEEN:
HOUNDED

Via a circuitous path, Nipper led Ascot to a barren, scrubby bit of ground at the mountain's foot; nothing but sere, rugged earth and patches of gnarly grass. Every outwardly pretty flower bristled with thorns. A few trees were scattered about the landscape, but judging by their dry, peeling bark, they'd all made a pact to grow to exactly the same size, then die.

"Miss! Nipper! You're safe!" Rags-n-Bones bounded up the last stretch of the path to greet Ascot in dog-form. His scruffy, rust-colored tail wagged. Nipper hopped onto his back. Spotting a squirrel, Rags-n-Bones dashed off to chase it.

Dmitri rose from where he was resting in the shade of the lightning-blasted trunk of a long-dead juniper. "I'm glad your deductions about Cavall proved correct."

And wrong, she thought, staring down at her hands. She spread her fingers, the better to watch her ring sparkle in the sunlight. "He let me go so you and Rags and I could return to Widget." Her voice shook, which surprised her. "I suppose I'm supposed to twiddle my thumbs and hope they release Moony after they execute Catch."

Her hand trembled. Glints thrown by her ring skittered across the yellow ground. Not fear, not sadness. Anger. In Widget, she'd ridden a helhest to save Rags-n-Bones from a mob, and still Cavall imagined she'd just give up?

I'll find whatever Magden Le Fou stole from Rune and throw it in Cavall's face. No, in Gildar's face.

No; that was too easy. She'd—she'd catch another frabjacketing helhest and drag it into Holdfast and threaten to feed whatever Le Fou stole to it unless Gildar let Catch and Moony go, and worked with the Hide Aways, and promised her a lifetime supply of chocolate on top of it.

There; she felt better. Folding her hand, she looked up. "Has Condorella located this 'green and hidden' place yet?"

"Let's go see." Dmitri, who had waited patiently while she composed herself, now stretched fore and aft and padded off, leading her to an overhang in the mountainside. Starley's red coat and white hair shone through the fronds of the long weeds concealing its entrance.

"Hello?" called Ascot, brushing the weeds aside.

Brightening, Starley rose in one fluid motion from his cross-legged posture. "Eh, you're back. Didn't sit right, leaving you to leather-britches."

Ascot shrugged one shoulder. They'd improvised the best they could, considered the brief time they'd been given. "He's not off the scent."

"No surprise." Starley kicked a pebble. "Jolt went off hunting rabbits. I'll fetch him."

"I'll accompany you," said Dmitri quickly.

Probably a good idea, considering Starley's poor eyesight, thought Ascot as they set off. Hearing muttering, she peered into the shallow cave. Condorella sat against the wall, her spellbook and the letter spread over her skirt. "Sorry about your cottage."

Condorella scowled. "Cavall will pay for that," she said, savagely flipping a page. Then she looked up, expression turning thoughtful. "Of course, it gives me the opportunity to try something new when I rebuild. Children like pasta, don't they?"

Ascot decided not to comment. "Learn anything new from the letter?"

Condorella brightened instantly. "It's another example of Le Fou's genius. It's enchanted to repair itself." She pointed to a scraped-off word. "Given time, it should mend itself entirely." She frowned thoughtfully at the curly purple writing. "Actually, it's rather odd it hasn't already."

"No it isn't," said Ascot, feeling absurdly clever for knowing the reason. "Until recently, it's been kept in Widget, and there's no magic in Widget."

"Widget?" Rags-n-Bones charged under the overhang, ears pricked. "Are you talking about Kay and Lindsay?"

"No," Ascot replied. "I was telling Condorella there's no—"

"Oh." Rags-n-Bones thrust out a paw. "Look, I remembered how to shake hands."

Gravely, Ascot shook it. "I doubt you forgot, Rags. You're not really a dog."

He cocked his head, his funny, inside-out ear lifting. "But I was once, miss." He grabbed up a nearby stick with his teeth and scampered out.

Ascot stared after him worriedly. Rags-n-Bones had originally been a dog named Rufus. Could this transformation make him forget his present life in favor of his old one? *We're not safe in the Clawcrags if we can't fake shifting*, she reminded herself. *Besides, it's only for a few days.*

Six days, to be exact. Six days before the Moonless Night. She glanced up at the sky. *Soon to be five.* Her throat tightened.

Starley, Dmitri, and Jolt returned to the overhang at a noticeably faster clip than they'd left it. "Pack up, Condie," said Starley. "We're going."

"So suddenly?" said Condorella.

"I received word through our network while I was out hunting," said Jolt, crouching to gather up the bundle of objects he'd taken from Condorella's cottage. "Cavall's heading for a garrison on Mt. Skylash's western side. Likely, he means to assemble a posse of Sniffers and track us in earnest."

"If you stay with the Hide Aways, I'll track you like the Hide Aways." Ascot touched her neck, feeling the marks left by his teeth. "Where will we go?"

"We have hiding spots, but…" Starley scratched his head.

"The trouble is you, to be blunt," said Jolt, rising with his bundle. "Star and I can hide in a burrow, in a pinch. But a lot of the people who'd usually shelter us might not risk their guts for non-shifters and a wolf. Especially a wolf."

"This feels familiar," grumbled Dmitri.

"We're not abandoning you." Starley patted his head, apparently oblivious to Dmitri's indignant growl. "We said we'd help you, and we meant it. It's just going to be dodgy."

"Would we be safe in this hidden green place, if we could find it?" asked Ascot.

"Safe." Condorella picked up her staff, which still had a few broom bristles clinging to it. Long gown flaring about her, she levered herself to her feet. She beat her staff against the cave floor, and the crystal flashed. Also, quacked. Scowling, Condorella muttered a rapid stream of gibberish and tried again. This time, the crystal chimed. She gave a satisfied smile.

"Let it be known the way is perilous," she said, raising an arm in a gesture that failed in being dramatic by virtue of looking too much like an eager student trying to win a teacher's attention. "How much are you willing to risk?"

"Everything," replied Starley instantly. "No joke. I don't care if I die if it means getting a chance to live first. Hang it, all the ambitions, all the soddin' *dreams* that die because of our system—the stupidity of it makes me want to bite my own arse."

"Don't challenge him to actually do that, because he will," said

Jolt.

Starley punched Jolt's arm lightly. "Let me see the day we can choose our own lives, and I'll be satisfied."

"I'm with him," said Jolt simply when Condorella looked at him. She turned to Ascot next.

Ascot folded her arms. *My feet are sore, and I have to walk on them anyway.* Sometimes, that's how life was. "We don't have many options. Let's get going."

"Agreed," said Dmitri.

Scowling, Condorella dropped the drama along with her arm. "Fine," she muttered, tying the bundled spellbook over her shoulders. "We head south." After taking a moment to assume a far-off visionary air, she strode out of the cave, and tripped over Rags-n-Bones, who was chasing his tail. He yelped.

"We're going, Rags," Ascot told him as Starley helped Condorella rise.

His tail wagged. "I can help track in this form. It's fun, smelling." To demonstrate, he sniffed Condorella's feet. Her outraged expression almost made Ascot laugh. But her earlier fears quelled it. Worse, going by the strained expression on Dmitri's face, he was worried about exactly the same thing. Would continuing with this plan to save Catch and Moony mean losing Rags-n-Bones?

Night caught them all too soon. *Tomorrow's only five days before the Moonless Night,* thought Ascot, kicking a pebble into the pretty, rippling creek whose bank they walked. To her left, the mountains rose in a jagged yellow line. *Five days. One, two three*—She stopped herself before she counted them all compulsively, and glanced up at the sky, darkening like a bowl of water that an inky quill kept repeatedly dipping into. Soon, someone would suggest they'd stop. She didn't think she could bear it, not when every step seemed to be taking them farther from Holdfast, Catch, and Moony. Five days. *One, two, three*—would it be enough?

Dmitri moved to her side. "We should probably—"

"Oh, don't say stop," she said.

He walked silently, gaze going to the creek. He was limping noticeably. Their recent exertions had to be straining his injured shoulder. Ascot ran her hands through her hair, fingers snaggling on tangles. "Sorry."

He looked back at her. "Fretting won't help them. Or me."

"Good advice. Too bad I can't follow it." She kicked another pebble. *Sploosh*, it went, into the river. Another *sploosh* as a trout leaped out of the water. *Moony's eyes would go so wide if he were here. He'd probably swoop over and try to catch it.*

Catch. Frabjacket, why did his name have to be a common verb?

"Bark, bark," Rags-n-Bones shouted excitedly, spotting the trout. He leaped excitedly about the bank and chewed a pebble. Jolt paused also, gazing at the water with a speculative air. Starley, in stoat-form, rode on his shoulder. His white fur almost glowed, but if there was a difference between stoats and weasels, Ascot couldn't see it.

"However, if we stop, light a campfire, and convince Rags to return to his human—er, usual—form for a while, it might help him," said Dmitri, watching as Rags-n-Bones dropped to the pebbly bank and rolled. "I have nothing against canines, naturally, but…"

"But he's taking an illusion too seriously." Ascot tried to summon the energy to kick another pebble, but just scuffed the ground.

"Are we stopping?" asked Condorella, coming up.

Ascot nodded, reluctantly. "We'd better. Is this a good spot?"

"Good as any and better than some," said Jolt, turning from the creek. In the distance, a howl rose above the wind's soft whoosh. "I might be able to rig poles and catch some trout."

There it was again: Catch. Ascot started a sigh and broke it off, noticing Dmitri's pricked ears, the fur lifting along his spine. "What's wrong?"

"Hush," he snapped, cocking his head. Another howl rose in the distance. Condorella's gaze snapped north. Rags-n-Bones stopped rolling and whimpered.

"Wolves?" asked Ascot.

Starley exploded off Jolt's shoulder, transforming in mid-air. "There are no wolves in the Clawcrags," he said, grabbing his clothes from Jolt. "Those are hounds. Sniffers."

She'd known that. She just didn't want to believe it. *He's hunting us, just as he said he would. Hunting me.* A bitter taste filled her mouth, and her throat refused to swallow it.

Another faint, quavering howl. "They're talking," said Dmitri. "'I found the scent,' they're saying. 'Follow me. Follow the scent.'"

A fourth howl rose to the northwest, one with a slightly raspy quality to it. Ascot did swallow, then, and the sides of her dry throat stuck together. Dmitri met her eyes. "'Keep after them. Find them. Don't let them rest,'" he reported.

Condorella tapped her staff against the ground and the crystal lit up, throwing out an eerie, blue-violet light. "So, we're not stopping after all." She strode ahead.

"Pick up the pace," said Jolt.

"Will you be all right?" Ascot asked Dmitri.

"I'll manage," he said grimly, and set off, limping. Ascot followed, fretting, her own feet rubbing themselves raw inside her boots, and— deep inside herself—amazingly, guiltily happy that they wouldn't be stopping after all.

❧

Double-ringed irises...a feather that shines like metal...

"Captain?"

Catch lifted his head. He'd been leaning against the Underway's wall, methodically twirling his father's ring between his fingers. He didn't know how long he'd been doing it. "I thought you were sleeping," he whispered as Moony hopped onto his knee. Savotte was, bundled against the opposite wall, or at least lay with her eyes closed, her breathing deep and regular.

"I was," said Moony, yawning hugely. "But Vicardi cats can sleep and think at the same time. We can write books, too. Dostoyevsky's actually a Vicardi cat. He's working on a new novel called *Mischief and Getting Away With It*. I just never told Dmitri."

Probably wise to keep that particular story to yourself. Catch touched the clip on Moony's wing. "Maybe we can convince her to remove that tomorrow."

Moony twisted his neck for a look at the clip. "She's probably afraid I'd fly off and fight those phony tengu some more. They're what I was thinking about, Captain. You think Glider had them made." Catch nodded. "Why?"

Catch glanced at Savotte. Her eyes remained closed, dark lashes glistening faintly. "To make sure something happens."

Moony tilted his head from side to side.

"Every cub in the Clawcrags learns of the Moonless Night," Catch explained. "Gildar's always been obsessed with it. He thought Glim—" his throat clenched briefly "—his son, Glim, was the golden star."

Moony lifted a paw for a few quick licks. "That's odd, because making an army of fake tengu implies he doesn't expect the real ones to show up."

Real tengu...double-ringed irises, glaring down...Catch's imagination had been hard at work, trying to convince him that what he'd glimpsed had been a trick of the light. Not entirely successfully. "I don't think he does," he said, pulling himself back to the conversation at hand. He glanced at Savotte. Had he caught a brief gleam of light shining off eyeballs? Her chest rose and fell regularly. "I think he wants to use it to gain more power."

Jumping onto Catch's legs, Moony settled into a cat-loaf. "Then why did Glider agree to the deal with Widget?" he said, blinking up at Catch. "If he doesn't believe in the prophecy, he doesn't need you."

Catch stared. He hadn't considered that. Maybe there was something to this Vicardi cat sleeping-and-thinking tale. "Maybe he wants me there in case the prophecy's real."

A huge yawn split Moony's head. Amazing there was room for a brain in his little skull, actually. "If the prophecy's real, you would've returned in time for the Moonless Night no matter what. I think there's something else going on, Captain. We have to keep our eyes open."

Then, in absolute contradiction to his words, he snuggled his chin to his paws and began snoring. Across the way, Savotte's eyelashes fluttered, but Catch couldn't say for certain if she slept or woke.

He stared at a patch of dimly glowing lichen, trying to match it to a shape, but its irregular outlines defied classification. Maybe a duck. With six arms. Wearing a crown.

Eyes open…ringed eyes. The notion that Gildar may have created an army of fake tengu only for the real ones to appear was almost hilarious. Except—

Catch's hand tightened about his father's ring. "No," he whispered to the unhearing walls. "There's no such thing as fate."

CHAPTER FOURTEEN:
THE FOREST FOR THE TREES

They were dragging. *Dragging.* Having granted Ascot's wish to travel through the night, the luck-fairies compounded their generosity by making them run all through the next day and night as well. Ascot berated herself for selfishness as blister after blister burst within the soggy recesses of her boots. Dmitri staggered on three legs, stifling whimpers whenever the lame one touched the rocky, half-frozen ground. Rags-n-Bones—still in dog-form—panted openly, and Condorella dragged herself along on her staff. Only Starley and Jolt remained relatively fresh.

Still the howls came on. Even if she'd had the breath to inquire, Ascot wouldn't have asked what they were saying. She could guess. *Hunt them. Catch them. Tear them.*

"Fleas *drain* you, leather-britches," shouted Starley, stopping halfway up the hill they were climbing to scowl northwards. Dawn threw rosy stripes across his pale cheeks and white hair.

"Save your breath," said Jolt, tugging him onwards.

"I got plenty." Starley gazed back again. "Look, it's me he wants most—"

"*No,*" growled Jolt, yanking his arm.

A bird chirped nearby; a cheerful morning sound. A hound's howl drowned it out. *They're gaining*, thought Ascot, clutching a cramp in her right side. Desperation lent her enough energy to make it up the hill's last stretch at a run.

Cool dampness brushed her ankle. Her next footstep squished softly underfoot, releasing the smell of crushed greenery. Startled, she lifted her boot, staring down at a patch of lush, low plants with heart-shaped leaves. The hill's other side sloped gently toward the beckoning shadows of a beech forest, as green and incongruous, in the Clawcrag's sere yellow landscape, as an emerald in a sandbox.

"Is this the green and hidden place?" she asked as Condorella came stumbling up beside her.

"No, it's the Forlorn Forest," said Starley. "Any mumper with a map can find it. You'll have to do better, Condie, if we want to shake leather-britches."

"There are odd rumors about it, though," said Jolt. "Stories of travelers disappearing and the like."

Two howls rose as one. The wind made their exact location wander, but they were unquestionably nearby. Another howl answered from a distance to the west, followed by another from the east.

Dmitri dragged his head up. "They intend to encircle us."

"Any idea how many there are?" asked Jolt.

Dmitri licked his dry nose. "I believe seven."

Starley laughed harshly. "So, if we include the rat, our numbers are evenly matched, should it come to a fight." He kicked the caps off a clump of white mushrooms. "Don't like the odds."

"I fear we'd be outmatched," said Dmitri.

Starley flashed a grin. "Actually, I was thinking I'd give him seventy to our seven. I'd love those odds."

Standing tall and impassive, Condorella stared into the forest, pointed chin lifted high, the wind dancing her spiky hair about her cheeks. Her staff's crystal sparkled.

"You led us here," said Ascot, a howl wailing a counterpoint to her words. "Where we can hide before Cavall's posse surrounds us?"

As if Condorella had been merely waiting to be consulted, she lifted her staff and tapped its butt twice against the leafy ground. The crystal's facets flashed deep blue and purple. Condorella drew in a breath and bolted down the slope. "Run, you chumps!" she cried over her shoulder.

Oh, brilliant, thought Ascot even as she started running, slipping every other step. The dew-damp plants made for treacherous footing. She caught up with Condorella at the forest's edge. "'Run'? That's your great plan?"

"Better than everyone else's plan of standing around gawking," Condorella shot back, tearing her long skirt free of a grasping twig.

Greenery crunched behind her. Glancing back, Ascot saw that Rags-n-Bones was supporting Dmitri while Starley and Jolt brought up the rear. "But we have to have somewhere to run *to*, or there's no point," she shouted to Condorella, slapping a dangling vine out of her path.

For reply, Condorella leveled her staff like a spear. "*Orientus!*" she snapped. Several of the crystal's facets turned sky blue. The color wandered around the crystal, now darkening, now lightening, as Condorella swung the staff before her. Abruptly, the crystal keened. Its top facet turned pure white and emitted a thin beam of light that arrowed between the beeches' trunks.

Condorella let out an excited yell. "We're close!" She sped up, arms swinging like she meant to elbow the trees aside. Ascot followed on her heels, the others close behind. They burst into a glade. The crystal's light shone directly on a large, conical rock, surrounded by powdery-smelling blue flowers, rising from the glade's center. Condorella dropped to her knees beside it. "Here," she said, touching a pale gray striation running through the rock's middle.

"Yes, here," said Cavall, stepping out from the shadows on the glade's far side. Leather creaked as he folded his arms and regarded them down his nose.

Tucking his tail, Rags-n-Bones ran to hide behind Ascot. Starley and Jolt whipped knives from their belts. Dmitri merely swayed, his right foot dangling several inches from the ground.

Cavall whistled two sharp, clear notes. Howls answered him on all sides. "You're surrounded," he said. "I thought you Hide Aways might have a nest in the Forlorn Forest, with all the rumors about the place."

As if alone in the clearing, Condorella ran a long-nailed finger down the striation.

"Please don't, Mr. Black Knight, sir," said Rags-n-Bones, pressing against Ascot and trembling. "It won't make you happy."

Cavall laughed softly, throatily, his blue eyes narrow and cold. "Actually, I believe it will." He drew his sword with a whisper of steel. "But if you surrender, Mr. Bones, I'll allow you and Miss Nuisance and the wolf to return to Widget."

"The wolf declines your offer," said Dmitri. Rags-n-Bones shook his head vigorously.

Muttering in a singsong, Condorella dragged her fingernail up the striation.

"Some folk have principles, locklegs," said Starley, making his favorite gesture.

Cavall's brows contracted. But only briefly. Throughout the forest came the sounds of panting, soft grunts, and the squish of footsteps over wet leaves. Six bristling hounds appeared through the trees and took up position around the glade's perimeter. Cavall's gaze traveled in a slow circle. With a nod of evident satisfaction, he pointed his sword at Starley. "Before I give you the gratification of dying for your cause, tell me what you know about my father."

"He had a bastard for a son," Starley replied with a malignant grin and without the slightest pause, as if he'd had the answer in mind for a long time and could hardly believe his luck in getting to say it. Even Jolt winced.

Lips tight, Cavall advanced. Condorella rubbed her finger

furiously over the striation, as if trying to erase it. *If she's doing magic, she needs more time,* thought Ascot. "I wish!" she shouted.

Cavall paused. Sword still poised, he turned his head just enough to look at her.

"I wish," she repeated, looking into his eyes. "That's what you said in the graveyard." That night, with the trickle of snow despite the clear sky and big moon, beside the crypt with the simpering carved angels. "That things could be better, or at least different. It won't happen if you keep choosing to hate, Galen. Different means change."

Actually, "different" means "diverse," "unalike," or "dissimilar."

Get out of my head, Catch, Ascot thought fiercely. He was the last person she needed whispering suggestions to her right now. He'd probably prompt her to say something rude and rile Cavall again, just when he might be listening. He scowled at the ground, face drawn into knife-sharp lines, but his sword tip lowered. Ascot held her breath. Condorella spat on the rock.

The sword whipped up again. "No," grated Cavall. *No,* like the voice of stone, eternal and unyielding. "Not so long as this tail-chewer's alive."

Starley laughed—almost a cackle. "Fair enough, leather-britches," he said, flinging back his head. Jolt hovered beside him, glaring death at Cavall. "I'd like you to know the truth before I go." His laughter cut off. "Your father founded the Hide Aways. We're his group."

Cavall staggered back, shaking his head.

"He was a slipskin among slipskins," Starley added mercilessly. "And he'd be ashamed of you."

With a painful, guttural sound, almost a roar, Cavall raced forward, raising his sword. Simultaneously, Condorella lifted her staff, gripped it in both hands, and slammed it down on a plain, grayish-brown stone lying at the foot of the large, conical one. It shattered into many fragments.

The conical rock split along the striation, gaping it wide as a shark's mouth. Then, as if it had indeed become a hungry, living thing, the gap began sucking in all who stood in the glade's center. Ascot leaned away, frantically wind-milling her arms, to no avail. "Grab a shard!" cried Condorella, snatching up a piece of the shattered stone.

Ascot grabbed at the sluglike fragments, which seemed to recede even as she reached for them. She managed to snag a small, speckled chunk. Dmitri snapped frantically at the ground, as did Rags-n-Bones.

"Biscuit!" shouted Ascot. Rags-n-Bones returned to himself with a soft pop. "Use your hands," she told him.

Rags-n-Bones blinked at her, blinked at his fingers, then snatched a piece of rock as quickly as he might have snatched a tempting tea cake. Nipper snagged a pebble. Grabbing two fragments, Jolt pressed one into Starley's hand.

Did everyone get one? wondered Ascot as the shark's mouth sucked her in.

Darkness closed over her head.

An instant later, the sky returned, and the breeze, and the green, dusty scent of ferns. She was on her feet, in the glade, Rags-n-Bones behind her, quivering. Cavall was still—again?—charging, sword raised, but a little of his rage had leached away, replaced by bafflement.

Ascot's thoughts felt heavy and slow, as if someone had poured syrup into her head. She opened her hand. The speckled chunk of rock lay in her palm.

"Don't lose those," said Condorella, giving her staff a cocky spin before thrusting it out to block Cavall's path.

He nearly folded in half around it. Jumping back, he glared at Condorella. "Keep out of this, witch." He turned, scowling, to his followers. "What's the delay? Capture them."

Raising her arms, Ascot braced for the impending attack. Frowning, she lowered them again. The sun shone right through

Cavall's posse, as if the six hounds were mere images painted on water. One's mouth hung open, but no howl emerged. Seconds elapsed, and none moved.

"Petrified?" Walking over, Starley poked a finger at a posse member. It went right through. "What did you do, Condie?"

"Whatever it was, it appears the odds have shifted." Jolt hadn't sheathed his knife. Grinning, he advanced on Cavall, the skin around his brand stretched tight.

Two hounds stood behind Cavall, barely audible whines rising from their misty throats. Looking from them to Jolt, Cavall drew himself up. "I'll take you with me, slipskin."

The back of Ascot's neck tickled. *Probably another frabjacketing cicada tangled in my hair.* Promising herself the pleasure of swatting it later, she stepped between Cavall and Jolt. "Stop it. It's more important to figure out what happened than fight." She looked to Condorella for an explanation and froze. Condorella stood calm and composed, an arrow pointed directly at her ear. A very real and solid-looking person, dressed in a hooded green cloak that hid their face, stood behind her, aiming the bow.

"Perhaps we should deal with *them* first," said Condorella with a slight backwards nod. She didn't examine her nails, but radiated the same nonchalance as if she had.

More green-hooded people stepped out of the forest, leveling bows at Starley, Jolt, Dmitri, and Cavall. The tickle at the back of Ascot's neck transformed into a prickle. A very pointed prickle, centered on one, very small, point. *I think that's called a 'prick,' actually.* Her survival instincts, galloping ahead of her thoughts, had already raised her hands defensively and started her heart pounding. Her eyeballs, less sensible, rolled inward, trying to see who stood behind her.

Whoever it was spoke in lilting tones. "The giant breathes so loudly we could've tripped him six times in the dark."

Ascot held hers. Her pounding heart filled the silence. *One, two, three, four...*

"Um?" Rags-n-Bones raised a hand. "Am I the giant? I don't grind bones to make bread. That doesn't sound yummy. I don't think I'm tall enough to be a giant, either. Or is there an actual giant out there? Because if there is, maybe we should run. They sound scary, and the Mighty Terror isn't here to protect us."

The hooded people exchanged glances. Ascot could forgive them a certain befuddlement. Meanwhile, Cavall's posse grew even more translucent, their edges blurring.

Clearing her throat, Condorella stepped forward, assuming a dramatic pose. "*Venvowza.* I am a Keeper of the Secret Colors. In the name of the mystic spectrum, I claim sanctuary."

It sounded like a bunch of rot to Ascot, but the prickle in her neck softened. "The Order of Colors? You're here to see the Lady, then?"

"The Lady?" Condorella dropped her pompous tone. "Magden Le Fou is *here?*"

"How is that possible?" asked Ascot. *I mean, you're wearing one of her teeth, for goodness' sake.*

"Never underestimate the powers of the great Le Fou." Condorella's mouth stretched in a pumpkin grin. Addressing the hooded folk, she lifted her chin. "Aye. We be here to see the Lady."

"Oh, don't start with the 'ayes' and 'bes'," muttered Jolt. Dmitri groaned agreement.

The atmosphere in the glade darkened. "You brought a *wolf*," said the woman standing behind Ascot.

Ascot closed her eyes. *Oh, frabjacket, no.* Dmitri was going to explode if he was accused of public wolfy-ness again. Already, a growl trickled out of his throat.

"We will grant you entrance, but the wolf and your weapons stay behind," said one of the bowmen.

"The wolf's name is Dmitri, and he does not," snapped Dmitri, ruff bristling.

"If he does, I'm staying, too," said Ascot.

"And me," said Rags-n-Bones, raising his hand. "And I'll never let you pet my hen that lays golden eggs, so just think about that."

"He be not a werewolf, thine ancient foe," said Condorella.

Dmitri twitched, shedding clouds of loose fur. "Would you kindly let us pass before she proceeds to 'thines' and 'hasts'?"

The small, pointed pain at the back of Ascot's neck vanished. A sigh gusted over it instead. "Very well," said the woman with the lilting voice. "Just be warned that our bows are trained upon you."

Rubbing the small, stinging spot on her neck, Ascot turned. The woman who'd held the bow on her was slender and middle-aged, with blonde hair and arched dark brows that gave her a look of aloof wonder. She was delicately licking the back of her hand. A cat-shifter? "Thank you for seeing reason," said Ascot.

"Well, if we stand here much longer it'll interrupt my nap," she replied. Giving her hand another lick, she rubbed it against her face. "My name is Lacey Karenina, and I will escort you to the Lady."

"Karenina!" said Dmitri with sudden, focused interest. "Any relation to Anna?" Lacey's brows rose as her head tilted to the side. Settling back on his haunches, Dmitri harrumphed. "Right. Unlikely to encounter a fellow Tolstoy enthusiast in such surroundings, I suppose."

"More slipskins!" Cavall found his voice. It was somewhat higher-pitched than usual, but he glared around defiantly. "So, this is your nest, Reftkin. I don't know what magic your witch worked, but it can't hide you forever."

Unimpressed, one of the hooded women prodded Cavall with an arrow. "Hand over your sword."

Instead, he whipped its point up and backed defensively toward the glade's edge. Two archers moved to intercept him. Less solid than a whisper, his posse's outlines wavered and vanished.

"T'would be wise to heed her warnings," said Condorella.

"Come and take me, slipskins," Cavall spat.

He was too wrapped in wrath to see how the strange, hooded shifters tipped their heads in evident confusion at the word.

"Weapons are not allowed in the Lady's presence," said Lacey, drawing back her bowstring.

"I will not surrender." Cavall bared his teeth.

Ascot had had enough. "Yes, you will." Plucking Rags-n-Bones' purple muffler off his shoulders, she wrapped it around her hand, strode over to Cavall, and, with little resistance, yanked the sword from his grip. As if she'd cut a string holding him up, his shoulders sagged. His arms dropped to his sides.

"You would see me humiliated," he muttered.

"I would see you alive," she said, tossing down the sword. One of the hooded people picked it up. Ascot returned the muffler to Rags-n-Bones and set her hands on her hips. "Maybe you'll finally listen."

The corner of Cavall's lips quirked. Maybe a grimace, maybe a smile.

"Oh, love—" said Starley.

Ascot spun on him. "No jokes about that never happening."

He held up his hands. "Actually, I was going to say if you ever get bored of Starthorne, and me of Jolt, let's run away together. You have *panache*."

Her cheeks heated, but so did her heart. "I think we're ready," she said with a cough, turning to Lacey.

"Finally." Lacey yawned, curling her tongue, and gestured to the glade's opposite side, where rounded white stones cut a path through the forest's soft covering of moss. Ascot could've sworn it hadn't existed a moment ago.

Lacey finished her yawn. "Outsiders, welcome to Lorrygreen."

CHAPTER FIFTEEN:
OUT OF TIME

The path meandered through the forest, often seeming to lead precisely nowhere. Once, it took them across a slab of cracked gray stone spanning a trickling stream, and they had to wait as Lacey crouched on its edge to watch the fish. But, at last, the path ended, spilling them into Lorrygreen proper.

"Magden Le Fou's green and hidden land," murmured Condorella, shivering as she looked about. It had to be excitement, not cold. The air, balmy and only slightly damp, smelled of some sharp, woody spice Ascot couldn't place.

Condorella gasped and "oohed" as if viewing a marvel, but to Ascot, Lorrygreen most closely resembled a city park run slightly to neglect. Sanded paths, overgrown with moss, crisscrossed an open green space dotted with tiny white flowers. Ascot studied a graceful, carved boulder standing at an intersection, but it was so covered with vines she couldn't begin to guess what it meant to depict.

At least, with the slower pace, Dmitri could put weight on his bad leg. "How are you holding up?" Ascot asked him.

"Tolerably. But even as he spoke, a small ripple of pain shuddered through his fur. "No matter," he said, forestalling her. "We have no time for convalescence. The Moonless Night is only four days hence.

If an object of value resides here, we must swiftly formulate a plan on how best to utilize it."

"Actually, we needn't rush," said Condorella.

"Why not?" asked Ascot. They passed a group of people in yellow robes sauntering along with more ceremony than a morning stroll seemed to require, humming, palms held horizontally by their hips. Rags-n-Bones, back in dog-form, woofed uncertainly at them, then stopped to sniff an enormous tree with peeling gray bark. Another robed person stood on its other side, hugging it just a shade lasciviously.

Instead of replying, Condorella quickened her pace to walk alongside Lacey. "You are taking us to Magden Le Fou, right?"

"To the Lady. Yes." Lacey jumped at a butterfly.

"This place is weird," grumbled Starley. He walked shoulder-to-shoulder with Jolt, rubbing a finger beneath his nose. Several steps behind them came Cavall, staring at the ground and flanked by two bowmen.

"You're the last person I'd expect to make such a complaint," said Ascot.

Starley pointed to his temple. "Head-weird, not regular weird. My thoughts are slowing. Never been the sort for afternoon naps, but I feel I could lie on my back and watch clouds all day."

Ascot had almost forgotten the strange, syrupy feeling inside her skull. Now it came squelching back, and with it, the realization that Dmitri's mention of the closeness of the Moonless Night had raised no worry in her, no compunction to count the days. It seemed…distant. She tried for alarm and managed mild concern. "Uh-oh."

Starley nodded grimly. "Hold onto that."

Hip-high bushes, bursting with almost offensively exuberant magenta blossoms, brushed against them as they traveled down a narrow track. From below came the soft burble of water. Condorella stopped in the middle of the path, her hands flying to her chest.

"Could that be the mystic pool of Magden Le Fou?"

"Oh, the pool's delicious," said Lacey. She licked her lips. "Fishies!"

It apparently wasn't the response Condorella expected. Her brow knotted before she continued on. Ascot glanced back at Cavall. His head hung too low for her to see his face.

Near its foot, the path grew wide and slippery. Ascot slid down the last two feet, recovered her balance, and looked around. Lacey crouched beside a small, round pool, lined with gray-blue stones, peering at three orange koi swimming languidly in its depths. A weeping cherry grew beside it, its trailing branches so thickly covered in pale violet blossoms they hid its trunk.

"Mistress Le Fou?" Condorella scanned the grove. "Mistress Le Fou, I am a humble supplicant."

Lacey snatched at a koi, recoiled at the splash, and shook water off her hand. Condorella spun on her. "Where's Le Fou?"

Still fixed on the koi, Lacey pointed to the cherry. "Mistress?" said Condorella. Going to the tree, she parted its branches, revealing the worn, black marble oblong of a headstone.

Sighing, Dmitri lapped from the pool. "So, she is dead, then."

Ascot's stomach rumbled. She glanced down at her midsection, surprised. Of course she should be hungry. Condorella had been sitting on her heels, staring at the headstone for...quite some time, and they'd been running...a while before that, and it had been...sometime prior to that since she'd eaten.

The *whens* were vague, but the *what* remained vivid: some kind of bread Jolt created by mashing up thistle seeds. The resulting product managed to be both hard and chewy. Likely, a chunk of it lingered in her stomach, defying all attempts to digest it. *Maybe it's lonely in there*, she thought, prodding her belly with a forefinger. "We should..." She stopped. Already, whatever she'd thought they should do was sliding from her mind.

But Dmitri, sprawled on the mossy ground beside the pool, roused himself with a shake. "Yes, we should…" He shook himself again, harder. "We came here for a reason."

"Oh yeah." By the slope, Starley propped his sagging chin on his hand. "The whatsit. The letter whatsit."

The letter that Catch had slipped into her coat. Yes. Catch. Moony. Their images wavered hazily in her mind. They were fine. She'd see them soon.

No! cried a tiny part of her brain. *It's only four days until the Moonless Night. Catch. Moony.* She'd run her feet raw, trying to rejoin them. Why didn't it matter now?

She thrust her hand into a bar of sunlight. Her ring's tourmaline threw out glints sharp as splinters. Ascot studied them. She touched the itching scab in front of her left ear. When she pressed down, pain trilled through her temple. Still touching it, she stood. "Wake up."

The grove swallowed her words. Starley and Dmitri stirred listlessly. Rags-n-Bones snored in a nest of leaves, his inside-out ear twitching. Nipper lay belly-up beside him, pink feet wriggling as he scampered through dreams.

Ascot scooped him up. "Mm, rat," she said loudly.

Nipper woke with a squeal. Having often heard Ascot lament the roast rat sandwiches she'd enjoyed in Shadowvale, he must've believed he'd awakened into a nightmare. His eyes bugged. A warm trickle ran down Ascot's wrist. Ignoring it, she opened her mouth.

"Miss!" Rags-n-Bones leaped up. "No—biscuit!" Popping back into his normal self, he threw his arms around her and began wailing like one of Widget's steam whistles. "Please, don't. Look, I might have some bread left in my pocket."

Shaking him off, Ascot brought Nipper to her mouth. He bit her thumb, and the pain further sharpened her thoughts. Rags-n-Bones' already epic wails redoubled. No one could sleep through that. Dmitri, Starley, and Jolt roused, Lacey sat up, and even Cavall, sitting cross-legged by the tree, lifted his head to regard her with weary cynicism. Only Condorella remained on her knees, staring at the tombstone.

Spitting out a bit of fur, Ascot handed Nipper to Rags-n-Bones. "I wasn't going to eat him," she said as he cuddled the rat, sniffling. She went to soak her hand in the pool. "Condorella. I don't understand this place, but it's dangerous. We should leave."

For a moment, it seemed Condorella hadn't heard. Then, slowly, creakily, as if she'd aged two decades, she dragged herself to her feet. Taking her satchel off her shoulder, she rummaged in it, drew out a handful of dried herbs, and scattered them over the grave. "*Temporum stabilis*," she said with a perfunctory wave of her staff. The crystal flashed once. A tiny tremor ran through the ground and dissipated before it could properly be called a quake.

Ascot shook her head. A little of the syrup sloshing in her skull seemed to have drained out her ears. "What did you do?"

"Stabilized the temporal seal," said Condorella, looking gray and weary. "I think it started disintegrating when Le Fou died."

Dmitri's ears torqued. He licked his snout. "And when exactly was that?"

"Ah, you got it, did you?" Condorella mustered a smile. "Some time ago. The 'when' can't really be measured. We're out of time."

"Wait." Jolt leaned forward. "That's not a colloquialism, I gather. We're really—"

"Think about it," said Condorella. "What *place* could there be in the Clawcrags that the Sniffers couldn't find? Le Fou took a few seconds and just...stretched them."

A land outside time. Ascot took her hand from the water to see if the bleeding had stopped. She remembered reading stories like that. Something about it being always summer, but never berry season. A witch was responsible for that mess, too.

"What's that?" said Condorella suddenly, crowding beside her and staring into the pool.

"Koi," said Rags-n-Bones. "They like being petted, if you're gentle."

"Fishies," murmured Lacey. She yawned, rolled onto her back, and resumed napping.

"Not the fish," said Condorella. "Below them." She pointed.

Ascot squinted at the bottom of the pool. There wasn't anything there. Maybe there was. No, it was just water currents. She tilted her head to the other side, and the barely visible object grew a little clearer. "It's…a bubble? A piece of a bubble?"

"Wouldn't it pop, miss?" asked Rags-n-Bones. He scrounged a chunk of thistle bread from his pocket and chewed it with every evidence of relish.

Ascot bent closer to the water, her nose nearly breaking its surface. Her left ear brushed Dmitri's cheek, her right, Condorella's hair, as they also crouched over the pool. Starley and Jolt knelt at the opposite edge. "Look, there's another fragment." Oddly bright colors moved over their curved surfaces.

"I can't see anything," said Starley, squinting.

"Of course not." Tugging his torn ear, Jolt sat back. "I think they're fragments of a Seersee."

Letting out a yell, Condorella made to dive head-first into the pool. Jolt grabbed her by the shoulders. "Careful. You know how fragile Seersees are."

Starley laughed. "I hear they break if you fart too close to them."

Condorella swelled, her face darkening to a shade that approximated her *nom de guerre.*

"What's this whatsit you're talking about?" asked Ascot before she exploded. She clapped a hand to her mouth. *Frabjacket, did I pick up that habit already?*

"Seersee," said Jolt, his glower asking the same question. "They're like crystal balls, only they show the present instead of the future. Or the past. The last five remaining are all in the Roundgrounds—that's a big arena, in Holdfast."

Without fuss, Cavall stood and walked up the slope through the hip-high bushes, raising clouds of pollen from the magenta blossoms. Ascot watched him go, troubled. *The Lorrygreens will stop him if he tries anything,* she decided.

"Magden Le Fou created the Seersees," said Condorella, staring longingly into the pool. Rags-n-Bones slid his hand into the water to pet a koi. His knuckles brushed a Seersee fragment. After hearing of their fragility, Ascot held her breath, but it just rocked slightly.

Dmitri's ears shot up. "Magden Le Fou brought something to 'a green and hidden land.' Could this be it?"

"If they show the past, maybe this one could show us why Le Fou came here," said Ascot. "Assuming we could repair it."

Condorella sucked in her lower lip. "Theoretically possible, but even getting the fragments out of the pool without breaking them further—"

Ever helpful, Rags-n-Bones plucked a Seersee shard from the pool's gravel and held it out. Condorella shrieked, and he quailed and fumbled it. It dropped against the pool's edge—Condorella shrieked again—and it still, obstinately, refused to shatter. Ascot gave her lungs permission to start breathing again.

"Did I do wrong?" asked Rags-n-Bones tearfully.

"No," Ascot replied. Either the Seersees weren't as fragile as rumored, or Rags-n-Bones had the special touch they needed. "Retrieve the rest of the fragments while Condorella looks through her spellbook."

Smiling again, Rags-n-Bones dipped into the pool for the rest of the fragments. Condorella looked as if she might try another shriek. *"Don't,"* Ascot mouthed at her, and she swallowed it.

"I'll see what I can do," she said instead, opening her spellbook. Dmitri took up an overseeing position beside her.

Of course, thought Ascot. Her ring flashed again, but she focused more on her hands. Dirt caked the whorls of her fingertips. The lank, sweaty feel of her hair, falling about her neck, abruptly revolted her. They were all worn and filthy. One look at Dmitri's matted coat would have the students of Widget's Academy grabbing their hairbrushes.

She stood. "Lacey, is there anywhere we can get some clean water, and something to eat?"

"Mur?" Lacey lifted her forearm from her eyes. "Oh, food. Yes. Come with me." Yawning widely, she peeled herself off the ground.

"Food, miss?" said Rags-n-Bones, still chewing away on the thistle bread. Apparently even his jaws couldn't break it down quickly.

She patted his shoulder. Nipper darted under Rags-n-Bones' muffler and glared suspiciously out. "Yes, I'll bring you something. You're doing a wonderful job." Helping with the Seersee might distract him from dogginess for a while.

Finished yawning, Lacey took a new track up the slope, lined with weeping cherries covered in the more usual pink flowers. Ascot, Starley, and Jolt accompanied her.

"D'you know, I think the trees are humming?" said Starley, glancing about as they walked. "Driving me crazy."

I hoped that was just my imagination. Ascot watched Jolt shake out his mantle and rewrap it around his shoulders, careful not to let it snag in the cherries' dangling branches. Its color looked more coral than vermillion in Lorrygreen's dreamy sunlight.

"That's pretty," she said, touching the white embroidery.

He draped a fold over his hand. "Don't care for dragonflies, actually," he said. Starley snorted.

"Why'd you buy it, then?" asked Ascot.

Jolt slid a side-eyed look at Starley, slick black hair falling over his face. "It was a gift."

Ascot glimpsed the threads of a tale behind the mantle—a real tale; not a storybook one. "Why—?"

Leaves rustled. That wasn't what cut her question short. What did it was the silvery flash as Cavall stepped out from behind the curtain of a cherry's branches and put a knife to Starley's throat.

CHAPTER SIXTEEN:
POOLED RESOURCES

Condorella flung up her hands as they came trudging back to the pool. "Merlin, magic, and mayhem!" she swore, rolling her gaze to the sky.

"I know," said Ascot, feelingly. She was sick of this particular dance as well. Moreover, she worried that, any moment now, Jolt would shift into devil-form and begin screaming. Nearly incandescent with rage, he kept pace with Cavall and Starley, the former still holding a knife to the latter's throat.

Dmitri rose, tail swishing. Rags-n-Bones, squatting beside the pool, the Seersee shards laid out before him like so many puzzle pieces, whimpered. Cavall walked Starley right past them, onto a spot of bare ground between the pool and violet-flowered cherry.

"You're undoing this magic, now, witch," said Cavall. His knife dented Starley's throat. Starley spat onto the moss and folded his arms.

"Hiss! Hiss!" cried Lacey, swatting at Cavall. A creditable snarl scratched its way out of her throat.

Lowering her arms, Condorella studied Cavall. "You mean, re-synch Lorrygreen's time with the rest of the world?"

"If that's what it takes to escape this mad place, yes," said Cavall, standing rooted. But there was a wild look in his eyes and his hand holding the knife shook.

It's sad, thought Ascot. What did he hope to accomplish? Lacey hissed again, threw off her robe, and transformed with a series of pops and crackles—

—into a tiny, green-and-white hummingbird. She circled Cavall's head, wings beating furiously, and shot off up the slope.

Although he may have a point about Lorrygreen being rather odd.

"All right," said Condorella.

Cavall gaped, apparently not expecting such easy acquiesence. "All right?"

She shrugged. "Either I do as you say, or someone dies, as I see it," she said, rummaging in her satchel. "I'd rather avoid that. Blood makes my stomach go all squishy. Keep matching up the pieces, Mr. Bones."

Rags-n-Bones dragged his sleeve across his eyes and tremblingly resumed piecing together the Seersee shards. Cavall's eyes narrowed. "What does that have to do with escaping this place?"

"I theorize that time shattered when it did," said Condorella, setting out various herbs. "What do you know about magic? Let me work."

What do you know about magic? Ascot watched that realization sink into Cavall. Being inherently magical creatures, shifters were incapable of spell-work. There was absolutely no way he could know if Condorella was fulfilling his demand, or working on some nasty little cantrip to turn his nose into a rutabaga. Meanwhile, it was only a matter of time—whatever that meant in Lorrygreen—before Lacey reappeared with a squadron of archers.

"What do you really want, Galen?" asked Ascot as Condorella mixed up goo in a mortar. She'd asked before, when it had just been them and the cicadas, and he'd avoided an answer.

Not this time.

"*I want to know if these tail-chewers killed my father!*" His scream seemed to shock even him. The knife trembled, and a trickle of red ran down Starley's throat, bright against his pale skin. Yelling, Jolt dashed forward, but Dmitri seized his shirt hem in his jaws, bringing him up short.

Into the silence Starley spoke, using the calmest, most rational tone Ascot would never have suspected him of possessing. "I don't know."

Cavall might not have heard. Maybe his ears rejected the answer. He stood, taut and shaking like an overstretched string.

"I'm younger than you," Starley continued. "I probably hadn't settled into form when your father died, and I certainly wasn't with the Hide Aways." His cockiness returned. Setting a fist on a hip, he tossed his head. "Maybe you could explain why you hold me responsible for your father's death."

"First rule of leadership," said Cavall, coldly. "Everything's your—"

"I'm not the leader," said Starley.

Rags-n-Bones grabbed up another shard with a happy cry, so absorbed in the Seersee puzzle he'd apparently forgotten the hostage situation.

The simple statement had left Cavall with his mouth hanging open, so Ascot asked Starley the question. "Who is the leader?"

"Don't know," snapped Jolt, pacing in a short arc, his furious eyes nailed to Cavall. "The Hide Aways have a network. We never gather in groups larger than five, because it makes us too large a target for the Sniffers."

Dmitri released Jolt's tunic. "Then, it wasn't your idea to abduct Catch?"

Starley shook his head. "We received orders to pick him up in Highmoor and bring him to a place outside Merryvick. Haven't heard anything since then, so I've been following my own, whatsit, initiative."

Dmitri gave Ascot a meaningful look. Unfortunately, she couldn't quite infer what she was meant to gleam from this new information, so she scratched her nose and watched Rags-n-Bones line up two more Seersee fragments on the mossy ground. Condorella handed him her mortar, brimming with goo, and a small brush.

Cavall's chin dropped to his chest. He still held the knife, but Ascot suspected Starley could've broken free without repercussion. "You don't know who killed my father."

Over the slope came a series of rattling, jangling sounds. Ascot blinked, frowning. Was that Lacey returning with reinforcements? Bows didn't make such a noise, nor swords, unless you liked hitting random bits of metal with them—which, she understood, damaged their edges.

Stern-faced and clad in a fresh robe, Lacey came striding down the slope at the head of a party of six Lorrygreens. The two at the back held bows, but the three in the middle carried steaming pots and cups. "Everyone sit!" cried Lacey imperiously. The archers aimed arrows at no one in particular.

Glad of the intervention, Ascot knelt beside Rags-n-Bones. Ducking out of Cavall's grip, Starley went over to Jolt, pressing him down with a squeeze on his shoulder. Cavall simply dropped onto the muddy patch, vacant gaze fixed on the ground.

Lacey passed around cups filled with some steaming dark brew. Starley sipped, turned his head, and spat it out. "What's this muck?"

Dmitri sniffed his serving. "Roasted dandelion root tea. It's said to have a calming effect, which I believe is the point." He took a few laps. Nodding approval, the Lorrygreens withdrew, save for Lacey, who thrust a cup virtually in Cavall's face. He made no motion to accept it, so Ascot went over and took it from her. Satisfied, Lacey returned to her sunbeam.

"Drink some. You'll feel better," said Ascot, holding out the cup. He was probably suffering from coffee withdrawal, and in her opinion, burnt weed roots were a good enough substitute.

Cavall shook his head. His hair hung over his face. Pollen from the exuberant blossoms streaked his black leather.

Delicately setting the last Seersee fragment in place, Rags-n-Bones smeared it with goo. "Finished!" he cried, holding up the completed globe.

Condorella cupped her hands around his. "*Nilus fragmenti,*" she said, spitting onto the Seersee with remarkable accuracy. It sizzled, glowing with such a hot, white glare that Ascot averted her gaze. The light died down, and—

Well, the seams where Rags-n-Bones had glued it were still visible, crisscrossing the globe like threads of glowing white silk. Colors reflected off the fractured sections, save for one small, triangular dark spot gaping amongst the brightness. "You missed a piece," said Condorella, scowling.

"I think a koi ate it," replied Rags-n-Bones with an apologetic shrug. He tilted the Seersee, and all the shimmering colors focused into a single, blurry image, segmented by cracks.

"Wait, that's a face," said Ascot, who'd just taken a sip of dandelion tea and was hoping to direct everyone's attention elsewhere so she could dump her cup unobserved.

Rags-n-Bones tipped the Seersee this way and that, but the image remained obstinately blurry, save for the face's left nostril. "Hold it steady," said Condorella, laying a hand over Rags-n-Bones'. She muttered under her breath. The image jerked, and the face shot back, shrinking, but sharpening.

"Rune!" cried Starley and Jolt in unison. Cavall glanced up and sucked in a breath.

"The Great Alph, Rune?" said Dmitri. "Are you sure?"

Starley leaned forward, squinting, but Jolt nodded. "Sure as fleas. One of the Roundgrounds' Seersees holds an image of him. He's been sculpted and painted. Everyone in the Clawcrags knows what Rune looks like."

Ascot stared at the dark-haired face in the crystal. Handsome enough, with high, rounded cheekbones and a straight nose, but there was something squinty about the eyes and the mouth seemed inclined to smirk.

Lacey cast the crystal a brief, disinterested glance. "Oh, Runey-pruney," she said, tongue curling in a yawn. "The Lady was very angry with him." She snuggled into a patch of moss.

She knew Rune? Ascot—fortunately—stopped herself before she blurted the question aloud and earned an exasperated look from Dmitri. Of course she could've known Rune; Lorrygreen was just a couple of seconds stretching from his time to…whenever.

She decided not to think too deeply on it. It made her head fill with syrup again.

Muttering, Condorella waved her staff, and the small image lurched again. Now Rune bent over a prone body, lying on some dark, silvery-smooth floor. The crystal buzzed as the image moved in fits and jerks. Rune put his hand to the body's neck, nodded, and shrugged off his hooded cloak. His outline folded in on itself, wavered. Seconds later, a small bird took flight. A mockingbird; the white patches on the undersides of its dark gray wings were unmistakable.

Thump. Ascot glanced to the side. Starley had, quite simply, fallen on his rump. She thought people only did such things in cheap novels. Both Jolt and Cavall looked stricken beyond words. "What?" she asked.

Dmitri huffed and rolled his eyes. *Well, there's my quota of exasperation for the day,* thought Ascot, glancing back at the image, frozen on a vague blur of wings. *Wings.* A breath later, she understood. "But…wasn't Rune a lion-shifter?"

The branches of the violet-flowered cherry rustled, whispering over the slick marble of Le Fou's headstone. Going to the pool, Jolt splashed water over his face. "So we've always been told." He shook his head until his hair flew. "It's why our leaders have always been big cat-shifters. It's natural. Ordained. But I was right. Le Fou didn't mean 'fly' metaphorically. Rune—"

"Was a poxy, bleedin' little chirpy-bird," burst out Starley gleefully. "Our system's a lie!"

Find the lie. All of it—everything shifters based their lives on. Catch laughed in Ascot's head. *Glad you're happy,* she told him.

"No," whispered Cavall, still seated. His fingers clenched, gouging mud. "Someone would know. There'd be records."

Dmitri gave an annoying cough. "This letter *is* a record. I suspect Petryovan was ordered to alter or destroy it by someone who didn't want its contents known."

"They tried." Condorella's eyes gleamed like tiny, avaricious stars. "But LeFou outsmarted them." She brought out the letter.

She'd said the writing would mend itself, given time, Ascot recalled. And time had little meaning in Lorrygreen. So…

Clearing her throat, Condorella began reading. *"To Rune, My Former Beloved."*

"Beloved?" cried Starley. He was quickly shushed.

"My crystal witnessed your deed," Condorella continued. *"I know your reasons, and find them inadequate. A friend is a friend, and treason is treason, and to lose the former by the latter is more than I can excuse, even from you. Perhaps especially from you. I believed better of you, and can barely endure the pain of that belief shattering.*

Should I find myself beginning to forgive you, I've kept the record of your treachery. I've also taken what you stole. I am going to a green and hidden land, beyond your ability to locate. Fly as far as you wish in search of it, and me. Search until your wings ache, as my heart does.

Ah, my poor Ginkiku!

Magden Le Fou."

There didn't seem to be any cicadas in Lorrygreen, so they were spared the *bloc-bloc* of one rushing in to fill the silence. The pool bubbled instead, while the cherry's branches rasped over the grave.

"She loved him," said Ascot. Her reflection gleamed faintly in the tombstone's black marble. She transferred her gaze to the blurry image in the globe. "She loved him, and he killed her friend."

Appalled, she shook her head. "Who could do such a thing to someone they loved?"

"I killed my father," said Cavall.

The branches whispered across the grave again.

Cavall scrubbed his sleeve across his face, smearing pollen over his nose. No one laughed. "I was raised in Holdfast by my mother," he said in a tired drone. "When I settled into hound-form, I was sent to train with my father in Highmoor.

"I wasn't pleased. Mother raised me to be proud of my name. Cavall's an old family among hound-shifters. But Father treated all shifters as equals. He made coffee for the hare-shifter messengers who came to the ranch, offered hawk-shifters beds for the night. He even befriended *humans*."

"What a kind man," said Rags-n-Bones, nibbling a pebble.

Cavall's laugh sounded like a handful of rusty nails rattling in his chest. "It revolted me. We argued, frequently. One day, Father found an injured shifter in the woods and hid him in our barn. I was furious. Our job was to catch slipskins, not harbor them. So, when some shifter came around asking questions, someone with authority, wearing an embroidered mantle, I—I—"

"You told him about the shifter in your barn," Ascot finished for him.

Cavall nodded, head hanging between his shoulders. "The next evening, the shifter in the barn vanished, and I— I found my father—"

You found him? Ascot didn't need the details. The words, his broken tone, were enough. Sobbing sympathetically, Rags-n-Bones dropped the Seersee to hug him.

"No!" hollered Condorella, diving for it. It shattered in her grasp.

"Oh, hell!" cried Starley. "That was the letter's proof."

Condorella scrabbled at the shards, wailing. Ascot pulled her away and counted the pieces. There were definitely more than before. "Maybe we can fix it again." Her hope faded even as she spoke. The image had been blurry before. The letter alone likely wouldn't be enough to convince most shifters, not with five hundred years of false history slanted in Rune's favor.

"Maybe." Condorella didn't sound particularly sanguine. She brightened slightly. "Or, perhaps I could transfer the image to an intact Seersee."

Starley stood on one leg to scratch his heel. "Right. So all we have to do is infiltrate the Roundgrounds and hope no one's farted too close to the remaining Seersees recently. Should be simple enough. Perhaps Bel—" Jolt pinched his arm. Starley shot Cavall a glance and coughed. "Well, it's a plan. Gather the fragments."

Condorella stooped, but Ascot stopped her. "Let Rags do it." For whatever reason, the Seersee seemed less inclined to break for him. *Maybe it's hoping he'll sing to it.*

Scooping up handfuls of water from the pool, she scrubbed her face and neck and dampened her hair. No substitute for a thorough wash, but she could feel her thoughts starting to coagulate again. "We should get out of here," she said, standing and flicking off water.

"Agreed," said Dmitri. "There's an issue, however. Am I right in assuming that we will return to the exact instant of time we left?"

Condorella nodded, hawkishly watching Rags-n-Bones gather shards. "That's why we need those stone chips. Outside, the rock's just been broken. It remembers that moment. We can use it to pull ourselves back."

Shivering, Ascot felt in her pocket for the unremarkable little piece of rock. It was still there, wedged in a corner of the cloth. *I hope Rags hasn't chewed his.* Then she remembered. "Galen. You didn't grab a piece, did you?"

He looked at her dully. Ascot wondered if he'd even followed the last few minutes of conversation. All at once, comprehension flooded his face. His eyes widened. "You mean I can't leave Lorrygreen without one of those chunks of rock?"

Lacey lifted her forearm from her eyes. "Chunk of rock?"

"You can," said Condorella. "But you might emerge a hundred years in the future, two hundred in the past…you get the idea."

Dmitri stomped twice against the pool's rim. "Returning to my point, we can't leave Lorrygreen, either," he said, having gained everyone's attention. "Cavall's posse will still be there, hunting us."

Cavall rose in one swift motion, extending his hand. "Give me one of your rock chunks, and I'll call my posse off."

"Rock chunk." Lacey stood, stretched, and meandered off past the violet-flowered cherry, pushing aside its trailing branches.

"You're asking for one of us to stay here, forever," said Jolt. His nails dug into his opposite elbows, as if he had to hold himself tight lest he strike Cavall. "After *you* chased us in."

"It's either that, or face my posse when you emerge." Cavall didn't waver.

Appallingly, Ascot found herself running through a list a candidates. *Maybe Condorella wouldn't mind staying near Le Fou.*

Self-disgust hit harder than a slap to the face. No, none of them should have to remain here forever. Yet, without Cavall to call them off, the six hounds were sure to attack the instant they left Lorrygreen.

Tail slowly waving, Dmitri approached Cavall. Was he going to volunteer? *No!* thought Ascot. *You still haven't found a satisfying translation of* The Gambler, *remember?*

Then she noticed Dmitri's ears; perked forward, and slightly cupped. Having played enough poker with him to recognize his tells, she swallowed her protest.

"If I give you my stone," said Dmitri, assuming a magisterial stance before Cavall, "you will not only call off your posse, but cease pursuing the Hide Aways altogether."

"It's my duty—"

"Pox on your duty, leather-britches," said Starley. "You know it's based on lies now."

Ascot waved him down. Dealing with Starley really wasn't much different from anticipating Moony's antics.

Cavall drummed his fingers against his thigh. "I can promise not to pursue you until after the Moonless Night."

"I can accept that," said Dmitri. "Do you swear, on that sense of honor and loyalty we canids are known for?"

Cavall made a rueful noise; acknowledgement of a point well-struck, perhaps. "I swear. And...thank you, Dmitri." He looked away. "I can't stay here. I have a daughter."

A daughter? Ascot's breath froze.

"Some of the Hide Aways you Sniffers killed had daughters," growled Jolt, but very softly.

A daughter. Ascot breathed out, accepting it. *Thank goodness I didn't accept his proposition. I'm not ready to be a stepmother.*

"Very well," said Dmitri, nosing into the satchel that contained his books. His jaws worked. Something clicked. Withdrawing his muzzle, he spat a piece of rock onto the moss. Cavall let out a tiny sigh as he picked it up.

Dmitri spat out a second piece of rock. Then a third. Ascot gauged the size of his jaws, remembered him snapping frantically at the ground, and swiftly clapped a hand over her mouth to stifle giggles. "I may have swallowed a fourth," said Dmitri, blinking like a contented cat. "Your promise remains heard and witnessed, however."

Cavall rolled the shard of rock on his gloved palm. "Outplayed." A hint of a grin curved his lips.

"So long as you keep your promise," said Jolt, still grim and clutching his arms.

Ascot thought it best not to push the issue. "Let's go, if we're ready," she said, shouldering her knapsack.

Her companions filed up the slope. A touch to her shoulder stayed her. Turning back, Ascot found Lacey standing behind her, extending a faceted lump about the size of a grape.

"Rock chunk," she said.

"Thanks, but we already have them," Ascot replied.

Lacey shook it, emphatically. "No, this is the good one."

It wasn't worth arguing. "Thank you," said Ascot, accepting it. Its dull, metallic gleam looked like gold's embarrassed cousin. *Pyrite*, she thought, tucking it in a pocket.

Lacey licked her hand, satisfied. "No more buzz. Used to singe my whiskers."

Don't you mean your beak? No; best not go there. "You could leave Lorrygreen if you like, Lacey," said Ascot, thinking of the extra shards Dmitri had grabbed.

Lacey tossed her head. "Leave Lorrygreen? Why would I do that? You outsiders are so silly. Mew!"

Shrugging off her robe, she transformed into a tiny green hummingbird, and led the way back to the forest's edge.

CHAPTER SEVENTEEN:
ANTI-HERO'S WELCOME

Pulling a lock of hair in front of his eyes, Catch examined it for signs of gray. Amazingly, he found none—they must've been walking the Underway at least seventy years. Moony, draped across his shoulders, snored in his ear. That had been going on forever, too. Catch hoped he wasn't expecting to be awakened with a kiss.

Ahead, Savotte paused. "Ah."

Alerted by her satisfied tone, Moony sat up. "Are we there yet?"

Savotte's grin faltered. "Had to grab your last chance, didn't you? Yes." She pointed. Twenty feet ahead, the floor's gentle, upward slope met a series of steps hewn from the yellowish rock. A pattern of golden light seeped down from some unseen opening overhead.

"Sunlight," said Catch. *I could roll in it, like a patch of catnip.*

"Whee!" Eagerly, Moony paced to Catch's other shoulder. "Let's see this city of yours."

"If it were mine, I'd sell it for a handful of magic beans," Catch replied, following Savotte up the staircase.

"Coffee beans?" asked Moony.

"Naturally." He could smell coffee. The scent spilled down the stairwell, along with the smell of cheese bread, spiced cicadas, and a dozen other aromas that roused dormant memories. Distant voices exchanged words, accompanied by the rumble of carts and an occasional trill of music.

The skin between Savotte's brows creased. "Do you remember where this particular tunnel comes out?"

"No," Catch replied.

"Sounds lively," said Moony, purring and kneading. Wincing, Catch unhooked his claws from his shoulder. The staircase doubled back on itself. When they climbed it, a final, short span of the Underway stretched before them, blocked by a grating. A city guard in a red-cuffed uniform slouched by it. Hardly more than a cub, with close-cropped black hair and a beaky nose, her folded arms and outthrust lip said exactly what she thought of the justness of the world at this moment.

"Mistral," murmured Savotte, sounding surprised.

The young guard straightened. Beyond her, another short flight of steps led to an open doorway with a splendid view of a yellow wall patched with gray where the clay had cracked off to expose the brick beneath. "Rainy," she said.

"That's 'Lieutenant Savotte' to you, Cadet Cavall," replied Savotte sternly, approaching the grating.

Cadet Cavall? Catch did a double-take. On second inspection, that nose was unmistakable.

Mistral feigned deafness. "That's not Dad," she said, standing on her toe-tips to peer over Savotte's shoulder.

Dad? Catch, who had been expecting "Uncle Galen," nearly fell backwards down the steps. *The black-clad nightmare has spawned?* On his shoulder, Moony made a small, squeaky "mur" noise that could've come from Nipper.

Savotte blew out her lips. "Your father left on another assignment. This is—"

"Is it him?" asked Mistral, inserting a key into the lock. Her eyes were the blue of cornflowers, pale, like Cavall's, but with a warmer, lavender tinge. "The golden star?"

The gate swung open. Collecting his wits, Catch stepped through it. "Yes, 'tis I," he said, bowing low enough to sweep the gritty yellow floor with his fingertips. "The blazing golden star foretold by Magden Le Fou. Behold me, brief mortals, and quail."

"Oh, don't," muttered Savotte, dropping her forehead into her palm. But Mistral laughed. Catch smiled up at her.

Moony giggled. "I don't see any quail." He licked his lips at the thought.

"Means 'tremble,' 'cower,' or 'cringe,'" Catch replied. Straightening, he smoothed his hair—always a losing prospect. *Cavall's daughter*, he thought, studying her. She regarded him back with equal interest. "I take it your father's mentioned me?"

Her scowl made her the image of her father. "Just that he met you in that human town he was posted in. He didn't say anything interesting—I mean you're *only* the golden star of prophecy."

Sarcasm. It was something that just blossomed with adolescence, like spots. "I am a very dull fellow." Catch bowed again. "If you'll escort us to the Aspire, I'll have you asleep before we reach Halfpace Lane."

Mistral lit up, but Savotte shook her head. "Cadat Cavall will remain at her post."

Catch exchanged a glance with Mistral. Simultaneously, they rolled eyes. Catch supposed he could anticipate such expressions because he'd never fully grown up himself. "If she accompanies us, she can fetch us coffee," he said.

They'd been deprived for days. Catch watched Savotte's internal struggle. It was heroic, but brief. "Oh, very well," she said, trying to sound grudging. Mistral tried to sulk and smile all at once.

"Come *on*," begged Moony. Catch unhooked his claws again.

Mistral led them up the steps. Moony lifted his head, whiskers twitching. "What's that smell?"

For a second, the name belonging to the tart, fruity fragrance with the lingering bittersweet notes floundered in the depths of Catch's mind. *I couldn't have forgotten*, he thought, annoyed.

Then suddenly it was there, neatly as a note handed on a silver platter. "Bitterseed oranges," he replied, ascending into the sunlight. His eyes were too dazzled to see. He didn't need to see. He knew exactly where he was, as if twenty-five years had never passed: Buy-Your-Leave Way, the grand thoroughfare cutting northeast through Holdfast. The domain of merchants, its name jested that you'd be practically forced to purchase something before you could escape it. *Who said shifters had no sense of humor?*

Moony's raspy giggle tickled his ear. "Foo! Grapes, peaches, and now oranges. You shifters are fruit-obsessed."

"Rather cuts into our reputation as scary predators, doesn't it?" he agreed. The last spots faded from his eyes, leaving him with a plain view of the plain alley he stood in. A short length to his right, it dead-ended. To his left, it opened onto Buy-Your-Leave. Carts passed the alley's mouth, loaded with food and trinkets. Mistral loped off, presumably in search of coffee.

"Buy-Your-Leave," said Savotte. She brushed a lock of hair back from her ear. "Our original path emerged closer to the Aspire."

Indicating Gildar wanted him to enter Holdfast unobtrusively. Catch pursed his lips.

"Make way!" Mistral shouted from the street. "This is for the golden star." There was the sound of a scuffle. Voices rose in a startled murmur. Moony, unable to contain his excitement any longer, leaped off Catch's shoulder and ran into the street.

"Oh, no," said Savotte, clapping a hand to her face.

So much for Gildar's plans, thought Catch with satisfaction as Mistral came running back.

"Here," she said, thrusting a mug at each of them. His was larger than Savotte's, Catch noticed as he took it.

She noticed it, too. "Let's get going," she said, accepting her mug from Mistral with the vague suggestion of flattened ears. "Quietly."

She spoke to empty air. Mistral darted back out onto Buy-Your-

Leave. "Make way for the golden star!" she bellowed.

Savotte clapped her hand to her face again. "No point shouting after flown bats," said Catch, shrugging. Ascot frequently quoted that at him when he discovered she'd eaten all the chocolate.

He stepped into a sea of eyes. They stared from the windows of the yellow clay shops on Buy-Your-Leave's north side, decorated with colorful tiles. They gawked in front of the vendor stands lining the street's south side, brightly striped awnings rippling behind them. Some even gazed from the branches of the bitterseed orange trees planted at intervals between the stands, providing the customers with patchy shade.

Something inside Catch stopped breathing. He'd always preferred shadows. He'd been groomed for them. Those eyes were like a thousand glow-globes, all focused his way.

Savotte nudged his shoulder. "Flown bats, Starthorne. Start walking."

I can do this. Brushing back his hair, Catch slid into an air of indifference as he would his brown coat. A sip of coffee helped, after he got past the first taste. He'd forgotten the Holdfast fashion of flavoring it with bitterseed orange syrup.

He started walking. Mistral and Moony led the way. Moony's tail arched so high over his head it tickled his tufted ear tips.

A susurrus of voices trailed in their wake. "Starthorne…the golden star." The words traveled along the street, handed from lips to ears reverently, like a rare bauble none felt worthy of wearing. "The golden star…Starthorne." Flower-draped banners snapped overhead in sharp counterpoint to the whispers. Catch's feet kept moving, mechanically. He supposed it could be called walking.

They passed the Bottomless Fountain, with its six tinkling spigots and orange sunburst tiles. Catch remembered how he and Glim used to sit on its rim, dunking chunks of cheese-laced bread into mugs of coffee.

He was *not* going to think about Glim.

A vendor struggled to drag his heavy cart out of their path, his cheeks flushed with panic. Bundles of gaily painted feathers tipped over the sides, but when Catch stopped to help gather them up, the poor man practically fainted. "Let him be," said Savotte, grabbing his arm.

"Why is everyone so scared?" Catch murmured. Holdfast stank of it. Tomorrow was Yawning Day, a grand holiday, yet the preparations for it looked less than joyous. Where were the groups of youths preparing for the Rising Tournament, drinking too much syrupy coffee and tossing flowers in the fountain?

"It *is* the year of the Moonless Night," said Savotte, avoiding his eyes.

It was more than that. Catch frowned, studying the onlookers. "What's this new fashion?" Everyone dressed in a single color. The tunic might be a lighter or darker shade than the trousers, but when all was said, they would both be green or yellow or brown. Very few wore mantles, and almost none with embroidery. The ragged, gray stuff one woman at the crowd's forefront wore could have easily been dishclouts as clothes. Under Catch's curious gaze, she lifted her head. The raised, white scar on her left cheek formed an "F."

Catch stopped, staring. The woman's dull, unhappy eyes met his a few seconds before dropping to the ground.

Moony settled on Catch's shoulder. "Jolt had a brand like that," he whispered, his claws prickling through Catch's coat, all crackling fur and stiff little bones.

I hoped it was just an unfortunate fashion choice. "What does that brand mean?" Catch asked Savotte. She tugged at his arm. His foot pulled reluctantly away from the smooth, yellow street, as if he'd stepped in glue.

"It stands for 'feral,'" she said.

Ferals—those who transformed into such unusual animals that the Shifter Registry had no designated role for them. Twenty-five years ago, they'd been assigned drudge work: cleaning and hauling and the like. Evidently, things had changed.

"They started branding them eight years ago," Savotte continued. Mistral dropped back a pace to listen in. "To keep better track of them, said Gildar. They're so much more likely to slip their skins."

Catch wrenched out of her grasp. "Perhaps because they're being *branded?*" he hissed. *If I weren't a big cat, I'd probably be classified as a feral.* Why not? Whoever set down the ridiculous rules in the first place made no more specific provision for Smilodon-shifters than they did for wombat-shifters.

Bones and blood, the Clawcrags had always been a horror. He could hardly believe he'd returned to find them worse than he remembered.

"The outfits are also new," whispered Mistral. "It's illegal for certain shifters to wear certain colors."

Catch closed his eyes. He'd feared that was the reason. Now he recognized the smell accompanying the stink of fear; the one that trailed him like a pungent perfume: hope.

After five hundred years, the Moonless Night was nigh. Once it was passed, everything would change. Even if nothing happened on the day, everything would change, because once it was past, the hope that it would bring change would be gone.

"Captain, we have to do something about this," Moony whispered. His whiskers scraped Catch's cheek. "This isn't something you can run from, not even dashingly, with a really long feather in your hat."

I'm not your savior! Catch raged silently. *I don't want to be here. I'm a rogue, a thief, and a liar.*

I might be a killer. Glim.

The Bottomless Fountain splashed remorselessly on. Several young shifters perched on its rim. Their eyes widened when his gaze fell on him. Several bobbed their heads convulsively. Catch looked away.

I'm not your savior. Can't be. The prophecy's a sham. But as he walked on, the memory of that branded cheek kept burning into him, as if the hot iron had scorched his own flesh. *Hold your chin up, keep your hands out of your pockets, and stop worrying about your damned cowlick.* At any moment he might laugh, if he could avoid screaming. Surely this was some dream, the kind of self-centered, self-important child's dream that became a nightmare with age and sense.

"Are you all right, sir?" asked Mistral

"Oh, I'm brilliant," said Catch. He suspected he'd gone pale. His head felt light as thistledown. "How could I not be? I'm the golden star, the savior of the Clawcrags. Means 'rescuer,' 'redeemer'—"

He choked on the third synonym: *liberator.* He glanced back, but a multitude of bodies hid the branded woman from view. "How could I be other than brilliant?"

&

The Aspire, seat of the Alph and his Pack, loomed over Holdfast's eastern side. Someone must've earned a prize for cleverness in naming it, for it was indeed little more than a collection of spires. Its central part, the Heartspire, consisted of a tall, sharply pointed cone, like someone had placed a giant dunce cap on the plateau, glued smaller cones to its sides, then smaller cones to theirs, and simply kept going until the whole thing was covered in spikes. It looked as if it were waiting to impale a giant melon falling from the sky. Light flowed off silvery-sleek gray sides that resembled hematite without, probably, actually being hematite. No one knew for certain—Clawcrag geologists were all rhinoceroses for reasons Catch neither understood, nor cared to. As rhinoceros-shifters were rare, and mostly supremely uninterested in their occupation, the Aspire's mysteries continued unfathomed.

Unknown, undiscovered, unplumbed. Fur and fangs, but we're a daft race. Catch waited with Savotte and Mistral in the great cavern under the Aspire while a draft horse-shifter worked the treadmill that operated the lift that would carry them to the Heartspire's heart. Savotte watched the horse-shifter covertly, perhaps pondering how close she'd come to sharing his fate.

"It wouldn't burn very well," said Moony, sniffing a gray wall. Catch had forgotten their sour, metallic scent that the peacock-shifter servants tried to sweeten by burning incense.

The lift came squeaking down, settling into its allotted depression with a thump that should've shaken the floor, but didn't. Catch and Savotte stepped on. Savotte held up a hand when Mistral made to follow.

"No," she said. "Really, no." Mistral looked pleadingly at Catch, but Savotte shook her head. "The lion-shifters will growl if an unauthorized cadet is discovered in the Heartspire."

"But—"

"Be patient, and I'll send Moony with a Starthorne sigil after I'm settled," Catch said over Mistral's protest. "That'll give you the run of this place while I'm here."

Curiously, Mistral's mouth twitched, as if at a private joke. She hastily twisted it into a scowl after a sidelong glance at Savotte, and stepped back. "Oh, very well," she said, making a show of grumbling.

The peacock-shifter attendant pulled a lever. The lift door shut and the platform rose. Shiny gray walls slid past. "She didn't want to be a guard," said Savotte. "But she's a hound-shifter, so what choice does she have?"

Catch held his tongue with difficulty. "Where's her mother?"

"South, in Fairfallow. Galen's marriage was arranged. It means nothing on a personal level."

Of course. Was there anything the Clawcrags couldn't suck dry of joy? Then again, going by the way Savotte's lips had thinned, she probably had her own reasons for wanting to dismiss Cavall's marriage.

The lift slowed, coming to rest at a large, circular hallway surrounding a core of inwardly sloping, maybe-metallic walls. Stepping out of the lift, the peacock-shifter strode over to the high-arched door deeply recessed into the inner wall and waited expectantly.

Catch started to follow. Savotte touched his arm. "Don't mention the fake tengu," she whispered. "I should report that."

He shook his head. "Take my advice, and don't."

Her mouth pressed into a stubborn line. "You believe Gildar's behind it. I still say it could be the work of slipskins."

Catch turned up a palm. Outside of tying her up, he couldn't very well prevent her speaking. "Do as you must. I won't say anything."

"Thank you, Starthorne."

Catch nodded. No, he wouldn't say anything until he'd determined to his own satisfaction if Gildar was behind the not-tengu. *As for the real tengu, if that was a real tengu...*

"Catch, Smilodon-shifter of house Starthorne," announced the peacock-shifter, opening the Heart Chamber's door.

...I'll decide later.

A great patch of light, almost as solid as a coin, fell out the open door, reflecting brillinatly off the metallic walls of the surrounding corridor. Shading his eyes, Catch stepped into it. Two perfectly round windows pierced the Heart Chamber's walls, one to the east, the other directly opposite, as if a giant arrow had pierced the room. *If only one had. It'd almost certainly have hit Gildar's swollen head.*

"Starthorne," rumbled a voice, a rich, rolling, remembered voice. "Do not keep us waiting."

Catch squinted down the length of the golden carpet stretching to the Heart Chamber's far end. There, a single thick, twisted spike, known as the Claw, thrust out of the wall at a twenty degree angle. A man reclined on the red cushions piled atop its slightly scooped point.

Alph Gildar Ambersun. He crooked a finger.

Ignoring the half dozen or so other people standing below the Claw, Catch started down the carpet. Traces of white veined Gildar's almost glowingly golden locks and finely shaped beard. His sun-bronzed skin hung more loosely about his throat than Catch recalled, but his limbs, under his sleeveless gold tunic, loose trousers, and gold-fringed red mantle, remained fit and athletic. Shifting revitalized the body to a certain extent. Most shifters remained relatively youthful until they passed a hundred and thirty-five, then went into wrinkles and a rapid decline. Gildar was around one hundred, so with luck, he still had another thirty years of merry despotism to go.

In practicality, he had to be looking over his shoulder for the challenger who'd tear out his throat and take his place as Alph of the Clawcrags.

"Alph Gildar." Catch stopped before the point of the Claw and bowed, stretching out his wrist in the formal way. "I am pleased to return to my homeland."

Only the faintest crows-feet marred the corners of Gildar's small, but piercing, dark gold eyes. "Lethe's son. Welcome back."

Lethe's son. Catch frowned at the floor. An odd salutation. According to Cavall, Lethe had been dead twenty-four years. On his shoulder, Moony began grooming himself with wet, sloppy tongue-smacks. Catch hoped he was restricting his ablutions to polite portions of his anatomy.

Gildar tented his fingers. "You arrived later than expected."

Was that a statement, or is he expecting a response? Gildar's tone gave little clue. Catch shrugged mentally. It was probably one of those circumstances where, whichever you chose, you were wrong. He elected to remain mute, bent over and quite certain that Moony was gaining weight.

After a moment, Gildar snapped his fingers. "Fetch Lieutenant Savotte." She was hurried in. Three paces behind Catch, she knelt, crossing her wrists before her. That was new, too.

"Alph," she said.

Seconds stretched. Under the cover of his unruly hair, Catch watched Gildar stare at Savotte. It was his trick, to unnerve people. Lethe had pointed it out to Catch as they watched Gildar confer with his Pack.

"Gildar's a fool," Lethe had whispered to him. Then, he'd smiled.

"But not so much of a fool that he can't learn...which makes him not such a fool, after all."

"Where is Captain Cavall?" Gildar asked at last.

"We were ambushed by the Hide Aways," Savotte replied. Her ringing voice sounded just a little shrill; Gildar had succeeded in unnerving her. "They attempted to abduct Starthorne. My partner left to round up a posse of Sniffers and pursue them."

More seconds strained. "Captain Cavall should be commended for his sense of duty," Gildar spoke mildly, but his unwavering stare voiced a different opinion. "That does not explain your tardiness, Lieutenant Savotte."

A muscle twitched in Savotte's cheek. "My apologies, Alph. We encountered trouble in the Underway."

Don't say it, Catch begged silently. His back was about to snap. Moony had to weigh as much as Dmitri by now.

"I see." Gildar gestured, and the peacock-shifter stepped forward. "Thank you, Lieutenant Savotte."

She dared look up. "Alph—"

Gildar's hand slashed. "Dismissed."

The peacock-shifer took Savotte's arm. Defeated, she let him escort her out of the chamber. As the door closed behind them, Gildar propped his cheek on his knuckles. "Horse-shifters," he grumped. "Flighty. Unreliable. You may stand, Starthorne."

With an effort, Catch lugged himself upright. The crick of his spine snapping into place echoed softly through the Heart Chamber. Moony kept his balance without losing a beat in the rhythm of his licks.

"What is that on your shoulder?" demanded Gildar.

Moony's head snapped up. "'That?'"

"Alph Gildar, this is Moony, a Vicardi cat from Shadowvale," said Catch, lifting a hand to soothe him. "Moony, this is Alph Gildar Ambersun."

Moony and Gildar regarded one another. Neither seemed

impressed. "So, the rumors of your traveling with a Shadowvalean were true," said Gildar. "Is that where you've been these last twenty-five years? Shadowvale? Consorting with our banished wolf-shifter kin?"

"Mostly," said Catch. Moony's snigger at the lie was, fortunately, quickly stifled. "They call themselves werewolves and have run quite to barbarity, I'm afraid." *It'll please Gildar to think that all wolf-shifters immediately descended into sniffing bottoms and howling at the moon the instant they left the Clawcrags.*

Indeed, a smile swept over Gildar's lips. "Of course they did," he said, nestling back on the Claw.

The lull in conversation gave Catch a chance to study the Pack members currently in attendance. He recognized the burly, black-haired young man standing to the left of the Claw as Bandersnatch Falxus, a panther-shifter who'd been a couple years ahead of him at school. The past twenty-five years had changed him. He'd gotten bigger. Panthers were generally thought of as sleek, lithe cats, but Bandersnatch had opted for the "able to balance a bull on either shoulder" build instead. His biceps, nicely exposed by his sleeveless tunic, rolled like belligerent grapefruits with every flex. Stubble tinted his jaw blue.

Catch didn't know the other Pack members, neatly clad in dark gold tunics, but they shared a familial resemblance, with golden-brown hair, heavy brows, and flaring nostrils.

"It's because their society lacks structure, isn't it?" said Gildar suddenly, taking up the former thread of conversation as if the long pause hadn't interrupted everyone's interest in the subject—another of his habits. "If everyone's a wolf, how can they know who's fit for what place?"

The gold-tunics nodded, murmuring their agreement. "I'd like to go to Shadowvale and teach them their place," said Bandersnatch, slamming a fist into the opposite palm.

"Let's sweep out our own lair first," said Gildar, waving him down with a humoring, paternal sort of gesture.

Maybe a little too condescending, come to that. A faint line appeared between Gildar's brows, as if he didn't think anyone should be voicing their preferences in his presence. Was Bandersnatch the one who had him glancing over his shoulder? "I had no idea our lair had grown so filthy while I was away," Catch offered, just to see where Gildar would go with it.

"Hadn't you? And yet, you were nearly abducted by slipskins on your way." Gildar's face darkened. "There's nothing worse than a slipskin."

"Not even the tengu?" asked Catch. *They're certainly awful poets.* Moony continued grooming, but the slurpy quality of his licks had diminished, indicating he was listening in.

Gildar brushed that aside with the same ease he knocked over people who didn't get out of his path quickly enough. "The tengu are mindless brutes, bred for violence, and—now that you've returned, of course—we'll make short work of them on the Moonless Night."

Catch muffled a snort. *How convenient the tengu dolls fit Gildar's description perfectly.*

"Our real enemies are slipskins," Gildar continued. "They're the rot inside our society. Five hundred years ago, we were disorganized, ready to fall. Rune found us our path and our home, and these Hide Aways would have us diverge from the way he showed us." Gildar pounded the Claw's silk drapery. "I won't have it. After the Moonless Night, I'll put shifter-kind right for once and all."

The gold-tunics applauded. "I'm bored," whispered Moony in Catch's ear. "When can we start razing this place?"

"Soon," Catch murmured back, staring at a portrait of the Great Alph Rune, set on a stand behind the golden-tunics on the Claw's left. No one had ever discovered nails that would pierce the material of the Aspire's walls, so all paintings and tapestries had to be displayed on wooden frames around its curved perimeter. After a certain height, all attempts at ornamentation were abandoned, and bare, silvery walls met the eye.

Rune's artist had probably been going for an expression of lofty contemplation and had achieved deep boredom. *Can't blame you, Rune. But you can't fly away. They've stolen even the memory of your wings.*

Bandersnatch noticed Catch's abstraction. "Perhaps you don't agree, having spent so much time amongst our traitorous wolf cousins," he said, folding his arms. Even that small movement made his muscles ripple. "Perhaps you've forgotten that shifters obey their Alph."

"Now, now." Again that slightly paternal wave of indulgence from Gildar. "Lethe's son will have a chance to prove himself a true shifter on the Moonless Night."

Lethe's son. Catch scratched his cheek. *Has he referred to me by name once? He hasn't, has he?*

Bandersnatch scowled at the floor. Gildar clapped his hands. "Enough for now. Starthorne, you may take up residence in Lethe's old chambers. Tomorrow, we celebrate Yawning Day. At the traditional banquet, I will outline my plans for not only the Moonless Night, but a map for shifter-kind to follow for centuries after."

Centuries? Catch tilted his head. Except for Rune, Alphs didn't get centuries. They clung to their office until some fool like Bandersnatch challenged them and took their place.

A second thought followed hard on the heels of the first. *If Gildar leads shifter-kind successfully through the Moonless Night, he'll be a hero. The Pack will probably vote to make him Alph Eternal, like Rune, and he'll never have to fear a challenge again.*

But for that to happen, the Moonless Night couldn't pass without event. How convenient a flock of fake tengu waited in the Underway.

But where do I fit into this scheme? He had the feeling it had something to do with being Lethe's son. *And I know a way to find out.* "Change of plans," he whispered to Moony. "This isn't a swashbuckler, after all. It's a spy intrigue."

"Oooh!" Moony's ears shot up. He danced from shoulder to shoulder, sparks snapping from his fur. "Those are good, too. When do we get started?"

Catch smiled. "Tonight."

CHAPTER EIGHTEEN:
STAR QUALITY

Without enthusiasm, Ascot watched Starley roast cicadas over their campfire. *I suppose it's nice the little nuisances are good for something other than tangling in people's hair,* she thought. But she couldn't quite muster enthusiasm for eating them.

"Smaller steps," called Jolt. Ascot glanced outside the cave, where he was schooling Dmitri's manipulations of his fennec form. Tomorrow, they'd enter the town of Merryvick, and they couldn't risk the commotion a wolf's appearance would rouse. Condorella had swept out announcing she intended to consult with the stars—which Ascot suspected was a euphemism for hitting the bushes—and Rags-n-Bones had burst into slightly perfunctory tears at the sight of the cicadas and been sent to fetch water.

Dmitri minced past the cave, oversized ears flapping. "No, no," called Jolt. "Widen your eyes and look about as if you expect everyone to grab you up and cuddle you at any moment, and are smugly aware of the fact."

Ascot certainly would've liked to do just that. "What do fennecs do?" she asked Starley to distract herself from Dmitri's rampant adorableness.

"Foxes make clocks," Starley replied, skewering another cicada.

"Clocks?" Ascot shook her head. "Why?"

"Because 'fox' and 'clocks' rhyme?" Starley clicked his tongue. "You're acting like our system makes sense, love. It doesn't."

Obviously not, yet some people would fight to the death to preserve it. *Like Cavall,* she thought. He'd let them go after escaping Lorrygreen, without any significant glances or throat-clearing from Dmitri; just called off the posse and headed north without another glance back.

"What about weas—stoats?" she asked, accepting the skewer of roasted cicadas Starley offered her.

"We're lawyers." He grinned at her sound of surprise. "Don't think it suits me, right? Well, half of lawyering's pure theatre, and I'm dead good at that. As for the justice bit, I didn't give it much thought until I was hired to defend someone they didn't really want defended. I was supposed to just make a show before they declared him guilty."

Ascot bit into a cicada, willing herself not to taste it. "What did you do?"

"I started thinking about real justice," Starley replied. "And then, I bought him a mantle." He pierced another cicada. Its bulging eyes regarded him accusingly.

"Trot more briskly," called Jolt outside the cave. Ascot caught a fleeting glimpse of vermillion.

"You can change yourself, if given a chance. A choice." Starley slid another cicada onto the skewer. "That's what I fight for. I think it's what Starthorne wants, too."

Change. Ascot swallowed and the cicada went down in a fibrous lump. Was it really what Catch wanted? Every time she thought he'd finally stopped running, he took off again.

Until Highmoor. Until the one time when she'd really wished he'd flee.

Who gave you the idea Starthorne wasn't a killer?

The words she'd fought down ever since Cavall spoke them again popped up like a stubborn spring. "Do you know anything about Catch's escape from Holdfast?" she asked, rolling the skewer between her fingers.

"A bit." Draping his arm over his knee, Starley chomped into a cicada. "It happened on Yawning Day, twenty-five years ago. They were holding a Rising Tournament—"

"What's that?"

"A flag hunt through an obstacle course, for prizes. They're a Yawning Day tradition." Starley twirled his skewer. "That particular tournament, there was the understanding that whoever came in ahead, Starthorne or Glim Ambersun, would be declared the golden star. They had some scuffle right at the Roundgrounds' edge, and fell off Holdfast Plateau. Or jumped, or—well, no one knows."

Ascot shaped her next words very carefully. "Did the fall kill Glim?"

"Don't know," he replied gently, and she knew that despite her efforts, he'd heard the hope in her voice. "The Seersee everyone was watching them in was too dusty to make out details. But Starthorne's father, Lethe..." Starley scuffed the gritty cave dirt. "Love, you should know. He was the Clawcrag's most notorious assassin. He might have taught his boy something."

Ascot set her skewer aside. Even forgetting that it was, well, a cicada, she didn't think she could eat anymore. She folded her arms around her knees. *Oh, Catch.* Maybe he had good reasons for wanting to run.

Another thought raced on its heels, sharp enough to drive the breath from her. Maybe he was right to be reticent about his past. Because if he *had* killed Glim, she wasn't sure she could—

"Forgive him," said Starley. Startled, Ascot lifted her head. He smiled with half his mouth. "You have to judge people on who they are, not who they were in the past."

That still leaves Catch a liar. Sighing, Ascot laid her cheek back on her knee. "Is that what you believe?"

The other half of his mouth joined in on the smile, but the expression didn't touch his eyes. He glanced out the cave.

"Better," came Jolt's voice as Dmitri minced past again, "but hold your head higher. And quit flapping your ears."

Starley's gaze returned to Ascot. "It's what I hope."

※

"There must be some around here somewhere," muttered Catch, hunting through the shelves above the cushioned alcove in his father's bedroom. An alabaster lion statuette caught his eye. Picking it up, he stared into its face, which wore an expression of suffering constipation nobly.

"Gildar," he said, and tossed it into the alcove.

It narrowly missed Moony. "Careful!" he cried, leaping up from the blue quilt.

"Sorry." Catch resumed searching.

"What are you looking for?" Moony groomed. His eyes crossed with the effort of trying to reach that spot in the middle of the chest that defied all but the most heroic tongue-efforts.

Catch opened the compartment concealed beneath the alcove. All of his father's furniture was wooden, deceptively simple and pragmatic at first appearance. The polished mahogany's warm color made a pleasing contrast to the cold, silvery walls, but once you found the first knife hidden under a chair cushion, you never sat with confidence again. "I'm looking for a Starthorne family sigil to give to Mistral. I'm sure my father must've kept some around."

The compartment contained a leather satchel. Opening it, Catch discovered a collection of some of his father's more interesting elixirs. He closed it before he became too intrigued. Lethe's old quarters consisted of three rooms in a small, northeasternly spire known as the Shardspire. A ladder built into the wall connected the bedroom with the sitting room and kitchen below.

"Can we start spying now?" Moony whined.

Catch shot him an annoyed glance. His ire melted away at the sight of Moony's huge, innocently blinking orange eyes. "How *do* you do that?" he grumbled.

"Secret kitty technique," replied Moony smugly. "You're not ready for it, Captain. Can we start spying now?"

A metallic yellow gleam from the top shelf caught Catch's attention. Investigating, he discovered several sigils etched on bronze disks, tucked behind a small vase filled with a powder that a cautious sniff revealed as the dried residue of a Laughing Death potion. *Father so loved his work*, thought Catch, plugging the vase with a lump of clay.

He held out one of the disks to Moony. "The city guards quarter in the southwestern spire. Mistral should be there. Give this to her. It'll allow her to act as my agent."

Moony tucked the disk under his unclipped wing. "Savotte might be in Watchspire, too," Catch added, reminded. "See if she'll take that thing off your wing."

"I'd appreciate that," said Moony, giving the clip a quick lick. "What are you going to do in the meantime, Captain?"

A chill draft stirred the green curtains around the window set in the eastern wall. Catch repressed a shudder at what was coming next. "I'll be having a private chat with Gildar."

Moony bounced up. "Ooh, you aren't going to challenge him to a duel, are you?"

Catch made an impatient noise. "We've been over that, remember? Beat Gildar, become Alph. I'd prefer bees."

"Would be dashing, though," Moony grumbled. "We'd better have one rooftop duel before this is over." He leaped off the cushion.

"Don't cause any mischief," said Catch as he jumped down into the sitting room.

"You're no fun, Captain," Moony called back. The front door squeaked open, then shut.

Alone, Catch stared at the window. The window stared back. Its sharply arched tip almost touched the high ceiling, like a brow raised in challenge. Catch clasped his hands until the suction pulled his palms together. He pulled them apart. Pressed. Pulled.

You're only stalling. Going to the window, he opened the latch and leaned out.

He swallowed. Hard. Cold air tugged his hair. A small shelf jutted from the window's base, just wide enough to step onto. Beneath it, the Aspire's slick, sloping, silvery-dark sides fell away, studded with spikes. There wasn't even a comforting glimpse of a garden below. This window overlooked the Roundgrounds. Night had fallen, but a few figures scuffled in the smaller arenas around its perimeter. Distance turned them beetle-sized.

Shuddering, Catch leaned out just far enough that he could see the great, semi-circular balcony thirty feet to his right and fifteen above. Gildar's chambers. Lamplight flickered through the balcony's glass doors, soft and golden.

Drawing back inside, Catch sank onto the cushion in the alcove. *The world spun behind his closed eyelids, alternating bright pink with dull gray...*Ascot never knew how much scaling Terruga Falls to look down into the great, foaming basin had cost him. She'd seen it as a great adventure. He'd wished he'd swallowed his damn pride and, like Rags-n-Bones, looked at the climb, said, "Nope. Too scary," and stayed happily ensconced at Tellomore Lodge at the base, drinking coffee—or, in Rags-n-Bones' case, eating avocados. And spoons.

He forced himself to stand. The wind, grown stronger, battered his hair about his ears as he leaned out the window and ran his fingers under the ledge's narrow lip. *It's been twenty-five years. Maybe it broke off, or someone discovered it and chiseled it—*

His thumb brushed a little knob, divided into three bumps, like the bud of some flower. He gritted his teeth. *All right, maybe it won't turn.*

It didn't. He actually started smiling before realizing he was twisting it the wrong way. He glanced at the softly lit balcony, took a breath, and twisted counterclockwise. The knob turned. As it did, a decorative spire located between this window and Gildar's balcony rotated. A faint tremor ran through the wall, as whatever hidden machinery that was required to pivot the spire churned away. The wind's unremitting wails drowned any scraping sounds.

With a faint chuff, the ornamental spire's base struck the ledge's underside. Its tip rested against the edge of Gildar's balcony, forming a narrow walkway. Now, all he had to do—

Catch sank to his knees. The solid floor swayed beneath him. *Get moving*, he ordered himself. The walkway would rotate back to its former position after seven minutes. He couldn't waste time.

Yes, I can, he thought rebelliously. He could take the lift to the next floor, knock on Gildar's door, and ask politely to be admitted. Except, Gildar might refuse, and even if he didn't, it would put Catch in the position of a supplicant. And while Lethe Starthorne might nod to Gildar Ambersun, he'd never kneel.

Sparing no time for further thought, Catch rose, swung out onto the ledge, and stepped onto the two-foot-wide walkway created by the rotated spire. The wind insinuated itself between his belly and the Aspire, pushing and tugging. Catch pressed as close as he could to the smooth, sour-smelling, maybe-metal wall and side-stepped along, inching his way up the slick incline. *Faster. Move faster.* How many minutes had elapsed? He kept fancying he heard a creak, felt a shiver under his feet. If it happened, he'd be gone. No handholds here. Only the screaming chasm. *I fell off the Roundgrounds once; maybe I could fall into them now.*

The wind tore away his mad chuckle.

There. The balcony, only a few feet ahead. Catch conquered the distance inch by inch, certain every second that the spire was about to twist back into place and slide him to his doom. The path thinned as the spire came to a point, forcing him to abandon the wall's comforting support.

He ran the last few feet and jumped, welcoming the twinge in his knees as he landed on the wonderful solidity of the balcony's red-and-gold tiled floor. While he crouched, trembling, waiting for the wind to dry his sweat, the ornamental spire gave one click and spun back upright. *No going back that way.* Catch smoothed his hair, ignoring the added, whispered thought: *not that I could force myself to return that way, anyway.*

He stood. The balcony, shaped like half a silver bowl protruding from the Aspire's side, was perhaps fifteen feet wide and seven deep. Plant-filled pots lined its walls, set on fancy, tiled benches. Catch inhaled the sour-sweet tang of a bitterseed orange tree, smiled at the cluster of bonfire lilies—his mother's favorite flower—and paused over a single terracotta planter containing a miniature custard peach tree. He barely stopped himself from plucking one of its tiny fruits.

On second thought, he didn't stop himself. Selecting the lushest of the thumb-sized peaches, he twisted it off its branch, slid open the glass balcony door, and sauntered into Gildar's private quarters.

Inside, everything blazed with a golden luster. *Gildar would've found Albright Castle's décor a trifle underdone,* Catch mused— although, thankfully, there were no cupids in evidence. A great, gilded mirror over the washstand reflected the flash of all the other shining objects. Cloth-of-gold drapes framed the patio doors. Golden velvet cushions gave the sleeping alcove a honeyed glow. A marble coffee table with gold scrolling down its legs stood in the room's far corner. Atop it sat a golden bowl containing fruit, including a couple full-sized custard peaches. Beside the table, settled in a gilded armchair with a glass of sunberry wine at his elbow, was Gildar, absorbed in a sheaf of papers.

Excellent. Gliding to the chair opposite Gildar, Catch took up an insolent, lounging position, dancing the tiny peach over his knuckles.

Gildar kept reading. Minutes passed. Catch's hand started aching. *Am I going to have to cough and attract his attention?* Resisting the impulse, he hooked his leg over the chair's arm for greater affront.

Gildar kept reading. Catch considered throwing the tiny peach at his head. *I'll count to a hundred. If he hasn't noticed me by then, I'll do it.*

Gildar kept reading. Catch counted. Slowly. He'd reached ninety-seven when Gildar set aside the papers, rubbed his eyes, and reached for his wine. Halfway through the gesture, he gave a great start and, unfortunately, didn't spill his wine.

Catch smiled, doing his best to make it look wicked and knowing instead of relieved. His hand was definitely cramping. "Good evening, Gildar."

"How—" Gildar's eyes darted around his vast room, as if expecting to find a newly chiseled hole in one of the walls.

Catch turned his little peach over, stroking its sides, soft as baby velvet. "I *am* my father's son." He touched a pocket. Let Gildar imagine a knife there; wonder if he hadn't considered taking certain measures.

Gildar did blanch. But a calculating expression swiftly hardened around it. "Your father's son. Yes. I've missed Lethe these many years."

Have you? Catch remembered the months before his…departure from Holdfast. Gildar and Lethe might've played at friendship, but their quarrels over whose son was the golden star seeped through the tightest-closed doors. They'd arranged that last, fatal Rising Tournament to end the debate for good and all. "How did he die?"

Gildar took up his wine. "Your disappearance unhinged him. A year after you vanished, he apparently jumped off Holdfast Plateau, almost exactly where you fell. We found a jaguar skeleton and a pouch containing his belongings some months later."

Father committed suicide? Catch spread his hand. The black pearl sucked in the oil lamp's yellow light greedily, only giving back the faintest, foggiest gleam. A brighter yellow flashed as Gildar lifted his glass. Glancing up, Catch noticed Gildar watching him over its rim.

Perhaps Father was murdered. The thought washed over Catch like a cold wave, soaking him from crown to toe. He'd convinced himself that the Hide Aways had slipped his father's ring onto Cavall's pendant, to lure them to the corral. But perhaps it represented Gildar's silent boast that he had killed both Lethe Starthorne and Arctic Cavall.

Catch's hand stilled. He'd loved his father. It was pitiful, it was stupid—possibly even straight-up wrong, morally speaking—but there it was. "How sad," he managed.

"I found it especially hard, coming so soon after Glim's death," said Gildar, setting his glass down with a click. His eyes met Catch's. *Your move*, they said.

My father's death—vengeance for his son's? "I had more flags, so Glim attacked me." Catch met that golden gaze steadily. "He threw me over the edge, but lost his balance and tumbled after."

What happened then was really quite startling. Gildar dropped his brow into his hand, pressing his closed eyelids. "Ah, my boy. I underestimated him."

Catch's heart slogged damply, like a collection of wet, squeezed tissue. He rolled the little peach between thumb and forefinger, silently apologizing to Glim's memory.

"Well, well," Gildar managed to produce one small tear. Wiping it away with the pad of his thumb, he leaned forward. "Glim had more of the true blood in him than I realized. Perhaps he would have been a fine Alph, in time."

Doubts welled again. There'd been little love between Glim and his father. Gildar had never made a secret of his disdain for Glim's quiet, scholarly nature. Difficult to imagine Gildar needing to avenge him.

"Why did you not return until now?" asked Gildar.

Catch had anticipated this question. "I hit my head when I fell. It gave me amnesia." It was *always* amnesia in the stories. Ascot would so approve. He stifled a snicker. "It was years before my memory fully returned. As for why now…" Shrugging, he settled deeper into his chair's lush upholstery, practically letting it swallow him. "I incurred a debt to the Shadowvalean I was traveling with. That little affair with the Muscatel."

"Or, it could've been fate," said Gildar.

A water clock by the door dripped away several seconds. Fate. *Destiny, providence, fortune.* The red fury Catch had quelled so often rose. Spinning his tiny peach, he fought it down yet again. *I am not a puppet.*

"Your father was quite interested in fate."

Catch answered with a brief, stiff nod. He knew, and did not wish to discuss it.

After a moment, Gildar shifted his weight. His chair's upholstery sushed as his rump slid over its velvet. "Lieutenant Savotte told me a wild story of some mishap in the Underway."

Of course she did. Stifling a sigh, Catch spoke the lie he'd prepared. "After we came upon that cave-in, she mistook the rumbling of snow falling off the peak for voices, or some such nonsense." He shrugged. "Horse-shifters are a skitterish bunch."

"Quite true." Gildar shook his head sadly and sipped wine. "They're not really fit for guard duty. Or, perhaps..." Catch lifted a brow, waiting. "Captain Cavall simply abandoned his duties, saying he was going to track the rebels?"

"Yes."

Gildar's frown deepened. "It may have been a subterfuge. He could've crept ahead and caused the collapse in the Underway. They had plenty of time to scheme with the rogue alchemist, Porpetti, in Widget. They could've been planning this all winter."

Oh, that's a nice lie, Gildar, thought Catch. It had just enough shine of the possible about it to allow it to pass for truth. "That's feasible," he said, and threw out a little bait, watching Gildar covertly. "Cavall's father was a known slipskin."

Gildar's shoulders relaxed a trifle. "Exactly." Picking up the carafe, he refilled his wineglass. "In any case, Lieutenant Savotte cannot be allowed to alarm the populace with her lies."

"So send her away," said Catch.

"That wouldn't stop her mouth. No, a more permanent solution is needed." Gildar ran a finger around his glass's rim. "Are you truly your father's son?"

A bead of juice seeped over Catch's thumb. He softened his grip on the little peach. *Oh, hopefully I missed out on a few of Father's traits: the lack of empathy, the attention span of a distracted gnat, and the notion that killing people is a great way to settle a debate.*

Gildar flicked a nail against his glass. "Even if you're the golden star, you have no control over what happens on the Moonless Night."

There. Catch seized on the tiny emphasis: *you have no control. I do.* Catch's attention was suddenly drawn to the mantle over Gildar's shoulders; crimson red, embroidered with golden suns. *Everyone thought Glim and I were the only candidates for the prophecy. But with some careful marketing, Gildar looks like a viable third.*

"But as for what comes after the Moonless Night—" Gildar continued.

"You want Rainy Savotte dead," said Catch brightly. "Consider it done."

If there'd been any justice in the world, Gildar would have spat out the sip of wine he'd just taken, but he managed to swallow without choking. "Good man," he said, only slightly red in the face. "I believe in making your own fate."

"Oh, indeed," replied Catch. "You so rarely get what you deserve when you trust to any other."

If Gildar felt the jab, he let it pass. Draining his wine, he stood and offered his hand, as if he had called the meeting and therefor had the right to end it. "Accomplish it before the end of Yawning Day."

Catch stood, too, but not before swapping his tiny, mauled peach for one of the regular-sized ones. He relished Gildar's fleeting scowl. "Just Lieutenant Savotte, or shall I deal similarly with her partner?" he asked, ignoring Gildar's hand.

"Mm." Brows raised, Gildar gave Catch a thorough appraisal. "Perhaps you truly are your father's son. You have his eyes." Sitting, he shuffled his papers. "Cavall as well. I trust you can exit the same way you entered?"

"I could," Catch lied smoothly. "But I don't care to." Biting into the peach, he sauntered out the front door, startling the guard patrolling the corridor outside. "I was just reading Gildar a bedtime story," he said, waving airily. "He never tires of 'The Princess and the Pea.'"

The guard slapped a hand over her mouth. Her shoulders shook.

It's the little things in life you treasure. Catch's own smile dropped off his face as he made his way back to his father's chambers. So, the fake tengu were part of Gildar's plans to get himself named the golden star—and from there, Alph eternal.

And me? Does he just want me to be a more pliable version of Lethe? Catch wondered, opening the door to his father's chambers. It made some sense. Not everyone would be pleased about Gildar being declared Alph eternal. Some mouths would have to be stopped.

Starting with Savotte and Cavall, he thought, lighting the oil lamp on the table just inside the door. *Well, at least Cavall's a dog—he might be good at playing dead.* Catch started to laugh, broke it off, and rubbed his eyes.

He was more tired than he realized. Only after the scrape of the match and soft crackle of the little flame broke the silence did he notice the room wasn't entirely silent after all. Someone close at hand was breathing—rather loudly, in fact.

He turned too late. Two hands, roughly the size of melons, seized him by the collar. "I'll show you how we treat traitors in Holdfast!" cried Bandersnatch.

CHAPTER NINETEEN:
HIDDEN AWAY

"You don't want to do this." Catch spoke calmly. No matter your personal discomfort, you want to speak calmly to the person who is currently dangling you by your ankles out of a window located a hundred feet up the side of a miniature mountain. Agitated people are more likely to drop things.

"Yes, I do," Bandersnatch replied with absolute certainty.

Blood pounded in Catch's ears, almost drowning out his thoughts. The darkness should have been a blessing, concealing exactly how much distance there was between him and the ground, but, somehow, he could feel every inch of empty space reaching for him. *Can you throw up when you're upside-down?* He wasn't eager to attempt the experiment.

The wind tore at his hair and coat. Even knowing it would be disastrous, the urge to thrash and kick was almost overwhelming. "I'm the golden star. If you drop me, the tengu will kill you all," Catch called.

"The golden star's supposed to fall," said Bandersnatch. Catch couldn't see his face, but would've bet the promise of solid ground that he was grinning ear-to-ear in stupid, happy malice. "Let's see you rise from *this*."

Bandersnatch's grip on his ankles slipped, just a little. Blind, white panic engulfed Catch. He tried to fold himself in half; climb Bandersnatch's arms. "I already fell, for—"

"What are you doing?" shrieked Mistral. "Haul him in!"

The wind's howls half obliterated her words. Almost, Catch believed he'd imagined this rescue. But seconds later—long seconds, agonizing seconds—the pressure on his ankles shifted. First the backs of his legs, then his rump, bumped over the window's lip. Bandersnatch flung him to the floor, rattling him from tailbone to crown. The wind's after-whine shrilled in his head.

Slowly, he uncurled. He began to thank Bandersnatch, but stopped himself in time. "Not my usual way of taking the air before bedtime, but refreshing all the same," he said, rubbing his ears.

Bandersnatch wasn't even looking at him. "What are you doing here, cadet?" he growled at Mistral, who faced him defiantly, gripping her sword's hilt.

"She's in my service." Catch stood. "You, however, can leave now." Opening the door, he made a gesture as of shooing out an annoying fly. "Go on, or I'll have her poke you full of holes."

Booming a laugh, Bandersnatch folded his arms. "Getting a cub to fight your battles, Starthorne?"

"You're not worth his effort," said Mistral. "He could swat you without blinking."

Bandersnatch rounded on her. "I just grabbed him up and swung him out a window without raising a sweat! Without raising a drop of sweat on a single hair under one of my arms!"

Thank you, Bandersnatch, I didn't require so visual a detail. Giving up on Bandersnatch leaving any time soon, Catch dragged himself to a chair and plopped into it, hoping a secreted knife didn't skewer his rump.

Bandersnatch stamped about, shaking the floor. Furniture rattled. "I could break him in half easy as…as breaking wind." Metaphors were clearly not his forte. "I could rip his false hide from his body."

"False hide?" Mistral bristled. "Are you calling him a slipskin?" Catch stopped surreptitiously feeling the cushion for hidden blades and peered at Bandersnatch. In Holdfast, "slipskin" was a killing insult; no metaphor.

Bandersnatch didn't back down. "Yes. I am. Slipskin." Folding his arms, he threw the word at Catch with all the maturity of a cub hurling a clot of mud.

Mistral gasped, paling. Slowly, she turned to Catch. "I...he accused you before a witness, sir. You can't just ignore it."

Half-listening, Catch studied Bandersnatch under his hair. Bandersnatch's scowl was too broad, his stomps a bit too emphatic. Most people were bad actors, but Bandersnatch seemed to be a bad actor in the very specific way of a person ordered to play a part he would've rather refused.

"Of course I can't ignore it," Catch replied. "A challenge, then."

Bandersnatch's eyes, the green of grapes, lit. "You mean, you'll fight me?" He sounded surprised.

Catch shrugged. "Certainly."

"That's the style." Grinning broadly, Bandersnatch bounced on the balls of his feet, limbering up. The pops of his enormous muscles were astoundingly loud.

Catch held up a hand as Bandersnatch took up a fighting stance. "Not here. We'll do it properly, in the arena."

If he'd made Bandersnatch any happier, he'd have floated straight through the ceiling, like Artful Prince Alec after being dosed with the Moonlight Muscatel. "Tomorrow?" he asked, his grin now wide enough to make a second continent of his large chin. "How about eleven o'clock in the Half-walled Arena?"

Catch inclined his head. "See you there."

"You're a better man than I thought, Starthorne." Bandersnatch shook his offered hand and bounded out. "I'm going to go train." The door clicked shut behind him.

Sinking back into his chair, Catch exhaled a long hiss of breath between pursed lips. "Thank you for interrupting before he dropped me," he told Mistral.

She shook her head twice, slowly. "What was that about?"

How far to trust her? Catch scratched his cheek. Savotte said she hadn't wanted to be a guard. *Chance it*, he decided. "I believe he was following Gildar's orders."

"Why—oh." Her widened eyes narrowed. "Because otherwise, Bandersnatch might've challenged *him* tomorrow. What a dirty scheme."

Catch raised a palm. That was one favorable outcome. Gildar might also want to see him fight, to see how he compared to Lethe.

Or, possibly, he'd really hoped Bandersnatch would drop him out the window.

Mistral fussed about the room, straightening furniture and repositioning ornaments in their alcoves with angry clatters. "I suppose if you'd fought now, Gildar was counting on Bandy being too beaten up to challenge him tomorrow."

Catch winced. "Don't call him Bandy."

Her chin rose. "Too disrespectful?"

"Too precious. Like tying a pink bow around a Cerberus's neck and calling it 'poochie.'"

Her scowl melted. Stooping, she retrieved his peach from the chair it had rolled under when Bandersnatch grabbed him. "Here's your custard peach, sir," she said, holding it out.

"Where's Moony?" asked Catch, accepting it. He was lifting it to his mouth when it struck him.

Looking down, Mistral dug her toe into the thick, white rug. "I, uh, didn't see Moony."

"Then how did you get up here unchallenged?" he asked, the peach poised halfway to his mouth. She kept twisting her toe deeper into the rug. Catch lowered the peach. "How did you know this was a custard peach?" Her father hadn't been able to recognize one.

Mistral glanced up. Her black hair was cropped too short to peer through it, but her thick lashes provided much the same effect. Reaching into her sleeve, she pulled out an oval, coppery pit. "Tigers have no spots."

The words sank into Catch's brain. His memory folded around them, leaving a maddening little knot that hid any actual revelations. "Actually, in my saber-toothed tiger form, I do have spots," he said, frowning. "Cream-colored ones, on my back and rump." He chomped into the peach, savoring its almost offensively rich flavor. Its aftertaste lingered like a shot of brandy.

Mistral sagged slightly. She held the pit higher, turning it so the lamplight threw coppery glints off its surface. "Where did you get that?" Catch asked, mouth full.

"Around," she replied, avoiding his eyes.

Such an adolescent answer. Catch took another bite of peach. *Tigers have no spots.* And why was she holding it up so significantly?

"Fur and fangs." He closed his eyes. Custard peach trees only grew in two places, and one held particular meaning for a certain group. "You're with the Hide Aways."

She broke into a grin. Answer enough. Catch stared at the rug. He remembered that sweep of soft, cream-colored wool stretched vividly across the cold, maybe-metallic floor. He'd fallen asleep on it, nestled against his father's side. If he searched, he could probably find black hairs from his father's coat embedded in it. *Tigers have no spots.* "Cavall's daughter, a slipskin rebel."

"I never wanted to be a guard," she flared, hands balling into fists. Catch suspected that, in her mind, she faced a taller person, dressed in black leather. "It's *boring*, watching the Underway's gates. Why should that be my whole life, just because I'm a hound-shifter? And my nanny, he wanted to be a doctor, but—"

She reminded him of Lindsay Ashuren and her tirade against Widget. "I know." Getting up, Catch put an arm around her shoulders. It's—"

His stomach dropped. "And leopards no stripes."

Mistral spun. "I knew it," she crowed. "You're a Hide Away, too. You were just testing me, weren't you?"

"Testing you. Yes," said Catch. His lips felt numb. *Tigers have no spots, and leopards no stripes.* The first two lines of a lullaby his father used to sing to him, curled on this very rug. A lullaby the Hide Aways were using as a password. *A ring, a pendant, and a custard peach pit...* Catch's head spun. Just when he'd convinced himself that that was Gildar's doing, the evidence spun the other way. Or, had Gildar killed both Lethe and Arctic for being Hide Aways?

"Did I pass?" Mistral jogged his arm, interrupting his thoughts. "You have some plan, right? To bring down Gildar on the Moonless Night?"

Just for spite and my father to requite. Catch bit deliberately into his cheek. He was not going to switch synonyms for rhymes. *Poems, verses, jingles. Better.*

Then again, if Gildar had killed his father, Catch *would* see him regret it. "You passed," he told Mistral. She was owed some vengeance for her grandfather, after all.

Mistral practically skipped to the door. "I'll bring you breakfast before your bout with Bandy. You can beat him, right?"

"Don't call him—" Catch blew a lock of hair out of his eyes, giving up an already lost battle. "It's under control." A few drops of one of his father's concoctions, and the only fighting Bandersnatch would be doing for a while would be wrestling aside people who tried to enter the privy ahead of him. "Get my sigil from Moony before you come up here again."

"Will do. Goodnight, sir," said Mistral.

"Wait." Catch's weary brain spat up a fresh question as she opened the door. "How did you sneak up here in the first place?"

Her grin was a masterpiece of adolescent smugness. "I have many tricks, sir. You don't know the half of them." She slipped out before he could press her, shutting the door behind her.

Catch slumped in his chair. "And neither does your father, I'd wager."

Fathers…In the darkness, the white rug almost glowed. Catch sat staring at it a long time, his father's voice singing softly in his memories.

Tigers have no spots,
And leopards no stripes,
Daggers no teeth,
But beware their bite.

Hawks don't have horns,
And bulls have no wings,
Poison is fangless,
But watch for its sting.

Wherever you lack,
Learn to contrive.
Harbor your secrets,
And you'll long survive.

We sleep to awaken
'Til we sleep in death,
Beginning and ending
In every soft breath.

CHAPTER TWENTY:
COMPETITIVE NATURE

Merryvick smelled of honey. *Catch would hate that*, thought Ascot. He hated anything bee-related, ever since one had killed his friend, King Alastor. Even glowered at beeswax candles.

Catch. Asassin's son. Friend, killed. Killed friend. Stop that. She looked around. Actually, Merryvick's general shape reminded her of a honeycomb, with its rounded, yellow clay houses lining the canyon walls. Crowds of people, both human and animal-shaped, filled its single street. Many wore flowers braided into their hair, or garlands around their necks. Colorful banners proclaiming "Yawning Day!" swayed overhead, interwoven with more blossoms, and leafy twigs. Ascot stepped on one of the tattered-looking, mauve flowers growing flat against the hard-packed ground, and it broke with a soft crunch, bringing a fresh honey waft to her nostrils. Rags-n-Bones sneezed.

"Sorry," she said.

"It's all right, miss." He wiped his nose. "Should I transform now?" He looked hopefully at Dmitri, mincing in fennec-form nearby. One of Dmitri's oversized ears kept flapping, but even that was adorable, much to his evident disgust.

Frabjacket, she'd hoped Rags-n-Bones had gotten past that obsession. "You need to carry the Seersee fragments."

He tugged at his muffler. "I could carry them in my mouth. They wouldn't mind," he muttered. It was the nearest he'd ever come to pouting.

Ascot tried another tactic. "Besides, you can't talk in dog-form without rousing suspicion." Another huge sticking point for Dmitri, who could no longer dispense the advice he adored giving. *Of course he could overcome that problem by transforming into human form, instead of fennec.*

Rags-n-Bones poked a finger through his muffler's weave. He even thrust out his lower lip a little. What was going on in his head? "Rags," Ascot began.

Jolt pushed through the crowd, a kind of contained excitement in his manner. "Bellmonte has some news," he said, pointing to a bronze sundial set atop three tiered, square chunks of clay placed in the street's center. Both Starley and Bellmonte stood before it, gesticulating. Condorella hovered between them.

"All right." Taking Rags-n-Bones' arm, she followed Jolt over to the sundial, dodging around a man carrying a pole covered in tiny cages containing butterflies. Dmitri minced behind them, growling softly every time his ears flapped.

Condorella started speaking the moment they approached. "They just announced the prizes for this year's Rising Tournaments," she said, in high glee, waving her staff. She'd once again wrapped straw around the crystal to disguise it.

Ascot repressed a sigh. *You honestly think carrying a broom around is less suspicious than what could be taken for a fancy walking stick?* "That's that flag hunt you told me about this morning, right?" she asked Starley.

"Exactly," he said, removing his bandana and running a hand over his hair. He twisted the length of red cloth between his hands. "This year, the top two winners from each tournament win entry to a masked ball that will be held in Holdfast on the Moonless Night."

"And the two runners-up get to serve at the ball," added

Bellmonte.

"You mean, if we win, we can enter Holdfast—go straight to where Moony and Catch are?" asked Ascot.

"Right into the Roundgrounds—containing the last Seersees!" cried Condorella, waving her staff/broom and nearly clouting a passing shifter in the nose.

"Exactly." Starley retied his mauled bandana. "If we can transfer the broken Seersee's image into the ones there, everyone present will learn the truth about Rune."

Ascot was hardly listening. *Moony. Catch.* As the golden star, Catch was sure to be at the ball. And Moony would never miss a party, with all the opportunities for mischief. Perhaps while everyone was watching the Seersees, they could sneak away.

Or jump off the plateau. Frabjacket, where did such venomous little thoughts come from? This one popped the bubble of her freshly rising spirit.

"I'm in," she said, kicking it aside. She'd always done well at the annual Bat Hunt back in Shadowvale, and that required much clambering around in caves, and the little critters were very quick. *Of course Vincent always nicked my bats and took all the credit afterwards.*

"I only managed to obtain four entry tokens," said Bellmonte, producing several leathery, orange disks.

Condorella snatched one so quickly her fingers blurred. "You need me to transfer the image."

Ascot stared at the remaining three. *One for me, one for Dmitri, one for Rags...* if only she could be so selfish. Sighing, she took one. "You and Jolt can have those."

"Eh." Starley rubbed his neck. "Actually—"

"I'm not eligible." Jolt flicked his branded cheek. "Ferals aren't. Help yourself. I'm going to get some coffee."

"Ferals?" asked Ascot, but, wrapping his mantle about his shoulders, Jolt stalked off.

Ascot was left staring at Starley. "Unusual shifters," he explained.

"Shifters without status. Hmm…" He stared at the sky. "I think most societies would call them 'slaves.'" Taking the last two tokens from Bellmonte, he handed one to Ascot. "The competition starts in fifteen minutes." He walked off after Jolt.

Slaves. Ascot picked at the tokens. A bitter-tart smell came off them, clinging to her fingers. Bellmonte gave her a sympathetic look. "Do you want one?" she asked.

He spread his hands. "Cows aren't particularly nimble. Besides, there's someone I need to speak to." He moved off, leaving Ascot with Rags-n-Bones and Dmitri.

"Fyodor," said Dmitri. With a *pop*, he rose on two bare, human legs. He grimaced, but it swiftly passed. "I'll take the second token."

Ascot stared at him. Perhaps his illusory human face didn't translate his wolf expressions very well, but she couldn't guess his thoughts. Whatever they were, they were dark enough for him to take on his hated, human shape.

"I'm making amends," he said softly.

His supposed wrongs of the past. His expression begged her not to ask. "Can you manage, without hands?" she asked, holding out a token.

"I've managed very well without hands," he replied, a little tartly. "Alyosha." Popping into fennec form, he took the disk between his jaws and trotted off, left ear flapping.

They should really sew an image of him in plush, Ascot thought.

"Do you like him better as a fox?" asked Rags-n-Bones.

Starting, Ascot turned to see him watching her closely. "No. He's adorable that way, but Dmitri is a wolf."

Rags-n-Bones plucked his chin. "Biscuit."

"Oh, no!" she cried, but he was already sprouting rust-colored fur. Pricking his crooked ears, he jumped about, unbalancing the dozing Nipper, who toppled off Rags-n-Bones' shoulder with a squeak even Ascot recognized as indignant. "Why is everyone acting so oddly?" she demanded, picking him up as Rags-n-Bones bounded away.

Nipper, thankfully, behaved perfectly in character, glaring at her pop-eyed and squirming furiously. Ascot released him next to the sundial and studied the shadows across its surface. Its lines and numbers made no sense to her, but then, no Shadowvalean ever considered telling time by the position of the *sun*.

Another shadow fell over its surface. Ascot lifted her gaze to the even blacker object that cast it, clad neck-to-toe in gleaming leather. "Cavall," she breathed as his blue eyes met hers. He held a steaming mug of something undoubtedly bitter as ground wasps. She quickly pinched herself. "What are you doing here? You promised."

Strangely, Cavall looked hurt. The expression sat oddly on his thin, sharp-angled face. "Am I screaming for your arrest?" He glanced around. "Still with the weasel?"

"That's *stoat!*" cried Starley from twenty feet away, and began pushing furiously through the crowd, Jolt at his heels.

Ascot flung up her hands. "How the *frabjacket* did he hear that?"

"Leather-britches," said Starley, coming up and jutting his chin at Cavall. "Can't get your nose out of our arses, I see."

Cavall swirled his coffee. Little flecks of spice danced on its dark surface. "I didn't come here because of you. I—"

Starley rolled his eyes. "Yadda, yadda, right, it's about the price of cheese on the moon. Fine, why are you here, leather-britches?"

In reply, Cavall flicked his index and middle fingers. Like a magic trick, a leathery orange, bitter-tart-smelling disk appeared between them.

"Ticks and fleas." Jolt slumped against Starley. "He's a competitor."

The word echoed mockingly in Ascot's head. *Contestant, challenger, opponent.*

"Eh, he's a promise-breaker," said Starley. "No matter. I can beat him without breaking a sweat." Turning away, he folded his arms.

A moonstone pendant hung around Cavall's neck, teardrop-shaped, gleaming milky blue. She remembered seeing it in

Highmoor. "Is this about your father?" It had to be something important, something he needed to confront Gildar formally about.

Cavall touched the pendant. "It's about family." His gaze seemed vacant, but when Ascot followed it, her eyes landed on Bellmonte, leaning against a pole wrapped in yellow blossoms. "Someone reminded me that it's possible to get so caught up in the past that you neglect the present."

A horn sounded in the distance. Cavall drained his coffee in a series of long gulps and handed the empty mug to Starley. "That's our cue. See you in the arena, weasel." He strode off.

"That's sto—oh, forget it." Starley hurled the mug at Cavall's head.

Jolt caught it—it was going to miss by feet anyway—and gave Starley a push. "Get moving," he said as the crowds around the vendors' stands began ambling eastwards.

Following the shine of Cavall's black leather, easily glimpsed through the flower-clad revelers, Ascot reached an arena that had been created by the simple act of erecting two woven twig fences to the west and east, enclosing a slightly rounded section of the canyon. The rocky grounds included a splendid, twisted juniper with ropes hanging off its branches, and two good-sized cedars with a fragile-looking rope bridge swinging between them. Small caverns pocked the canyon walls, with ramshackle ladders propped nearby. Strewn through it all were lengths of bright orange silk.

"Contestants, here," called a green-jacketed official perched on a thick post by the arena's gate. She indicated a cordoned-off area. Dmitri, Condorella, and Cavall already stood inside. Another official collected the orange tokens and distributed lengths of knotted cord. Meanwhile, a crowd of onlookers gathered around the fence, climbed trees, or claimed seats on a boulder overlooking the arena.

Ascot bumped elbows with another contestant as she entered the cordoned area. "Sorry," she apologized, looking away. The boy she'd collided with was young, pudgy, nervous, and completely naked.

Looking away was no good. Cloth rustled around her as the contestants not already bare began disrobing.

"Strip," said Jolt, standing just outside the cordoned area. "You'll be targeted if you don't. It's like a boast: 'I can beat you without shifting.'"

"Condorella's not—" Ascot began.

A smug smile from Condorella cut her off. "*Voluptu expose.*" She made a small, twisting gesture. Her clothing shimmered and vanished.

"That is *not* your real body," Ascot whispered furiously, glaring at the far-too-voluptuous and pearl-skinned figure beside her.

Condorella sniffed. "Reality is in the eye of the beholder, my dear."

And being clothed in illusion was not the same as public nudity. Slowly, Ascot undid her blouse's top button. Her second button caught a ray of sunlight, as if winking at her. She stared back at it.

"What are you waiting for, Starley?" asked Jolt.

Ascot looked up. Starley was still dressed, arms folded across his chest, the wind flapping the tails of his faded red coat. "He's not undressing," said Starley, nodding toward Cavall. Cavall smiled back, insolently.

Jolt sighed. "Ignore him, he's taunting you."

Starley's chin lifted higher. "It's too sunny. I'll burn." To emphasize the point, he took out his jar of balm.

Jolt growled—apparently all shifters were prone to that particular silliness in human-form. Tugging his ear, he turned to Ascot.

"I'll burn, too," she said. What a wonderful excuse! "Noble Shadowvaleans burn very easily." Besides, if Rags-n-Bones saw her without clothes, there was every possibility he'd simply explode. *Rags-n-Bones.* She sighed. *Probably off barking and sniffing feet.*

"I give up." Jolt took out a licorice root.

The head official clapped her hands. "Competitors," she announced. "Fifty flags are scattered around the arena. You have half an hour to collect them. "After twenty-five minutes, I will blow two short bursts on the horn. You may exit through the gate at that time, if you wish. If you leave the arena before I blow the two blasts, you will be disqualified. If you haven't left by the time I blow the final blast at thirty minutes, you will be disqualified. The top two contestants win invitations to Alph Gildar's ball, while the third and fourth place finishers will be allowed to serve there—which is a great honor," she added cajolingly.

The gathered crowd muttered. Several leaned over the fence, rubbing their hands in anticipation. Pretending she wasn't disconcerted, Ascot examined the red cord she'd been handed. Each knot held a small hook.

"It's an alchemic cord that expands or contracts as you shift," Jolt explained in an undertone. "You hook the flags into it."

"I see," said Ascot. Running around naked did mean forgoing pockets. After looping the cord over her shoulder, she helped Dmitri arrange his across his back.

Condorella bumped her with a sharp elbow. "Get ready," she said, tossing her hair. It had changed along with her body, growing long, lustrous, and richly red. Actually, her current form reminded Ascot of Tanya Roebanks, from Albright.

"And if you must nobble someone, go for that bloke there." Starley canted his head toward the pudgy youth Ascot had bumped into. "Beaver-shifter. Nearly bit Fairflax's leg off last year."

"Nobble someone? *Bit?*" Ascot took in the thirty or so people crammed inside the cordoned area. The sunlight found Cavall's black leather and made it gleam. "Is this a flag-hunt, or a battle?"

Starley grinned. "You're in the Clawcrags, love. It's sometimes hard to tell."

The official put the horn to her lips.

CHAPTER TWENTY-ONE:
CAT FIGHT

The door flung open, smacking the wall with a bang. Catch leaped off the rug, and possibly out of his skin. Landing in a fighting crouch, he bared his teeth.

"What's this I hear about you getting into a duel, Captain?" demanded a small, raspy voice.

Mistral and Moony stood in the doorway. Mistral carried a silver pot and covered plate. Slowly, Catch's shoulders came down. "Good morning to you, too," he grumped, running a hand through his hair. A bit of white lint clung to his cheek. Mange, he'd slept on the damned rug. He brightened when he sniffed the air. Coffee. Mistral had brought coffee. *What a fine girl she is.*

"Well, Captain?" Fur crackling, Moony advanced into the sitting room with as much menace as a tiny cat could muster. "You said you wouldn't."

Stepping over him, Catch headed for Mistral. "Technically, I only promised not to duel Gildar," he said, swiping the pot and going to the kitchen. "There is, beside, the little matter of you knowing full well that I lie."

"Oh, foo." Deflating, Moony licked a paw. "I'd forgotten that."

"You lie?" said Mistral with deep disapproval.

"Only as a hobby," he replied, finding a sturdy mug with thick drops of green glaze frozen down its sides. He poured it full of coffee, set down the pot, and fixed her with a stare. "And I think you've lost the moral high ground, Miss Secrets."

Ducking her head, Mistral set the plate down onto the counter. "Honored to serve you, sir."

A show of subservience. Nice tactic, but it won't work. Sipping coffee, he lifted the plate's cover to reveal smoked fish mixed with scrambled eggs, fried cicadas, and two berry-studded buckwheat cakes. *It's been ages since I've seen a Clawcrags breakfast.*

He didn't get to see it long. Moony jumped onto the table, stuck his face in the eggs, and began smacking up bites of fish. "What did you learn last night, Captain?"

Catch snatched a cicada before Moony engulfed all of his breakfast. "That Cavall's daughter is a slipskin rebel."

Mistral threw him a reproachful look and tried to scoop up Moony. He pivoted expertly, keeping his rump pointed at her while his gobbling mouth remained centered on the plate. Mistral gave up. "We'd better hurry, sir. It's almost eleven."

The cicada dropped from Catch's fingers. "Almost eleven?" Bells in the Timespire rang to proclaim the hour, but clearly he'd slept through them.

"Half past ten," Mistral affirmed.

Catch wasted seconds staring before bolting toward the bedroom. Thinking the better of it halfway there, he turned back, chugged his coffee, and poured himself a second cup. *Then* he ran for the ladder. A minute's rummaging through the satchel under the alcove located the vial he wanted. He tucked it in his sleeve and was down the ladder again in seconds. Back in the kitchen, he gulped the second cup of coffee and crammed a cicada into his mouth.

"Let's get going," he said, chewing.

Moony finished the eggs, licked a paw, and rubbed it over his muzzle—just to show he was in no hurry—before jumping onto

Catch's shoulder. Catch frowned at the alchemic clip, still clinging tick-like to Moony's right wing. "Couldn't you find Savotte?" he asked, opening the door.

"I forgot, in last night's excitement," said Mistral, loping after him. "She wants to talk to you. She had an interview with Alph Gildar last evening. She came out of it stomping and saying your name like a curse."

"I have that effect on people." She'd probably intended to show Gildar the feather, and found it missing. "I'll speak with her after this Bandersnatch nonsense," he said, barreling down the squat Plainspire's winding steps. Sunlight slanted in through narrow window slits, striking viciously bright glints off the metallic walls.

"She might be in the garden, with the others," said Mistral.

"What do you mean, 'with the others'?" asked Catch, reaching the narrow corridor at the Plainspire's base. Did he hear voices? He walked slowly to Midspire, located at the Aspire's rear. A set of wide, shallow steps, carved from the same maybe-metal as the rest of the place, led to a topiary garden bordering the Roundgrounds.

"Why, all the guards," Mistral gestured to the small corridor waiting at the step's bottom, like a pursed mouth. "And servants. The Pack. Students."

Catch took a fortifying breath. "So, basically, everyone in the Aspire?"

Moony and Mistral looked at each other. "Everyone, you think?" said Mistral.

Moony nodded. "Everyone." Hopping off Catch's shoulder, he scampered down the steps. "Come on, Captain. You don't want to be late."

No, I certainly don't, if you mean "deceased," "departed," or "dead." The first steadying breath hadn't helped much, but Catch took another before descending the stairs. Their treads dipped in the center through centuries of wear. Moony preceded him like a herald, tail curved jauntily over his back while Mistral hovered by his side, hand on sword.

Put her in black leather, and she'd be the image of her father, thought Catch, stepping out of the dark corridor into blue skies and sunlight. As he raised an arm to shield his eyes, the general babble faded.

"The golden star," someone whispered.

Catch squinted, and the blobby green clump before him sharpened into a topiary lion, lying on its side. It gave the impression of watching him lazily. Beyond it stood the people. The *crowds* of people, leaning against the railings of the small training arenas surrounding the great, squashed-circle expanse of the Roundgrounds, or sipping coffee in the shade of some beast-shaped bush. Some wore red-cuffed guard uniforms, others, the double-tailed blue coat of an Aspire servant. Still others, by their embroidered mantles and lounging postures, could be pegged as members of Holdfast's elite. Flowers strewed the ground and banners snapped overhead in celebration of Yawning Day.

"Wow, look at all the people!" cried Moony, puffing out his chest. "Can I act as your second?"

Catch stopped himself before he tried to smooth down his cowlick. "Certainly." Crackling excitedly, Moony bounded toward the Half-walled Arena. Bandersnatch was already inside it, going through some stretching exercises.

"Starthorne!" cried a familiar, dulcet voice. Gunmetal hair gleamed like a stormcloud.

She does say it like a curse, thought Catch as Savotte approached. He let her grab his arm and, ignoring the crowd's curious murmurs, drag him to a far corner, under the shelter of a topiary eagle's wing.

Her mouth opened.

"You informed Gildar of the false tengu and he pretended not to believe you," said Catch.

She let out an angry huff. "You picked my pocket with the feather, didn't you? That was my only proof."

Catch scratched his cheek. "What did it prove?"

"It proved I wasn't scared by the mountain rumbling," she said, slamming her fists on her hips. "That feather's peculiar. Maybe it's alchemic, but it might be something else." Her voice rose. "Either way, Gildar must see it."

No, thought Catch instantly. It was as final as some door slamming inside him. If the feather was…something else, he and Gildar could face the Moonless Night together, and let chance decide the golden star—because that was the only way to snatch choice from the situation; to be a man, not a puppet.

Gildar would likely dismiss the feather as a trick, anyway. Catch peered under the eagle's wing. Despite Mistral's efforts, the crowd was growing restless. "You might be right about the feather," he told Savotte, digging in a pocket. He brought out a loosely closed fist and offered it to her. She reached forward, then jerked back with a cry when he scratched the soft skin under her wrist.

"What did—" Her eyes clouded.

Catch shook the drop of clear liquid off his father's ring. "Must brew more of that stuff," he muttered, grabbing Savotte's shoulders as she sagged. He stretched her along the grass. Even unconscious, she looked reproachful. "You'll thank me for it in the end."

Dipping under the eagle's wing, he waved to the nearest peacock-shifter. "She swooned suddenly. Fetch help."

He rejoined Mistral. "What happened?" she whispered, watching a flock of peacock-shifters tend to Savotte.

"I had to kill your Auntie Savotte," he replied out of the corner of his mouth, walking toward the Half-walled arena. She gasped. "Don't worry; she'll get better. We'll have to keep the vultures from eating her later."

She leaned closer, glaring the onlookers back. "Gildar?" she murmured.

"Yes. She saw something she shouldn't have."

Mistral's lips, fuller than her father's, pulled tight. A petal came fluttering down from a banner above and landed in her hair. She swept it off with a quick, brusque motion. "I know a vulture-shifter," she whispered. "We'll go see him after you beat up Bandy."

Catch stopped. "Beat up Bandersnatch?" Why'd she say it so confidently?

Oh, right. Because last night he'd implied he could do exactly that. But last night, he'd expected the challenge to be a private affair. Now, with so many watching, if he gave Bandersnatch dosed coffee, someone would be smart enough to connect it to Bandersnatch's sudden need for the privy.

Maybe I should drink it myself, he thought, feeling the weight of the little vial in his pocket.

Mistral tugged his sleeve. "Sir, the Alph's beckoning you over." She pointed to a row of benches arranged before the Half-walled Arena. Gildar, dressed in resplendent golden velvet, his red mantle blazing over his shoulders, sat with six Pack members; all blond and heavy-browed, like him.

"All lion-shifters," whispered Mistral as Gildar rose and strolled over, teeth displayed in a lazy smile not unlike the topiary lion's. "He wants to make it law that only they can lead."

Another change. Quickly schooling his frown into a blander expression, Catch bowed as Gildar stopped before him. "Alph."

"Has Lieutenant Savotte suffered an indisposition?" asked Gilder, failing at an expression of concern.

"Sadly, yes," Catch replied. "Perhaps we should cancel the forthcoming challenge, out of respect."

"Nonsense. She was only a horse-shifter. Besides, duels are a Yawning Day tradition. Mustn't disappoint the audience." He gave a paternal chuckle, clapped Catch's shoulder, and strode back to the bench.

No surprise there. Catch blew a lock of hair out of his eyes. Bandersnatch was so keyed up, Gildar probably feared he'd immediately challenge him, if deprived of his duel with Catch.

"Everyone's ready to begin," said Mistral, walking him toward the

Half-walled Arena. Moony sniffed about its interior.

"By all means, begin without me," said Catch, staring with glazed fascination at the flexing Bandersnatch. "Bones and blood, I think he grew overnight. Is that possible?"

Bandersnatch heard them approaching. His face lit up. Bounding over, he leaped the railing without breaking stride, eliciting "oohs" from the spectators. Catch smothered a mad laugh.

"Commander Falxus, your challenger has arrived," said Mistral, pushing Catch face-to-face with Bandersnatch—or, more correctly, face-to-chest.

Bandersnatch offered an enormous hand. "I'm so glad. I admit I thought you a coward, Starthorne, but you have claws."

"My fangs are much more impressive," said Catch, letting Bandersnatch engulf his hand. *His fingers are the size of carrots.* Big *carrots.*

Bandersnatch beamed. "I'm looking forward to this. Your parents' fight was *brilliant.* I still remember it, after all these years. Velocity actually got Lethe down once before he snapped her neck." He sighed, face taking on a dreamy cast.

I'm pretty sure he means it as a compliment. "It was something to watch," said Catch between his teeth. It was an event he still occasionally watched, in nightmares.

Bandersnatch turned to Gildar. "Alph, we're ready to commence. Is this a free-form duel, or should we confine ourselves to one shape?"

Catch held his breath. His Smilodon form might have a slight advantage over Bandersnatch's panther one.

"Human form," said Gildar, stroking his beard.

Catch closed his eyes. Why did he bother?

Nodding, Bandersnatch vaulted the railing again just as Moony jumped onto it. "The ground's smooth and resiliant, Captain," Moony reported, tail curling. "I recommend you topple him. He must be top-heavy, with shoulders like that."

Topple him, and he'll sit on me. Catch took another look around the garden. Eyes everywhere, staring at him. If he tried to bolt, he might well bounce right off the combined force of their gazes. Even the topiary bushes seemed to have moved closer, herding him in. He wracked his brain for a possibile escape, and his brain laughed at him.

Oiled muscles flexing, Bandersnatch took up position in the northern corner of the arena. Catch smoothed his hair, which felt tangled as a bird's nest, rubbed his eyes, forgetting the bruised one again, and gave it up as a bad job. *Chances are, however scruffy I look now, it'll be far worse within a quarter hour.*

He jumped the railing. The two walls that gave the arena its name met in a right angle. Bricks and small ledges jutted out of the east wall; if you were acrobatic enough, you could leap off them. The south wall was perfectly smooth, yellow clay, topped with spikes. It continued past the arena, becoming part of the wall sealing off the grove of custard peaches. Occasionally, their heady aroma wafted over its top. Gildar must've kept alchemists working overtime to ripen them out of season.

Undoubtedly more than he can eat, thought Catch. Gildar wouldn't care if some peaches rotted, so long as they all were his.

Gildar stood, raising his arms. "Bandersnatch Falxus. Catch Starthorne. Are you ready to defend yourselves?"

"Ready," sang Bandersnatch. He dropped his weight, settling it evenly between his legs. Not so top-heavy after all, in that stance.

Catch flexed his shoulders, sore from days of travel. "I'm fairly indefensible, but I'll do my best."

It furrowed Gildar's brows; there was that, at least. But it smoothed quickly. Gildar lowered his arm. "Begin!"

CHAPTER TWENTY-TWO:
DUELING CONCERNS

Brrrzzaaawwwwtttzzz!

The deep, guttural buzzing of the official's horn raised the fur down the spine of Ascot's phantom skunk-self; a disquieting sensation. For a moment, she thought some quick-legged insect had scurried down her back.

Meanwhile, the gate swung open and her fellow competitors raced through, some crackling as they shifted. Cavall barely took a step into the arena before Starley, whooping, tackled him. The grunt of the air whooshing out of his chest echoed off the canyon walls.

The spectators cheered. Bouncing up, Starley grabbed the banner Cavall had been targeting, flourished it, and dashed off. Growling, Cavall pushed to his feet and pursued.

"Get moving, Ascot!" shouted Condorella, bounding past. Her red hair had grown so long and flowing she could've ensconced herself in a tower and waited for a prince to climb it.

Choking back a retort, Ascot headed toward the arena's eastern half, where there were fewer competitors. An orange flutter ten feet overhead caught her attention. *Mine*, she thought, spying a flag dangling out of a small hole pocking the canyon wall. She grabbed one of the ladders lying on the ground; a crude thing made from thick branches lashed together with vines. She muscled it into position, bracing it against a rock protruding from the canyon wall. The rungs bent under her feet as she climbed. Halfway up, one snapped.

The spectators cheered.

I hate you, thought Ascot, clinging to the ladder's splintery sides. The wind made it sway. Her left foot floundered a few seconds before finding the next rung. She climbed the final six rungs as quickly as she dared and reached out. At the last moment, a sly breeze blew the flag out of range. Gritting her teeth, Ascot stood on the very top rung and reached out again, feeling along the cliff wall.

The flag's fringe tickled her hand. She grabbed for it, gripped it with her very fingertips, and yanked it loose. *Victory*, she thought, hooking it to her cord.

The ladder crumpled beneath her, tipping sideways and back.

Too startled to yell, Ascot clung to its sides. Her rump swung heavily, seemingly eager to make acquaintance with the ground. Desperately, she leaned left, trying to shift the balance.

Crack. Something below her gave way. Flinging out her arm, Ascot grabbed the rock spur she'd braced the ladder against. She clung on at the expense of a wrenched shoulder while the ladder collapsed beneath her. Gravity's doing, but it felt very personal. Her left foot found a toehold, which was good, because the spur had a wobbliness to it, like a tooth about to come out of its socket.

Now, to find another dozen or so handholds and toeholds and climb down, she thought grimly, nose pressed against the yellow clay. If she sneezed, would she propel herself right off the wall?

She didn't sneeze, but halfway down, a handhold tore out of the wall in a spray of dust. Ascot dropped. She bent her knees, but the shock of landing still flared all the way up her hips. Pebbles and dirt rained down on her. She wrapped her arms around her head until it subsided.

The flag whipped from her cord. Gasping, she grabbed for the trailing end and missed by inches. Its other end was clenched between the buckteeth of a pudgy, brown-furred creature with a broad, flat tail.

The frabjacketing beaver-shifter! A glance at the broken ladder revealed evidence of some busy chewing. Heat shot up her neck until steam might well have poured out of her ears. Ignoring her knees' protests, she charged after the beaver-shifter. "Give it back!" she yelled, flinging herself onto him.

He dropped the flag, but only to snap at her. Drawing back her fist, she punched him right in his wet, black nose. *I rode a helhest into a mob. I'm not going to let some chunky rodent defeat me,* she thought as he squalled. Scooping up the flag, she ran, retucking it into her cord. *One.*

One, out of a fifty, and her climb and subsequent fall had to have taken almost ten minutes. Maybe going for hard-to-reach flags wasn't her best idea.

She spotted another flash of orange in a dimple in the ground, with weeds combed over to conceal it. Falling to her knees, she yanked the flag out and hooked it to her cord.

Two. *Oh, yes, you're the clear victor here, Ascot.* She ran on. Spying another flag snagged in the split of a hollow log, she dove for it. The same instant, a blue jay swooped down and grabbed it.

A literal bird's-eye view of the arena, thought Ascot bitterly, beginning a curse. But just then, the flag, still snagged, stretched to its fullest length and snapped back, ripping out of the jay's grasp. Ascot reconsidered. *Then again, fingers have their uses.* She pulled the flag free. Squawking, the jay banked. Its wings slapped air around her head. Ascot swatted at it and the jay crackled. A naked woman with wiry black hair and darting eyes landed before her.

"Mine!" she screamed, grabbing for the flag.

Ducking around her, Ascot ran. The jay-shifter gave chase until she stepped on one of the thorny weeds that grew so copiously in this area and stopped with a yelp. *Something to be said for boots also.* Ascot ran on.

Three. Three flags, and half the time gone.

Orange flashed atop a tall boulder shaped like a smashed bowler hat. Ascot circled it. Then circled it again, desperation rising inside her. How to climb its smooth, rounded sides? A breeze tugged at the flag, and she briefly dared hope it might blow right over the side and into her hand, but apparently, it was weighted down. "Frabjacket," she muttered.

"Need a leg up?" asked a voice in her ear.

Ascot spun. Cavall stood behind her. A dimple showed in his cheek when he smiled.

❧

Bandersnatch remained in his stance, watching, eyes probing. Catch waited, feeling like he was standing on a stage with no memory of his lines. A mad, bull-like rush would've been easier to handle.

Then again, if I never move, maybe Bandersnatch won't, either. A slow tickle crept down the back of Catch's neck, electrifying each vertebra one by one. A cold burn filled his stomach, as if he'd swallowed a chunk of ice whole.

Battlelust. It had been twenty-five years, but the telltale symptoms were unmistakable. Shifters throve on fighting. Apparently, he hadn't scraped as much of his upraising off his boots as he'd hoped.

Bandersnatch moved forward, keeping his weight evenly balanced, holding his hands a distance from his chest. Catch licked his fangs. *Does he prefer to punch or grapple? Why didn't I watch him practice last night, study his fighting style?*

He shook himself. That was his old training kicking in. It was quite simple, really. All he had to do was strike a few poses while Bandersnatch hit him. Eventually, the crowd would get bored, forcing Gildar to call it off. Then, maybe, Bandersnatch would still have the energy to challenge Gildar.

At some point, Catch had lifted his own hands. He let them drop. Spotting the opening, Bandersnatch sped forward and slammed his fist into Catch's eye.

His right eye, of course. *Do I have a target painted on the lid?* he wondered as he fell. He rolled on the landing and came to his feet. It got him out of the way of Bandersnatch's follow-up body-slam, which might've ended the match right there.

I should've let him sit on me. His training hadn't allowed it. It had already settled him in a fighting stance. He couldn't see out of his right eye. Colored flashes throbbed in his head. The purple ones hurt the most, but it was a distant pain, of little importance.

He felt *wonderful.* The electrified ice he'd swallowed earlier melted, racing along his nerves. Bouncing lightly on the balls of his feet, he grinned widely enough to display his elongated canines.

Bandersnatch picked himself up and grinned back. "All *right*," he said, and closed again, fists raised.

Thinking ceased for some time. Thoughts were too slow to keep up with the action. Catch circled about Bandersnatch, distracting him with light jabs and following up with punishing kicks and leg sweeps. With size and range in his favor, Bandersnatch's preferred tactic was to land a disorienting blow, then try to move in and use his weight to settle the issue. His kicks were slow, but—as Catch discovered when one came up on his blind side—powerful.

It folded him over. The accompanying crack, wet and internal, sickened him. Dropping to his knees, Catch clutched his ribs, breathing in gasps while the spectators' horrified/thrilled "Ooh!" rolled over him, flattening him further. He supposed they'd been making sounds all along, but this was the first he'd heard them.

"Get up, Captain!" Moony's yell penetrated distantly. "He's coming for you!"

Who—oh, Bandersnatch; right. Still fighting. I'd better—Catch turned his head in time to be treated to a close-up view of Bandersnatch's knuckles.

Crack. Catch sprawled into the dirt while Bandersnatch reeled back, wringing his hand. Catch's last second head-turn had caused him to hit the solid bone above his forehead, rather than his chosen target above Catch's right ear.

He should have pinned me instead of throwing a punch. Pain returned from its short holiday. Breathing felt like sucking in shards of glass. His right eye was a compressed ball of agony, and his forehead pulsed hotly. Other, smaller pains waited in an eager queue to register their complaints. Catch exhaled, blowing a spray of dust off the hard ground. It was all right. All he had to do was lie here until Bandersnatch pinned him, and it would be over.

Above him, Bandersnatch chuckled. "Kissing the ground, Starthorne? Maybe you'd like me to bury you in it."

Catch stiffened. If a small thundercloud had passed over with the express purpose of shooting a lightning bolt at his rump, it couldn't have annoyed him more. *Oh, you didn't. All you had to do is sit on me to win, and you had to* talk *instead?*

What an amateur!

Pain took another respite. Rising to his hands and knees, Catch ran his tongue along the backs of his canines. His fangs. His wonderful, wicked, cruel, curving Smilodon sabers.

Bandersnatch strutted over. He'd been strutting for several fractions of a second—an eternity. Catch's fingertips clawed into the dirt. Power and strength surged between his shoulder blades. At the end of his spine, an intangible tail gave a predatory flick.

When Bandersnatch crouched, Catch shot off the ground. No finesse; just his two outstretched palms slamming into Bandersnatch's chest. Bandersnatch flew back, smacking into the orchard wall with a *bang* loud as a muffled thunderclap, and hard enough to dribble crumbs of yellow clay from the point of impact. He crumpled. Landing atop him, Catch sank his sabers into his neck where it connected with his shoulder.

❧

"I didn't mean 'leg up' in an improper way, if you were wondering," said Cavall. His grin, already edging into sleazy, widened. Ascot flushed, glad that she'd refused to strip, and even gladder that he'd decided to remain clad as well.

"Why would you help me?" she asked.

Throwing back his head, he laughed, motioning toward what she would've noticed if she hadn't been distracted by his smile: a dozen or more flags dangling from his knotted cord. "You're no competition, Miss Nuisance."

"Mine!" screamed the jay-shifter, running up. "Mine!"

Cavall pivoted. One of his hands shot out to grip the back of the woman's neck. His other hand plucked the single, sad flag from her cord and tucked it amongst his own trophies. "Excuse me a moment," he said. He walked the struggling woman to the fence and hurled her over it.

The spectators cheered. Cavall swaggered back. "That's the fourth I've gotten disqualified."

Oh. "Intending to take mine as well?" asked Ascot, bracing back against the boulder.

He smiled down at her, those well-remembered blue eyes crinkling at the corners. Ascot relaxed, looking into them. He was about to say, *"No, we're friends of an odd sort,"* or, *"I understand your reasons, even if I don't agree."*

Leaning in close, he spread his hand against her breastbone. "Of course I am," he whispered in her ear.

Snap, snap, snap. A little jerk accompanied each snap. Pressed against the rock, all Ascot could do was stare, frozen more by the betrayal than his grip.

"This is shifter business," he whispered. "Return to Widget, Miss Nuisance." Stepping back, he held up her three flags. "That's sixteen for me. The official should sound the two warning blasts soon. Think I'll go wait by the gate." He sauntered off, in no apparent hurry. "The mongoose-shifter has almost a dozen," he called back, passing under the juniper tree. "If you target her, you might have a chance."

Ascot gathered her wits. Zero flags, and less than ten minutes remaining. Pushing off the boulder, she charged Cavall.

In a blur of gleaming leather, he spun, kicking both her legs from under her. She fell hard, several rocks slamming into her rump, as if they'd leaped up to meet her halfway. She sat up dizzily, clutching handfuls of yellow dirt.

Cavall stood over her. "Not a chance, Miss Nuisance," he said, shaking his head. Not—"

"Flying ferrets!" yelled Starley, leaping out of the juniper's branches. Five flags streamed from the cord looped around his left shoulder.

Calmly, Cavall dropped his weight and raised his arms. *He expected an ambush*, thought Ascot as he caught Starley in mid-fall and used his own momentum to hurl him to the ground.

"Oof!" Starley didn't have time for more exclamations before Cavall knelt on his chest.

The spectators cheered.

"Maybe your lot didn't kill my father, Reftkin." Brutally, Cavall ripped the flags from Starley's cord and held them up. "But that doesn't mean I'll forgive you for the other things you've done."

Flags. They dangled temptingly from his hand. *Must get them.* Ascot tried to rise, and a spasm curdled her right thigh. She squeezed it, frantic to stop the twitching. Meanwhile, Cavall stood, kicked dust in Starley's face, and continued toward the gate.

Ascot managed one, lurching step after him before her right leg seized up. A peep squeaked between her teeth. *No! Must keep trying!*

"Leather-britches!" Starley pushed onto his hands and knees. He swayed there a moment before hurling himself at Cavall.

Cavall side-steppped. Starley belly-flopped onto the patch of ground he'd just occupied. "Nrg."

Cavall snorted. "Give up, Reft—"

Starley jumped to his feet, faltered drunkenly, then starting spinning in wide, meandering circles. He flipped onto his hands, and just as quickly sprang back, as if the yellow dust burned his palms.

Next came a not entirely successful cartwheel that ended in him rolling on the ground. Swaying even more, he staggered upright and tried it again.

What's he doing? Ascot couldn't stop gaping. *Is he hurt, or...?* She couldn't think of an "or."

Cavall's head turned to follow Starley, his brows forming a line above his pale eyes. He made a small grunt of surprise as Starley jumped five feet straight up in the air and clicked his heels. Landing, Starley flopped on the ground and writhed before staggering up and beginning the drunken spins again.

All at once, Ascot noticed how close Starley's crazy gyrations had taken him to Cavall. Too late, Cavall noticed it, too. In fact, he might not have realized it until the very moment Starley bounced off the last piece of ground he'd thrown himself at and came flying foot-first at Cavall. His heel impacted solidly with Cavall's midsection.

Cavall doubled over with a wheezing guttural noise, too deep and ugly to be called a grunt. Snatching up Cavall's flag-covered cord, Starley bolted for the gate. "Think you're over time, love," he called to the head official.

Only then did Ascot realize that everyone in the area, competitors and spectators alike, had frozen in place to gawp at Starley's antics. Now, the spectators let out a belated cheer.

The head official started. "Oh, right." Hastily, she blew two short blasts on her horn. "That's, er, twenty-six minutes, competitors," she called. "Under four minutes remain."

Four minutes. Zero flags. Drawing back her fist, Ascot slammed it into the quivering muscle in her right thigh, hoping to stun it into submission. Amazingly, the tremors abated. Meanwhile, Cavall straightened, murder in his eyes, just as Starley vaulted through the gate, waving his handful of flags cheekily.

"Twenty-one," called one of the helpers, quickly tallying Starley's flags. The spectators burst into wild cheers.

Twenty-nine remain, thought Ascot. *Cavall said the mongoose-*

shifter had almost a dozen. Where was the mongoose-shifter?

There, running for the gate, like a ripple of furry, brown water. She wasn't fast enough. Cavall, already near the gate, coiled himself and leaped, transforming in mid-air. When his leap ended, he was in hound-form. One snatch of his jaws grabbed up the mongoose-shifter. He shook her hard enough to make her squeal, then bit off her cord of flags. Letting her drop, he dashed through the gate.

"Eleven!" shouted the helper.

"Three minutes!" shouted the spectators, applauding.

CHAPTER TWENTY-THREE: THUNDERSTRUCK

"Stop, *enough*, I say."

The voice was rich and rolling, golden. Catch recognized it without interest. Hands tugged at him, and he shrugged them off with offended ease, baring his fangs. How dare they pull him off his prey? He'd make them his prey, too. A snarl pulled out of his throat—

"Captain!" A tiny, gray paw swatted him across the bridge of his nose.

Catch blinked. The world was orange. No; he was just staring into Moony's eyes. The little Vicardi cat hovered directly in front of him, so close Catch felt the tickle of his whiskers.

"It's over, Captain. You won." Moony landed on his knee.

Knee? Tentatively, Catch ran a hand over his face, pressing his lips against his teeth. Human lips, human teeth. He hadn't shifted.

"Lethe's son, indeed," murmured Gildar, standing over him, gaze disquietingly intense. His golden-eyed stare lingered before he directed it over his shoulder. "What say you, Bandersnatch? Do you yield?"

Seven feet away, Bandersnatch pulled himself into a sitting position. A trickle of blood from his neck soaked into his shirt, and his eyes were slightly unfocused, but he was grinning hugely. "That was amazing! How did you do that, Starthorne? It was like being hit by an avalanche. Can you show me?"

Putting an arm around Catch's waist, Mistral helped him up. "You were channeling, weren't you?" she murmured in his ear.

Catch started. Few shifters knew the trick of tapping into their animal forms while in human shape. He'd almost forgotten it himself, having lived among humans, concealing his nature for so long. "How do you know about that?" he murmured, and got a secretive smile in return.

Gildar grabbed his wrist, pulling up his arm in a gesture of victory. "The bout goes to Starthorne," he boomed to the crowd. They'd spilled over the arena railing, but kept a respectful distance. The cool spring wind billowed Gildar's red mantle. Embroidered suns flared, brightly golden.

Struggling to his feet, Bandersnatch clasped Catch's other hand in his huge mitt. "You won, Starthorne," he said earnestly. "You really are the—"

With a sudden rumble, Mt. Skylash erupted.

❧

Eighteen flags left. Three minutes. If I find all of them, I'll beat Cavall. A hysterical laugh threatened to bubble out of Ascot's throat.

The beaver-shifter lumbered past, head jerking from side to side as he scanned the arena. A single flag trailed from his cord.

A flag. Grabbing up a stick, Ascot hit him across the shoulders— not hard, she told herself; just forcefully enough to hold him down. "Sorry," she said, snatching his flag. "But—"

He snapped at her, so she punched his nose again and ran. "Two minutes!" shouted the spectators.

"How many flags do you have?" squawked a great, ugly, bald-headed bird running up beside her. Four flags dangled from its cord.

"Just one." Ascot did a double-take, recognizing Condorella's voice. *A condor? After all those efforts to make yourself pretty? And why choose a flying animal if you can't actually fly?*

"One?" Condorella screeched. "Is that all? Well, give it to me." Flaring her wings, she shuffled forward.

Ascot clutched it. "No."

"You can't win with one!" cawed Condorella. "The marten-shifter has four also. I must go to the ball, or the plan won't work. You don't have to."

Ascot hesitated. Condorella was right. Without her to manipulate the Seersees, the truth about Rune would remain hidden.

"Miss!" Rags-n-Bones' voice penetrated from beyond the fence. Somehow, even with Condorella scrabbling at her, she met his eyes. Big, watery gray eyes—he was back in his normal shape, half bent over the railing. "Miss, there's a flag under the tree. Get it! The Captain and the Mighty Terror need you."

They need me. It penetrated like a sunburst. Like the *truth*. He was right. Moony needed someone to listen to his tales of lassoing comets, and Catch—Catch needed someone to believe that, despite his tricks and lies, he was, at heart, a good person.

She ran for the flag, tangled in the juniper's roots. Throwing herself onto her belly, she clawed for it. She touched it, and Condorella dragged her out, pushed her aside, and dove in herself.

"Five," she chortled, voice muffled by dirt.

"We shouldn't fight each other," Ascot yelled at her. Teeth closed around her ankle. Panicking, she kicked, nearly fell, and saw it was Dmitri, fennec ears fluttering like maddened butterflies wings.

He released her. "Take my flags and run."

Four hung from his cord. She stared. "But—"

"One minute!" shouted the crowd.

"Quickly," he snapped.

Grabbing the flags off Dmitri's cord, she ran for the gate. The badger-shifter blocked her path, swelling with growls. Two flags hung from its belt. Ascot jumped over it, but when she landed, it snapped sideways, sinking its teeth into her calf. Ascot hopped frantically, suspecting if she went down this time, she wouldn't get up soon.

"My apologies, sir!" cried Dmitri, hurling himself at the badger-shifter. It must've been awfully shocked when the tiny fennec hit with the force of a giant wolf. Its teeth wrenched free of Ascot's leg.

"Thirty seconds!"

"Thanks, Dmitri." Ascot limped through the gate, thigh spasming again. Resurfacing from under the juniper, Condorella came running, dirt-covered and clutching five flags. Ascot took satisfaction in how incredibly stupid a running condor looked.

"Ten seconds!" shouted the spectators as Dmitri cuffed away the badger-shifter and padded through, flagless.

Ascot crouched before him. "Thank you, Dmitri."

"There's someone else you should thank." Dmitri bowed his head to reveal Nipper, peering around one of his huge ears. "Bringing him with me was a touch duplicitous, but I fancy Catch would approve."

"Oh, thank you, Nipper." Ascot tried to pet him, but he whisked off, probably afraid she'd succumb to her lust for rat sandwiches.

"Five flags. Better be enough," grumbled Condorella, popping back into her usual shape and finger-combing her sea urchin hair.

Jolt clasped Starley's forearms. "Weasel war dance stuns 'em every time, doesn't it?" he said as they bumped foreheads.

"That's 'stoat,'" Starley corrected, grinning.

"Miss!" Rags-n-Bones raced over, tears pouring down his cheeks. "I'm sorry. I should've been human. I should've helped."

"It's all right, Rags," she said, squeezing his hand. "There weren't enough entry tokens for everyone anyway."

But he shook his head. "No, it's not all right. You're bleeding, miss."

Surprised, Ascot looked down. Darkening fabric stuck to her right calf. The badger-shifter must've bitten deeper than she'd thought. "It doesn't hurt," she said, only to be belied by an instant throb from her leg. Evidently it was one of those injuries that only hurt when noticed.

Rags-n-Bones unwound his beloved purple muffler. "Rags, no," she said as he began tying it around her leg.

"We can wash it later, miss," he said, securing the knot. His lower lip quivered just slightly.

The head official blew her horn. "Let's thank our competitors for a fine Rising Tournament," she said, tucking it under her arm. "With five flags apiece, winning the right to serve at the Moonless ball, are Condorella Verydarkblue and Ascot Abberdorf."

To a smattering of applause, one of the helpers handed dully gleaming silver badges to Ascot and Condorella. *Wow*, thought Ascot, running her fingers over the crescent moon inscribed in its surface. *I won the right to be a maid. Well, so what? Maggie was a maid, and she was worth a dozen Tanya Roebanks.*

"In second place with eleven flags, is Captain Galen Cavall," announced the official, giving Cavall's name a little extra sparkle as one of the helpers handed him a shiny gold disk. He took it with a grudging bow. "And in first place, with twenty-one flags," she held up a golden disk half again the size of Cavall's. "Starley Ref—"

Releasing Jolt, Starley raced up, swiped his prize out of the official's hand, and leaped onto the nearby boulder, pushing through the spectators until he reached the crest. The crowd quieted as he inhaled, holding up the brightly gleaming disk. Ascot, expecting some rambling speech peppered with "whatsits," blinked when he broke into song instead.

"I have no words, not a single song,
To sing to those who've done us wrong,
To sing to those who've chained us tight.
I'll save my voice, raise it up and rejoice
To remember those who made the choice
To go walking into that—"

Starley beat his heel twice against the rock, sharply enough to startle the cicadas from their eternal *bloc*-ing.

"—moonless night."

His voice was strong, if not entirely on key, and what he lacked in training, he made up for in enthusiasm.

"When you're on your knees, afraid to rise,
There's no blame if you shut your eyes,
But when fear ebbs, look to the light.
Lift your head, give a nod, salute the dead,
Remember it could be you instead
Who went walking into that—"

He stomped twice again. Several members of the crowd stomped along with him. The beaver-shifter clapped the double beat, eyes shining.

"—moonless night."

Stepping forward, Jolt joined his voice with Starley's. The officials exchanged uneasy glances. Out in the arena, Cavall re-donned his black leather with quick, jerky motions. Sucking in a fresh breath, Starley practically hurled the next words at the crowd.

"Not one more; I've drawn a line.
You don't get to cross what's mine.
Here I stand, and here I'll fight.
For those gone unbowed, I make this vow:
Not one more soul will I allow
Not one more's walking into that—"

The stomps were like paired thunderclaps this time.

"—moonless night!"

Aside from the officials, Cavall, and a few holdouts on the fringe, the entire crowd took up the chant, stomping as they shouted. *"Not one more's walking!"*

The head official raised her horn, but lowered it again, unblown. Ascot glanced around. The crowd's energy buzzed in her bones, almost demanding she stomp along with them. Her companions seemed likewise affected; Dmitri quivered, eyes and nose arrowed on Starley. He looked like he might howl, and she had never heard him howl. Quivering, yet smiling, Rags-n-Bones tapped his leg, Nipper perched on his head. Condorella swung her staff/broom out of synch with everyone else.

"Not one more's walking," whispered Ascot. Something that had been growing in her chest abruptly burst into exuberant bloom. For a while, she'd been wondering if she'd lost her way. Rescuing Catch—yes, of course it was important, but when she looked at Jolt's branded face, it seemed a bit petty. Now, for the first time, she realized it was all of a piece. In helping Catch, perhaps she could help them all. Wrapping her fingers tightly about her silver disk, she lifted her voice along with the rest.

"Not one more's walking!"

Dmitri did howl, although he looked embarrassed immediately afterwards. Cavall watched, running his hand over his jaw, as some of the revelers tore flowers off posts and punched the air. More vehement outbursts might have occurred if a sudden scream hadn't risen above the cries of "Not one more."

"Mt. Skylash!" yelled the screamer. "Look, the top of Mt. Skylash!"

The cries broke off. Heads turned, even Starley's. A dying blue haze dusted Mt. Skylash's forked crest. Suddenly fingers were pointing everywhere. Voices rose a pitch in octave, then quieted to the hum of a sleeping beehive as another blue flash burst from Mt. Skylash's peak.

"The tengu."

It started as a whisper. It was repeated as a shout.

"The tengu! The tengu have returned!"

It was a sound you felt in your marrow rather than heard. It was too big for ears, hitting like the slap of an angry giant. Catch imagined his blood actually reversed its course briefly. At the same instant it struck, a piercing blue light drenched the topiary bushes, the watching faces, the arena. It lingered before fading, as if it wished to stain all it touched with its cerulean hue. The moment it did fade, a second *boom* rang out and the blue light flared anew. This time, Catch felt the earth shake. A bench's leg snapped, toppling it over.

People might have begun screaming earlier, but their cries slammed into him all at once, as if they'd been held back briefly to make space for the eruptions. A third *boom*, more tentative than its predecessors, shook leaves to the ground and blotted out the cries. When it faded, the world kept still and silent for a few seconds, like a man who has just fallen hard and is waiting for any broken bones to make themselves known.

Five seconds…ten…twenty. No more explosions rocked Holdfast Plateau. Catch wondered how long it had been since he'd exhaled. He did it now, and a pain in his chest eased.

"The tengu." Diverse voices spoke, but all sang the same tune. "The tengu! The tengu have awakened. The Storm Queen has returned!"

Then, inevitably, it came: "The golden star." Catch felt the prick of a dozen sidelong glances.

A pounding hot-coldness filled him; kept filling him until he couldn't contain a drop more and it burst from his chest like some terrible monster. Only then did he identify it as outrage. He glared at Mt. Skylash's crest, which should at least have had the decency to be blackened and smoking after the eruptions. Perhaps the faintest gray wisp trailed into the sky.

There is no such thing as fate. I am not a puppet!

His hand, bruised, two knuckles bleeding, dove into his pocket and clenched around the odd silver feather. In the midst of whipping it out and hurling it at the not-smoking mountain, he glimpsed Gildar's face. His calm, composed, and *completely unsurprised* face.

Catch's fingers uncurled. The feather dropped back to the depths of his pocket.

A fold of Gildar's crimson mantle unfurled as he raised his arms. "Shifter-kind," he boomed, and waited. Gradually, cacophony of babbles quieted. "Be not alarmed," he went on once it had. "Our ancient foes have shown themselves. This is only to be expected, and we are prepared."

Prepared. Catch rubbed his thumb over his ring. A drop of blood sparkled between its amber petals. *Arranged, organized. To have plans.*

Gathering his mantle's loose fold about him, Gildar lifted his chin like he was presenting his profile for a portrait. The wind, smelling of brandy and peach cream, rippled his golden hair. "I will address the citizens of Holdfast now in Daybell Park to assuage their fears. Let it be known that the children of Rune do not quail before brutes!"

After a moment, people applauded. "I still don't see any quail," Moony whispered to Catch, but subdued.

Bandersnatch moved to join the other Pack members, who'd stepped forward to flank Gildar. Gildar waved him back. "No," he said. "Your present appearance does not inspire confidence."

"Nor mine, either?" said Catch, touching his swollen eye.

Gildar shook his head. "Rest and wash. We'll speak at tonight's banquet." Gold-clad Pack members in tow, he swept out of the garden at a brisk, knock-over-anyone-in-his-way pace.

"But I'm Pack," said Bandersnatch, staring after Gildar, face twitching with bafflement.

You're also not a lion-shifter. Catch clapped his shoulder sympathetically.

Bandersnatch glanced down at him. "You should be with him. You're the golden star."

"Not if Gildar has his way," Catch muttered, watching the last, bright splash of Gildar's mantle vanish around the corner of a clipped green hedge.

Now Bandersnatch's brow furrowed outright. "What do you mean, Boss?"

"Boss." I suppose if you beat a Bandersnatch, you have to keep it. He probably wasn't stupid, Catch reflected. It was just that, all his life, being strong had been enough. "Let's get some coffee."

He looked around for Mistral, located her gazing at Mt. Skylash's peak. He started to call to her, closed his mouth and took a second, closer look at her.

No trace of surprise showed on her face, either.

CHAPTER TWENTY-FOUR:
SHIFTING POSITIONS

The thunderclaps died, and the mountaintop went still. Despite the shouts of "tengu," no large, grunting, dark-skinned creatures appeared in Merryvick's streets and started snatching up children and munching them down like roasted cicadas. Little by little, the crowd's cries dwindled to mutters.

"No more lightning," said Rags-n-Bones, sadly.

Starley leaped down the boulder to rejoin them. "That's inserted a gnat under the communal tail," he grumped. "Just when I had 'em nicely fired up, too."

"Only you would take the tengu's return as a personal affront," said Jolt. But his fingers shook as he stuck a licorice root between his lips.

Dmitri coughed, setting Ascot's teeth on edge. One day, she vowed, she'd train him out of making that noise. "Are we certain it was the tengu?" he asked. "The timing's suspiciously convenient."

Frowning, Condorella shook the straw off her broom. Muttering arcane gobbledygook, she began walking in circles, taking exaggeratedly huge strides.

"I suppose you could get such an effect with alchemy," said Ascot.

Rags-n-Bones' hand shot up. "Master Porpetti could. He could pet the Mighty Terror and get a little *snap*," he clicked his fingers, "from his fur, then put the *snap* in a special jar and make it bigger."

Ascot rubbed her nose, again boggled by how much he'd learned from Master Porpetti. "Do you think it was alchemy, Rags?"

Plucking his chin, he stuck out his tongue and licked the air. He smacked his lips. "Yes."

"You!" The shout made Ascot jump. She didn't recognize the speaker when she turned: a big, rough-looking man with a pale streak in his dark hair, standing at the front of a small, scowling crowd. He leveled a forefinger at Dmitri. "I heard you speaking in the arena. What's up with that?"

The badger-shifter! *Oops.* Ascot's bitten leg twinged. Not for the first time, Dmitri's mouth made her wish she could pass herself off as a clever ventriloquist.

"Yarp?" Dmitri wiggled his oversized ears.

Ascot winced. While working on his stride, he should've given some thought to his voice as well. His yips were far too deep and raspy to sound anything but absurd, coming out of his little fennec throat.

"There's something odd about you." The badger-shifter took a belligerent step forwards. "Something non-shifter."

Ascot surveyed the situation. Bad. They were backed against the boulder. Vendor stands, flower-wrapped poles, and a throng of people stood between them and a hasty exit from Merryvick—a throng of riled, scared people, looking for a way to take control of a suddenly upended reality.

Always sensitive to disapproval, Rags-n-Bones trembled. "Biscuit," he whispered. *Pop.* Tucking his tail, he rolled over, exposing his belly.

Oh, frabjacket, thought Ascot as the angry eyes facing her narrowed.

"That wasn't a proper transformation," roared the badger-shifter.

"Back off," said Jolt, showing his teeth.

One of the badger-shifter's followers hefted a cudgel. "Keep quiet, feral, or I'll thrash you."

In a flash of red, Starley joined Jolt. "Oh, no, mate. Not that," he said, glaring fiercely enough to give Moony pause. "Were you singing along just now? Well, it's not 'I got mine, so the rest of you can chew tail.' You're either breaking locks, or a jailer."

It might've been all right if he hadn't followed the statement with his favorite gesture. As one, the badger-shifter and his gang growled.

That particular silliness is rampant among shifters, apparently. Ascot picked up a rock. A pitiful defense, but she'd bruise at least one eye before she let them hurt her friends.

"Stand back!" snapped a voice. A deep, sand-and-silk voice. It carried enough authority to halt the badger-shifter's party's advance.

"Captain Cavall," said the badger-shifter, turning. "These are outsiders."

Cavall glowered. The hard angles of his face made the expression particularly vicious. Bellmonte stood behind him, big and quiet in a way that had nothing to do with not speaking. "When does a badger-shifter's duty include apprehending outsiders?" Cavall demanded. "Go back to your weaving, before I arrest you on suspicion of slipping your skin."

The badger-shifter glanced back as two of his followers melted away, mingling with Merryvick's crowd. He looked again at Cavall, who favored him with the briefest frown.

"Don't make me wait," he said.

That did it. With a few final, resentful glares, the badger-shifter's group dispersed.

"Thank you," said Ascot when it became clear neither Starley nor Jolt was going to say it.

Cavall sighed. Unfolding his arms, he ran a hand through his hair. "I should've chucked you over the fence, Miss Nuisance. I should've known you'd find a way through at the last second."

"All right, leather britches." Starley blew out his lips. "Why the rescue? You could've let that mob rip us up without tarnishing your promise."

Before he could reply, Condorella, having missed the earlier excitement, came stalking back, holding her staff/broom before her, its crystal glowing sour green. "Bone-man is right. The explosion was definitely alchemic in nature."

"What?" Cavall's head jerked up.

Starley pointed to Mt. Skylash. "The blue boom-boom wasn't the work of the tengu, but some alchemist." He grinned. "Aren't all the alchemists in the Clawcrags in Gildar's employ?"

"Why should I believe you?" said Cavall. But there wasn't much conviction behind the words. He stared down at the moonstone pendant, milky blue against his black leather jacket.

"Why did you help us?" asked Ascot.

Bellmonte stepped forward. "Because I told him the truth." Cavall groaned, dropping his head so low it hung between his shoulders, but Bellmonte continued, looking at Ascot. "His daughter's one of us."

"Mange and maggots, we never out each other," said Starley, pulling at his bandana.

"Mange and maggots yourself," retorted Bellmonte, turning sharply on him. "I was her nursemaid. I raised her, and I see her growing strange, keeping secrets. In your fervor to make things *right*, you don't see a cub in danger. I introduced her to the Hide Aways. If anything happens to her, it's my fault."

Starley spread his hands. Bellmonte addressed Cavall. "Please. Talk to her."

Cavall laughed rustily. "Right. Because I've been such a good father. Didn't even see her the two years I was posted in Widget." His laughter ebbed. Lifting the moonstone off his chest, he turned it in the light. "Why did I help? Because apparently slipskins run in my family. My father. My daughter. The only way I can see to salvage a scrap of honor is if you're right. Rune was a mockingbird-shifter and our system's a lie." His throat worked. "Of course, that leaves me having devoted my life to that system." Letting the pendant drop onto his chest, he ground one of the ragged pink flowers into the dust with his heel. A honey smell rose up, overly sweet and faintly rotten.

"Consider myself your ally," he said. "I can get you into Holdfast safely and find a place for you to stay until the Moonless Night."

Without waiting for Dmitri's nod of approval, Ascot took his hand. "Thank you. We appreciate your help."

"Wait—wait a minute," sputtered Starley.

Ascot glanced around. Starley was shaking his head. Jolt, brand stark white in his livid face, bit his licorice root clean in two. "You judge people on who they are now, not who they were in the past, right?" she said, cocking her brows.

After a moment, Starley sighed and scratched beneath his bandana. "Could've sworn I didn't mean it that way," he grumbled.

Dmitri started trotting down the path out of Merryvick, big, bushy tail whisking his heels. "Even if you change everything, you're still going to have to contend with one another," he called back. "Might as well make a start."

Cavall and Starley exchanged a look. Of all possibilities, neither had ever seemed to have considered the one where they shared the world peacefully. Jolt still seemed disinclined to consider it. His jaw ground harder. But, after a moment, Cavall shrugged. Starley rubbed his neck.

"Come on, Jolt," he said, picking up the fallen licorice piece. "Let's make a start."

❧

"Eww!" said Moony as they emerged from under the natural stone arch of Mortalis Pass and picked their way down Bone Slope. Yellowed shards littered this steep, rocky stretch of ground on Holdfast Plateau's southwestern edge. Yellow shards, and less pleasant objects. Some still bore the remnants of faces.

Shifters didn't bury their dead. "Lucky for you," muttered Catch as Mistral led the way to Savotte's not-quite-final resting place. A tall man with a long face and scraggly, shoulder-length hair kept watch over her. A flock of vultures wheeled overhead. Another one, hungrier or more optimistic, crouched twelve feet from Savotte, waiting hopefully.

"I'm sorry, Captain." Moony's whiskers tickled Catch's cheek as he turned his head from side to side. "This is *gruesome*. They may go overboard in Shadowvale, what with all the monuments, obelisks, and occasional yachts, but *this*—"

"Yacht?" said Bandersnatch.

"A Von Hoyterbach family tradition," said Moony. "They believe the afterlife's one big ocean cruise, so they put yachts on their graves." He licked a paw thoughtfully. "Come to think of it, they should probably stop making them out of marble."

Catch glanced back through Mortalis Arch. The Aspire glinted in the distance, towering over Holdfast's boxy, yellow edifices. Even with Gildar's propensity for public bombasticy—which wasn't a word, but should have been—he probably only had a couple of hours before his absence was noted. Crouching, he lifted Savotte's wrist. Still no trace of a pulse.

"Sure she isn't dead?" asked Moony, leaping off Catch's shoulder and sniffing her hair.

"Looks dead to me," said Bandersnatch, also bending over. In his interest, he nearly spilled the container of cold, nectar-sweetened coffee he held.

"It's only temporary." Catch pulled out the antidote, made from special green figs and a certain crushed beetle. He could virtually taste its sourness through his skin. Carefully, he dribbled a couple drops in Savotte's mouth.

"Any trouble, Ty?" Mistral asked the scraggly-haired man.

"Naw. She hardly been here twenty minutes." Ty chewed, stone-faced, on a bone chip. It wouldn't actually belong to anyone left on the slope (Catch hoped), but the effect was still disquieting. The vulture-shifters who tended Bone Slope were known for a macabre sense of humor.

Savotte gasped—a mistake, as she promptly inhaled the liquid in her mouth. *I suppose she can be excused*, thought Catch watching her choke and spit. The waiting vulture croaked, flapped twice, and settled again. *You never know*, its attitude seemed to say.

"Hey, she isn't dead after all," said Bandersnatch. His brow furrowed. "Or, she was dead, but now she's alive again?"

"Gildar ordered me to kill her." Catch sat back on his heels, regretting it when something crunched beneath him.

Savotte's eyes bugged. She was too busy coughing to cry "*What?*" with indignation, but Bandersnatch did it for her, although his version probably sounded more bewildered than hers would've been.

"He also ordered me to kill Cavall," added Catch, corking the antidote vial. "Well, to be honest, I suggested it, but he readily agreed."

With a final hack, Savotte cleared her lungs. "Are you asking me to be *grateful* for this little trick?" she rasped, sounding almost as sandy as her partner. Bandersnatch handed her the cold coffee.

Catch sighed. He hated being obvious. The wind blew rolls of yellow dust off the slope. A bit of bone rattled among the rocks. "Gildar wanted you dead. If I refused, do you imagine he'd have said, 'fair enough' and let the matter drop?"

Between sips of coffee, Savotte considered, cocking her head. Temporary death had, finally, mussed her coiffure. One hand set to work straightening it. "I'm still not forgiving you, Starthorne."

"Try to do someone a favor." Catch dusted off his coat.

"Why did Gildar want her dead?" asked Mistral. Catch glanced at Ty. She gave a flip of her hand. "You can talk in front of him."

"Tigers. Spots. Yup." Ty gnawed his bone shard.

Another Hide Away. How many were there? Soon, he had to sit Mistral down and worm out her secrets.

But not now, he thought, glancing at the sun. *Even Gildar can't pontificate much longer.* "We came across an army of fake tengu in the Underway. When Rainy told Gildar about it, he dismissed the story and told me to kill her to prevent her spreading lies."

"Fake tengu? What do you mean, fake tengu?" asked Bandersnatch.

"Alchemic dolls," said Catch, but Savotte recovered her voice before he could explain further.

"You could have told him I wasn't lying," she cried.

"Why waste the breath?" Catch ran his tongue along the back of his teeth, summoning patience. "Rainy, he knows about them. He had them made. Why else would he want you thrown to the vultures?"

With keen timing, the waiting vulture shuffled over to one of the huddled objects everyone was trying not to look at and tore off a piece. "Ew," said Moony, shuddering until his wings rattled.

Bandersnatch scratched his jaw, making audible rasping noises. "I'm still stuck on the fake tengus. Why would Gildar make such things when the real ones are going to show up on the Moonless Night?"

As casually as he might mention the sun rising tomorrow morning. Catch stared at a mottled stone. *As if the prophecy was as solid as that rock.* "Real tengu," he said. He bestowed a savage kick on the rock, hard enough to hurt his toes. It clattered off down the slope. "From where?" he demanded, glaring after it. "The Underway's been patrolled. Has anyone seen a creditable glimpse of one tengu, let alone an army of them?"

Savotte lifted her brows. *That feather,* said her gaze. Catch looked away, hands fisting inside his pockets.

"But...but Magden Le Fou prophesied their return," protested Bandersnatch.

"Magden Le Fou wrote a *poem*," Catch snapped. "Prophecies don't actually prophecy anything until after whatever they're supposed to prophecy happens and everyone starts matching reality to the rhyme."

That was too complicated for Bandersnatch. He grunted, still scratching. "What about the explosion?"

"Explosion?" asked Savotte, getting shakily to her feet.

"It happened while you were dead," said Mistral. "Blue lightning struck Mt. Skylash's peak."

"Alchemy also," said Catch. "Gildar was expecting it." *So were you,* he thought, watching Mistral kick dirt over one of the things they didn't want to see, much to the waiting vulture's disgruntlement. Moony stared at it and crouched, tail twitching.

Savotte looked skeptical. Catch raked a hand through his hair. "Gildar knows the Sniffers have never found evidence of tengu. He doesn't expect them to show up, but he does want to use the prophecy to gain more power. *That's* why he wants fake tengu he can control. *That's* why he was prepared to give a speech in Daybell Park after Mt. Skylash exploded. And *that's* why he didn't want me by his side while he did it."

Bandersnatch's hands dropped. "That's cheating," he sputtered, and began stomping about. Catch winced at the splintering crackles. "You're the golden star. And the Alph's Alph because he's the fittest and the strongest. That's why you have to listen to him." He stopped abruptly, and stared at his feet. "Gildar ordered me to challenge you. 'The golden star can't be a coward,' he told me."

"I know," said Catch.

"But he's the coward, isn't he, Boss?" Bandersnatch went on. He wriggled a toe. "I should've challenged him instead, but you got to obey the Alph."

Mistral snorted, but very quietly. Savotte, hair back in order, folded her arms. "It's an interesting theory, Starthorne, but where's your proof?"

"Gildar ordering me to kill you isn't proof enough?" Catch retorted.

She snorted. "All I have is your word that he did so. The word of a liar."

It's so irritating when one's hobbies come back to bite one, thought

Catch, scratching his cheek and flinching when his nails encountered fresh abrasions. But there had to be some way to convince her…

Darting forward, Moony swatted the vulture across its beak. It took off squawking, lurching along the ground for several steps before its wings deigned to lift it up. Catch idly followed its flight toward—

—Mt. Skylash. *Oh.* His blood congealed. An icy-footed centipede ran down his spine. There was a way.

No, there's not a way.

There is. He sighed. "If Gildar used alchemy, there will be residue on Mt. Skylash's peak. We can go there and find it."

"How?" asked Savotte. "None of the Underway's passages lead to the peak, and climbing the slope in the dark—"

"There's another path," said Catch. "If you need convincing, we'll follow it tonight."

Savotte's inky brows shot toward her hairline.

"Ooh," said Mistral. "A secret mission to bring down Gildar!"

"No." Savotte's hand sliced air. "Just me and Starthorne. A large group is more conspicuous."

"I'm coming, too," said Moony, leaping to Catch's shoulder and hulking like a miniature gargoyle.

"Fine," said Savotte, not even glancing at him.

She didn't fear discovery. She wanted to talk about the feather out of the others' hearing. "The three of us, then," said Catch.

Mistral sulked. "Rat pellets." She almost kicked a clump of matter on the ground, but thought the better of it. "Fine. I have a training session with my swordmaster anyway. But you'll need me to sneak Rainy into your chamber, sir."

"The same way you sneaked up that first night?" he asked, raising a brow. She pretended not to hear.

"I—I'm Pack," said Bandersnatch, still staring at his toe. His scuffing had half-buried it in yellow dust. "I gotta do as Gildar commands. But if he meets with any alchemists, I'll let you know."

"Thank you." Catch glanced at the sun. "Now, I really must

return to the Aspire." Gildar couldn't hide him during the traditional banquet, even if he wanted to. He hoped he had time for a nap beforehand; another long night loomed. *But not a moonless one,* he thought grimly.

"I'll go with you," said Bandersnatch. "Gotta get cleaned up."

"I'll sneak Rainy into your chambers during the banquet," chirped Mistral, waving a hand. Savotte grimaced and folded her arms. Ty offered her a bone chip.

Tomorrow, Catch promised himself as he and Bandersnatch walked back through Mortalis Pass. First thing tomorrow, he'd sit Mistral down and discover where she'd learned the Aspire's secrets.

Well, maybe he'd have a cup of coffee first.

"Boss?" asked Bandersnatch. They'd reached Holdfast's outskirts. These houses, the closest to Bone Slope, were mean, shabby things with gaping holes for windows, piled atop one another like so many yellow boxes, home to the rat-shifters who cleaned Holdfast's streets and the vulture-shifters who tended the dead.

"Yes?" Catch replied.

"If we prove Gildar's tricking everyone, what then? No one can challenge him until the solstice."

Catch ducked under a washing line strung with a few sad, withered boquets; the only evidence of Yawning Day festivities he'd seen in this district. "An Alph can be removed by unanimous vote of the Pack."

Bandersnatch shuffled his feet. "Unanimous? Half the Pack are related to Gildar."

"I know," said Catch. It wouldn't be easy, but having Gildar quietly removed, like a cowflop left on a banquet table, rather than allowing him a final, glorious fight, would be the perfect revenge, if Gildar had killed his father.

Lethe Starthorne, dead. Catch spread his hand. All the sunlight pouring in golden streams out of the flat, blue sky couldn't brighten the dusky pearl in the ring's center. During his years of exile, Catch had never imagined the possibility of his father's death. Maybe a black hole would open somewhere in the universe and swallow him up, but other than that, Lethe Starthorne didn't die.

Except, it seemed he had.

CHAPTER TWENTY-FIVE: WALKING ON AIR

Night wrapped the Aspire like an ugly package. Inside the Sparkspire, the most northerly of its spikes, the cold, stale air tasted bitter and metallic. Moony sniffed a collection of dead insects lying on the narrow window's sill and sneezed lustily.

Terrific; a squall, thought Catch as the wind whipped past the window, its wail echoing down the narrow, winding stairwell he and Savotte had just climbed. *Just what we need while embarking on this mad venture.* He glowered at Mt. Skylash. The bloated moon's light broke its silhouette into fragments of black and white.

"Well, Starthorne?" said Savotte, folding her arms.

"Give me a moment," he muttered. "It's been twenty-five years. Is this the right landing?"

"What's the grappling hook for?" asked Savotte, indicating the tool he carried over his left shoulder. She peered out the window slit. "Intending to pull Mt. Skylash closer to us?"

Catch gritted his teeth. She was in a bad mood. He allowed she had reason. Mistral had indeed smuggled her into his father's chamber during the Yawning Banquet, and she'd promptly sat on a wrong chair. *I could've sworn I'd cleared the knives from under that one.*

"We're going to walk to Mt. Skylash," he said. *The fourth landing,* he remembered, and retraced his steps back down a flight.

"Walk?" Savotte followed, her toes nipping his heels. "Is this another of your stories?"

"I once walked across the ocean," said Moony, scampering after them. "The waves were so scared of me they froze underfoot."

Savotte sniffed. "Why didn't you just fly?"

"Maybe because someone put a clip on my wing?" Moony snapped back. Savotte had pointed out that she couldn't remove it without revealing that she wasn't dead. Moony had responded to her very sound logic by hacking a hairball into her right shoe while she napped.

I wish I could fly, thought Catch as they reached the fourth landing. He stared at its window; a glassless gap in the shape of an elongated pentagon, its sill level with his chest. Taking a breath, he hefted himself onto it.

"What are you doing?" Savotte grabbed his coat. "It's a straight drop out there."

Oh, Catch knew it. His feet swung over empty air. The ground, a smear of pale yellow, lurked far below him. An upwards gust slapped both his cheeks, finishing with a yank to his hair. Darkness gaped. Nothing to break his fall. If he was lucky, he might end up impaled on one of the lesser spires.

On the other hand, Savotte was mistaken. "Don't distract me," he said between his teeth, hooking the grapple's barbs into the few inches of sill between his rump and the wall. He tugged the rope to make sure it was secure, checked the knot to make sure it would hold, and tied the rope about his middle.

Then—and he wouldn't have sworn that he didn't close his eyes—he clutched the rope and slid forward, right foot extended. Savotte and Moony's startled yells as he vanished from their sight only made his stomach plummet faster.

Just when he was certain his foot would keep going, with the rest of him flailing after it, it met a solid surface. A tear leaked from his eye, shocking him with its heat.

His left foot joined his right on the solid surface—more-or-less solid; it vibrated under the wind's buffeting. Knowing it was a mistake, Catch opened his eyes.

It was a mistake. He hastily shut them again before his stomach brought up everything he'd eaten in the past ten years.

He was standing on air. *On nothing!* On air.

Wings fluttered. "Wow, Captain, how are you doing this?" With a tickle of fur, Moony settled on Catch's shoulder. The slight addition of weight almost unbalanced him. He swayed, clutching the rope in a death grip.

Don't say "death grip." Red flares danced behind his tightly closed eyelids. *Clasp. Clutch. Very secure hold.* "It's a no-see-'em road." Fleas, he sounded almost as hoarse as Cavall. "They don't exist unless you're standing on them."

And even then, they were invisible. Clearly constructed by sadists.

"I never heard of such things," said Savotte, above him.

Tipping back his head, Catch looked, very carefully, and specifically, upwards, into her brown eyes as she leaned out the window. The wind fanned her hair in a rather fetching, shimmery, halo. "Few have. Think you can join me?"

She swung, far too easily, over the ledge. Holding onto the rope, she touched down a foot. The no-see-'em road rippled, and Catch swallowed bile. Savotte brought her other foot down and bounced experimentally. The invisible surface undulated in a way that made Catch repress a scream that would've awakened all of Holdfast.

"Don't. Do. That," he snapped, visions of falling two hundred feet and ending up a red paste decorated with bits of crushed bone playing merrily through his mind.

Moony, poised to leap off his shoulder, paused, his front paws pressing against Catch's chest. "What's the matter, Captain? This road's amazing. We could use it for a daring escape. Imagine fencing on it!" Giggling, he hopped down.

"Careful!" said Catch. "If you go off the edge, you can't fly."

That perfectly rational observation earned him a dismissive flick of Moony's tail. "Does this lead to that opening in Mt. Skylash's side?" asked Savotte, pointing.

"Yes," said Catch, tightly. Of all the Aspire, the Sparkspire lay closest to Mt. Skylash's side. It was still too far a distance. Far too far.

"Amazing." Savotte stood with her hands on her hips, at ease even when the wind gusted. "We should mark the path, however. Don't want to risk stepping off the edge."

"I brought some pebbles. In my right pocket," Catch grated. He couldn't retrieve them himself. It would mean letting go of the rope.

Of course he had to let go. The rope wouldn't stretch all the way to Mt. Skylash. The wind gleefully assaulted him, sneaking under his collar and billowing up the back of his coat, attempting to make an impromptu balloon and float him away. Only the rope, still tied about his middle, tethered him.

I can't untie it. No. No.

Moony's head butted his knee. "Come on, Captain. It's already late."

Late. Unfortunate word choice. Catch's fingers refused to unclench. His knees locked.

"Starthorne?" Savotte nudged his shoulder.

"I can't!"

"Captain?" Moony sat on his rump and blinked. "You're not afraid, are you?"

A laugh tore out of Catch's throat. "No, Moony, I'm petrified, terrified—" Giving up, he buried his face in his arms. There wasn't a word for a fear so powerful he almost wished it would simply stop his heart and be done with it.

Savotte's hand delved into his pocket, withdrew. A moment later came a muted patter, as of heavy raindrops over thick leaves. "Scout ahead, Moony." She untied the rope about Catch's middle, then bent his fingers back one by one, forcing his grip apart. "Starthorne."

Catch lifted his head. Her face filled his vision, blocking

out…everything else. "Good," she said. "Keep your gaze fixed on me." She gripped his wrist. When she rose, he had to, too.

Can't we just crawl? Standing just made them a target for the wind. But Savotte was already walking, stepping ahead of him and encouraging him to follow.

Pulling one foot off the path, he took a tiny step forward. "That's it," said Savotte. "Now another."

Why was she being so kind? Maybe she meant to push him off at the midpoint. *No, that's fear talking,* he thought, instantly ashamed. "I'm sorry," he said.

Her lips pursed. "That's a start." She eased him forward another step. "You ruined my life. What am I going to do now? My family was so proud when I became a Sniffer. They're all farmers. Just because my horse-form was more elegant…" She shook her head.

Don't, he thought. He needed her to concentrate on her footing. "Gildar believes horse-shifters are too flighty for guard work. I image he'll consign you all to farming if he gets his way."

"Why I should believe you?"

"I don't always lie." The wind roared, swelling a small bump in the no-see-'em road. Stumbling over it, Catch froze again. How far had they come? More importantly—"How far do we have to go?" he asked through his teeth.

But Savotte stayed put. "So, you're not lying now," she mused, glancing down. Catch almost followed her gaze, but he tightened his neck against it until its muscles screamed for pain. When Savotte looked back up, she wore just enough of a smile to raise her beauty mark. "Is this because of what happened in the Roundgrounds twenty-five years ago?"

"I still can't believe you're frightened, Captain," said Moony from somewhere near Savotte's feet. Of course he couldn't. Moony only feared geese and helhest, and he'd deny the latter.

Still Savotte didn't move. "What did happen twenty-five years ago?"

Another gust of wind swept the path. "The moon dropped out of the sky, pushing me and Glim over the edge," said Catch, rapidly. "Simultaneously, Holdfast Plateau flipped onto its side and we slid off—" *No! Don't think of sliding!*

Savotte had judged rightly; he couldn't form a coherent lie right now. He sagged. "I don't remember, exactly. Glim and I hated the golden star nonsense. We were so young, and the Moonless Night so far off, like something that would never happen."

Glim. An image of his first best friend rose, his almond-shaped golden eyes alert with humor and curiosity. So young. He'd never grow older. "When our fathers decided the Rising Tournament would settle it, Glim and I made a pact. We'd gather exactly four flags each and throw them over the plateau's side while everyone watched via the Seersees. Glim met me at the edge, as planned. But—"

"Yes?" Savotte prompted.

Catch shook his head. "Something went wrong. I remember Glim being angry, or frantic, but I don't remember anything we said. I remember the falling—"

—the world whirling around him, the wind gusting beneath him, mockingly, as if it could catch him, but never would.

"—but I don't remember the landing. My memories only solidify a few months later, in an apple orchard, outside the town of Derving."

"Fruit again!" The wind's roar half-drowned Moony's small, raspy laugh.

Not roar. Catch frowned, concentrating. Nor wail, moan, whisper, or any other sound he'd ever heard the wind make. More of a constant, metallic buzzing, accompanied by a clicking rattle, such as might be created by fanning together several strips of thick paper.

A bird wearing a suit of armor? he guessed. Cautiously, making sure his balance didn't shift, he looked up.

A pair of two-toned eyes, the irises ringed with distinct bands of copper and pale bronze, glared back.

"Oh," said Catch.

It was all he had time to say before the person bearing those peculiar eyes swooped down and grabbed him by the lapels. In the half second before he was taken, the dim figure resolved into the shape of a young woman with ochre-gold skin, a sharp nose, and black hair tied in a long queue. Two short wings protruded between her shoulder blades, covered with a wild burst of silver feathers.

Then he was aloft. Below him—*below!*—Savotte let out an incoherent cry. "No, you don't!" shouted Moony, and a small weight added itself to the hem of Catch's coat.

His feet dangled, skimming open air. *She's going to drop me, she's going to drop me.* He clenched her forearms, putting all his strength into maintaining his grip. Let her try dropping him. He'd take her wrists with him.

Mercifully, the journey lasted scant seconds, ending before the shock fully wore off and blind panic set in. Grunting, the flying girl hefted him into a cavern on Mt. Skylash's side, several feet above the one the no-see-'em road led to, and unceremoniously released him.

"Let go," she said, shoving a foot into his chest when he didn't return the favor.

Catch risked glancing down. The cavern's floor was only a couple feet beneath his toe-tips. Moony hung off his coat's hem, teeth buried in the tough leather.

"Let go." The winged girl kicked him again. This time, Catch obeyed. Usually, he'd land on his feet, but his knees buckled. He only narrowly avoided sitting on Moony, who spit out his mouthful of coat and leaped eagerly at the winged girl. She shot back, bumping her head on the cavern ceiling.

"Come down and face me, varlet!" cried Moony, dancing on his hind legs.

The winged girl seemed happy to oblige. Kicking off the ceiling, she swooped, wings trailing black ash. Hooking out an arm, Catch swept Moony to his chest and held him there despite his yowled protests.

The winged girl stopped ten inches away and hovered, her stubby wings throwing off a shower of sparks. She wore a short burgundy tunic, belted and loose-sleeved, like a robe, and black leggings that looped over the arches of her bare feet. A polished metal ball weighted her braid's end. "Scared to fight me, lightning thief?" she demanded. Her Alumbrian was sharp and rapid, almost staccato.

Double-ringed irises. Sparking silver feathers. She was no alchemic chicken experiment gone awry. "You're a tengu," said Catch.

"And you're a shifter," she replied, clearly unimpressed by his observation. "Shifters are all thieves and liars."

You have no idea. Catch got stiffly to his feet, still clutching Moony. This cavern curved into the mountain's side. He couldn't see how deep it went, but its walls were rough and irregular, quite unlike the Underway's rounded smoothness. Roaches scurried across the floor.

"I heard you talking." The tengu swept closer, making herself taller than Catch by hovering eighteen inches off the floor. "Where is it?"

"Where's what?" asked Catch. Moony went limp, trying to ooze out of his grasp. Catch squeezed him warningly. He knew all about felines and their pretentions to liquidity.

The tengu buzzed closer. "What you stole."

"I've only just met you," Catch objected. Even he couldn't pick a pocket that quickly.

She stamped air. "Not you from me! Your kind from my kind. The *kinhoshi.* That *fizzle* Rune stole it after murdering Lady Genkiku."

"Genkiku?" The name struck a familiar chord amongst all her baffling accusations.

Hotter, fatter sparks popped off her wings. "You shifters are more stupid than I expected. Lady Genkiku," she spoke each word distinctly, "was our Rai-sama. That mucky bit of damp ash, Rune, killed her and stole the *kinhoshi*."

The Storm Queen, Catch remembered. Shifter legends never bothered naming her, but now he remembered where he'd seen it; near the end of the mangled letter he'd slipped in Ascot's coat. The stories claimed Rune defeated her in fair combat.

Of course they do, thought Catch, clicking his tongue. Since Moony had stopped growling, Catch set him down on the pebbly cavern floor. "Where did you come from?" he asked the tengu.

It seemed a fair question. If the tengu were indeed lurking inside Mt. Skylash, how had the patrols missed all sign of them for five solid centuries?

The tengu having responded with nothing but fury thus far, reacted to this question by shifting her gaze, thrusting out her lip, and tugging her braid.

Rebellious guilt. Catch recognized the symptoms.

"What's your name?" asked Moony, watching her wings buzz with fascination. He batted at a cast-off spark. "I'm The Mighty Terror from the Deepest Shadows, also known as Moony, and this is the Captain."

"Catch Starthorne," said Catch.

The tengu tossed her head, swinging her braid over her shoulder. "Koyuki. Sasakade Koyuki." Her wings stilled, dropping her lightly to the ground. "I'm Genkiku's grand-niece. I should be the next Rai-sama."

"And you're looking for the...*kinhoshi*." He pronounced the unfamiliar word carefully. "What is it?"

Her irises whirled. "It commands the lightning."

Sighing, Catch smoothed his hair. "Now I know why you called me 'lightning thief,' but not what it looks like, which is rather critical if you wish me to find it."

Koyuki thrust her tongue into her cheek and rolled it around, created a moving bulge. "It's a...thingy." Catch's incredulous look ignited her fury all over again. "Rune stole it before I was born," she yelled, kicking pebbles. "All the pictures just show Genkiku holding aloft a handful of lightning. Maybe it's a wand."

"All right, quiet down," said Catch. The cavern amplified her voice. Mt. Skylash had already exploded today; people didn't need to think it had started shouting at them also. Pacing to the opening, he looked down. Several feet below and to the left, Savotte walked along the no-see-'em path, scattering pebbles before her. Of course she'd kept her head and continued on after Koyuki spirited him off. *And Gildar thinks horse-shifters are flighty.*

"I once stole an ogre's shadow," Moony told Koyuki. "The ogre had grown so large its shadow blotted out the sun and people's tomatoes wouldn't ripen. I locked it in a chest and buried it in a crater of the moon."

"Are ogres anything like oni?" asked Koyuki, squatting opposite him, arms tucked around her knees. "We have trouble with them where we come from."

"And where is that?" asked Catch, drawing back inside. Her lip thrust out again. She fingered the ball on her braid. Catch nodded. "You're not supposed to be here, are you?"

She threw her braid aside so fiercely it whipped around her neck and caught her a glancing blow on the opposite cheek. "Fine, no," she said. "We're not supposed to return until mourning for Genkiku is officially over, and that's still three nights away."

"You've been mourning for *five hundred* years?" he asked, incredulously.

"She was our Rai-sama. It's only respectful."

Not excessive? Extreme, disproportionate, overdone. Catch scratched his cheek. "The Moonless Night. That's when your mourning ends. Magden Le Fou must've known. That's not prophecy; that's cheating." He tried for outrage, but couldn't quite summon the hypocrisy.

"But where are you returning from?" asked Moony.

She answered him when all Catch's attempts had met with resistance. "The Etherlands," she said, pointing out the cavern's mouth.

But there's nothing there, thought Catch, staring up at the deep black sky, wispy clouds, stars, and crooked white moon.

"You live in the air?" asked Moony, staring wide-eyed. "Wow!"

Koyuki made a face. "The Etherlands are on the other side of the sky. They're thin and cold and boring. This solid land is much nicer. It's warm. The ground pulls at you. I can't wait to live here, but everyone says we'll have to fight you shifters the instant we return. I think they just want to fight because they're still angry about Ginkiku. But what if we lose? We'll have to return to the Etherlands. I think we should try talking with you lot first, but no one will listen to me without the *kinhoshi.*"

And what if you don't lose? Catch licked his fangs. What if everyone was so busy congratulating themselves about defeating Gildar's tengu dolls they were completely unprepared when the real ones showed up? *Even if we are prepared...a whole army of angry tengu...*

"Hello?" Savotte called from a lower passage, voice echoing and distorted.

"Up here," Catch replied.

"I'll fetch her," said Koyuki, and flew off. Shrugging, Catch sat down against the wall and waited.

Moony hopped onto his knee. "An army of tengu." His tail flicked thoughtfully.

"Please tell me you're not thinking of challenging the lot of them to a duel."

Moony licked a paw. "I'd win, of course, but would it be just? Rune killed Genkiku, so the tengu were the victims. Still, it was so long ago, it's not like you're to blame. All in all, I think Koyuki's right. Everyone should sit down and figure it out." He stretched out a leg, starfishing his paw. "Maybe a duel between champions. But which side would I fight for?"

Smiling wearily, Catch stroked Moony's head. "If we want the tengu to listen, we should find this *kinhoshi* and—"

He stopped. Oh, bones and shards. Rune stole this *kinhoshi* from Ginkuku. According to her letter, Magden Le Fou had taken something from Rune in turn and vanished into some green and hidden land.

Then *he'd* taken that letter and slipped it into Ascot's pocket, thereby pointing her straight at the thing the conflict revolved around. Groaning, Catch knocked the heel of his hand against his brow. *Why am I surprised? If I'd given her a torch, she'd undoubtedly have walked right into a paper forest.*

Moony nuzzled his wrist. "What's the matter, Captain?"

"So very much," Catch muttered through his fingers. A sharp yelp echoed through the cavern. He lifted his head. "I think Koyuki's found Savotte."

Half a minute later, Koyuki buzzed back into the cavern carrying a kicking Savotte, and dropped her unceremoniously on the floor. Annoyingly, Savotte landed on her feet. She pushed back her unmussed hair, eyes sparkling. "Alchemic chicken."

"Yes, I was wrong." Catch sighed. "Gloat briefly, please. Having learned there is an army of enraged tengu headed our way, I'd very much like to figure out how to appease them."

More significantly, how to appease them without him having to be present for the Moonless Night. Because there was no such thing as fate, and he was not a puppet.

Explanations took less time than Catch feared. It was the arguments afterwards that dragged. And the recriminations, mostly aimed at him by Savotte.

"You had a letter indicating Rune wasn't a lion-shifter, and you hid it from us?" she demanded, voice rising an octave.

"Because you've always been so willing to criticize the system rather than uphold it." Catch stifled a yawn. How long had it been since he'd had a full night's sleep?

"Who cares if that muck-sucker was a lion-shifter or a newt-shifter?" Koyuki demanded. "He murdered our Rai-sama and stole our home."

Savotte's brow furrowed. "Your home?"

Koyuki pointed out the cavern. Moonlight cascaded down the Aspire's sleek sides. "That big, pointy building? The Raishiro."

"The Aspire? We stole that, too?" Catch shook his head.

Savotte swelled, possibly beginning a heated denial, but abruptly let out her breath in a gusty and very horselike sigh. "It makes sense," she admitted. "We don't even know what it's made of." She rubbed her eyes. "You must meet with Gildar, Koyuki. I see no other way."

"No," said Catch and Koyuki at once.

Taking her hand from her eyes, Savotte raised her brows.

"Without the *kinhoshi*, I have no authority," said Koyuki. "I'd be labeled a traitor if I made a deal with the enemy behind my people's back."

"And the last information I want to give Gildar is that there's a device capable of commanding lightning within his reach," added Catch.

"You'd think he'd try to take it for himself?" asked Moony, looking up from playing some game that involved herding roaches across the cavern floor.

"Would Rags-n-Bones try to eat the moon if you told him it was a giant avocado?" Catch replied. At the very least, informing Gildar could set off a hunt for Ascot. "No, our best bet is to return the *kinhoshi*."

He expected Savotte to immediately protest that they didn't know where it was, but her lips pursed. "Miss Abberdorf has the letter, yes? Then she'll have investigated it. I cannot imagine Miss Abberdorf able to resist diving neck-deep into such a mystery."

Catch spread a hand. She'd read Ascot perfectly, to his thinking.

"Galen went back. I wouldn't be surprised if he kept an eye on her." She nodded, tallying up some sum in her mind. "Unfortunately, considering how quickly Gildar had me dumped on Bone Slope, word of my demise has probably reached the entire Sniffer network."

Catch sighed. She was never going to forgive him for that, was she? "So, you can't contact him."

"No. But Mistral probably can."

"It's something," said Catch, after a moment's consideration. A reed to cling to, at any rate. He'd meant to speak to Mistral in the morning anyway.

But Koyuki scoffed. "That's all? A promise that you'll look for the *kinhoshi*? I can't return to my people with so little."

"Then we'll give them the Aspire," said Catch. Savotte gasped and he whirled on her. "Oh, so?" he snapped. "It's ugly, smelly, and half-empty. Not worth dying for."

After a moment, Savotte nodded reluctantly. Not all shifters would be so reasonable. He didn't care. One way or another, everyone had to learn to share the world.

"The Aspire." Koyuki's cheek bulged with her tongue. "Who'll make the offer on the shifters' behalf?"

"You mean, go into the Etherlands?" asked Catch. She nodded.

Moony's wing shot up. "Ooh! I'll do it."

Moony? Our ambassador? Catch's brain stepped carefully around the notion.

"He can't speak on behalf of shifters," protested Savotte.

But Koyuki took her tongue from her cheek. She seemed to like the idea. Tucking away his own reservations, Catch drew off his father's ring. "Then, I'll give him permission to speak for me." Finding a length of cord in his pocket, he threaded it through the ring, and tied it around Moony's neck. Moony purred, whiskers fanning in the most enormous cat-smirk of satisfaction Catch had ever seen. "Please don't start a war."

"The Etherlands!" cried Moony. "Up among the clouds! You

usually have to climb enormous beanstalks to reach them. Maybe there will be giants."

"Business first," said Catch as Savotte buried her face in her hands. "Report back on the eve of the Moonless Night." Two days. He hoped it was enough. He turned to Savotte. "Take the clip off his wing."

"Of course." She sighed, tucking back a lock of her hair. "There's another problem we must address. Koyuki, can you fly me to the chamber with the fake tengu before you go? I'll see if I can sabotage them. We don't need Gildar being proclaimed a hero five minutes before the real tengu arrive."

"So, you finally accept that Gildar's behind the fake tengu?" said Catch.

"Shut up, Starthorne." More quietly, she answered his real question. "I saw you on that invisible road. That wasn't a lie. You'd never have subjected yourself to that if you hadn't expected to find proof at the other end."

Catch looked down. A roach was clambering over his toe. He flicked it off, glanced up at Savotte, and nodded. "Thank you."

She nodded back.

"No time to waste," said Koyuki, wings already buzzing. Rising off the floor, she gripped Savotte under her armpits. Moony jumped to her shoulder. "See you in two days, Starthorne."

"Bye, Captain!" Moony called. The trio swooped off, trailing sparks and ash. Only then did Catch realize his plan's greatest flaw.

Somehow, he was going to have to make it back across the no-see-'em road alone.

Pulling himself through the Sparkspire's window, Catch collapsed, quite simply, on the landing's floor. *Now I know what hell looks like, should anyone ask.* His synonym for it would forever be "crossing a no-see-'em path." No; crossing a no-see-'em path during a storm. That was the only thing that could make it worse.

After several shaking minutes, he staggered to his feet and descended the Sparkspire, pausing every other step to lean heavily against the wall. The sky outside the window slits was already changing from blue-black to slate-gray; dawn was only hours off. *Wonderful,* thought Catch. *I'll get three hours' sleep, at best, and after this trip, they'll all be plagued with nightmares.*

A light flickered under the door to his father's chambers. Catch paused in the hall outside, staring stupidly at the strip of yellow while his tired mind tried to work out what it signified. Had he left a lamp burning, or had Mistral returned, or…?

Soft thumps emanated from inside the room, accompanied by shuffling footsteps and the occasional grunt. Someone was definitely inside. *At least whoever-it-is isn't an assassin, or at least not a good one.* Shrugging, Catch opened the door.

He froze on the threshold, hardly breathing, incapable of more than staring. Two people holding reed batons, caught in mid-spar, stared back from the middle of the room. They'd pushed aside the furniture and rolled up the white rug.

One was Mistral. "You're back, sir," she said, wiping sweat off her cheek. She gestured to her smiling, black-haired opponent. "This is my swordmaster—"

Catch recovered his voice. "Father."

CHAPTER TWENTY-SIX:
ORIGINALS AND COPIES

Mistral gaped. Over her shoulder, Lethe smiled at Catch, eyes twinkling, as if he found her simply endearing.

"No," she finally squeaked. "This is my swordmaster, Evoke Moon—"

"I was told you were dead," said Catch, not so much talking over her as hardly noticing she was speaking.

Propping his reed baton against a wall, Lethe dragged up one of the chairs and sat, crossing his ankle over his opposite thigh. "Perhaps we should take displays of astonishment as read and move on," he said, tenting his fingertips.

"You procured a jaguar, killed it, and left its body beneath the cliff for Gildar to find," said Catch. He could've laughed. Had he truly ever believed the story of his father's demise? Lethe Starthorne didn't die—he killed.

"Well done," said Lethe, smiling. Difficult to even imagine him dead, seeing him lounging there in his plain, dark clothes, a mantle the color of smoked malachite tossed carelessly over his shoulders. Catch saw why Gildar had compared their eyes. It wasn't the color—the green in Lethe's was more prominent. It was the size of them, the shape of them, the wideset-ed-ness of them, how their slightly thick lids gave them an expression of innocence when opened wide, and sulkiness or condescension when lowered.

Perhaps Mistral spotted the resemblance. Her brows lowered from their high, incredulous position. "Is it true, Master Moonbranch? Are you really his father?"

"I truly am," Lethe replied. That calm, pleased voice. Catch remembered it better than his father's face, or the way his black hair stuck up in back, just as his own did. How unfair that Lethe should look so unchanged. Shifters aged gradually, but it seemed Lethe had evaded time's effects as easily as he'd evaded Gildar's notice these past twenty-four years.

Leaning forward, Lethe patted Mistral's hand. "I meant to inform you in due course, and here we are." He slipped her baton from her grip and propped it with the other. "But for now, pupil, to your tasks. My son and I must talk."

Pouting slightly, Mistral bowed to Lethe and headed to the door. Her shoulder brushed Catch's as she passed. "Mistral," he said. She stopped. A *"don't"* lodged somewhere in his throat. He just stood there, mouth working silently.

Don't. Whatever he's asking you to do, don't do it. But she'd ask why, with Lethe sitting there, not twenty feet away, smiling, smiling.

"Goodnight, sir," she said, and continued on. The door clicked shut with the sound of opportunities lost.

Lethe smiled. "Still here," he said, waving.

Catch moved. Every step seemed to carry with it the possibility of some horrific explosion, but he dragged up another chair to face Lethe's and sat. "You're Mistral's teacher."

That was how Mistral knew about channeling, he realized. And the Aspire's secret passages. Lethe had taught her. Likely, he'd taught her many things.

Perhaps he'd taught her to be a killer.

"Yes, I felt I owed her that much." Lethe tapped his fingertips together. "Tigers have no spots."

"It was you," said Catch. A ring and a pendant, bound together with a custard peach pit. "You're the Hide Away's leader. Was Arctic your partner? Did you kill him?" *And just think, five minutes ago, I was exhausted.* He wondered if he'd ever sleep again.

Lethe flicked away the lock of hair that fell over his right eye. It swung back again. "I regretted the necessity." He did sound remorseful, but it was on the scale of a person treading on a butterfly by mistake. "It was a good partnership while it lasted. He used the Hide Aways to help slipskins escape, and I used them to gather information from beyond our borders. But when he found you, he wanted you to join them. That didn't fit my plans."

A lava rock slammed into Catch's gut, burning away his innards. "You killed Arctic because of me." *Cavall gave me trout chowder, and in return, I got his father killed.* Jumping up, he ran to the kitchen to find a cup of water to quench the heat boiling inside him.

"I couldn't have you mucking about the Clawcrags being a Hide Away," Lethe called. "You needed to be free."

Mistral, praise her, had left a jug on the counter filled with juice-sweetened water. Catch filled and drained three cups in rapid succession. His gut still burned, but at least his throat no longer clamped tight.

"What's wrong, son?"

Turning, Catch spotted his father leaning against the side of the rounded opening between the kitchen and sitting room. In one hand, Lethe absently manipulated a peach-sized sphere as clear and fragile-looking as a bubble. A furrow traced a line between his brows.

Our almost identical brows, thought Catch. *Damn him.* He banged the cup down on the counter. "Galen Cavall's spent the last twenty-five years obsessing over who killed his father. It turned him into a fanatical slipskin hunter. How many died because of that?"

Lethe's eyelids dropped, giving him that petulant look. "I *am* sorry about Arctic. That's why I made his granddaughter my pupil."

Catch leaned against the counter. The cup's sides trembled

warningly under his fingers. He eased his grip before it shattered. "What are you doing here, Father? Why play dead for twenty-four years?"

He jumped at a touch on his arm. Somehow, Lethe had crossed the distance between the opening and the counter without a whisper of sound. "Come, sit down," said Lethe, guiding him back to the sitting room. "You haven't properly rested since reaching Holdfast." A tongue click. "If only my agents had apprehended you in Highmoor, as they were supposed to, you would've known everything already."

His doing all along, thought Catch, settling into his chair. Lethe had taught him to pick pockets. It would've been a simple matter for him to steal the ring, add the pit and pendant, and return them without Cavall being the wiser.

The Hide Aways he'd met in Highmoor would never realize how lucky they were he'd chosen to go with Cavall. Undoubtly, Lethe would've disposed of them once they served their purpose.

"Perhaps that, too, was fate." Reclaiming his own seat, Lethe resumed rolling the bubble-sphere over his knuckles.

Fate. Catch squeezed the chair's arms. A rough edge on a tiny nail tacking the upholstery to the frame cut his thumb. "Why are you here, Father?"

Lethe cocked his head. "I wish you were happier to see me. I've missed you, son."

And I've missed you. That was the worst of it; that a part of him wanted to fling his arms around his father and sob into his shoulder. He held himself straight and tight.

"I'm sorry for all you've suffered. But this year, we'll finally have our revenge on Gildar." Lethe smiled like a cub treated to his first sip of coffee.

"That's what this is about? Revenge? That's why people have died?" Catch hunted through his pockets for his drinking flask.

"Revenge..." Picking up the bubble-sphere, Lethe gave it a

careless, ceiling-wards flip that should have shattered it into splinters. He caught it, unbroken. "…and fate. Possibly."

"Fate." Catch lowered the flask.

Lethe nodded. Wedging the sphere into a corner of the cushion, he leaned forward, resting his forearms on his knees. "You know I've always wondered if it exists. It's hard to believe our lives could be laid out before us, like a line on a map that we must walk, and yet I've always felt chosen. Some people are worth more than others."

"Gildar thinks the same thing," snapped Catch, flashing back to the woman with the "F" branded into her cheek.

Again Lethe's eyelids dropped petulantly. "No, Gildar thinks being born with a particular *trait* makes you worth more. Blond hair. Lion-shifting. Whatever puts him on top. Gildar's someone who can't accomplish anything without his entire circumstance being slanted in his favor. The definition of mediocre, really." He tapped his lips, as if the thought had just struck him and he liked it very much.

Middling, thought Catch. *Second-rate. Unexceptional.* He drank.

"Gildar desires power and glory without earning them," said Lethe, toying with his sphere again. "That's where it started. When you were born, it was obvious—if there is such a thing as fate—that *you* were the golden star. *I'm* the death in the Clawcrags; that's quite clear."

An edge came into his voice; a sharp one. Catch took another drink from his flask.

"All I had to do was wait until the Moonless Night," Lethe continued. "If you saved us, well, fate's a real thing. But Gildar saw the prophecy as a chance for power. He killed his own wife just so he could claim Glim was 'born of death.'"

"He…killed Glim's mother?" Catch started to take another drink, corked his flask, and stuffed it into a pocket. It wasn't helping.

"I mixed the poison myself," said Lethe. Setting aside the sphere, he interlocked his fingers over a knee. Always restless, Lethe

Starthorne, unless intent on a kill. "I didn't know he meant it for her. But getting an alchemist to charm that star-shaped whorl into Glim's fur was really pushing it. How could I tell what was fate and what was his manipulation?"

Cavall's father, Glim's mother..."Did Mother die for your obsession, too?" Catch rasped.

Lethe's eyes widened. Horrified, Catch recognized delight. "That was my greatest fight. Velocity forced me to make an effort. She gave everything she had, and it was more than I suspected she possessed. Such a delightful surprise." Turning thoughtful, he gazed up at the ceiling. "I should've taught her how to channel. A cougar can't match a jaguar, but with her determination—" Abruptly, he refocused. "Your mother, yes. She feared that, unless we publicly proclaimed Glim was the golden star, Gildar would have you killed. I agreed with her on that," he shrugged, "but she didn't like my solution of killing Glim."

Mother. Catch shut his eyes. Velocity hadn't been the nurturing sort. She was boisterous and impatient, eager for pranks and a game of skittleball, ready to tousle hair and eat honeyed seed cake. She'd always returned him to his caretakers when, as a cub, he'd wanted more from her than rough-and-ready attention.

Yet, she'd been willing to give her life to save his. "You killed my mother just so you could continue your experiment with fate," said Catch, staring at the undersides of his closed lids. The burning wetness would fall if he opened them. "Did you kill Glim as well?"

He heard the surprise in his father's answer. "As far as I know, son, that was you."

❧

The world was very quiet. The pocket of warm air surrounding him smelled of coffee, black cherries, and spruce gum. His face was wet. No; soaked, and resting against something soft and damp that rose and fell in gentle intervals.

"There, there," soothed a voice. A hand stroked his hair. "You're exhausted."

Lethe's voice. Lethe's hand. Lethe, crouched beside his chair. Appalled, Catch jerked away from his touch, banging an elbow against his chair's arm. Lethe's hand trailed from his head to rest on his shoulder. "Calm down, son. You'll sleep soon. But first, I must tell you about the Moonless Night."

Catch scrubbed his sleeve over his nose and eyes and lips, smearing tears and snot uncaringly across his face, ignoring the pain of his bruised eye. "I know about Gildar's fake tengu army."

"Good." Lethe sat back. "If my agents had brought you to Merryvick as planned, I'd have shown them to you. As it was, I had to set off the charges I'd planted in the Underway and hope you'd find them. That makes this easier. Yes, Gildar's trying to sell himself as the golden star now. Even putting it about that *his* mother died in childbirth, too. Of course, changing documents to reflect more flattering history is an Ambersun family tradition."

Catch heaved himself upright. "Father. Drop your vendetta. The tengu are real, and—"

"Oh, I know," said Lethe cheerfully. Getting up, he went to the kitchen.

Catch stared after him. "You know?"

"Gildar's not the only one who's had documents changed," Lethe called back. "I was spymaster, remember?" A chuckle floated out of the kitchen. "Wait until historians read the bit about Alph Veer and the pickled eggplant I inserted. Anyway, I know the tengu will return after finishing their mourning period." He peeked around the opening, eyes twinkling. "I had to silence everyone else who knew it. You're lucky you're my son." Chuckling, he again vanished from sight.

More deaths. Catch pulled a hand over his scalp. *Deaths. I killed Glim.* It rocked him all over again. Heaving, he clenched his teeth, pressed a hand to his stomach. *No. I didn't. Couldn't.* "I spoke with a tengu," he called. "They won't attack if we return what Rune stole from the Storm Queen."

Lethe poked his head around the opening. "They won't? Where is it?"

Like I'd tell you. "I don't know." Catch rested his hands palm-up on his lap. He closed them. Opened them. "Magden Le Fou took it somewhere."

"Hmm." Lethe ducked back into the kitchen. He emerged carrying a tray containing the pitcher, two cups, and a plate of seed cakes. He righted a table that had been pushed aside and set the tray on it. "Drink," he said, putting a cup in Catch's hand. "You cried a long time." Taking a seed cake, he reclaimed his seat.

Catch did feel entirely wrung out, like an old cloth. He drank, set down the cup, and clasped his hands loosely between his knees. "Maybe you saw some reference to where Le Fou went while you were amending old documents."

"I don't want the tengu appeased." Lethe toyed with his bubble-sphere.

Catch should've been beyond surprise. Maybe he was; his heart gave a single lurch before resuming its steady glug. "You don't."

"Everything's planned," said Lethe. "When the fake tengu arrive in the Roundgrounds, my Hide Aways will be there, armed and waiting." He smiled broadly. "Then, after the dolls have been revealed as frauds, and Gildar thoroughly shamed, the *real* tengu will appear. Seeing us prepared for battle, they'll naturally assume the worst and attack."

"You *want* that?" cried Catch. "Why?"

Lethe tossed the sphere high. "After the shock of Gildar's betrayal, we'll be in disarray," he said, watching its downward trajectory. He swiped it out the air and looked at Catch. "The tengu should defeat us easily."

A noise of protest smothered itself in Catch's throat.

"We're dying here." Lethe turned his face to the wall, watching his reflection slide along its shiny, inwardly sloping surface. "You must've noticed half the Aspire's empty. Shifters are very good at killing—well, it *is* amusing—but for centuries, we've only been turning it on ourselves. Defeat will force us to abandon our system and band together against a common enemy." He smiled. "Really, I am serving the Hide Aways' interests."

Only Father would believe he deserves praise for planning mass slaughter. "People will die," said Catch, faintly. Gray shadows crept into the room's corners. The lamp was burning low. He should get up and attend to it.

"They'll also fully live, for a change," said Lethe. He paused. "Of course, if fate is real, you'll stop that all from happening. Won't that be interesting? Here." Abruptly, he tossed the bubble-sphere straight at Catch. Catch, sinking deeper into his chair, watched his hand lift, vaguely realizing it would be too late to intercept the oncoming object.

It was. The sphere struck his fingertips and bounced onto the floor. Catch yelped as it fell, but it didn't chip, let alone shatter.

Lethe laughed. "Amusing aren't they?" Scooping it up, he banged it against the wall. "The more delicately you treat them, the more likely they are to break."

"It's a Seersee?" asked Catch. He'd never seen one so clean before—no one dared polish them for fear of breaking them, which, if his father was right, only made them more likely to shatter.

"Yes." Setting it in his lap, Lethe patted his shoulder. "Fathers should give their sons gifts," he said, smiling into his eyes. "It's been years since I've been able to do so."

Catch tried to move away and his body didn't react. It seemed coated in a layer of fluffy cotton that was slowly sinking into his skin, into his nerves.

Oh, mange and ticks and leaping fleas! "You drugged me." His voice slurred. Rolling his head to the side, he strained to look at the cup, innocently dripping a bead of juiced water down its side.

Lethe laid a hand across his forehead. "I said you'd sleep. Two full days of it. You'll awaken by the Moonless Night, and then…" He shrugged. "I don't believe in fate, and yet, look! Here you are, after twenty-five years, returned in time for the Moonless Night. It *does* make me wonder."

Catch stared down at his reflection, distorted in the Seersee's sides. Other images danced faintly in its center. *I have to stay awake. I have to speak to Mistral. Moony and Koyuki will return, and if I'm sleeping…*

He was almost asleep now. The room had turned very gray. Lethe stroked his hair, light as the brush of a wafting cobweb. "I'm so happy to see you again, son. It'll be wonderful after the Moonless Night. I've also traveled outside the Clawcrags. I spent four years in a seaside village called Gorse Cliff, pulling pints at an inn called The Drunken Gull. I knew the names of every regular. The owner, Nat Cody, told the most wonderful stories every night."

This was a nice story, too. Catch leaned into his father's hand.

"Have you ever smelled gorse?" Lethe continued. "It's like coconut and pineapple mixed together. Myrtle, Cody's daughter, kept vases of it on the tables, so the Drunken Gull smelled of it, and salt, and malty beer. These elaborate fisherman's knots hung on the walls. They held competitions to see who could tie a particular knot the fastest." He laughed. "I never won; can you imagine?"

With an effort, Catch lifted his head. "Father. Confront Gildar and appease the tengu, and I'll go to the Drunken Gull with you. I promise."

Ascot would understand if he left her for a while. He was planning on seeing her again, wasn't he? He'd forgotten.

"Oh, it's gone." Lethe waved a hand. "It started getting popular and noisy. Then, Nat Cody died, and the new owner planned to repaint and enlarge it. It really wasn't worth letting it go on. I poisoned everyone the day of Cody's wake."

Catch let his eyes close. For a moment, his father had almost seemed a normal person.

"I like to think of them like that, gathered around Cody's bier, as if listening to his last tale. I placed a bouquet of gorse in Myrtle's hands." Lethe kept stroking his hair. "But they were just humans. We'll probably have to fight them, when we're driven out of the Clawcrags."

Giving Catch's hair a final pat, he bent down to whisper, "Remember, the softer the touch, the more likely to shatter."

"I won't shatter," said Catch. The words took all his strength to say, and he wasn't even sure what he meant. But he forced them out before darkness took him.

CHAPTER TWENTY-SEVEN:
ROCKS AND HARD PLACES

Several feet ahead, Cavall halted suddenly. A huff grunted out of his throat.

"What is it?" Ascot called, instantly on edge. The sound suggested surprise and dismay, and neither was reassuring, particularly in these surroundings. Her old phobia about being buried had reawakened the instant the Underway's alchemic door crunched shut behind them. *So much for leaving that particular fear behind in Albright's wine cellar.*

"There's been a cave-in," Cavall replied.

Exchanging worried looks, everyone went to join him. Sunlight flowing through the gaps in the right-hand wall mixed with the blue lichen light, turning everyone corpse green—except for Starley, whose white hair glowed like an incandescent cabbage. Cavall stood at a branch between two passages. Fallen rubble choked the left one.

"Does this happen often?" asked Starley, toeing a rock.

"Never," Cavall replied. Dmitri snuffled amongst the rubble. Ascot seized Rags-n-Bones' collar before he joined him. Cavall rubbed his jaw before adding, "This is the path Rainy and Starthorne would've taken to Holdfast."

It took a second for the import to sink in. Then, it pierced like an arrow. *Moony! Catch!*

"Calm down," said Dmitri, muffled.

Ascot blinked. She was on her knees, which stung, digging through the rubble. One nail had already broken. She picked at it wonderingly.

Dmitri spat out her coat hem. "There's no blood. It didn't fall on them."

"Blood?" Belatedly piecing together the potential tragedy, Rags-n-Bones burst into tears.

"No blood," repeated Dmitri, conferring with the ceiling for patience. "The dust's settled. The rocks likely fell before our comrades passed through."

"Before." Jolt tugged at his ear, scowling. "I *hate* the timing."

"So do I," said Cavall. They exchanged a grim look. Remarkable progress, considering he and Jolt had refused to speak to each other since joining forces.

Rubbing grit off her hands, Ascot got to her feet. Her heart still pounded. "What do we do?"

"Investigate," said Starley promptly. "Something that's never happened before happens just as Starthorne comes through? Not a, whatsit, coincidence."

Raising a paw, Dmitri wiped away the dust smearing his glistening black nose. "Tomorrow's the eve of the Moonless Night. Can we spare the time?"

"I think we must," said Cavall, staring down the blocked channel. "The Underway's checked by alchemists regularly. This shouldn't have happened. It'll mean backtracking."

Blue-violet light burst into existence; a concentrated ball of it, hovering six feet above the tunnel's floor. "Have you forgotten you've a witch in your party?" demanded Condorella, posing dramatically beneath it.

"Not likely, with you blinding us," said Starley, throwing an arm over his eyes. "Shutter it, will you?"

Ascot peeled a loose shred off her fingernail. "Are you suggesting you can move all those rocks by magic?" she asked, giving the rubble blocking the passage a dubious look. It had to weigh tons.

Condorella puffed out her meagre chest. "They'll float like feathers."

"That's silly," piped up Rags-n-Bones. "Rocks are nothing like feathers."

Scowling, Condorella waggled her brows at him, trying to make her eyes flash. Ascot chewed another shred off her nail. How much time would they lose in backtracking? "Do it," she said.

Condorella's chin came up. "Give me space," she said, flapping her hands at them like they were so many chickens. Taking Rags-n-Bones' arm, Ascot drew him away. He plucked his chin, eyes troubled.

"Why does she need so much space if the rocks are going to float?" asked Starley, not particularly quietly. Ascot stepped on his foot, in gentle warning.

"Because rocks don't float?" said Rags-n-Bones.

Condorella scowled over her shoulder. "Hush," begged Ascot. Part of her would feel, well, wobbly, until she saw for certain that no bodies were squashed under all those rocks.

Condorella spun her staff. The bobbing blue-violet ball brightened, beginning a low-level hum.

Rags-n-Bones tugged Ascot's sleeve. "Let's move a bit further, miss," he whispered, urging her further down the passage. Dmitri and Cavall followed their example.

The hum intensified. Condorella's face turned purple. Cords strained in her neck as she lifted her arms. The fallen rocks vibrated, clicking together. Exchanging glances, Starley and Jolt shuffled a few steps backward.

Sweat dripped down Condorella's cheeks. Her fingers curled into claws. "*Proteo plumero,*" she rasped.

With an enormous, heavy crack, the wall to their left crumbled.

Then, the ceiling fell in.

Then, part of the outside wall collapsed, and all the fallen rocks rumbled down the mountainside. The whole sequence of events was probably extremely loud, but all Ascot heard was her brain sloshing inside her skull. Instinctively dropping into a crouch, she clutched her head and tried not to choke on rising dust.

The world shuddered around her for quite a while. When the floor stilled, and she believed she could actually hear silence over the buzzing in her ears, she considered uncoiling.

Rags-n-Bones touched her arm. "Are you all right, miss?" Beside him, Dmitri shook himself until yellow dust and creamy hair flew.

Slowly, Ascot straightened. "I'm all right." She popped her cheeks, but the buzzing continued. "How about everyone else?"

Reassuring murmurs answered. Cavall had a nasty cut along his cheek from a bit of flying rock, and Condorella wheezed, clutching her midsection, but that seemed the worst of it.

"I appreciate the fresh air," said Starley, climbing halfway out the new, large opening in the mountainside. "Ah!"

Jolt dragged him back. "We're lucky the whole mountain didn't collapse on our heads."

"Objects that have been treated with alchemy don't like magic," said Rags-n-Bones. "Alchemy brings out innate qualities, while magic makes them do things they shouldn't, see? So they get confused and go boom." He brought his palms together in a resounding clap.

He really did learn a lot from Master Porpetti this winter. Ascot shook pebbles out of her hair. "Let's investigate before something does fall," she said, stepping into the new, wide channel created by the wall's demolition.

She stopped. Ahead, bright in the darkness, winked a yellow-green light, tiny as an errant firefly. "Is that a glow-globe?"

"It's the right color," said Cavall, moving to her side. He touched her shoulder. "Could be a Sniffer patrol. Better let me go ahead."

"Wait." Dmitri snuffled, nostrils flaring. "It smells like Savotte."

"Rainy?" Cavall's grip on his sword loosened. "Rainy?" he called.

"Galen?" Savotte's answering voice sounded every bit as incredulous as his.

Cavall's face brightened. With lighter stride than before, he jogged toward the firefly dot, which grew bright enough to illuminate the sheen of gunmetal hair. They met mid-tunnel. "What are you doing here?" asked Cavall.

Savotte snorted, running her gaze over the group gathered behind him. Except for a rough bandage wrapped around her right arm, the woman remained ridiculously well-groomed for someone found lurking in a tunnel. Ascot sighed, tugging her own, snarled, locks. "Same question," Savotte replied. "Only I'll add 'what are you doing in such company'? Reftkin's head is still attached, I see."

Starley's teeth flashed. "So are my—"

Ascot wasn't the only one who stepped on his foot. She thought even Rags-n-Bones might've gotten a toe in.

"Long story," said Cavall. "But..." He looked away. "I learned something about Mistral."

"That she's a Hide Away?" asked Savotte, gently. Cavall's head jerked up and she raised a hand. "I only recently learned it myself."

"Moony and Catch." Ascot couldn't contain herself any longer. "Are they all right?"

For a moment, Savotte stared at the floor, her jaws chewing invisible grass. "Yes. They're fine." Turning, she gestured them up the path she'd come from. "You must see this."

❧

"Apples, peaches, and little green cherries," breathed Starley as they surveyed the chamber lined with hulking, dark-skinned figures. Sunlight beaming through ceiling holes shone off glassy, slit-pupiled eyes.

"We came across them by accident when that cave-in forced us to divert from our path," said Savotte, setting her glow-globe on the floor. "Starthorne's certain Gildar ordered their construction."

"Why?" said Cavall, slowly spinning in place to take them all in.

Savotte rubbed her wrist, looking grim. "So he can defeat them on the Moonless Night and be proclaimed the golden star, savior of the Clawcrags."

The back of Ascot's neck tingled the longer she looked at the huge, slumped figures. Whoever'd designed them had a flair for menace. "I suppose he has some key word to control them."

"It isn't right." Rags-n-Bones walked the circle slowly, staring deep into every slack face. His eyes glistened. "It's not fair."

"Careful." Savotte stopped Ascot as she reached out to touch one. She lifted her bandaged arm. "They're not harmless. I attempted to sabotage them, and one attacked me. Some defense mechanism. But we have a larger problem." She rubbed two fingers between her brows. "There are real tengu. We met one."

She should've melted under the force of all the stares directed her way. Only Rags-n-Bones didn't look at her. He patted a doll's hand. "You're real, too," he murmured.

"They've been...well, behind the sky for the five hundred years, mourning their leader, Genkiku," Savotte flashed a grim smile. "Whom Rune killed. Needless to say, they're rather angry."

An army of fake tengu, another of real ones, and Catch in the middle of it all. Ascot fell back against a fake tengu. It was vaguely leathery and malleable, with some kind of armature inside. "Our plan," she croaked. "The tengu won't care that Rune wasn't a lion-shifter."

"Rune wasn't a lion-shifter?" Savotte's eyes darted to Cavall.

He pinched the bridge of his nose. "It's been a week for revelations. We found proof in a Seersee. We planned to reveal the truth at the ball, but like Miss Nuisance says, that won't impress the tengu."

Starley, standing in the entranceway with Jolt hovering behind him, laughed. He kept laughing while everyone stared at him. "Whatsit?" he asked, slapping his leg. "We make a smart little plan, but Gildar's smart little plan messes with it. Then along come the tengu with their own smart little plan to wreck his." Chuckling, he adjusted his bandana. "The Moonless Night's been brewing for five hundred years. Not surprising everyone has a different idea how it should go." He strode into the chamber.

When Jolt followed, one of the tengu dolls rumbled. Its eyes flared yellow, losing their haze. Stiffly, yet with greater speed than the big, awkward thing seemed capable of, it swiped out at Jolt.

"Oy!" Jolt jumped back, showing his teeth. Another tengu doll on his left rumbled to life and lurched toward him. All around the chamber, yellow glints seeped into glassy eyes.

"What's up with these flippin' things?" demanded Starley. Whipping his knife from his belt, Jolt brandished it at the first doll.

Rags-n-Bones dove between them. "Don't," he begged.

Jolt glowered. *Any moment now, he might shift and scream,* thought Ascot. *And if he screams, it'll echo off the walls and we'll all go deaf.*

"Jolt," barked Dmitri. "Cover your left cheek."

A rapid flux of emotions twisted Jolt's features, before, almost spasmodically, he clapped a hand to his face. The tengu dolls instantly sagged, the yellow light draining from their eyes.

"What happened?" asked Savotte, crouched and wary, blade drawn.

"They reacted to the brand," said Dmitri. Ascot had never heard him sound so grim, like every word was a bite out of someone's flesh. "Gildar needs these fake tengu to prove themselves a threat, so it seems a valiant deed when he defeats them. Ergo, they need to terrorize someone. Ergo, he's created them to menace a group of people he deems dispensable."

Silence raked the cavern like a killing-cold wind. *Expendable,* thought Ascot, shivering. *Superfluous. Disposable.*

Jolt's amber eyes narrowed to slits. Still clasping his cheek, he raised his knife over the now-inert doll that had menaced him.

"Don't!" Rags-n-Bones grabbed his arm. "It's not their fault."

He held on, even when Jolt glared. After a moment, Jolt let out a long breath and sagged. Rags-n-Bones released him.

Jolt's arm whipped up, burying the knife hilt-deep in the doll's chest. Rags-n-Bones cried out, but, pushing past him, Jolt stalked into the tunnel.

Rags-n-Bones tugged at the knife. "They're like me," he said, tears streaming down his face. "They're not as...alive, but we're the same."

Ascot helped him pull the knife out. It wasn't that he wasn't strong enough; he just hated sharp things. She ran her finger over the gash in the doll's chest, seeping thick, blue-black liquid. "Like you. Does that mean there's an electro-magniphager around somewhere?"

The electro-magniphager, also known as the Egg, was the alchemic device that had brought Rags-n-Bones to life five years ago. It had also, incidentally, exploded and given Kay and Lindsay Ashuren unusual abilities—after nearly killing them. Thinking of this, Ascot warily scanned the walls' crevices for glowing ovoids.

Rags-n-Bones' sniffling trickled off. He plucked his chin. "The Egg was Master Porpetti's special invention, but I think he got the idea for it from some earlier work. Maybe this." He pulled his chin harder, staring sadly at the tengu doll before them. "I think whatever's powering them gives them energy, but not life. If they were alive, they could think for themselves, and maybe wouldn't do bad things."

"Could you give them more life?" asked Ascot.

Rags-n-Bones shook his head. "Oh, no, miss, I'm not an alchemist. I just listened to Master Porpetti, and—"

"Then they must be destroyed," said Starley.

Rags-n-Bones gasped. Ascot swung around. Starley stood in the entranceway, arms folded across his chest. She'd never imagined his amiable face could look so stern. "They're going to *murder* ferals." His voice cracked on the verb. "They'll probably attack other shifters Gildar doesn't give a scrap for. All these new rules about what colors certain shifters can wear. If these dolls can be commanded to attack people with brands, why not people wearing brown, or yellow?"

"You think those laws were passed in preparation for this?" asked Savotte, paling. Perhaps she was wondering if horse-shifters were on Gildar's "allowable" list.

"Gildar's obviously been planning this for years," said Starley. "With one swipe, he can win eternal glory and rid himself of those shifters he considers unfit for society."

"I'll give them life," said Rags-n-Bones.

Ascot almost didn't recognize his voice. It had a hard, clear steadiness that was very unlike him. She looked at him, and he was standing without a trace of a slouch or a hint of wetness in his gray eyes. "I'll give them life, and teach them it's wrong to hurt people, and if I can't—" Here he broke. Tears dribbled, but he held himself straight. "If I can't, I'll—I'll make sure they can't hurt Devil-Jolt."

No, you won't, thought Ascot. Destroying them might prove necessary, but she wouldn't put him through it. "You'll need a helper," she said, hoping someone caught the significance behind her words.

Savotte nodded. "I'll do it. I'm dead, anyway." Smiling sourly, she turned over her wrist to reveal a little brown scab.

Ascot touched the matching mark on her cheek. "Catch?"

Savotte nodded. "Gildar wanted me dead before I could spread word of this find. Starthorne obliged."

I must get that vial from Catch, thought Ascot, and snorted. He was having such fun with it; sorting out the tengu mess might be an easier task.

"I will also stay," said Dmitri. He'd been prowling the chamber restlessly for several minutes, fur raised in spikes along his back. Ocasionally, Ascot thought she heard him growl. "An alchemist might come to activate the dolls, and we may need to detain them."

Ascot bent over him. "Something wrong?" she asked quietly. Realizing that could be a long list, she amended the question. "I mean, specifically?"

Dmitri slowly shook his head, hackles still raised. "Just stop Gildar," he replied in an undertone. "The troubles in Albright and Widget were petty compared to this." He showed his teeth.

Abruptly, Ascot realized the truth: Dmitri *hated* Gildar, even having never met the man. "I'll do my best," she replied.

He regarded her silently for ten solid seconds. "I know you will. Sorry." Sighing, he dropped his head to rub his nose against his leg. "Ascot. Don't feel guilty if it's not enough this time."

She swallowed, and the saliva went down in a cold gob, settling like a lump of ice in her stomach. How did one manage that? "Be careful, Dmitri." She hugged him, then went to Rags-n-Bones, who crouched before a copper box half-concealed in an indentation in the wall, staring at his hands.

He turned a wondering gaze on her as she came up. "I couldn't do this with paws." He wriggled his fingers.

"No," she replied, puzzled.

"Miss." His brow furrowed. "Am I supposed to be a dog, or," he looked down at himself, "this? I mean, I was born a dog, but then I was reborn like this." He rolled his fingers into his palms. "I thought Kay and Lindsay would be happy to see me as a dog again. They lost so much. But…"

They'll love you whatever you are. It would've been easy to say, and probably true. But it didn't feel right. "It's your choice," said Ascot, glancing at Dmitri. "You have to live in your body, so it should make you happy."

Rags-n-Bones wiggled his fingers again. Abruptly, his lips spread in a wide grin. "I'm not sure dogs like avocados." Rising, he hugged her. "Save the Captain, miss. Sir Dmitri and I will make all these tengu friendly."

Ascot hugged him back, then went to Cavall and Savotte, who were holding a hurried conversation in the chamber's center. Starley had gone after Jolt, which left only Condorella unaccounted for. Glancing about, Ascot located her sitting in the entryway, eyes closed, face pale, apparently not recovered from breaking the mountain.

"The real tengu are looking for something called the *kinhoshi*," said Savotte, turning to Ascot. "It controls lightning. Rune stole it from Genkiku, and Le Fou took it from him."

"To 'a green and hidden land'," added Cavall, voice heavy with irony.

"Oh, frabjacket." Ascot rubbed her forehead. "We thought it was the Seersee. Does this mean we have to return to Lorrygreen and dig up Le Fou's grave or something?"

"No time," said Savotte. "We have to hope your cat's a better ambassador than I fear he is."

"Moony's...negotiating with the tengu?" Laughter fought its way up Ascot's throat. She choked it down.

"We didn't have many options." Savotte ran a hand over her sleek hair. "He'll return tomorrow night. Hurry to Holdfast. Take the Seersee you found in Lorrygreen. Even if Moony fails, if you discredit Gildar, someone else will have to negotiate with the tengu, and they can at least promise to return the *kinhoshi*."

Her eyes met Ascot's with no mutual rancor, for once. *If. If.* They both knew what thin ropes they clung to. Ascot blundered for words. "If Rags can't—"

Savotte nodded, glancing at the dolls. "I'll take care of it."

"Thank you, Rainy." Ascot looked at Cavall. "Ready to go?"

"Yes." His determined expression briefly collapsed. "My daughter's in the middle of this."

So much pain. Ascot looked back into the chamber, keenly aware she was leaving the last of her original party behind. Under Rags-n-Bones' direction, Dmitri tugged at some of the wires connected to the copper box.

Dmitri. From all she'd heard, Gildar had earned his hatred, but she hated to think of him hating. It had to end somewhere.

So let's end it, Ascot thought. Facing resolutely forward, she went to join her new companions.

CHAPTER TWENTY-EIGHT:
RUDE AWAKENINGS

A collection of sounds added themselves to Catch's brain one by one: the click of pottery, footsteps, a subdued hiss, followed by a trickle. In a state of consciousness that could not be labeled "asleep" or "awake," he leaned back against the softly supportive frame behind him and stared at the ceiling. Its details slowly painted themselves into his mind.

He frowned. Although all Aspire ceilings bore a certain resemblance, each possessed its own peculiar whorls and ripples. *That's not the sitting room's ceiling*, he thought, blinking the gumminess from his eyes.

The smell of coffee hit his nostrils. This sensation required no leisurely filtering. He sat up, and only then realized he'd been lying down. *I remember falling asleep in the chair.*

Or, being drugged in his chair. *Father. Father!*

The pleasant lethargy fled. Catch swung his feet to the floor, encountering a smooth, blue rug instead of a soft, white one. He also didn't recall taking off his boots. Glancing around, he met the prim gaze of the constipated lion statuette, sitting on a shelf by the window. Peachy light streaming through the glass turned its alabaster sides pink.

"Good morning," Catch told it, running a hand through his hair. He was sitting in his father's sleeping alcove. He'd slept in his father's bed. Had Lethe moved him there? The thought made his skin bump up and quiver.

More clicks emanated from below. "Mistral?" he called.

With a series of thumps, footsteps climbed the ladder. A head of close-cropped black hair, far too large to be Mistral's, appeared in the opening. Grape-green eyes met Catch's.

"Bandersnatch?" said Catch.

"Boss." Bandersnatch ascended the rest of the way into the room, carrying a cup on a ludicrously dainty saucer. "I was worried. Mistral couldn't wake you."

He didn't sound worried. He sounded flat, and tired. The creases around his eyes did look worried, however. His gaze flicked from Catch to the window and back again.

Standing, Catch took the cup of coffee without asking if it had been intended for him, and drained it in several quick gulps, not caring that it burned his tongue. Aside from being hungry and thirsty, he felt remarkably fit. "I probably needed the sleep."

He knew he was lying to himself. Something in his brain screamed it was so even before Bandersnatch heaved a noisy sigh and went to stare out the window. "You slept for two days, Boss."

Catch set the cup into its frilly saucer with a click.

"It's the morning of the Moonless Night." One of Bandersnatch's hands rose toward his stubbled chin, then fell back to his side, leaving it un-scratched.

The cup didn't rattle on its saucer as Catch set both aside. "Where's Mistral?" he asked, voice steady as his grip.

"I don't know. Last night, she learned her father had returned to Holdfast, and she asked leave to visit him."

Two days. While Bandersnatch spoke, Catch fully absorbed the information. He'd missed two days. "Did Moony come by? Or—" No, Bandersnatch didn't know about Koyuki.

"Your winged kitty?" Bandersnatch shook his head, gaze fixed on the scene below. "Haven't seen him."

He should've been back last evening. Horrible possibilities rose into Catch's mind. Maybe Moony couldn't breathe in the Etherlands. Maybe the tengu had thrown him in prison.

Or, perhaps most likely, he'd gone looking for giants and was at this moment dueling over a singing golden harp.

Catch joined Bandersnatch at the window. Blue specks moved around the Roundgrounds' shiny silver surface; peacock-shifters, preparing for—

The ball, he realized. It was happening tonight. Both tengu armies would arrive tonight. The Hide Aways were assembling tonight. It was *all* happening tonight.

And he'd missed two days! Burying both hands in his hair, he scrubbed his scalp, trying to think. "I need to talk to Mistral."

"I'll try to get a message to her, but the peacock-shifters are pretty busy," said Bandersnatch, still in that odd, flat tone.

Catch sank inside. Why would Mistral avoid him now, unless Lethe had told her to do so? She'd been under his tutelage for years, unknowingly imbibing his poison. *I can't rely on her,* he decided regretfully.

Which left...Savotte, gone. Moony and Koyuki...where? Ascot, Dmitri, Rags-n-Bones...for all he knew, they'd returned to Widget. *I'm alone.* It was a forlorn thought. Cold. Hollowing. It felt like *bees.* Leaning over the window sill, Catch stared into his palms.

Bandersnatch picked up the cup and saucer. "Gildar wants to speak to you before everything starts," he said, heading toward the ladder. "He sent over some clothes for you. There's warm water in the ewer. Wash and dress, and I'll take you to him."

He descended the ladder. Catch continued staring at his palms. Between his spread fingers, the business of the Roundgrounds continued below. Its semi-circular expanse gleamed like a coin hammered flat over the plateau's rear.

Three armies waited to descend upon it tonight. And, according to the prophecy, it was up to him to stop them.

What can I do? I'd be an ant in a coffee grinder, smashed amongst all the beans.

Why should he even care? Glim's phantom face rose, and he banished it, savagely. Let them all tear each other. Surely he could hide in an empty corner of the Aspire for the night. Tomorrow, the survivors would be too busy picking up their scattered teeth to care about him. He could sneak out, find a path through the Underway, return to Ascot—

Running again? The little copy of her he kept in his mind glared, hands on hips, one toe poised to start tapping.

I don't know what else to do, he admitted, dropping his brow to his crossed arms.

He could tell the truth.

Catch lifted his head. Gildar wanted to talk to him. Gildar didn't know Lethe lived, or that an army of real tengu would break through the sky as the moon went dark. Gildar was arrogant and power-mad, but he was also Alph. Perhaps, if he were given the facts, there'd be time to avert a catastrophe.

Fur and fangs. Brushing a hand through his hair, Catch laughed; a wry chuckle, deep in his throat. *The truth.* He should've expected it would come to that.

But he owed it to Glim—had he killed Glim?—to at least try.

Briskly, he went to the ewer. A pile of fresh clothing sat on the chest beside it. Catch scrubbed, shaved, and dressed. Half an hour later, his mirror showed a surprisingly elegant reflection clad in a sleeveless, pale green shirt, and black, drawstring trousers. A length of gold ribbon tied back his newly combed hair. Catch hesitated before picking up the mantle: dark green, embroidered with golden stars.

Subtle, Gildar. He glanced at his brown coat, hanging over the back of a chair. He'd have preferred its familiar armor, but if he wanted to persuade Gildar, dressing in the attire he'd chosen would probably help. He arranged the mantle about his shoulders.

One of the coat's pockets bulged. Curious, Catch reached inside. *The Seersee*, he remembered an instant before pulling it out. He weighed it in his hand; as heavy as air. *Why did Father give me this?*

"Boss?" called Bandersnatch from below. "We better get going."

A maddening smear of colors swirled in the Seersees' center. Catch turned it, squinting, but if it contained an image, it refused to clarify. He debated a few seconds. Then, shrugging, he stuffed the Seersee back into the pocket, and descended the ladder to join Bandersnatch.

❧

Cavall slipped into the stifling, square room and shut the heavy door behind him. They'd entered Holdfast before dawn, while the sky was still gray. Cavall had taken them to this square, windowless detention center under the pretext of interrogating them. It fooled the guard at the Underway's grating, and possibly Starley and Jolt as well. They kept throwing uneasy glances at the bare, clay walls, lit only by a small pair of glowglobes.

They still don't entirely trust Cavall, Ascot realized. Dmitri would probably say they had cause. Condorella, in contrast, sprawled against the far wall, snoring lightly, her arm hooked around her dimly sparkling staff.

"No one's seen Mistral since last evening," Cavall reported. "The guards said she heard I was returning and asked for leave—how did she hear that? I didn't send word."

"The Hide Aways?" asked Ascot. "We know she's one of them." She was a little sorry she'd mentioned it when Cavall winced.

"If the Hide Aways are planning something, I should know about it." Starley removed his bandana to swipe sweat off his brow. Only the slightest draft managed to squeeze under the thick door. "I haven't heard anything from them since you started chasing us, leather-britches."

"Which is odd," said Jolt, frowning and tugging his ear. "It's the Moonless Night. You'd think our leader would have something planned."

"Whoever your leader is," muttered Ascot. Someone else with "a clever little plan" perhaps?

Cavall spun. "Bellmonte. Maybe he knows where Mistral—"

Starley was already shaking his head. "I told him to gather Afleeta and a couple others and sit tight." Cavall swore and kicked the door. Starley shrugged. "If Gildar wins tonight, the Hide Aways have to survive. I wanted them safe."

"And I want my daughter safe." Cavall kicked the door again. It had to hurt his toe; the door didn't even quiver under the blow.

Ascot lifted her hair off her neck, hoping to cool it. "Rags and Rainy are handling the fake tengu. Let's focus on the real ones. If only we'd known about this *kinhosi* thing in Lorrygreen."

"Hmm?" Condorella opened her eyes.

A knock, muffled through the wood's thickness, rapped on the door. "Dad?" said a voice.

Cavall's shoulders sagged. "Mistral." He opened the door, dragged a tall, crop-haired young woman through it, and hugged her roughly. Two seconds later, he pushed her to arm's length and shook her. "Where have you been? What in the name of sharp, white fangs do you think you're doing? The Hide Aways? My own daughter—"

"Easy, leather-britches." Peeling himself off the floor, Starley went to the pair and loosed Cavall's grip on his daughter. Ascot would've guessed the relationship if she hadn't known; Mistral was a shorter, less angular version of Cavall. Jaw clenched, she shook off Starley and stepped back, twitching her red-cuffed uniform into place.

"You're not my commanding officer, Dad," she said. "I don't have to divulge my whereabouts." Her voice turned snide. "Or was I supposed to send daily reports while you were in that human town for two years?"

"That was duty," snapped Cavall, glowering down on her. "And it's one thing to come and go on your own time, and another to turn slipskin." His sandy voice cracked. "Your grandfather was killed by slipskins." Starley coughed, and Cavall grudgingly added, "Maybe."

"The slipskin thing is stupid!" Mistral threw up her arms, pouting like the adolescent she was. "I wanted to act, but you said no, I was a hound, not some primping cat-shifter."

"Reminds me of my fights with my sister," said Condorella to Ascot as Cavall's cheeks darkened.

"You have a sister?"

Condorella nodded. "A twin. Ravenna."

"Your parents named her Ravenna and you Condorella?" Ascot grimaced, sliding down the wall to sit beside her. "No wonder you fought."

"Yes, Ravenna never forgave them," Condorella replied smugly.

Clearly, the Verydarkblues had different standards. Ascot shrugged mentally. "I have a twin, too. Vlad." Abrupt homesickness welled over her for Shadowvale, the mountainous country of her birth, where even at noon, the light shone murky. She missed the howlings of the wargs and the wights, and the spicy smell of the black roses in Abberdorf Castle's garden.

She swallowed it down. Shadowvale was miles and months away, and her older brother, Vincent, would probably have her arrested for stealing the family silverware if she returned.

The argument between Cavall and Mistral raged on. Since it appeared to consist mostly of the standard "you never understood me" accusations, Ascot felt she could ignore it until it ran its course.

Apparently Condorella felt the same. "What were you saying about something we missed in Lorrygreen?" she asked.

"You must've been sleeping when Savotte mentioned it in the cavern." Ascot rested her chin on her knees. "Catch and Savotte met a tengu who's looking for something called the *kinhoshi* that can summon lightning. It's probably what Rune stole from Genkiku, after he killed her."

"After he killed her." Condorella rummaged in her sleeve.

Ascot nodded. "Then, Le Fou took it to—"

Condorella brought out a cloth. Barely visible shards glinted in the dim light as she unfolded it. Ascot frowned as Condorella delicately turned over the largest fragment. A piece broke off its corner, even under that light touch. "Toad spit!" Condorella muttered, making a pass with her hand. "Look closely."

Ascot peered at the faint image frozen in the shard's center. A man—Rune she now knew—bent over a prone body. "Oh." She swallowed hard. The first time they'd watched this, she hadn't fully appreciated what she was seeing. "Is that...?"

"Rune just murdered Genkiku," said Condorella grimly. "Look at his hand."

His tiny hand was just a blur, smaller than a split pea. Ascot bent, squinting. Her efforts were rewarded by a glimpse of the tiniest of gold sparks, clenched in his fingers. "You think that's the *kinhoshi*?"

In reply, Condorella lifted her staff and ran a finger down its shaft. All at once, she brought it down over her knee. Ascot gasped at the sharp crack. But Condorella nonchalantly worked her long, yellow-lacquered nails into a split on the top piece's broken end, widening it until the blue-violet crystal clattered onto the floor. Condorella picked it up.

"Wood's willful," she said. "Not really good for spells. It just likes to grow. Stones, on the other hand...read your fairy tales, and you'll see witches and wizards really love sparklies. The tengu would probably use alchemy, not magic, but I suspect there are similarities."

Rags-n-Bones would know, thought Ascot. From what she remembered, Master Porpetti's inventions worked on metal, and electricity, and yes, bits of stone. "You think the *kinhoshi's* a stone?" She peered again at the image. It would have to be a golden stone—

"It used to singe my whiskers," Lacey said, passing over the little piece of pyrite.

Ascot slapped her pockets frantically, trying to remember where she'd put it. Just a stupid chunk of rock, she'd thought. There; the right pocket. She pulled it out and held it up. Green light glinted dully off its rough facets.

"Is that the *kinhoshi*?" asked Jolt.

Looking up, Ascot discovered everyone was staring at her. She'd completely blotted out all other conversation for the past few minutes. "I don't know. Lacey gave it to me."

"Is it just my shoddy eyesight, or is that thing star-shaped?" asked Starley.

Ascot held it up. Yes, its facets sprayed out from a central point. You had to use your imagination a little, but Starley was right; it was star-shaped.

With a golden sheen. "The golden star," she gasped.

The thick walls muffled all outside sound. Held breaths and accelerated heartbeats filled the room for several seconds. "Can't be," said Cavall at last, sounding strangled. "The golden star's a person."

"Does the prophecy ever actually say 'person'?" Ascot asked Condorella.

"No," she replied. "I suppose the 'draw breath' line got everyone thinking that way, but Le Fou probably meant 'still have power.'"

Does it? Ascot squeezed the stone, to no effect. Well, maybe it only worked for tengu. "If Rune killed Ginkiku for this, that satisfies the 'born of death,' requirement."

"There never was a golden star." Cavall sagged, convulsively shaking his head as he clutched his pendant. "Rune wasn't a lion-shifter. Everything we were taught is a lie."

Mistral didn't seem to share her father's dismay. Her lips twitched, as if fighting off a smile. Ascot expected Starley to grin as well, but he just looked tired, running a hand repeatedly through his hair.

"So, we have the golden star, probably," he said. Jolt crouched at his feet, viciously snapping stray bits of straw between his fingers. "Let's say Bone-man stops the fake tengu—"

"He'd better," muttered Jolt. *Snap.*

"—that leaves Gildar. If we give him the *kinho*-whatsit, who says he returns it to the tengu? He might claim it for himself, to fight them." Starley shook his head. "We should follow our original plan. If we discredit Rune, Gildar can't claim the *kino*-whatsit as fair spoils. He'll have to return it."

He looked guardedly around, perhaps expecting dissent, but Cavall released his grip on his pendant and straightened. "I've given too much of my life, serving a lie. If I must realize the truth, everyone should. Can you make the switch, Condorella?"

She scowled at the clothful of fragments. "If this blasted shard doesn't shatter into dust. And if I don't get caught. All five Seersees will likely be guarded."

"So, we'll need with quick hands and a distraction to make the switch," said Starley, beginning to pace.

"Quick hands. A good task for Catch." Ascot's heart thumped. He'd be at the ball. She'd see him in a matter of hours.

"I can take the shards to him." Mistral reached out, but Condorella snatched the cloth to her chest.

"No. They're too fragile."

More likely she didn't want to relinquish a memento of Magden Le Fou, thought Ascot. "We'll bring them to the ball. You could take a message to him, however."

"I might not be able to. I haven't seen him since last night," Mistral replied. "He's always wandering off and coming back without an explanation."

Then why offer to take the shards to him? Wandering off and refusing to say where or why was just like Catch, but it seemed to Ascot that Mistral spoke a bit quickly.

"I'll try, though," Mistral added. "And I can maybe get myself stationed by a Seersee tonight. That would make it easier, wouldn't it?"

"*You're* staying away from the Roundgrounds tonight," said Cavall.

Oh, Galen. Ascot closed her eyes. His authoritative tone raised *her* hackles, and she wasn't his daughter.

Unsurprisingly, Mistral bristled. "Since you insisted I become a guard, I may as well do my job." She stomped toward the door, but Cavall held it shut. Mistral stopped and glowered. "Going to keep me locked up, Dad?"

"I have a good notion to do just that," he replied, staring down at her.

"Oh, that always works," said Jolt, still crouched on the floor. He twisted a handful of straw together. "Lock people up, force them to do your bidding. Such love it engenders." Throwing down the straw he rose and stalked toward the door. "Move aside, Sniffer."

Starley paused in his pacing. "Oy, Jolt, where are you going?"

Jolt thrust Cavall aside. "If Rags-n-Bones fails to stop the fake tengu, they'll come into the city and *murder* ferals," he snapped. "Maybe you're willing to go on faith that he'll succeed, but I'm not. They have to be warned."

"Jolt." Starley reached out. "What if a Sniffer arrests you? Besides, I could use your help tonight. We can cause the distraction. We're good at that, yeah?" He tried to smile, but to Ascot, the intangible thorn in his shoe was once again evident.

"Ferals aren't allowed on the Roundgrounds unaccompanied," Jolt replied, so softly a sigh would've drowned him out. "You'd have to pose as my keeper. Is that what you want?"

Starley dropped his gaze. "Of course not, but—"

Jolt opened the door. "Coming, Mistral?"

She started walking. "Mistral," said Cavall.

She didn't even pause. Brushing past him, she left. Cavall slumped. Jolt lingered a moment to slip off his mantle. "The Sniffers might wonder where I got this. Keep it safe," he said, holding it out to Starley.

When Starley didn't take it, he let it drop and went out, closing the door behind him.

Wishing she didn't have to be the one to break the silence, Ascot cleared her throat, instantly wondering why she'd chosen such a rude, juicy noise. "When should Condorella and I report to the Roundgrounds to learn our maidly duties?" she asked Cavall.

"Might as well go now." Cavall pulled himself up as if his bones ached. "I'll escort you. There's tension in the city, and you two aren't dressed like proper Clawcraggers."

"I'm ready," said Condorella, pushing off the wall. "Going to a ball to be a servant. Feh! They probably won't even let me cook my special cauliflower au gratin."

"Maybe we can spill wine on someone's shoe." Bending, Ascot picked up Jolt's mantle. The vermillion cloth was soft and heavy, with a faint scent of anise. The embroidered dragonflies shimmered softly. "He knows you care," she said, giving it to Starley.

"Yeah." Starley tried to grin, and for the first time, utterly failed. "See you at the ball."

Whatever had put the brand to Jolt's face, it wasn't something that could be wiped away with words, or time, or possibly even with love. Ascot squeezed Starley's hand. "See you at the ball."

They went out. Ascot took deep breaths of the cool, fresh air as she got her first real look at Holdfast. It smelled of coffee, of course, and hot spices from a fried cicada stand. Strings of paper golden stars swung overhead. Others hung in windows outlined with colorful tiles. Every building, no matter how grand, was constructed from the yellow clay. Even the fancy hotel they passed, three stories of arches covered with climbing bougainvillea, accented with a layer of mica chips, couldn't disguise the fact that, underneath the glitter, it was basically a box of hardened mud.

Except for the Aspire, she thought, looking ahead to the darkly gleaming, spikey thing rising above the sloping roofs. Many pedestrians' eyes went to it repeatedly as they conducted their business. For the number of people crowding them, the streets seemed subdued. The atmosphere reeked of an impending storm, although the sky remained clear. Odd to think that, tonight, it would crack like an egg and let a swarm of angry tengu through.

Absently, Ascot glanced up at it. Moony dropped onto her head.

CHAPTER TWENTY-NINE:
GOING UP IN THE WORLD

Bandersnatch suddenly stopped beside a large, cracked boulder marking the foot of a trail that wound a northwesterly track up Mt. Snagtooth's side.

"What's wrong?" asked Catch, stopping as well. Mt. Snagtooth was decidedly the uglier of the two mountains straddling Holdfast Plateau: squat and lumpy, with only a few sour, wind-twisted trees garnishing its bald pate. Why had Gildar chosen it as their meeting place?

Bandersnatch began scratching his jaw rapidly, nails scraping stubble. "I should've challenged Gildar on Yawning Day," he said, gaze fixed on the ground. "I was going to. But he told me to fight you and...you gotta obey the Alph."

He looked at Catch with a kind of pleading in his eyes. Catch stared back, nonplussed. "I know Gildar ordered you to fight me." Inwardly, he raged. *You could've disobeyed him. Why can't anyone think around here?*

But then, no one was encouraged to think in the Clawcrags. That was the thing about assigning people roles: they started forgetting they had choices. Catch swallowed his anger. "What's troubling you?"

Bandersnatch's hand dropped, leaving a patch of reddened skin.

"Things would've been different if I had."

"Everything will be different after tonight, one way or another." Catch glanced up the path. No sign of Gildar. He must be higher up. *The sooner we speak, the better*, he thought, feeling the worm-like crawl of passing minutes.

Still Bandersnatch stood, staring at the ground, seemingly on the verge of speaking. But in the end, he shook his head and climbed the path in silence. Catch followed. To their left, Holdfast Plateau repeatedly vanished and reappeared behind ridges and boulders and stands of straggly trees. These obstructions lessened the higher they climbed.

Mt. Snagtooth commanded a splendid view of Holdfast, Catch admitted, pausing to admire the city, held between the two mountains like a cake on a platter. A butter cake, with colored sprinkles.

He grimaced. That was a Rags-n-Bones thought.

"There's Gildar," said Bandersnatch, pointing to a trickle of black smoke curling into the sky. It originated from some source around the path's final curve.

No anticipation colored Bandersnatch's tone, or even relief. The fur Catch didn't currently possess lifted along his spine. He licked his fangs. *Run*, urged some instinct.

"Oh, Catch, are you running again?"

Not this time, Catch replied, to Ascot, the instinct, or both. Gildar had to be warned. Made to see reason.

He went forward. The narrowing path ended by a rounded outcropping overlooking Holdfast. Wrapped in a cloak, Gildar paced beside a small fire, methodically rubbing his hands. A cloak? Odd, but perhaps he feared tearing the Alph's crimson mantle before the ball. A twisted and bare-branched juniper, with a rough, triangular pit between two of its roots was his sole companion.

At the sound of their footsteps he turned, putting on one of his broad, white smiles. "Ah, Starthorne."

He must practice those in his gilded mirror. "Alph," Catch returned, bowing. "I'm glad you called this meeting. I must—"

Laying an arm across his shoulders, Gildar walked him to the outcropping's edge. Clearly not listening. *Of course; he must say his piece first.* Catch tamped down his impatience. He'd obviously chosen this setting carefully; probably practiced the pompous oration he was about to deliver.

Gildar swelled with a breath. "There it is," he proclaimed, sweeping an arm toward the scene below. The Roundgrounds shimmered darkly, casting back the sun's rays. The people toiling about its surface resembled flecks of pepper on a dinner plate. "Tonight, our ancient foes, the tengu will appear. I will face them."

"About that," Catch interjected, hoping to interrupt the flow before Gildar erupted into full-blown bombasticy—which still wasn't a word, but really needed to be, around Gildar.

Gildar kept smiling. "And you will not," he continued.

Something impacted against the back of Catch's head. The crunching sound sickened his stomach. His legs jellied beneath him. When Gildar released his shoulder, he fell to his knees, the echoes still reverberating inside his skull.

❧

"Ascot!" Moony's jubilant purr thrummed up her arms.

Moony! He was really there, smelling of ice and electricity. She tried to hug him, but he squirmed from her grasp and slipped to the street. His fur stood on end all over his body, making him look twice his usual size. His bristling tail resembled a gray cucumber.

"Ascot, I vanquished an oni," he chirped. "It was huge, with fangs and blue skin."

Something sparkled around his neck. "What's this?" Ascot asked, bending for a better look. There were two items, actually, hanging off a cord. One was a silvery medal shaped like a lightning bolt. The other was Catch's ring.

"The tengu gave me that for vanquishing the oni." Moony danced in place. "He menaced the gate between the Etherlands and Holdfast. Koyuiki said we had to sneak by him, but—"

"The tengu—you met them," said Ascot. Cavall and Condorella listened at either side. "How did the negotiations go? We have the *kinhoshi*." She hoped.

"The oni—" Moony looked into her face. He stopped whirling. With a disgruntled flick of his whiskers, he licked a paw. "You do? Good. They're demanding that, the Aspire, and the grove of custard peach trees."

Cavall laughed, slapping his leg. Moony's ears flattened. "They *were* demanding all of Holdfast Plateau until they learned I defeated the oni." His chest puffed. "You should've seen the size of him."

"The Aspire *and* the custard peach grove?" Cavall snorted. "Shifter-kind will never agree to it."

"The tengu expect the shifters to meet them in the Roundgrounds with a bowl of custard peaches and the *kinhoshi*," said Moony. "The Aspire should be empty. Otherwise, they say they won't stop fighting until they bring the mountains down on Holdfast."

Empty bluff, or the truth? Ascot chewed her lip. "At least they're open to negotiations."

After a moment, Cavall made an angry noise. "I suppose it's better than starting right in on the mountain-tumbling. Fine. The Aspire should be empty anyway, because people will be outside watching the skies. We have the *kinhoshi*, so we just have to acquire a custard peach or two. Gildar will probably have some by him at the ball."

"Maybe Catch can get one." Ascot refocused on Moony. "Where's Catch?"

"Don't know," he replied, washing his face. "Koyuki's looking for him. We went by his room last night, but Mistral said he was out. Which is odd, because he was very definite about talking to us."

He's probably up to something, Ascot tried to assure herself. "He'll be at the ball, right?"

"Of course," said Moony. "He's the golden star." He puffed again, wings unfurling. "Of course *I'm* the oni-vanquisher. Its eyes were yellow as mustard."

Lifting him, Ascot set him on her shoulder. "If we can't contact Catch, will you help Cavall snitch custard peaches tonight?"

"Fruit detail!" Moony wailed. "I subdue a monster half the size of the Aspire, and you put me on fruit detail!"

Ascot chucked him under the chin. *Moony and his stories.*

❧

Shifters didn't bury their dead. That was how the significance of the triangular pit between the juniper roots, even with the fresh pile of dirt nearby, had escaped Catch's attention.

Stupid, he thought. Wobbling lines of maroon-black surrounded the word. *You travel with a Shadowvalean. You should recognize a grave when you see one.*

"I'm sorry, Boss." Tears streamed down Bandersnatch's cheeks. "You gotta obey the Alph." A spade trembled in his grip.

So that's what hit me. Catch touched the throbbing spot on the back of his head. His hand seemed to float upwards through thick jelly to reach it.

"Your father believed himself superior to me," said Gildar, watching Catch with the same indifferent interest he might give a landed fish gasping itself to death. "I heard it in his voice every time he spoke to me. Me—a lion-shifter to his jaguar. He thought I'd be nothing without his support." Gildar's voice harshened. "He was a piece of selfishness who knew nothing of the sacrifices a ruler must make."

"What sacrifices?" Catch tried to stand.

Almost absently, Gildar kicked him over. "I grew stronger after Glim's death, but your loss broke Lethe. Look where his notions of fate led him—over the cliff."

No. That was a ruse. But Catch's mind seized on something else. *Sacrifices…Glim.* "You killed Glim, didn't you?" he choked.

"Mm." Gildar kicked him again, more meaningfully this time,

making the breath grunt out of his lungs. "I hoped he'd kill you before the drug I fed him killed him. It would've cleared my path, but I confess this is more satisfying. Look at you. Lethe's precious son. You look like a sick animal lying there."

The last kick was the hardest of all. Catch felt the thump in the small of his back, but none of the pain. Gildar stood above him, staring down.

"Fate is something one makes," he said. "*I* will make it. When the tengu arrive this evening, you will be nowhere to be found. Your name will die in ignominy as I step forward to save shifter-kind."

Catch struggled to his knees. A stab in his side warned of a broken rib. *But there are* real *tengu.* "Listen," he gasped.

Gildar nodded to Bandersnatch. Air whooshed. Catch heard the spade strike him again. He slammed into the dirt. It filled his mouth, gritted beneath his fingertips. His left eye seemed to be attempting to look out of his right socket.

"'Here lies fate,'" said Gildar. "Not that you'll have a marker. Not of that sort, anyway."

His shadow moved. Catch whimpered, protesting the cruelty of it as sunlight struck him blindingly in the face. But Gildar soon returned, holding something that made a hissing sound and reeked of hot metal.

"This mark you can have," said Gildar. "For all your airs, you always were a mangy feral."

Catch understood what the hot metal smell was an instant before Gildar put it to his cheek.

CHAPTER THIRTY:
A GRAVE MAN

Ascot's legs ached. "*This* is considered an honor?" she muttered. She'd presented her silver disk to the head of staff. In return, she'd been whisked into a sleeveless, peacock-blue uniform with an annoying, flapping swallowtail, and tasked with carrying drinks to the legitimate guests. She'd refilled her tray five times already; one fellow in an elephant mask crooked his finger every time she passed.

The masks were disconcerting. At Shadowvalean masquerades, people contented themselves with those half-masks on sticks that everyone tired of holding up before a quarter hour passed. Of course, Shadowvalean balls were a kind of competition to see who could act the most bored while simultaneously implying there was no place they'd rather be.

Here in Holdfast, the masks were full-faced, fantastically carved things, adorned with gold paint and sparkling beads. The false visages scowled, leered, and threatened, but the bodies beneath them moved with small, tight gestures that spoke of tension. Painted eyes frequently turned skyward to gauge the shadow creeping over the full moon.

Two hours until it's fully eclipsed, thought Ascot, checking it herself. As she placed another round of glasses on her tray,

Condorella bustled into the serving area; a small space erected in the northern corner of the topiary garden, shielded from the guests' view by painted screens. Like Ascot, Condorella wore a blue uniform and a scowl. She grabbed a haphazard handful of canapés.

"I can't manipulate Seersees and serve nibbles simultaneously," she whispered furiously. "I can't even get near the inner circle before being sent back for more candied crickets."

Wonder if Elephant-mask's crooking his finger at her, too. Ascot peered around a screen, focusing on the Roundgrounds' center, where the glow-globes shone brightly down on an arrangement of tables and cushioned chairs. Alph Gildar occupied the largest chair, its limbs bright with gilding that almost matched his hair. His posture reeked of buttery condescension, and a brilliant, crimson mantle draped his broad shoulders. Six gold-masked people of similar build and bearing surrounded him.

"Custard peaches," whispered Ascot. There had to be a few in that enormous, golden bowl of fruit by his side. Even one should be enough to satisfy the tengu.

Condorella pushed in beside her. "Seersees," she murmured back. "See them?"

Ascot did: six bubble-like spheres glistening dustily atop tippy-looking bronze stands around the inner circle's perimeter, each watched by two red-cuffed guards. "Six? I thought there were only five left."

Condorella shrugged. "Maybe they found another."

Noticing a supervisor throwing them a sour look, Ascot hastily snatched another glass. "If we could reach the inner circle, Gildar probably wouldn't even notice us," she whispered. He looked the sort to ignore servants. "Then Mistral—is one of those guards Mistral?" She couldn't tell. All wore blank white masks with slits for eyes.

"Ask Cavall," said Condorella, dumping a final handful of canapes on her tray. "He's over by the ice sculpture of the turkey."

"I think it's an eagle," Ascot replied. Condorella shrugged and whisked off. Ascot followed her, nerving herself to step on the Roundgrounds' strange, metallic surface, which seemed to cling to the soles of the loose boots she'd been given to wear. Yellow-green glow-globes, swinging from wires stretched between poles, made the masks sparkle. Strewn flower petals squeaked underfoot.

She kept alert as she passed though the sea of faces, but never saw what she was searching for. Even masked, Ascot would know Catch from how moved, held his head. No one scratched their cheek in that well-remembered way.

It was the Moonless Night. They believed he was the golden star. Where on earth could he be?

❧

A flame penetrated the stifling darkness Catch lay in. Not the orange, glowing kind of flame. He couldn't have seen such fire, anyway. Crumbs of dirt tickled his eyelids.

It was a flame of pain. His cheek, burning hot enough to ignite the inside of his skull. Gildar had erred, after all. Catch could've ignored the throbbing pain at the back of his head. The worst of that had subsided, leaving behind a heavy stupor. The crushing sensation over his chest was deeply worrying, but he thought he could ignore that, too.

But not the cheek. Not the heat, the stabbing, the...*make it stop!* He tried to claw away the pain and found his arms trapped, one beneath his side, the other curled loosely about his head, encased by rock and dirt.

He wriggled his legs. Also trapped. The muscles in his back and thighs flexed and strained, to no avail. The air stank in his nose, tainted by the scents of damp cloth and decay.

How am I breathing at all? He managed to twist his neck. Dirt trickled into his ear canal. Ah. His left arm's curl had saved him, creating a little pocket around his face.

Won't save me for long.

At that, panic struck. He saw the shape of it for one instant, like some terrible beast springing from the cover of brush, and then it was on him, shocking away the pain and dullness and lethargy. *Live! I want to live!* He opened his mouth to scream, and gritty, bitter dirt rushed in, turning his saliva to mud. He spat, and there was nowhere to spit, nowhere to breathe. His clamped limbs wriggled, finding space, forcing space, cracking the layers of earth covering him. A little looseness developed around his left shoulder.

Couldn't breathe. His throat worked convulsively. Dirt in his stomach, dirt in his lungs—

Live!

No air. Dirt in his teeth, his fangs—

Fangs. *I am a Smilodon!* Focusing all his strength into his left arm, Catch thrust it upwards.

His hand broke the surface. Cool, damp air brushed his skin. Clawing dirt, he tried to drag himself from his makeshift grave. A rock tore skin off his fingers without providing any useful purchase. Further, frantic flailing located something tough and vaguely knobby. *Root*, he thought. *Juniper tree. Now to pull myself out—*

A hand seized his wrist and pulled. His arm came loose, almost to the shoulder. A second hand gripped his elbow, tugged again, and his head broke through the dirt.

Air! There was air there, if only he could get to it. He gasped, and a clot stopped his lungs. Wheezing, he choked it out, those helpful hands pounding his back, and after a few, eternal seconds, he managed to suck in a gulp of wonderful, cool air. The dirt coating his face soaked up his tears.

"Sparks," said a horrified voice by his ear. The most welcome, metallic buzzing sound accompanied it. "You're a mess."

"Ko—Koyuki." Catch coughed, spit, and coughed again. "Thank you." He lifted his wrist to wipe his streaming eyes, and she tugged it back down.

"Don't. You'll get mud in them." Shifting her weight, she grabbed him under his arms. Only then did Catch notice he was still half-buried in dirt. "Let's get you out of there, and I'll take you to the river for a proper wash." She pulled, he kicked, and soon he was sitting on the edge of what had been meant to be his final resting place, leaning against the juniper's trunk. Crouching beside him, Koyuki touched his face with light fingers. Even that gentle pressure made him flinch. "That's going to get infected, if it isn't tended," she said.

Catch blinked his eyes somewhat clear. He'd been underground long enough for the sky to darken. The view below the outcropping showed the Roundgrounds gleaming like a still lake, throwing back the light of the slowly darkening full moon hulking above it.

"The Moon-*less* Night." Catch laughed. The shadow curling upwards from the moon's base seemed to grin sardonically at him. "Such a dishonest title."

"My people call it the Night of Reckoning," said Koyuki. "They're up there, readying for battle. They liked Moony. For his sake, they agreed to a truce if you returned the *kinhoshi* and gave us the Aspire and the custard peaches, but I think they were just humoring him." Sighing, she pinched a dried berry off the juniper and rolled it between her fingers. "I think they want to fight."

Finding a spot on his mantle that wasn't entirely filthy, Catch dabbed gingerly at his face.

"Fizzle!" Koyuki hurled the berry over the outcropping. "How can they be so stupid? Is it worth getting free of the Etherlands just to fly into a war?"

Catch paused mid-dab. "Free." He tasted the word. *Free*. Like rich coffee with something tart, yet sweet, perched beside it; a lemony biscuit, perhaps. Gildar believed him dead. He *should* be dead. No one was looking for him. Whatever was about to happen down on Holdfast Plateau could happen without him. His father's plans. Gildar's plans. Whichever. Why should he care? His hand, clenched in the mantle's dirty folds, shook.

"Starthorne?" Koyuki cocked her head.

"The prophecy's nonsense," he screamed down at Holdfast. The wind whipped his words away, so he screamed louder, ignoring the warm trickle down his left cheek. "It has no hold on me! I'm my own master, now. I can run! *Run!*"

His abused throat burned, but no matter how hard he screamed, the wind out-wailed him. None of the celebrants on the Roundgrounds could possibly have heard him. Brokenly, Catch dropped, pulled his knees to his chest, and hugged his arms around them.

"Starthorne?" Koyuki touched his shoulder.

"I didn't kill Glim," said Catch into his knees. He remembered now, a little. How Glim had flailed at him, shouting nonsense, eyes glassy and unfocused. They'd scuffled. A foot—his or Glim's—had slipped over the plateau's edge. They'd grappled for balance.

Lost it.

He lifted his head. Koyuki regarded him worriedly, ringed pupils whirling. "I didn't kill Glim," he repeated, and stood.

Koyuki steadied him before he toppled. "You're not considering going down there, are you?" she asked, a damnable note of hope in her voice despite her words. "You're more dirt, blood, and bruises than solid flesh. If you're not running a fever, you will be."

Not only was she right, but going to the Roundgrounds was the last thing he wished to do. But—

He hadn't killed Glim, but Glim had died all the same. If he ever wished to enjoy a sound sleep again, he had to see that the Moonless Night passed in a way that honored the pact he and his friend had made twenty-five years ago.

"Yes," Catch replied. "I mean to go down." He held out an arm. "Help me walk."

❧

Seven drinks later, Ascot finally had Mr. Elephant-mask comfortably slopped. Before anyone else could crook a finger, she jogged to Cavall, who stood beside the ice eagle—which did resemble a turkey—arms folded across his chest.

You don't really get the concept of a masked ball, do you? she thought. He was still dressed entirely in black, albeit silk instead of leather, with jet feathers fluttering from the sleeves. His half-mask curved into a raven's beak that didn't hide the tightness of his thin lips.

"Mistral isn't there," he said before she asked.

"Are you sure?" she asked, handing him a glass.

"I know my own daughter." He swirled the yellow wine and watched the ripples. "Maybe she decided to listen to me after all."

Ascot doubted that, but hadn't the heart to voice her misgivings about his daughter. "I haven't seen Catch, either," she said, dodging a couple that came twirling past, dressed in clinging red silk and flame-carved masks, laughing too loudly.

"I glimpsed him a moment ago." Cavall canted his head. "He's wearing a green cloak with a gold lining."

Foolishly, Ascot glanced over her shoulder, as if expecting Catch to be standing right behind her—which would actually be just like him. Instead, a peculiar mask caught her attention. Its left half depicted a more-or-less human visage, frozen in a leer. The right was carved to resemble a snarling bear.

Cavall beckoned her closer. "I've never seen split masks before, and that's the fourth I've spotted this evening," he murmured. "They're not dressed for the occasion, either."

The split-mask wearer vanished through the crowd, but not before Ascot noticed he was clad in a simple, short tunic and loose pants, in contrast to the fancy silks and trailing ribbons of other guests. *Dressed to shift quickly, if necessary,* Ascot realized. *Frabjacket. Is this someone else's "smart little plan"?*

Double frabjacket. Elephant-mask was crooking his finger again. How did he keep finding her, out of this enormous throng of people? "Mistral probably stayed home," she said. "Starley will just have to cause a big enough distraction that Condorella can sabotage the

Seersees without anyone noticing."

He snorted wryly. "Maybe he'll do another weasel war dance."

Elephant-mask crooked again. Ascot bit her tongue. "Keep watch. Help Moony with the peaches," she said, and hurried away. Elephant-mask took the last three drinks off her tray. *Frabjacket; I have to refill it again.* She headed back toward the serving area.

Green silk billowed in her peripheral vision. The edge of its gold lining flashed as it passed under a string of glow-globes. The cloaked figure paused, tilting its head to gaze at the moon.

Conversation, laughter, and the muted music of harps and fiddles faded. Ascot's feet stopped moving. A guest wearing a butterfly mask bumped into her and she hardly noticed the thump. "Catch."

The cloaked figure moved on, heading eastwards. Dropping her tray, Ascot followed.

"I don't care if you're a tiger-shifter, mate." The familiar, sharp voice stopped her. "I'll bite your arse off if you don't move aside."

Starley. Eyes on the billowing green, Ascot paused, then, reluctantly, looked back. Her breath caught. Starley stood at the Roundgrounds' entrance, arms akimbo and chin defiantly lifted. Jolt's mantle draped his red coat. His only concession to the festivities was a crude wooden half mask with a slanting "F" burned into its left cheek. Judging by the glares he was receiving, few appreciated his attire.

Thinking fast, Ascot grabbed drinks off another server's tray, ran over, and thrust them at two big, angry-looking shifters facing Starley. "Don't get yourself killed," she whispered, drawing him aside. "We need you to cause a distraction."

Starley flipped his golden disk into the air. "Looking forward to that."

"Good. Find Condorella. I'll be right back." Crisis averted, she turned away. Had she lost Catch? He should be the one to present the *kinhoshi* to the tengu. Scanning the crowd, she panicked, thinking she'd lost him, only to catch sight of gold-lined green vanishing into the shadows at the Roundgrounds' fringe.

There you are. Ascot darted after him, squeezing past two guests in trailing, striped robes. Someone shouted a demand for bitterseed cider after her, but she feigned deafness. Fighting free of the crowd, she spied Catch, striding toward the plateau's edge, green silk rippling.

Ascot frowned. "Catch?" What she'd meant as a call emerged as a whisper.

He was the right height, but his gait seemed…off. Moonglow highlighted the contours of his jaw. Its shape was correct, but—

He kept walking until his boot-tips protruded right over the plateau's edge. The wind billowed his cloak behind him, exposing flashes of gold lining.

"Catch?" said Ascot, moving closer.

"This is where he fell," he replied, pointing downwards. "There's a loop of a no-see-'em road that he landed on."

He had the burr in his throat. He rolled his "r"s gently, as Catch did. But his voice possessed a light, cheerful lilt that Ascot had never heard in Catch's. She stepped back as he turned, sweeping a hand over his head. It brushed away not only his hood, but the mass of pale brown hair beneath it. Darker locks tumbled down, spilling about his cheeks.

"Hello, Miss Abberdorf," he said, smiling. "I'm Catch's father."

CHAPTER THIRTY-ONE:
MOON MADNESS

"Nrrgghhhwwrrgrrr…"

What a horrible noise. Who's making it?

A moment later, Catch realized he was. Stopping, he spat a mouthful of bile into the bushes. Koyuki set him down and flew off, trailing sparks. *Abandoning me in the dark?* thought Catch, panicking.

An instant later, he decided he didn't care. He'd lay there until he stopped hurting, if such a future time existed. But she returned shortly, carrying a wad of soaked cloth.

"Here." She dripped a corner into his mouth. He spat it out, along with the foul taste of bile and mud, and squeezed a larger trickle into his mouth. She carefully wiped his face, patting the scalded skin. Nodding his thanks, he took the cloth from her and pressed it to his cheek. Its coldness helped a little.

"We have to keep going," he said, struggling to his feet at the expense of a briefly blinding headache.

She pushed him down. "*I* have to keep going." Her irises took on hard, metallic tints. "I'd be Rai-sama if I'd found the *kinhoshi*. You're just a bystander."

Catch would've laughed, had he the strength. Bystander? The Moonless Night had defined his life. "My father's responsible for half this mess. He's down there, now, like a spider in its web, getting ready to attack. Even if we found your *kinhoshi*, he'd cause mischief."

And he was the only one who could possibly stop Lethe, the only being in the world Lethe genuinely loved.

"It's just…" She sighed. "I'm not sure we're going to make it in time, at this pace. I could try carrying you."

She extended her hands and he waved her off. Even that small motion made his head pound like a fist was trying to split it from within. "I'm not sure I can take being lifted."

Still, there was no point in killing himself to reach the Roundgrounds only to arrive in time to watch his father do a victory dance on their smoking ruins—a scene he could picture all too easily. "Let's try it in short bursts," he said.

They tried it. Koyuki lifted him around the shoulders and flew a short distance. He blacked out and revived some indeterminate interval later, draped across a rock.

"Are we gaining time or losing it?" he asked, blinking up at the moon. Its shadowy smirk had widened to a broad grin.

"About equal. Wait." Koyuki craned her neck. "I hear something." She jumped into the air, wings spitting out a flurry of silvery-white sparks. "What are you doing here?" she snarled at the figure that came creeping around the bend, a spade propped against its shoulder.

Quite a large figure. "Bandersnatch," said Catch.

"Boss," cried Bandersnatch, falling back. "Who's this woman…with wings? Is she a…tengu?"

Swarming between them, Koyuki thrust her sharp nose into Bandersnatch's face. "You hit him," she snarled. "You *buried* him. I saw it all." Small stones rose beneath her dangling toes, clattering along the ground. Wilting without Koyuki's support, Catch watched them dance.

Bandersnatch gulped. "I didn't want to. Gildar ordered me, and you gotta obey the Alph."

Koyuki's hand snapped out, closing about the spade. Spinning about, she flung it over Mt. Snagtooth's side. "*That's* for your Alph! He tells you to kill, and you kill. Why not eat and sleep on his say-so? How far does it go?"

She hovered menacingly. Bandersnatch sank in on himself, arms raised protectively. "What's the point in having an Alph if—"

Catch slid off the rock Koyuki had laid him on and lolled in the dirt. "Help."

It was barely a peep, but both Bandersnatch and Koyuki flew to his side. Bandersnatch cradled his head while Koyuki patted his brow with the damp cloth. Catch repressed a smile that would've pained his cheek.

Bandersnatch futilely brushed off his clothes. "You need to rest, Boss."

"He hit you," said Koyuki, glaring at Bandersnatch.

"Most of my friends take a swing at me, sooner or later." Privately, Catch suspected he was only alive because Bandersnatch had neither hit him as hard as necessary, nor tamped down the dirt firmly enough to suffocate him. *Of course that also means I have to thank Gildar for forcing others to do his literal dirty work.*

Koyuki sat on her heels. Perhaps she was rehashing their own first meeting inside her head. "You're lucky you're still alive."

"Let's revisit that concept in an hour." Grabbing an overhanging juniper branch, Catch hauled himself shakily to his feet. The glow-globes spotting the Roundgrounds shone brighter as the night darkened along with the moon. "Come on. We have a war to stop."

With a puzzled glance at the glowering Koyuki, Bandersnatch scratched his chin. "Don't we fight the tengu, Boss?"

Koyuki's glare intensified. Tossing her head, she draped Catch's arm about her shoulders. Catch was pretty sure she'd meant to whack Bandersnatch with her braid's metal ball. "Coming?" she asked. "Or must you wait for your Alph's permission?"

Bandersnatch picked at his thumbnail. There was a spot of dried blood there. "Gildar did tell me I wasn't fit to attend."

Sniggering, Catch broke a twig off the juniper branch and waved it. "Presto! A new gown and glass slippers. Bring me a pumpkin, and I'll make you a coach as well."

Ascot would've enjoyed the reference, he thought. Bandersnatch and Koyuki's stares only made him laugh the louder, at least until his head gave a great throb and another surge of nausea rushed up his throat. Leaning over, he spat into the bushes. "Sorry." It occurred to him that he *really* wasn't well, even before the ground tried to slap him.

Bandersnatch steadied him. "You sure about this, Boss?" he asked, searching Catch's face, a great furrow between his brows.

Catch spat again and nodded, almost too tired for pain. "Unfortunately, yes. I'm sure."

The furrow smoothed out. Bandersnatch took Catch's arm. "The hell with Gildar's orders. Let's go to the Roundgrounds."

Catch's father? "I thought you were—" Ascot began.

He sighed, smiled, and shrugged all at once. "Yes, yes. Faking my demise allowed me to act unobserved, but I do tire of the gasps of surprise."

Catch's father. Lethe Starthorne. The most notorious assassin in the Clawcrag's history. *And I'm alone with him, right by the edge of a precipice.* Swallowing, Ascot inched back, hoping he didn't notice.

"Did my son really spend twenty-five years in Shadowvale?" asked Lethe. "That's what he implied, but I suspect he's acquired a talent for lying." He scratched his cheek, flicking it with his nails instead of curling his fingers inwards, but even that gesture screamed Catch.

You have no idea. "Not all of the last twenty-five years," she answered, mustering caution even as it ebbed. Lethe's serene cheerfulness made it difficult to find him alarming.

"Didn't think so." He looked at her curiously. "But he did leave the Clawcrags?" Ascot nodded. "Yet, he still returned in time for the Moonless Night." Whistling soundlessly, Lethe lifted his head. The shadowed moonlight struck red glints from his irises. "We may yet prove fate."

Fate? "Do you mean the prophecy?" asked Ascot. "That's all nonsense." There was no golden star, save the one she carried in the pouch tied to her belt. Her hand twitched toward it. Should she tell Lethe? Could she trust him?

"Yes, probably," replied Lethe, rummaging in a pouch of his own. "Before we can tell for sure, we must contend with Gildar's meddling." The lines of amusement drained from his face, leaving something cold and hard-edged behind. Ascot wished she could say this new expression didn't resemble Catch at all, but knew she'd be lying.

He brought out a stick with a small bulb at one end. Holding it up, he flicked a lever on its side. A shutter opened, and green light flashed. Seconds later, a black-clad figure emerged from the shadows, wearing one of split masks: half a human scowl, half a snarling dog. Hands reached up and lifted the mask off, revealing—

"Mistral!" cried Ascot. "Why aren't you guarding a Seersee?"

"She has more important tasks," said Lethe. "Is everyone in place, pupil?"

"Yes, sir." Mistral saluted. "We'll be ready when the tengu arrive."

"Ready to do what?" Ascot demanded. Mistral looked away. "We're going to negotiate with the tengu, not fight."

Mistral head whipped back. "That was *your* idea, outsider," she said, glaring. "But this is shifter business. Tonight, the Hide Aways will defeat the tengu. Then we'll make the rules."

"Exactly," said Lethe. A corner of his mouth quirked. It straightened almost instantly, but Ascot noticed it. Catch smiled exactly the same way before speaking some obvious and outrageous lie. "Go on, now, pupil."

Pupil. We found the Hide Away's leader—and it's Catch's father, thought Ascot. Saluting again, Mistral slipped back into the night. "No," cried Ascot, reaching after her.

Her momentum jerked to a stop. Surprised, Ascot glanced down. Lethe's fingers had closed about her wrist, so lightly and easily that only now did she realize she'd been grabbed.

"Youngsters and their belief in what's right," said Lethe, smiling. His eyes were warm, with crinkles at the corners. "You could build castles on it." He smelled of coffee, dark cherries, and soft leather.

And you're taking advantage of it. Ascot tried to wrench free with one, sudden lunge. His grip may as well have been steel. Her skin dented against his thumb. "Did Mistral tell you the real tengu are coming?"

"I already knew. I know about the fake ones, too." He might have shifted his weight slightly, to counter her action. Possibly. "I know it all, save for one thing." His gaze rose, lingering on the shadow filling up the moon, transforming it from an ivory orb to a coppery disk.

"If you care about Mistral at all, why set her up to fight?" asked Ascot, grabbing his thumb and trying to bend it back.

Lethe shrugged, hardly seeming to notice she was mauling his hand. "If tonight's fated, that's her part to play. Otherwise, it's just as well she learns how to fight. Shifters need a good helping of chaos, and that's just what I intend to serve up."

How could he wax philosophical with the Roundgrounds about to erupt? *Maybe because his brain doesn't work like normal people's, in case you haven't noticed, Ascot.* She rolled her hand into a cone, making it as small and narrow as possible, and yanked it downward while simultaneously bringing her knee up into his groin. He stepped lightly out of the way, clenching his fingers just enough to keep her captive.

"Sorry," he said, knocking aside the punch she threw at his face. Did something metallic glint in his palm? "My son cares for you, so I don't hold your meddling against you the way I do Gildar's, but—"

His head turned sharply toward the Roundgrounds' interior. The sounds of the celebration had continued, of course, but for Ascot, they'd been like something taking place on the other side of a thick sheet of glass. Now, abruptly, noises penetrated her brain: screams, accompanied by shattering sounds and the unmelodic twang of snapped strings.

The moon's top quarter still glowed white. Surely it was too early for either of the tengu armies to put in an appearance?

A howl rose above the shouts. A full-throated, quavering howl that Ascot would have recognized anywhere, having spent many Shadowvalean nights listening to the local werewolves serenade the moon. *There's only one wolf in the Clawcrags.* "Dmitri!" she hollered.

He came bounding out of the shadows, a length of silk trailing from his rear claws. "Ascot," he said. "Thank goodness." He glanced over his shoulder, flinching at the continuing screams and clatter. There were thumping sounds, too, heralding the approach of footsteps. Guards, most likely. "We have a problem," he said, turning back attention to her.

"More than one," she replied.

"A wolf? How fascinating," said Lethe. He leaned forward, looking, for all the world, as if he expected to be taken into their confidence.

"You're part of it," snapped Ascot, pulling with all her might. It was like trying to uproot a tree. "Dmitri, what's my word?"

"What?" he said, showing his teeth as two guards and three hounds bounded up.

"My, you know, the special word." *Frabjacket*, it was on the tip of her tongue.

"Kerfuffle!" he cried.

Pop. Ascot staggered forward as much as Lethe's grip allowed as the intangible weight pushed her down. She flung out her arms to catch herself, hardly able to tell if they *were* arms, or two stubby, clawed forelegs. Behind her, a great, fluffy, smelly tail arched like an ineffectual parachute.

She focused on it. *Yes*, she thought. *Stink. Stink!* She waggled her bottom, and Lethe reeled back. Yelping, the hound-shifters buried their noses in their paws. "Run!" she shouted to Dmitri, tearing free of Lethe's grip.

Kerfuffle, she thought as they ran. *Only I would forget "kerfuffle" in the midst of an actual kerfuffle.*

"Oh, that was wonderful!" Lethe's laughter burbled out of the darkness behind her. "That, I never expected."

❧

Scraggly bushes hid Holdfast Plateau from sight, but the screams still reached their ears. Koyuki and Bandersnatch stopped. Catch, draped between them, perforce stopped also.

"Already?" asked Bandersnatch.

Koyuki glanced at the moon. "Too early for us. Maybe it's the fake tengu."

Catch snorted and wished he hadn't when it made his cheek hurt, which made everything else hurt. "I'm sure Gildar's planned for maximum drama." Nor would his father act until all the pieces were in place. No, yet another party was responsible for those cries of distress. Who was unaccounted for? Who could somehow disarray everyone's careful schemes right before they came to fruition?

He pounced on the answer. Ascot. Unquestionably, Ascot.

Bandersnatch started to say something. "Hush," said Catch, straining his ears. Fortunately, the mountainside amplified sounds coming off the plateau. Catch's efforts were rewarded with a howl. "Dmitri." Smiling hurt, but he did it anyway.

A second later, it dropped off his face. Ascot! She was down there, with two tengu armies preparing to attack, and *his father*.

Adrenalin sizzled along his nerves, giving him a boost. He managed five solo steps before it fizzled out.

Mange take you, body! I'm a Smilodon. He took another three steps and collapsed, coughing. Apparently, he hadn't hacked all the dirt out of his lungs yet. His Smilodon-self pointedly informed him that the smart option was to find a nice cave, lick himself until he felt better, and take a long nap.

So much for his Smilodon-self. "You're done in, Boss," said Bandersnatch, crouching beside him.

Catch gritted his teeth. Ascot had ridden a helhest to save Rags-n-Bones. He wouldn't do less to save her.

*Ridden a helshest…*Catch contemplated his large companion. All right; so it lacked the panache of a helhcst…*Needs must.* He smiled grimly. "Still regretting obeying Gildar, Bandersnatch? Here's your opportunity to make amends."

CHAPTER THIRTY-TWO: LIGHTENING

Screaming guests threw themselves out of their path, knocking into the poles strung with glow-globes. The yellow-green lights swung crazily, creating dizzying illusions of skewed time and colliding space. Ascot wondered what they feared more: Dmitri, or the stench that trailed her like an honor guard. *If only this chaos could be enough to satisfy Lethe.*

She glanced back to see if he pursued, but the swinging lights confused her vision; it all looked a jumble of bodies.

"This way!" called Condorella's sharp voice. Blindly, Ascot oriented on it, catching what may have been glimpses of sea urchin hair and a waving hand. Dmitri loped beside her. As they fought free of the crowd, her eyes cleared enough to see that Condorella had guided them toward the serving area, with its painted screens.

Ascot dashed behind one. *"Alyosha, kerfuffle,"* she said, sighing with relief as the skunk-form dissipated. Dmitri let out a disgusted grunt as his ears grew enormous and began wiggling. "Look cute," she whispered.

Growling under his breath, Dmitri pulled his lips into a leering grimace, that, fortunately, still looked cute. "Aww," said one of the guards who'd just raced around the screen's edge.

Condorella slapped a hand to her bosom. "The wolf went that way," she cried, jabbing a finger to the south. She attempted to hyperventilate.

The guard looked puzzled. "I thought I saw it come here." Another, in dog-form, sniffed the ground only to draw back at the lingering skunk stench. The idea of a wolf transforming into a fox evidently didn't cross their minds. Exchanging puzzled glances, they followed Condorella's direction.

Ascot allowed herself to exhale. "Thanks, Condorella." She peered around the screen. Cavall was barking orders, trying to calm the crowd; apparently his guard-ly instincts wouldn't allow him to sit quiet during a crisis. But Starley—or more likely Moony, who perched on his shoulder—spotted her.

"What's the news?" Starley asked, jogging over.

Dmitri spoke first. "Rags-n-Bones changed the tengu dolls, but not enough," he said, brushing a paw over his flapping ear. "He attached a wire from that sparking box to himself. He's fine," he added quickly as Ascot gasped. "He can influence them a little, but they're still headed this way. There's some compulsion in them he can't override. And they're connected, so if you hurt them—"

"You hurt him," Ascot finished. And harming the tengu dolls was undoubtedly part of Gildar's plan.

"Did an alchemist come to awaken them?" asked Condorella.

Dmitri shook his head. "Rags-n-Bones had just awakened them when they started plowing through the Underway. They begged Rags to help them, but he couldn't uncouple himself from the box. Something's drawing them here."

How Ascot wished she'd spent more time talking to Rags-n-Bones about alchemy, now! "I got a peach," said Moony hopefully, shedding fur all over Jolt's mantle. He cradled a pink-cheeked fruit, sadly punctured and leaking, beneath one wing.

"Good," said Ascot absently. She rubbed her nose. "If the fake tengu are being drawn here, does that mean something here's giving them energy?"

"Something like an electro-magniphager, you mean?" asked Dmitri.

"It's a very nice peach," said Moony, nuzzling it.

Ascot stared toward the Roundgrounds' center, unsurprised when Elephant-mask crooked a finger at her. She ignored him. "Six Seersees instead of five," she murmured.

Dmitri followed her gaze. "You think one's the electro-magniphager."

"Gildar would want it near him," she replied. If Dmitri's appearance had worried Gildar, he'd regained calm. Lounging in his gilded chair, he surveyed the scene with only the faintest air of expectation. Soothed by his placid demeanor, the guests resumed chatting and drinking, only occasionally breaking off to peer up at the moon or glance into the shadows.

"What happens if you break this electro-whatsit?" asked Starley.

"It'll end their compulsion, but it'll probably suck all the energy out of Rags-n-Bones," said Condorella.

Ascot and Dmitri exchanged glances. That was what had happened to Kay Ashuren, back in Widget, when the first electro-magniphager exploded. It had left him a living ghost. "We don't want another alchemic accident," said Dmitri.

"We also can't have that lot murdering ferals." Starley glanced at the sky. Only a sliver of the moon still glowed silver-white. "They're going to emerge from the Underway any second now."

"Savotte's trying to hold them back," said Dmitri. "But if they attack, she might have to take stronger measures."

Ascot swallowed. That would also hurt Rags-n-Bones.

Moony jumped off Starley's shoulder. "So, split the electro-magniphager, take out whatever's fueling it now, and stick something nicer in it." He blinked around at them. "What? I'm a cat; I eavesdrop. Electro-magniphagers take energy from some living thing and amplify it. If an egg worked for Master Porpetti, why not a peach pit?" Unfurling his wing, he let the soggy fruit drop.

Ascot stared a full five seconds before sweeping him up in a hug. "That might work."

"Best plan we've concocted." Dmitri glanced at the moon. "Considering the little time we have."

"Less than you realize," said Ascot. "The man who was detaining me was Catch's father."

Briefly, she explained how Lethe meant to start a war between the shifters and the tengu, knowing all the while she couldn't capture his odd mixture of chill and cheer for her audience.

Condorella recovered from the flood of new information the quickest. "His plan will fail if we make peace with the tengu," she said, crouching to retrieve the peach. Using her long nails, she pulled out the pit.

Starley pushed his mask to the back of his head to scratch his hair. "I don't suppose we could transfer the Rune image into a Seersee while we're looking for the electro-whatsit?"

"Who'd be watch—" Ascot bit off her sharp retort. He was right. Rune was responsible for this entire conflict. His lies should be exposed.

"The image may prove useful, should some shifters balk at a truce." said Dmitri. "They believe Rune defeated Genkiku fairly. That fragment shows otherwise."

After a moment, Starley nodded. "All right. So long as people see it. Condie can play 'find the electro-whatsit' while I cause a distraction."

"Here." Condorella handed Ascot the peach. "You deal with the real tengu. I'll tell Cavall about the Hide Aways in the split masks. Maybe he can have them arrested."

Or reason with his daughter, thought Ascot. "Good luck," she called as Starley and Condorella dashed off. The head server beckoned angrily, but Ascot turned her back. She had more important matters to attend than serving Elephant-mask his fiftieth drink.

The peach dripped juice all down her hand. She hoped the mangled thing was enough of a gesture to satisfy the tengu. "Catch should be the one to present it," she said. "Where could he be?" *Did he run away again?* She couldn't help wondering.

Or was he missing for a more sinister reason?

Dmitri nuzzled her hand. "Hopefully, he'll appear. Until then, prepare yourself. Bring out the *kinhoshi*."

Ascot reached into the pouch tied to her belt. It was empty.

❧

Just as they reached the foot of Mt. Snagtooth, the sky rumbled overhead, distracting Catch from the possibility of being seasick all over Bandersnatch's back. Running panthers, he'd discovered, possessed a rolling gait that was doing queasy things to his already disturbed stomach.

Bandersnatch skidded to a stop and snarled. "Oh, no," said Koyuki, hovering beside him, staring at a patch of air above their heads. It looked no different from the rest of the invisible stuff.

Or did it? Catch squinted. He didn't entirely trust his vision just now, but on second glance, he seemed to see a hairline fracture through that particular patch of nothing, bending the light like a crack in a mirror.

Even as he focused on it, the fracture widened, spitting out a few sparks. A tengu slipped through it, first seeming as flat and translucent as a figure painted on tissue. The next instant, the tengu shook itself, transforming into a solid, breathing shape. This tengu was male, larger than Koyuki, with darker feathers, and gold braiding adorning the front of his knee-length robe.

He gave Koyuki the most unfriendly look. "There you are."

"Kaizen." Koyuki flung her braid over her shoulder. "You shouldn't be here before the mourning period expires."

Kaizen laughed humorlessly. His irises had three rings: bright silver, dull pewter, and a gray dark as smoke. They whirled as he cast a contemptuous glance at Catch. "Is this your shifter friend who bargains?" His lips curled. "A sad-looking creature."

"I've been happier," Catch admitted.

Kaizen shot back six inches, sparks shooting out his wings, as if he never imagined Catch would dare reply. Recovering, he scowled down his long nose. "We've changed our terms, shifter. "The injury done us requires further reparation. In addition to the *kinhoshi*, the custard peaches, and the Aspire, we demand your coffee groves."

Bandersnatch's rump dropped. Catch slid off his back as a growl of pure disbelief rumbled out of Bandersnatch's throat.

"I agree," said Catch, sprawled on the ground. The Aspire and the peach orchard were large enough demands, but their coffee orchards? Shifter-kind would mutiny.

"We want your winged cat, too," Kaizen added on a note of pure spite. "We like him. He can hunt oni for us."

Sighing, Catch hauled himself into a sitting position. "You never intended to bargain in good faith."

"Your leader betrayed and murdered ours. We're due our revenge." Kaizen pointed toward the Roundgrounds, the view obscured by brush and the square, yellow houses of Holdfast. "The Plain of Thunder," he said. "If you're not there with the *kinhoshi*, the peaches, a sack of coffee beans, and the cat by the time the moon fully darkens, we'll attack."

"This is madness." Wings buzzing, Koyuki swooped up until her eyes were level with his. "These aren't the shifters who wronged us. Why fight?"

Shoving his hand in her face, Kaizen pushed her down. "Quiet, you. Without the *kinhoshi*, you're just an upstart."

Koyuki ducked from under his hand, eyes blazing, wings beating so fast they hummed. "When the shifters return the *kinhoshi*, I'll be Rai-sama."

Kaizen laughed harshly. "So, never, then. The shifters don't have it. Ginkiku's golden star fell, and will not rise again."

Catch had been busy trying to convince his legs to hold him upright. His head shot up. "What was that about a golden star?"

Both Kaizen and Koyuki stared down at him. "That's what *kinhoshi* means," said Koyuki. "Legends say it fell from the sky a thousand—"

"I'm the golden star," said Catch.

It fell out of his mouth mechanically. He'd heard it so often it didn't even seem a lie. It bought him seconds, while they gaped. There was something he could use here, if he could just force his exhausted, aching brain to work.

Kaizen unfurled his wings with a snap. "The *kinhoshi's* an object, not a person."

"I'm the *shifter's kinhoshi*," said Catch. "Ask anyone in Holdfast; they'll tell you so." Bandersnatch nodded vehemently, tail lashing.

"I fell off Holdfast Plateau and still draw breath," Catch continued, ticking off points on his fingers. "My father is death, our most notorious assassin. *I'm* the golden star—and she found me." He nodded to Koyuki. "That makes her Rai-sama."

Oh, it was a beautiful lie. It glowed with a golden haze, fit for Gildar's bedchamber.

Koyuki's irises spun, exchanged places. But, quickly masking any confusion, she turned to Kaizen, lifting her chin. She rose while he sank, the sparks from his wings sparse and uncertain.

"The shifters' *kinhoshi*?" he muttered. "But—" His expression firmed. "You have to be able to control lightning. You're no Rai-sama if you can't."

"A simple matter," said Catch. "I daresay I can teach her the trick by the time the moon darkens."

Kaizen recovered his poise. "Very well. I can allow this farce to continue a few minutes longer. We'll await your presentation on the Plain of Thunder."

"You arrive ready to talk, not fight, understand?" said Koyuki, drawing herself up regally. With a grudging nod, Kaizen folded himself back into a thin image and slipped through the crack in the air, which sealed shut behind him.

Exhaling, Koyuki settled to the ground. "So, how do you control lightning?" she asked with a sidelong glance at Catch.

"No idea," he replied, hauling himself onto Bandersnatch's back. "Fortunately, we now have a few minutes before it matters."

CHAPTER THIRTY-THREE:
BLIND SIDED

Ascot didn't bother with the usual charade of turning the pouch inside-out, searching for a hole. She knew where the *kinhoshi* had gone. Catch often nicked small items from her pockets during their travels. *This time, it was the one who had taught him his tricks,* she thought, scanning the crowd.

"What's wrong?" asked Moony. Dmitri had already guessed. His ears, even the flapping one, pinned back.

"Fly above the crowd and see if you can find a black-haired man who resembles Catch," Ascot replied, cramming the dripping peach into her pouch. "That's Lethe. He stole the *kinhoshi*." Mistral must've told him about it. When her fingers had twitched toward her pouch, she'd given its presence away—assuming he hadn't already picked it, as a matter of course.

Moony gave an eager jump. "Should I challenge him, if I—"

"No!" Ascot exploded. Moony stared and she took a breath, pinching her nose. Even Moony would realize that was a bad idea once he met Lethe. "Just find him."

"I defeated an oni, you know," muttered Moony as he flew off.

A black-gloved hand closed about Ascot's bicep. "Condorella informed me of the latest developments," said Cavall. He'd ditched his half-mask, and torn most of the feathers from his shirt.

Black silk suits him as well as black leather. Acost kicked herself. Really, was this the time for such thoughts? "Have you found Mistral?"

"No, but I believe that's her handiwork." He nodded toward the Roundgrounds' interior. Just outside the circle of Seersees, four guards gripped Starley and Condorella by the arms. They struggled— Starley was clearly cursing; some of the guards' ears were turning red—but to no avail. "She must've told her fellows to be on the lookout for them."

There went their disturbance. More alarmingly, they needed Condorella to locate the electro-magniphager amongst the Seersees.

Only a thin silver frown topped the moon. As if to emphasize their dwindling supply of time, a scream rose faintly from the streets beyond the Aspire.

Swooping down from the sky, Moony settled on her shoulder. "I don't see Lethe, but the fake tengu have arrived and they're not stopping."

"No." Cavall's grip tightened on Ascot's arm as she stepped toward the Seersees. "Mistral will have warned them about you."

"But not me," said Dmitri. "She never met me. Ivan."

The head server, who'd just come stomping over, screeched as Dmitri transformed into his usual wolf-self. She sagged back against a painted screen as he dashed off toward the interior. Screams followed in his wake.

Racing right past the guards holding Starley and Condorella, Dmitri ran up to Gildar, spring coat gleaming with silvery markings. The Pack jumped. A couple threw off their clothes and crackled. Dmitri beat them to it. The air about him shimmered. Rising on human legs, he smiled at Gildar and wrapped his two inner fingers around his outer ones.

Conversation died, instantly. The last trickle of music squawked to a halt. "Greetings from Shadowvale's werewolves," said Dmitri into the newborn silence.

Face turning purple, Gildar stood so quickly his chair toppled. "Kill him," he choked, stabbing air.

Both Pack and guards rushed to obey, including the ones holding Starley and Condorella. All gave chase as Dmitri popped back into wolf-form and darted off.

"I'll try to prevent their catching him," said Cavall, releasing Ascot's arm. "You help with the Seersees. We have to stop the fake tengu before the real ones arrive."

I still have to get the kinhoshi back from Lethe, thought Ascot as they parted, she running for the interior, he toward the guards. Elbowing through the crowd, she realized she hadn't seen anyone in a split mask for a while.

The guards' mass exodus had left Gildar all alone. Starley wheeled just out of his reach, taunting him, while Condorella hurried from Seersee to Seersee, her lips moving in some muttered spell. She reached up to touch one, perched on its tippy-looking brass stand. Her fingernails barely grazed its surface, but it shattered.

Gildar spun around at the sound. "Guards—"

Starley tackled him, whooping, before it fully cleared his lips. Dmitri raced past again, leading the guards in another pass through the Roundgrounds. Guests screamed and scattered.

Couldn't this *be enough chaos for you, Lethe?* thought Ascot, hurrying to a Seersee. She touched it gently, with a single finger. It virtually exploded into needlelike fragments.

"It's this one," cried Condorella, across the circle.

Gildar threw off Starley with a jerky, panicked motion. His expression mirrored his alarm as he dove for Condorella.

"Moony, attack!" cried Ascot, nursing her bleeding hand.

Moony probably jumped before she shouted. Gleefully, all claws extended, he landed on Gildar's face. Starley ran past them, grabbing a heavy platter off a table as he went, and swarmed right up the brass stand Condorella indicated. Surprisingly, it didn't tilt under his weight; it must've been better balanced than it looked.

Condorella tossed him the peach pit. Starley caught it, raised the platter, but paused before he brought it down on the electromagniphager. "Look!" he cried, pointing.

Fresh screams rose. Ascot turned as huge, hulking dark bodies pushed their way onto the Roundgrounds. The fake tengu had arrived, and they didn't look happy.

❧

Bandersnatch loped through Holdfast's back streets. Despite the glow-globes shining at intersections, the city seemed dark and empty. Those who hadn't elected to stay home were likely gathered in Daybell Park, or along Buy-Your-Leave Way, or perhaps gathered at some coffee house for mutual comfort on this foreboding night. *I'd definitely choose a coffee house for the world's last night,* thought Catch, clinging to Bandersnatch's back.

Or, perhaps a café overlooking a stand of red maples, with Ascot sitting across from him, and a plate of cream puffs on the table between them.

Now his thoughts were wandering. "No, take Hookjag Alley," he told Bandersnatch when the panther started to turn down Spire Lane. "There's a back door that leads into the topiary garden behind the Aspire." Making a wondering noise in his throat, Bandersnatch obeyed.

"You know secret passages?" asked Koyuki buzzing along behind.

"I'll show them to you, once you're Rai-sama," he replied. *If we survive.*

They squeezed through curving Hookjag Alley, his left leg rubbing along the clay wall. Bandersnatch darted through the door he indicated, leaped the low hedge at its end, and nearly landed on top of a topiary tiger, caught in an eternal green crouch, its open jaws baring jagged fangs.

"Hello, son," called a cheerful voice.

Too late, Catch recalled he wasn't the only one who knew

Holdfast's secret ways. "Father."

❧

Snarling, the fake tengu lumbered forward, eyes and fangs gleaming. Ascot gasped as one lashed at a dark-haired, tan-skinned figure dancing ahead of the horde, just out of harm's reach.

"That's right, attack *me*," Jolt shouted, sweeping back his hair to display his brand. "Leave everyone else alone." The fake tengu attacked him again, but to Ascot, it looked half-hearted. Pale lines streaked its leathery cheeks; the tracks of tears.

The guests neither appeared to notice or care about such details. "The tengu!" someone shouted above the general shrieks. "They're here. Where's the golden star?" Several people gawked around, as if expecting Catch to glide in on a haze of light.

If only he would, thought Ascot, running over. "Jolt! Are you all right?"

"They don't really want to hurt me," he replied, dodging another swipe. "Something's forcing them to attack." He ducked another blow. "Still, I can't keep this up forever."

We don't have forever. Ascot cast a look at the moon: a great, dark copper disk topped with the faintest silver halo. "Hurry, Starley," she cried as Gildar threw Moony aside and rose. Condorella stepped into his path, arms outstretched, her glowing crystal clenched in a fist.

Starley raised the plate. "*Not one more*," he sang. "*I've drawn a line.*" He brought the plate smashing down. *Thunk.* The glassy sphere shivered.

Near Ascot, Jolt reeled, clipped by a fake tengu's fist. Ascot grabbed its arm before it could follow up with a blow that might have felled him. "Hold strong," she told it.

Looking pleadingly into her eyes, it whined. The immense muscles of its arm, strong as flexible steel, quivered under her grip. As Ascot fought to keep hold, a group of people in split masks charged out of the topiary garden. The one in front leveled a sword. "Kill the tengu," she cried.

"Mistral, no!" cried Ascot, recognizing the voice.

"*You don't get to cross what's mine,*" Starley gritted out. *Thunk.*

Recognizing a genuine threat, the fake tengus' demeanor changed. Several growled. The fake tengu Ascot held pulled free and lashed at Jolt as he came darting in. He dropped to his knees with a cry.

"*Here I stand—*" Starley brought the plate down, "*—and here I'll fight.*"

A purple glow blossomed as Condorella held her crystal aloft. "You shall not pass!" she thundered, standing at the base of the pedestal Starley clung to with the sides of his feet.

Snarling, Gildar cuffed her aside, but Moony dove onto his head. Ascot grappled with the fake tengu, trying to keep it from hurting Jolt.

"*Not one more's walking!*" cried Starley. *Thunk.* "*Not one more!*"

A Hide Away ran up, brandishing a knife. Staggering forward, Ascot knocked it from his grip before he could sink it into the fake tengu. The wind blew her hair about her face. Above, the sky felt like something about to fall.

"*Into that Moonless Night!*" Starley shouted, bringing down the plate with all his force.

The globe split. Blue-white light poured out. Ascot's eyelids clamped shut before she registered a fraction of its force. Even so, for a moment, it seemed bright as day inside her skull. She shouted along with the rest.

The light quickly faded, but the wind howled. *A storm's coming,* she thought, curling her arms over her head.

No, not a storm. Spots still flashed in her eyes, but she forced them to open. The moon, now a solid copper orb, shone overhead. The sky cracked open before it, and dark bodies poured through.

Ascot swallowed. *I don't have the* kinhoshi.

She had the peach. She stepped forward.

CHAPTER THIRTY-FOUR:
ECLIPSED

There was a marble statue of the Great Alph, Rune, in this corner of the topiary garden. Catch had forgotten that. The artist had captured him in lion-form, one forepaw raised, carved eyes gazing skywards.

Lion-form. So, not actually Rune, then. Lethe lounged on its back. As Catch slid to the ground, stepping into a patch of light cast by the distant glow-globes, his cheer morphed into horror.

"What happened?" Lethe demanded, leaping off the lion's back. Scowling, he answered himself. "Gildar happened. Tampering with my experiment again." He looked toward the Roundgrounds. Some kerfuffle was taking place on the vast, silvery disk. Screams echoed over the plateau. The fake tengu tussled with people wearing strange, split masks, apparently oblivious to the crack opening before the moon.

"We're coming," whispered Koyuki, hovering behind him.

Lethe cupped Catch's chin. "Listen to that. Such a lovely mess. You'll have your revenge. Gildar's sure to be torn apart by one faction or another."

Catch pushed his hand aside. "Not interested." Oh, he'd love to see Gildar strung up by his heels, but not if every shifter in the Clawcrags had to suffer with him.

He started walking toward the Roundgrounds. Lethe grabbed his wrist. "Son, don't go out there. You're injured. Your lady friend's here. We'll fetch her and leave. Find some quiet human town—"

"Where you can poison everyone once you grow bored of it." Catch channeled enough of his inner Smilodon to shrug his father off and kept walking, staggering slightly. Bandersnatch loped over to steady him while Koyuki buzzed around the side of the topiary tiger, glowering at Lethe as she passed.

Lethe tilted his head. "Perhaps it is fate." Folding his arms, he settled into a waiting attitude.

A wave of white light erupted in the Roundgrounds' center. Catch flung up an arm. It washed over them and vanished, leaving the world blacker than it had been a moment earlier.

Bandersnatch crackled back into human shape. "What was that, Boss?"

Catch shook his head. Whatever it was, it had affected the fake tengu. They'd stopped fighting. They cringed back from the split-masked people, whimpering like terrified children. "Mistral," said Catch, recognizing one of the people in the forefront. Teeth bared in a snarl, she raised her sword over a cowering fake tengu's head.

A tall, black-clad figure grabbed her wrist. "Don't."

Cavall. Catch would've recognized that sanded snakeskin voice anywhere. He dragged himself over just as Mistral, glaring, wrenched away from her father. Defiantly, she raised her sword again.

"My father killed your father," said Catch.

Mistral spun. "Sir." She gasped, seeing the mark on his cheek, but Catch looked past her, to her father. The blue of Cavall's eyes was the only color in his face, and even they looked drained, faded.

"Starthorne," he rasped. "What happened to you?"

Above, the skies tore. Catch heard the stiff, rattling sound of tengu wings, but he could spare a few more seconds. "My father killed your father," he repeated, because they might not have heard the first time, and it certainly hadn't penetrated. It did now. Cavall's legs buckled.

He grabbed for support that wasn't there. The fake tengu Mistral had been harassing helpfully steadied him. Mistral blinked at it.

"Our fathers were partners, until—" Catch dropped his head to rub his brow. "It was because of me. Arctic wanted me to fight for shifter freedom, but Lethe…"

How to explain that this was all because Lethe needed to know if he was special, chosen? Sighing, Catch met Cavall's eyes. "Lethe disagreed. So, he killed Arctic."

Cavall's throat worked, but no sound came out of it. Catch bowed his head. "I'm so sorry." Now, he looked at Mistral. "That's who your master is. I know the things he taught you, because he taught them to me. If you really want a better life, you'll be very careful choosing which lessons you keep."

She gulped and stared down at her hand, at her fingers, still wrapped around her sword's hilt. Abruptly, they unclenched. The sword clattered to the ground.

Reaching out, Cavall pulled Mistral to his side, hugging her roughly. "I'm sorry, too. If I'd been around to be your father, you wouldn't have gone looking for another."

The fake tengu tugged Catch's sleeve. "Av…" it grated. "Avoca. Avocad—"

"Avocado?" asked Catch. Its mouth widened in a huge, toothy grin. *I have no idea how Rags influenced it, but…* He patted its shoulder. "We'll get you one, later."

"Avocad!" cheered the other fake tengu. Waving their clawed hands, they did a happy jig. "Vacadado!"

"Boss," said Bandersnatch, touching his shoulder. Catch turned. Koyuki pointed to the east.

"They're here," she said.

Catch looked up at the darkened moon. Hundreds, possibly thousands of tengu hovered before it, the sparks from their wings falling in a thin, glittering stream on the Roundgrounds.

A solitary figure stood below them. The wind stirred her hair, revealing a white streak amongst her tangled, dark locks.

Of course.

"They don't really expect me to conjure lightning," said Koyuki.

"I know," Catch replied. A long pause limped after his words.

"You don't have to go out there, Boss," said Bandersnatch.

"Yes, I do," said Catch, and went.

❧

A host of strange, ringed eyes scrutinized Ascot, hostile and judging. Their wings beat the thick air to a froth as they waited for her to make an offer she sensed they'd already rejected.

"We agree to your demands," she called, holding up the pathetic, partially mashed peach. Juice ran down her arms.

The tengu stared down. "What right do you have to speak for shifter-kind?" one cried.

None whatsover. She glanced back toward the inner circle. Gildar was walking at a sharp clip toward the Aspire. Retreating. Did all shifters run?

No. Starley came to her side, supported by Condorella and Jolt. "Are they there?" he asked. "I hear this weird, buzzy-flappy sound." He turned his head, gray eyes glazed and staring.

"Breaking the electro-magniphager blinded him," said Jolt, quietly, through his teeth, as if biting back a scream. He raised his voice. "We don't want to fight, tengu."

"Then you shouldn't have betrayed us," said the foremost tengu. Gold braiding gleamed along the front of his robe.

"Wasn't us, mate," said Starley.

With a prick of claws, Moony settled on Ascot's shoulder. "Kaizen," he chirped. "Good to see you. They'll give you the Aspire and the peaches, so why not come down and be sociable?"

"Ah, Sir Moony." Kaizen smiled. "We've added a few terms to the agreement. You'll stay with us and be our champion, and we also demand their coffee groves and bitterseed orange trees."

"The orange trees as well now?" called a voice behind Ascot.

A familiar voice. A voice it seemed she hadn't heard in years, making a pathetic attempt at its usual nonchalance. "Catch!" she cried, turning. He was there, standing alongside a large, naked, dark-haired man and a slender tengu girl.

Oh, frabjacket. She stared. Her gut filled with mud.

He was a horror. A bruise shadowed his right eye, but that was fairly normal for him. There was worse. Far worse. He winced on every inhale, clutching his ribs. Mud created from a hideous mixture of dust and blood caked his pores. His hair hung in stringy ropes.

Then there was the brand. Fresh and livid.

He tossed her a smile and her heart thumped again. Despite his obvious pain, there was something in that look she'd never seen before. His shields were down. For the first time, and for all his injuries, perhaps he was ready to actually start mending.

"Hello, my diddle-darling," he said.

Ascot. Facing off against a horde of angry tengu. Catch couldn't have found surprise within himself with the aid of a dowsing rod. She stared at him in shock and growing fury. *Someone's nose is getting thumped, later.* He hoped he was conscious to see it.

He decided he liked her in that shade of blue; it contrasted nicely with her dark hair and pale skin. But he was distracting himself.

"So, it's the orange trees now," he called to Kaizen. "And if we grant that, what next? Our grapes? You know how we shifters are about our fruit."

Moony laughed raspily. Dmitri came padding up, and with his presence, all his friends were reunited again, even Rags-n-Bones, in the form of the fake tengu begging avocados. Cavall and Mistral stood by the Seersee pedestals with the Hide Aways, and Savotte came jogging in from the garden to join them.

No sign of Gildar. Or his father.

Catch turned back to the tengu as Kaizen swooped a little closer. "So, *kinhoshi* of the shifters, have you taught this upstart how to summon lightning?"

For half a second—no longer—Catch toyed with the notion of petting Moony vigorously. That would surely raise a snap. But the situation was too fraught to inflict his peculiar humor on it just now. "No," he replied.

Thunder rumbled along the tengus' ranks. "Then, will you cede the Aspire? Your custard peaches?" demanded Kaizen.

"I offer something better," said Catch.

Murmurs of surprise erupted, from the shifters as well as the tengu. Dubious looks were exchanged. Ignoring them, Catch threw back his filthy mantle and did something that took all his strength.

He knelt.

"I offer you an apology," he said, bowing his head.

The wind had died to a whisper. The Roundgrounds, always conducive to sound, carried his words to all the listening ears. A startled mumble swept the crowd. Someone laughed; the sort that hovered on the edge of disbelief.

"Our kind has profited by the wrong done yours five hundred years ago," Catch continued. "I apologize. We will make amends."

"This is your 'better offer'?" asked Kaizen, the rings of his irises whirling so fast they blurred.

Catch lifted his head. "Yes. Because it comes with the opportunity *not* to fight. You've been hidden away for five hundred years. You haven't seen bloodshed and contention. We have. We've been eating ourselves alive these five centuries."

His bent knee shook. He willed it to hold fast, just a while longer. *Holdfast.* A smile wisped across his lips. "I offer you the chance to not become killers. Believe me," he said, remembering the horrible, hollowing the moment when he thought he'd killed Glim, "such a thing is worth all the coffee in the world."

Ascot pressed his shoulder. Clasping his hand over hers, he glanced back. *"I didn't kill Glim,"* he started to whisper—and saw that it didn't matter. She'd have forgiven him anyway.

Koyuki stepped forward, feet firmly on the ground. "As the one who should be your Rai-sama, I say we accept their offer. We tengu have always been teachers before we were warriors. Why stain our legacy with unnecessary bloodshed?"

The tengus' wings buzzed more slowly. Fewer sparks rained down as they muttered amongst themselves. Kaizen glanced at the assembled army, then looked back at Koyuki. "Without the *kinhoshi,* you cannot be the Rai-sama. And, so long as we do not have a Rai-sama, we must avenge the one who fell by treachery."

Evidently, shifters weren't the only ones who got hung up on rules. "We'll find it," said Catch. "Just give us—"

Ascot coughed; an annoying, self-conscious type of cough she could only have learned from Dmitri. "Actually, we found the *kinhoshi.* Your father stole it from me."

Father. Catch iced, but unfroze an instant later. "He's in the topiary garden. Find him."

Koyuki flew off, followed by Moony. Cavall gestured to a handful of guards. Catch tried to rise and crumpled. "Easy, Boss," said Bandersnatch, steadying him.

What a joke, thought Catch, staring after the pursuers. Lethe Starthorne and the *kinhoshi* could be on the moon by now, rendering all his efforts to quell the war moot. *But what did I expect? I'm not some damned golden star of destiny.*

"Catch." Ascot put her arm around his shoulders. "You didn't run."

He'd never heard quite that note of approval in her voice. Of course he had to ruin it. "I ran quite a bit, actually. Five days solid, with Cavall and Savotte on my heels, just like a ranger in—"

"Don't mention rangers," she said, shuddering. She brushed his cheek. "You look awful."

"I'll mend."

"Captain!" Moony came fluttering up from the topiary garden. His orange eyes made perfect circles, slitted with black. "We found…come see." He dropped straight down, plump on the ground, and began to wash mechanically.

Exchanging a glance with Ascot, Catch trudged to the topiary garden, leaning heavily on Bandersnatch. Cavall, Koyuki, and the guards bent in a circle by the statue of Rune. Bandersnatch helped Catch push his way to the center.

Gildar lay beside the marble lion, his open eyes staring at the sky. A small chunk of faceted gold stone lay on his chest, alongside a note with four words scrawled in Lethe's well-remembered handwriting.

Perhaps it was fate.

CHAPTER THIRTY-FIVE: INVISIBLE INK

It wasn't fair, Ascot thought in the busy months that followed. Everyone had spent five centuries making a situation about as bad as it could possibly be, and now she and her friends were tasked with putting it all right.

But they tried. In the archives, Dmitri nosed amongst the documents with the owl-shifters, trying to sort old truths from new fiction. Rags-n-Bones escorted his troop of fake tengu—whom everyone had mutually decided to call "fengu"—about Holdfast, introducing them to the citizens, and teaching them manners and the love of avocados. Moony, now titled the tengu's champion, spent most of his time posing in sunbeams so everyone could see the medal sparkling about his neck. Condorella transferred the image from the Lorrygreen Seersee's shards to one of the remaining intact ones and showed it to the grumblers amongst the shifters. The last protests against the tengus' presence swiftly died, after that.

Still, in Ascot's opinion, the part they'd played in recent events wasn't an excuse for electing Catch Alph.

One morning, Koyuki, with an honor guard of four tengu, accompanied Bandersnatch, Cavall, and Savotte to Catch's room at the Agonvilla Hotel, where he spent most of his time curled up in the window seat. He listened gravely, rubbing the bandage over his left cheek, as Bandersnatch spoke, holding out the Alph's gold-fringed crimson mantle. Ascot stayed by the stove, brewing coffee for Catch. She'd decided she'd let him play up his injuries for another week, then kick him out of bed.

"We believe you're the best cadidate for the position, Boss," Bandersnatch summed up, either unaware of Savotte and Cavall's dubious glances behind his back, or determined to ignore it. "The tengu trust you, you're a big cat-shifter, yet you're also—"

Mistral elbowed him and he stopped, coloring.

"A feral," said Catch, taking his fingers from his cheek and looking at them. "Not that we're going to use that term anymore." He leaned back, folding his arms behind his head. The book on his blanketed lap threatened to slide off, and Ascot knew if it did, Catch would look piteous until she retrieved it for him. A smile tugged her lips even as she rolled her eyes.

"Anyway." Bandersnatch cleared his throat. "So much has changed recently that we feel we need some things to stay the same. Just for, you know, reassurance."

"Means, 'comfort,' 'support,' or oddly, 'assurance,' which seems redundant," said Catch, stretching. The book slid a bit more. He was probably trying to dump it on the floor.

He's going to decline, of course, Ascot thought, carefully scooping coffee grounds into the filter. *It's probably the only reason Cavall and Savotte agreed to ask him.*

"I accept," said Catch.

Ascot fumbled the scoop, spilling brown grains. Her head shot up in time to see the small smirk playing at the corner of Catch's mouth. *Oh, frabjacket.* He'd noticed Cavall and Savotte's grimaces, too. But that was no reason—

Too late. Beaming, Bandersnatch handed over the fringed mantle while Koyuki shot celebratory sparks from the *kinhoshi*. Wadding the mantle into a ball, Catch tucked it behind his head. "Let's think of constructive ways to restructure our society," he said, snagging his book an instant before it fell. He propped it on his knee. "We should also open trade with our human neighbors. And non-human ones. Oh, and appoint Condorella court witch. Pack witch. Must we keep the 'Pack'? Such an ugly word. Anyway, go discuss and bring me some good ideas."

He glanced up after a moment, when no one moved. "Shoo. I'm still convalescing."

They left, albeit not without casting him some looks as they went. Bandersnatch scratched his chin, clearly bemused by the idea of his thoughts playing any part in governance.

"Alph? You can't be serious," said Ascot when they were alone.

"Actually, it is within my capacity," Catch replied, flipping a page. "Means 'solemn,' 'thoughtful,' or 'grave.' I am an expert on grave matters."

She took a breath and held it, counting to ten. Of course his recent experiences hadn't completely changed him—and she was glad for it. But why did he have to be so contrary? "You can't accept the position just to annoy Cavall."

He looked at her. A brow rose. "What makes you think it's a jest?"

She stared at him. *Because we meant to go to Buenovillia. Travel north, see dragons and great libraries. How can we do that if you're here, being Alph?*

But maybe he didn't want to travel on, any more than Rags-n-Bones had truly wanted to leave Widget and come to the Clawcrags. Maybe she had to let go.

I don't want to let go. Not after all she'd gone through to reach him.

Catch's gaze slid out the window. "The lightest touch could shatter it all again," he said, watching a coffee vendor hawk orange syrup-laced coffee to passers-by below. Abruptly, he laughed. "It almost did. But I'll keep it out of his hands."

A rounded object tucked under his cushion gleamed. She'd

questioned him about it, but he'd always evaded an answer, so she wasn't going to ask again. Not now, anyway. Throwing down the filter, Ascot left, banging the door behind her.

❧

"Did you know about this?" asked Ascot. After wandering Holdfast a while, she'd found Starley and Jolt at—naturally—a coffeehouse called The Bad Black Brew. Rags-n-Bones and his horde of fengu were currently occupying half the round tables in its raised, brick-walled courtyard. Rags-n-Bones waved at her before returning to his lecture on how to use a silver tea service.

"You mean, Starthorne being elected Alph? Seems an obvious choice," said Jolt. Starley patted about the table, and Jolt patiently moved the pitcher of cream into his reach. Lifting it, Starley happily poured cream onto the table, a good six inches from his mug. Huffing, Jolt took the pitcher away.

"You're enjoying this," noted Ascot, propping her chin on her knuckles.

"Eh, when life hands you lemons, make lemon chiffon cake and a pitcher of iced whiskey flavored with lemon syrup." Starley picked up his mug, drank without spilling a drop, and set it down, grinning fiendishly. "Then, scarf the lot before anyone snitches it."

Surely going blind was good excuse for someone to mope. So, if Starley wasn't moping, what right did she have to do so? Sighing, Ascot doodled in the spilled cream.

"No, don't eat that," Rags-n-Bones said, taking a pair of sugar tongs out of a fengu's hand. "You use these to pick up the yummy sugar."

Obediantly, the fengu picked up a sugar lump with the tongs and dropped it right into its gaping mouth, then pinched up a second one for Nipper. Rags-n-Bones smiled approval.

Ascot started when Starley's hand settled over hers. "All I asked was to see the day we were free," he said, giving it a squeeze. "I didn't get my wish. But, I get to live instead. It's a better bargain, really."

"Much better," said Jolt, tucking his mantle about his shoulders. There was a small tear by the hem. Ascot wondered if she could persuade Jolt to relinquish it long enough for her to mend it.

I'll miss them, if I leave the Clawcrags. And Cavall and Mistral—perhaps even Savotte. She'd miss Condorella, too—certainly her baking—and she'd never thought she'd befriend a member of GEL since her misadventures in Albright.

Maybe Catch was right to want to stay. Holdfast was his home, after all.

"Ahem," said Starley suddenly, straightening. "Look sharp, loves. The Alph's here."

To Ascot's mind, that was still Gildar, so she jumped and stared about, only remembering it was Catch when she spotted him sauntering up the steps, hands tucked in the pockets of his brown coat, hair in his eyes, and the Alph's mantle rather haphazardly tossed over his shoulders. Perched on the left one, Moony rapturously kneaded the rich, red fabric. Dmitri paced at his heels.

Starley grinned. "Of course when I say 'look' sharp—"

Jolt elbowed him. "How'd you know he was coming?"

"With all the stuff in his pockets? The man clinks."

Grabbing a spare chair, Catch dragged it between Ascot and Jolt and sat. "The head of the city guard just made a rather interesting catch," he said, hooking his clasped hands around his knee.

"Means, 'Alph,' 'head honcho,' or 'boss,'" said Moony, purring with satisfaction.

"No, in this case means 'find' or 'discovery.'" Catch beckoned Rags-n-Bones over. "You'll want to see this."

After cautioning the fengu not to drink from the tea spout, Rags-n-Bones came over. "Nice," he said, fingering the gold fringe on Catch's mantle.

"What's this all about?" Ascot asked Dmitri. She wasn't sure she wanted to give Catch the satisfaction of answering.

Dmitri sighed. "Something we should perhaps have expected." He looked at Catch, who snapped his fingers.

"Bring them up," he called down the steps. Seconds later, a very put-upon Cavall came stalking up the steps, gripping the arm of a struggling girl with short blonde hair.

Ascot gasped, but Rags-n-Bones shot to his feet. "Kay! Lindsay!" he cried. He swooped in before Cavall reached the top step, one arm going around Lindsay, the other around empty air.

Or not so empty. "Oof, not so hard," said lanky, pale Kay, appearing suddenly.

The Ashurens. Ascot didn't remember standing, but she was on her feet. "How did you get here?"

"We walked," said Lindsay, with a roll of her eyes. Then grinned. "Or floated, occasionally."

Of course. With their combined talents, the Ashurens could go practically anywhere unnoticed. "But why?" she asked. "I mean," she added, hugging them when Rags-n-Bones finally let go, "I'm happy to see you, but it's such a long way."

"I always wanted to travel," said Lindsay. "This gave us the excuse." Rummaging in a knapsack, she produced a thick envelope sealed with a blot of dark red wax emblazoned with three bats, one flying upside-down.

The Abberdorf family crest. Ascot recognized the flowing black writing on the front. "Vlad. He answered."

"It came to Petroyvan Academy," said Kay. "We weren't sure when you'd get back, so we thought, why not bring it to you?"

"Come meet my friends," said Rags-n-Bones, drawing them toward the fengu eagerly.

The stiff paper purred as Ascot stroked it with her thumbs. She fancied it carried the scent of black roses. "Open it, Ascot," said Moony, leaning off Catch's shoulder to bat at her hair. "It's from home. I miss it sometimes."

So did she. No longer able to feign nonchalance, she ripped open the envelope and unfolded the letter inside. She skimmed it, then read it again, slowly, her eyes widening with every word. "Vincent's getting *married?* To a *human?*"

* * *

ABOUT THE AUTHOR

A. E. Decker hails from Pennsylvania. A former doll-maker and ESL tutor, she earned a master's degree in history, where she developed a love of turning old stories upside-down to see what fell out of them. This led in turn to the writing of her YA novel, *The Falling of the Moon*. A graduate of Odyssey 2011, her short fiction has appeared in such venues as *Beneath Ceaseless Skies, Fireside Magazine*, and elsewhere. Like all writers, she is owned by three cats. Come visit her, her cats, and her fur Daleks at wordsmeetworld.com.

A NOTE FROM THE AUTHOR

Sorry about the cliffhanger. Just as a spoiler, book four, *A Trick of the Moonlight*, is going to end on a cliffhanger as well. But I promise the last book, *A Pocketful of Moonglow*, won't leave you hanging.

As I write this afterword now, I can see the end of the journey. You're holding, (and have presumably finished reading) book three, *Into the Moonless Night*. The first draft of *A Trick of the Moonlight* is currently in the hands of my wonderful editor, Laura Harvey. I will start writing *A Pocketful of Moonglow* this summer. The *Moonfall Mayhem* series is so close to being complete.

The odd thing about writing a series is that past books recede so quickly into the past. I feel like I wrote book two, *The Meddlers of Moonshine*, a lifetime ago. *Into the Moonless Night* is already, in some ways, in the far past to me—and thank goodness, as it was an absolute beast to write. I mostly blame Catch for being an infuriating devil, but 2017 was a difficult year for me, as I know it was to many others as well. The world seems a little sharper and darker since then.

It's only coincidence that *Into the Moonless Night*, my most "political" book thus far, was written in 2017. I'd always intended it to concern a stratified society undergoing a revolution. I'm not a "message" writer—I wish to entertain—yet I hope a little thoughtfulness seeps through the humor, like a vitamin pill hidden in a chocolate drop. If, while you were reading *Into the Moonless Night*, you were nodding along in agreement with Catch when he remarked how ridiculous it was that people's worth should be judged on what animal they turned into, please apply that sentiment to our world as well. Isn't it pathetic, in our modern era, that we still privilege people according to such qualities as their skin color, gender, country of origin, and who they are attracted to? How much time and effort do we waste undercutting each other instead of helping one another to rise? How much *potential* do we waste?

It is an author's power that I can resolve such issues happily in my books. If, by some sympathetic magic, I could translate that into peace and understanding in the real world, I would write until both arms fell off at the shoulders. Unfortunately, all I can do is write and hope. Hope that the world gets better. Hope people choose understanding instead of intolerance, knowledge before ignorance.

Thanks to my fine team at World Weaver Press, including Sarena and Laura, and a special thank you to Nicole for her marvelous covers. Thanks to the Bethlehem Writers Group for their keen editorial skills. Thanks also to the Even Odders for beta reading, bourbon, and support.

Finally, a thank you to my readers. Thank you for following me on this journey.

Keep up the hope.

Thank you for reading!

We hope you'll leave an honest review at Amazon, Goodreads, or wherever you discuss books online.

Leaving a review means a lot for the author and editors who worked so hard to create this book.

Please sign up for our newsletter for news about upcoming titles, submission opportunities, special discounts, & more.

WorldWeaverPress.com/newsletter-signup

OPAL
FAE OF FIRE AND STONE, BOOK ONE
Kristina Wojtaszek
White as snow, stained with blood, her talons black as ebony...

In this retwisting of the classic Snow White tale, the daughter of an owl is forced into human shape by a wizard who's come to guide her from her wintry tundra home down to the colorful world of men and Fae, and the father she's never known. She struggles with her human shape and grieves for her dead mother—a mother whose past she must unravel if men and Fae are to live peacefully together.

Trapped in a Fae-made spell, Androw waits for the one who can free him. A boy raised to be king, he sought refuge from his abusive father in the Fae tales his mother spun. When it was too much to bear, he ran away, dragging his anger and guilt with him, pursuing shadowy trails deep within the Dark Woods of the Fae, seeking the truth in tales, and salvation in the eyes of a snowy hare. But many years have passed since the snowy hare turned to woman and the woman winged away on the winds of a winter storm leaving Androw prisoner behind walls of his own making—a prison that will hold him forever unless the daughter of an owl can save him.

"A fairy tale within a fairy tale within a fairy tale—the narratives fit together like interlocking pieces of a puzzle, beautifully told." — Zachary Petit, Editor *Writer's Digest*

CHAR
FAE OF FIRE AND STONE, BOOK TWO
An isolated fae must travel a century into the past to rewrite the book that will save her people.
Kristina Wojtaszek

HEIR TO THE LAMP
THE GENIE CHRONICLES, BOOK ONE
Michelle Lowery Combs

Ginn thought she knew all there is to know about how she became adopted by parents whose Number One priority was to embarrass her with public displays of affection, but that changes when a single wish starts a never-ending parade of weirdness marching through her door the day she turns thirteen.

Gifted with a mysterious lamp and the missing pieces from her adoption story, Ginn tries to discover who…or *what*…she really is. That should be strange enough, but to top it off Ginn's being hunted by the Order of the Grimoire, a secret society who'll stop at nothing to harness the power of a real genie. Ginn struggles to stay one step ahead of the Grimms with the help of Rashmere, Guardian of the lamp and the most loyal friend a girl never knew she had. But the Grimms are being helped, too—but by whom? As much as she doesn't want to, Ginn's beginning to question the motives of her long-time crush Caleb Scott and his connection to her newest, most dangerous enemy.

SOLOMON'S BELL
GENIE CHRONICLES, BOOK TWO
*Ginn thinks she has problems at home until
she magically lands herself in 16th Century Prague.*
Michelle Lowery Combs

CURSED: WICKEDLY FUN STORIES
Short Story Collection
Susan Abel Sullivan
"Quirky, clever, and just a little savage." —Lane Robins, *critically acclaimed author of
MALEDICTE and KINGS AND ASSASSINS*

World Weaver Press
Publishing fantasy, paranormal, and science fiction.
We believe in great storytelling.
worldweaverpress.com

Made in the USA
Columbia, SC
29 March 2018